When
Morning Comes

ALSO BY FRANCIS RAY

It Had to Be You
A Seductive Kiss
With Just One Kiss

SINGLE TITLES
Someone to Love Me
I Know Who Holds Tomorrow
Rockin' Around That Christmas Tree

ANTHOLOGIES
Rosie's Curl and Weave
Della's House of Style
Welcome to Leo's
Going to the Chapel
Gettin' Merry
Let's Get It On
Twice the Temptation

When Morning Comes

· · · · · · · · · · · · · ·

FRANCIS RAY

St. Martin's Griffin

New York

R

This is a work of fiction. All of the characters, organizations, and events portrayed in this novel are either products of the author's imagination or are used fictitiously.

www.stmartins.com

Library of Congress Cataloging-in-Publication Data

Ray, Francis.
    When morning comes / Francis Ray. — 1st ed.
        p. cm.
    ISBN 978-0-312-68162-3 (trade pbk.)
    ISBN 978-1-250-00986-9 (e-book)
    1. Neurosurgeons—Fiction.   2. Adoption—Fiction.
    3. Domestic fiction.   I. Title.
    PS647.A35W47 2012
    813'.54—dc23

                                        2012004639

First Edition: June 2012

10 9 8 7 6 5 4 3 2 1

Lovingly dedicated to three men who had a
tremendous influence on my life:

my father,
McCLINTON RADFORD SR.;

my brother,
McCLINTON RADFORD JR.;

and my husband,
WILLIAM H. RAY.

It was always a comfort knowing your love and
your support were unshakable.
I'll miss you forever.

8/12

Acknowledgments

· · · · · · · · · · · · · · · ·

Monique Patterson, executive editor at St. Martin's Press; Holly Root, agent with Scott Waxman Agency; and Holly Blanck, associate editor at St. Martin's Press—for your support and encouragement in making this book a reality. I love having you on my team.

Prologue

· · · · · · · · · · · · · ·

"It's a boy."

Carlton James heard his wife's softly spoken voice, the tiredness, the regret. Somehow he'd known his first grandchild would be a boy.

His long fingers braced on the fireplace, trembled the tiniest bit as he stared into the flickering flames. In mid-March in Dallas, Texas, it wasn't cold enough for a fire, but he had needed to keep busy once Christine's labor started. That had been over sixteen long hours ago.

His hands fisted with anger, then unclenched. He had to be strong for his family. He'd failed once, never again.

"Christine?" he asked, knowing before his wife answered that if their only child and daughter had had any problems with the delivery, she would have come downstairs to tell him before now. It was her emotional state he inquired about and they both knew it.

"Resigned."

Carlton felt every day of his forty-three years and then some.

His first grandchild and he would never get to know him, to love him. Blowing out a breath, he slowly turned to see Lawanna. The joy and laughter that he was used to seeing on her pretty, open face wasn't there. Her lips were pressed tightly together but they still trembled. There hadn't been much to laugh about over the past six months.

He opened his arms and his wife rushed across the room, burrowing against his chest, her hands gripping fistfuls of his shirt. He felt the dampness of her tears, blinked back his own.

"Carlton, I hurt for her. We were supposed to protect her."

Carlton's black eyes narrowed in anger. "I should have put a bullet in that no-good bastard the night she came crying to us."

Lawanna sharply lifted her head, fear gleaming in her tear-drenched eyes. "No."

Carlton's thumb brushed away the moisture from her dark lashes, then cupped her soft cheek. "He's taken enough from our family, he won't take any more."

"You're sure about what you're going to do?"

He nodded. "I wish there was another way, but Christine has made it clear she wants the baby placed for adoption."

Tears streamed down Lawanna's cheeks. "Carlton, he's beautiful with a full head of black hair and black eyes. He looks so much like your father. Maybe she'll change her mind in a few days. We've kept to ourselves since we rented the house. The few friends we have in the area don't know we're here."

They'd rented a house in Dallas in an exclusive neighborhood for the last month of Christine's pregnancy. He'd taken a leave from his medical practice in Houston for the past three weeks, wanting Christine to know how important she was to them, how much they loved her. It hadn't seemed to matter.

She could barely look them in the eyes, and when she did, tears always followed.

"Did she even look at the baby, ask to hold him?" he asked, hoping against hope.

Lawanna lowered her gaze. "No. She wouldn't even look at me."

"She's ashamed when it should be that bastard. He thinks taking advantage of naïve, unsuspecting women shows what a big man he is," Carlton spat. "He doesn't care about ruining their lives or about the child he refuses to claim. He won't ruin Christine. She's too gifted and has too much to live for. She just needs time and love."

Lawanna nodded. "I just wish there was another way."

There was, but Carlton wasn't going to tell her. This was one burden he planned to carry by himself. "You go sit with Christine and send the nurse down with the baby. The social worker is waiting for my call."

Lawanna bit her lower lip. "I don't mind telling you that once you see him I'm hoping you'll change your mind. We could tell everyone we decided to adopt."

"If we did, we'd lose Christine. We don't have a choice."

Tears sparkled in his wife's eyes. "We shouldn't have to choose. I hope that man finds a hell on earth. He's hurt too many people not to."

Carlton kissed her on the cheek. "Send the baby down and I'll make the call."

His wife nodded and then left the study, closing the door softly behind her. Carlton picked up the receiver on the desk and called his lawyer. The call was answered on the first ring.

"Yes."

"Is everything ready?"

"Yes."

"They understand and agree to the terms?" Carlton asked.

"Yes."

There was a knock on the study door. "Sir?"

"Just a minute," he said, loud enough for the woman to hear. "The nurse is here. I'll bring him out."

Disconnecting the phone call, Carlton opened the door. He told himself it would be best if he didn't look at the child, but the temptation was too great. He reached for the baby, felt the slight weight, heard the soft cry, and pulled back the soft blue blanket. His heart turned over. His chest felt tight. His wife was right. The baby did look like his father. He felt a fierce possessiveness, a fiercer love.

"If you don't need me, I'll go back upstairs."

He shook his head, still staring down at the squirming bundle. "No. Thank you. You can go back upstairs with the midwife." He heard the nurse move away, but his gaze remained on the now sleeping child. "I'm sorry. I wish there was another way."

Stiffening his shoulders, Carlton quickly went to the front door and pulled it open. A slender woman in a black business suit stood on the porch. Before he could dwell on what he was doing, he thrust the baby into her arms, stepped back, and closed the door.

It was done.

He just hoped and prayed for all of their sakes he had done the right thing.

One

. . . .

Sabrina Thomas clutched the leather-bound notebook to her chest and tried not to be impatient as the elevator in the south tower of Texas Hospital near downtown Dallas stopped once again on its climb to the eighteenth and top floor. But it was difficult.

Dr. Cade Mathis, the bane of her existence, would reach Mrs. Ward's room first and then there'd be hell to pay. Sabrina jabbed the button to close the doors as soon as the last person stepped onto the already crowded elevator. Evenings were always busy at the hospital with the staggered change of shifts and people dropping by to visit after work. Usually she didn't mind the crowd, but today wasn't usual.

Dr. Mathis wasn't going to be happy with Mrs. Ward's decision to postpone her surgery, and he wouldn't be shy about voicing his opinion.

The elevator finally stopped on the eighteenth floor. As soon as there was enough space to allow her to slip through the doors, Sabrina stepped off the elevator, excusing herself as she brushed by people trying to get on. Hurrying down the hall, she almost groaned on seeing Dr. Mathis's tall, imposing figure. At six foot three, he moved with a smooth, unhurried grace as he entered Mrs. Ward's room.

Sabrina increased her frantic pace.

Cade Mathis might be the best neurosurgeon in the country, but unfortunately, too often he had the disposition of a warthog in heat. And no one, at least as far as Sabrina knew, questioned him or went against his medical dictates. The hospital's board had gone all out to woo him from the Mayo Clinic. Housewife Ann Ward, in her mid-twenties, and her loving blue-collar worker husband a few years older, wouldn't stand a snowball's chance in hell of standing up against him.

No one on the staff even tried. As patient advocate for Texas Hospital, it was Sabrina's job to try. Her eyes narrowed. She'd do more than try.

Two steps from the door she heard Dr. Mathis's clipped, precise voice that could be as lethal and as cutting as the scalpel he wielded so skillfully. She didn't waste time knocking, she just went in. What she saw confirmed her fears.

Ann, in a patient's gown, was sitting up in bed. Her husband's work-worn hands clutched hers as he hovered over her as if to protect her from Dr. Mathis. Unfortunately, it would do no good. Dr. Mathis was a law unto himself and listened to no one, but that wouldn't stop Sabrina.

"Hello, Mr. and Mrs. Ward," Sabrina greeted. "Dr. Mathis."

The Wards' frantic gazes swung to Sabrina, clearly begging her to intervene. Dr. Mathis, hands on his lean hips, didn't even glance in her direction. Clearly he thought her insignificant. Tough. "Is there a problem?"

Ann nodded, swallowed a couple of times before she could

get the words out. "I-I just told Dr. Mathis I want to postpone my surgery like I mentioned to you yesterday."

Finally Dr. Mathis's gaze, cold and cutting, swung to Sabrina. Since she'd been subjected to his disapproval before, she didn't cower as most of the staff did. Her first responsibility was to the patient. A fact that had put her at odds with her last supervisor, and the reason she had made the difficult decision to transfer from a Texas Hospital affiliate in Houston to Dallas six months ago.

"You knew about this yesterday?" he accused.

"Yes," she admitted, aware that her chin had jutted.

"And did she tell you why?" he asked, his tone no less cutting.

"Her daughter's birthday party is Saturday, the day after her surgery and she doesn't want to miss it," Sabrina answered.

Dr. Mathis's midnight black eyes narrowed, then turned to his patient. "You have a tumor in the brain. Every second we wait to go in is a second too long."

"I feel fine," Mrs. Ward said, seeming to draw strength from her husband, who now had his arm around her shoulders. "The medicine you're giving me is helping the headaches and my other symptoms. Clarissa, my little girl, wants me there with her Saturday. I've missed so much because I was sick for so long and could hardly get out of bed, let alone play or take care of her. I can't disappoint her."

"If you don't have the surgery, you might not live to see her have another birthday," Dr. Mathis told her.

Ann's lips began to tremble, tears flowed freely from her big hazel eyes. She burrowed into the arms of her husband and sobbed. Her husband looked scared and angry.

"Dr. Mathis—" Sabrina began, only to be cut off.

"The next time one of my patients makes a critical decision, I'd advise you to tell me and not wait for the patient to
call me less than sixteen hours before the surgery," he said to
her, then strode from the room.

Sabrina considered throwing the notebook at his retreating
back, then wisely went to Ann to try to console her.

"What kind of doctor talks to a patient like that?" Mr. Ward
asked, his body trembling as much as his voice. "Don't listen to
him, honey. You'll be there to dance at Clarissa's wedding. Isn't
that right, Sabrina?"

Two pairs of eyes, begging for reassurance, fixed on her
face. "I hope you'll invite me," Sabrina told them. She'd made
it a practice never to lie to patients. They had to trust her. She
just hoped the evasive answer was enough.

"Let me talk to Dr. Mathis, and I'll be right back." Sabrina
left the room and went straight to the charting area for doctors
behind the nurses' desk. Dr. Mathis was there, his broad shoulders rigid, his mouth set in a tight line. The charge nurse, standing beside the secretary, kept throwing troubled glances at him.
When Dr. Mathis was unhappy, heads rolled. Two other nurses
decided they could finish charting elsewhere and moved their
carts away. Sabrina didn't hesitate.

"Mrs. Ward was frightened enough without you adding
to it."

Dr. Mathis finished making his notation on a chart in quick,
slashing motions before looking up. He stared at her as if she
were some icky bug that had dared cross his path. The look angered her just as much as the annoying unsteady pulse. He might
have the manners of a warthog, but he was as gorgeous as forbidden sin.

"It's critical that Mrs. Ward have surgery sooner rather than later."

Sabrina trusted his knowledge. It was his professionalism that set her teeth on edge. "You could have told her differently."

Dr. Mathis slowly stood, towering over her five feet four inches, his unblinking black gaze locked on hers. "She's playing Russian roulette for a birthday party that can just as easily be postponed. The surgery can't."

"She—"

"Is dying, Ms. Thomas. Enough time has been wasted already. Patients are too emotional. They don't always think clearly. I thought it was your job to help, not make matters worse," he said.

Her temper spiked at his accusing tone. Knowing she shouldn't didn't stop her from stepping into his space. "Making things worse is *your* specialty, Dr. Mathis." She spat out the last word as if distasteful. Clutching the notebook, she spun to see two other doctors there. Disapproval was clearly visible on their shocked faces.

Sabrina cursed inwardly. In the short two years Dr. Mathis had been at Texas his reputation as a top neurosurgeon had grown. He was revered as much as he was feared. No matter what Drs. Mims and Carter might personally think of Dr. Mathis, doctors stuck together against the lesser mortals on the hospital staff. Doctors were never reprimanded—and certainly not in public.

And before now, she'd had a good relationship with both doctors. Her rash actions might have endangered that relationship. Even the charge nurse frowned at Sabrina.

One thing life had taught her early was not to falter over

what couldn't be changed. Head high, Sabrina walked from the nursing station aware that the efficiency of the hospital grapevine would have their conversation all over the hospital in a matter of hours.

She didn't have time to think about it. Right now, a family needed her help. But how? She loved her job as patient advocate, but it wasn't an easy one. Often there were hard choices to make. Her job was to ensure that patients had the information needed for them to make the best possible decisions.

She knew firsthand how important that was. If someone hadn't been there to speak for her when she was too young to speak for herself, she wouldn't be alive today.

Stopping in front of Mrs. Ward's door, Sabrina took a calming breath. The patient's decision had been based on emotions, but reasoning—not anger—was needed to help her decide if her decision was the best one. She opened the door and wasn't surprised to see Mr. Ward still holding his softly crying wife in his arms. He glanced up.

In his gaze she saw helplessness, fear with a good dose of anger. "He had no right to upset Ann like that. I'm reporting him to the medical association."

Sabrina let the door swing closed. "Dr. Mathis is brusque, but he's also the best neurosurgeon in the state, possibly the country. He was at the Mayo Clinic for three years before coming to Texas two years ago. Patients come from all over the country to see him."

"That doesn't give him the right to scare my wife," Mr. Ward said, clutching his wife closer.

Sabrina knew he was doing his best to hide his fear. "Despite

Mrs. Ward doing better, Dr. Mathis believes it's in Mrs. Ward's best interest to have the surgery tomorrow as scheduled." Sabrina stopped at the foot of the hospital bed.

Mrs. Ward lifted her tearstained face from her husband's chest. "What do you think?"

Sabrina had been asked her opinion many times in her job and always answered truthfully. "Dr. Mathis might not have the best bedside manner, but few neurosurgeons have his skill in the operating room. He was sought by some very prestigious hospitals. Texas is fortunate to have a man of his gifts and accomplishments."

"He's rude," her husband snapped, clearly not wanting to let go of his anger.

"And gifted, as I said. He diagnosed your wife's condition when no one else had been able to," Sabrina reminded them gently. Grudgingly she had to give Mathis points for not pointing that out to her during their conversations. She'd never heard of him bragging. His accomplishments spoke for him.

Mrs. Ward glanced at her husband, then tucked her head. "The surgery has risks. He told us that. I just wanted to be there for Clarissa's birthday—in case—" Her voice broke, trailed off. Her husband pulled her closer.

Sabrina went to the bedside. "I might not have any children, but I understand why you made the emotional decision. Dr. Mathis made his decision based on your test results."

"If you needed a neurosurgeon, would you use Dr. Mathis?" Mrs. Ward asked, staring at Sabrina intently.

Sabrina didn't even have to think. "He'd be at the top of my very short list."

Mrs. Ward looked at her husband, then spoke to Sabrina.

"Thank you. If you don't mind I'd like to talk to my husband alone."

"Of course. If you need anything else, just have me paged. Good-bye." Sabrina left the room, hoping that she had helped, annoyed with herself that she hadn't handled things better with Dr. Mathis, and even more annoyed with him.

Sabrina Thomas annoyed the hell out of him, Cade thought as he went through the hospital's double exit doors and headed for his car. He paid no attention to the hot blast of June air that enveloped him. He might not have been in Texas for long, but he was used to the stifling heat. What he wasn't used to was being questioned.

His mouth tight, he activated the locks on the black Lamborghini. No one at Texas Hospital, not even the chief of staff, had questioned Cade in the years he'd been associated with the hospital. Doctors from all over the country sought his advice. He was respected, feared, revered. He knew he was maligned—but never to his face.

Except by Sabrina Thomas.

Yanking open the door, he slid inside and started the engine. His mind still on Sabrina, he backed out of the space and headed for the exit gate. At first he'd thought she was on a power trip until he'd seen her more than once holding a less than clean child while talking to a patient or family member or buying food from the vending machine for patient family members. Dirty bedpans didn't even faze her. She didn't appear to mind doing menial things for patients or working late to push departments and agencies to help a family in need.

Sabrina Thomas cared about her patients. But she had to

understand that patients didn't look at their medical conditions logically. Unfortunately, neither did she, which made for a bad combination, especially since he preferred a calm, nonconfrontational life at work and at home. His life had been too chaotic and uncertain growing up not to crave peace. He wasn't going to get that when they had the same patient.

The ringing phone interrupted his thoughts. He pushed ACCEPT on the wood grain control panel. "Dr. Mathis."

"Dr. Mathis, you have a call from Mrs. Ward. She says it's urgent," came the cool, efficient voice of his office manager, Iris, through his radio. "Your three late appointments just signed in."

He stopped at a red light. "Please tell them I'm on the way and put them in a room. I'll be there in less than five minutes." Some of his patients had difficulty getting off work so he had late appointments one day a week. "Put Mrs. Ward through."

"Dr. Mathis?" came the tentative voice. By all rights she shouldn't be alive. He'd stopped believing in a higher power for himself long ago, but he realized that for others there was such a thing.

He was different. He ruled his destiny, not some unseen force.

"Yes, Mrs. Ward." She sounded shaky. "Are you feeling all right?" As much as he disagreed with her decision, she was still his patient and deserved his best. He never wanted to give less.

He'd gone into medicine to show a man he hated that he wasn't worthless as he'd been told all of his life. Yet, somehow along the way he'd learned he could make a difference in people's lives, and perhaps make up for the fact that no one had been there to make a difference in his.

"Yes. I-I . . ."

"Mrs. Ward, I have patients waiting at my office."

"If it's not too late, I want to have the surgery in the morning as scheduled."

Frowning, he pulled through the light. "I haven't taken you off the schedule so there shouldn't be a problem. What changed your mind?"

"Sabrina."

Surprised, he turned into the underground parking lot of his office building. "Ms. Thomas?"

"She said if she needed a neurosurgeon, you would be at the top of her very short list."

Stunned—a rare occasion for him—Cade was momentarily at a loss for words, an even rarer occasion. He'd had the impression that Sabrina Thomas didn't think too highly of him. He hadn't minded. Usually, he could care less what people thought of him. Never had. Had always thought he never would. "I'll see you in the morning. Good-bye."

"Good-bye."

Cade disconnected the call, pulled into his reserved parking spot, and got out of his car. He had patients to see and then he was going to track down Sabrina Thomas. They were going to figure out a way to work together without all the friction.

Which meant she wouldn't interfere with his patients' care and he would have his calm, quiet life back, just the way it was before she'd come into it.

Two

. . . .

Still peeved, Sabrina opened the door to her office on the first floor of the hospital and came to a complete stop. Her tightly compressed lips softened. Her stiff shoulders relaxed beneath the red linen suit jacket. Slowly she continued across the room, past the woman standing quietly to one side, until she was behind her desk.

Where there once hung a bland reproduction of a lighthouse, now hung a vivid oil painting of children playing in a lush field of wildflowers. She could almost hear the laughter, smell the fragrance of the flowers, feel the sun on her face.

"Kara, your talent never ceases to amaze and delight me."

Kara Simmons's tense shoulders relaxed as much as Sabrina's had earlier. She came to stand beside Sabrina. "I'm glad you like it."

Sabrina turned to the woman who had become her best friend since her move from Houston. Tall, slim, with a striking face that often turned heads—which she never seemed to notice—Kara was the calmest, most forgiving person Sabrina knew, and woefully insecure when it came to her paintings.

The connection between her and Kara had been immediate. They'd met Sabrina's first day of work, when she'd gotten lost and asked the first friendly face with a Texas Hospital employee badge for directions. Kara, a social worker, had gladly shown Sabrina to her supervisor's office located in the same wing as Kara's department.

Hours later, in the cafeteria with a cold sandwich and a Pepsi, her head swimming with information and procedures, and a briefcase full of notes and forms, Kara had waved her over to her table. Over lunch, when Sabrina had mentioned she was looking for a place to rent or buy, Kara told her about a house near hers that turned out to be perfect.

"All of your paintings have been fantastic and this one is no exception." Sabrina folded her arms across her chest. "Although I'm still annoyed that you won't let me pay you for it." She touched the carved mahogany frame. "Unlike the particle board that masqueraded as a frame on the previous painting, this is real wood and expensive."

"I framed it myself, so that cuts down on cost." Kara smiled. "Besides, it's payback for letting me ride with you last week while my car was in the shop."

Sabrina waved the words aside. "We work at the same place. It was fun driving in together. I just wish our schedules weren't so erratic so we could do it more often."

"You won't get an argument from me, but neither one of us knows when we'll have to work late," Kara said. "Two days you had to wait over an hour while I worked with a nursing home to get a patient admitted."

"And I used the time to catch up on paperwork that I'm

always behind on," Sabrina reminded her with a wrinkle of her nose. Although she enjoyed helping people, she detested the paperwork needed to get them that help and document what she'd done. "The painting is worth way more than what I did."

"Not from my way of thinking. I didn't have to rent a car or ride the DART." Kara swept her hand over her head. "It rained two days and I would have gotten wet and this head would have been a hot mess."

Sabrina laughed with Kara. She had thick, naturally curly hair that hung several inches past her shoulders. Today it was loose, but most days she wore it in a ponytail. "You have beautiful hair. I'd trade you any day for this." Sabrina flicked straight strands of her smooth hair in a layered cut that framed her face. "I wish I had some curl, but one thing I wouldn't trade is your friendship."

"Same here. The picture before this was pitiful." Kara touched the corner of the wooden frame.

"No argument," Sabrina agreed. "It makes me smile, and today I need it."

"What happened?" Kara asked, instantly alert. Her compassion was only one of the reasons that made her such a wonderful social worker and friend.

"Dr. Mathis," Sabrina said. "Don't say it," she quickly added when Kara's mouth began to curve into a smile.

Kara grinned, showing even, white teeth in her dark chocolate face. "You do like to live dangerously."

Sighing, Sabrina placed her notebook on the desk. "Dr. Mathis sets my teeth on edge."

Kara folded her arms and leaned against the desk. "He also revs your engine."

Sabrina tsked and blew out a disgusted breath. "I didn't

know who he was at the time," she defended. A week after she'd arrived, she and Kara had been headed to the cafeteria for lunch. The elevator door opened and he was there. Tall, muscular, and incredibly handsome in a white lab coat, she'd almost sighed. Her heart had actually thumped. Obviously, he hadn't felt the same punch, because he'd walked past her as if she didn't exist. Naturally, she'd asked about him.

"And now that you do?" Kara asked innocently, her light brown eyes twinkling.

Sabrina made a face. "He needs to learn not to dump information on patients. He's so pragmatic."

"Unfortunately, so are a lot of doctors, but we both know he cares about his patients. He's spent many a night in the doctors' lounge when he's had a patient in crisis. If there's a problem, he's there. He's only had one vacation in the time he's been here."

"I know. I'd think he was on an ego trip if he didn't brush aside any and all accolades with that 'My patients deserve the best I can give them' speech. There's a heart somewhere under that Valentino double-breasted suit." Sabrina plopped into her leather chair behind her desk. "I trust you to get the full scoop of what the grapevine is saying about me."

"The nurses will applaud you," Kara said.

"The doctors will crucify me," Sabrina said, then smiled mischievously. "It won't be the first time. At least my direct supervisor won't be back until Monday."

"I'd say that calls for a celebration. Why don't you come over tonight for dinner? I'm doing a new pasta and shrimp dish."

Sabrina's smile wavered. As much as she liked Kara, her mother barely tolerated Sabrina. In all the four months since Sabrina had moved in two doors down and all the times she'd been to Kara's house, Sabrina had never seen the woman smile.

"It's Thursday, so Mama will be glued to the TV set, watching her programs," Kara coaxed, her smile a bit forced.

Sabrina immediately felt a twinge of guilt. "Since you're a fabulous cook and hostess, you talked me into it. I'll bring the wine."

"Deal. See you when I see you." Kara went to the door. "Bye."

"Bye," Sabrina said, then pulled the notebook toward her. She had one more patient to check on before she called it a day. Her mind tried to veer toward Dr. Mathis's sexy body, but she pulled it firmly away. He was off-limits.

Cade looked at the GPS, then at the one-story cottage home on the quiet street off Polk Street in an older, slightly affluent neighborhood in Oak Cliff and frowned. The quaint brick-and-stone home wasn't what he'd expected.

Sabrina Thomas dressed well, wore understated but expensive jewelry and the orthopedic-surgery-waiting-to-happen killer heels that women tortured their feet to wear. He thought she'd prefer a more happening and carefree place to live.

He had expected to see one of the new high-rise town homes or one of the apartments that catered more to an easy, affluent lifestyle that were popping up all over Dallas. A home meant work, permanence, and the very reason he'd chosen to live at Navarone Place.

He'd been lucky enough to purchase one of the highly prized penthouses that rarely came up for sale. The twenty-four-hour chef on duty meant Cade never had to worry about his dinner. He simply put in his weekly order on Sunday and the food was delivered to his penthouse at 7 P.M. each night. And, if he was going to be late, all he had to do was call and re-schedule.

Getting out of the low-slung car, he rounded the hood and started up the curved walkway. By the door and under the two large oak trees on either side of the neatly trimmed yard were blooming flowers in a rainbow of colors. He couldn't imagine her having the time to take care of the place herself.

However, if she liked flowers, perhaps he could smooth the tension between them with a bouquet or two. He wanted this animosity, or whatever it was between them, gone. Others on the staff might disagree with him, but they kept their opinions to themselves.

He just needed to get Sabrina to be the same way. He'd had enough chaos growing up to last several lifetimes.

Memories tried to surface of that forgotten time, but he ruthlessly pushed them away. He wasn't a man to live in the past. His long finger pressed the doorbell almost covered by English ivy. He waited, and then rang again. He glanced at the late-model red Audi convertible in the driveway. He had no idea if that was her car or if she lived alone.

"Are you looking for Sabrina?" inquired a scratchy male voice.

He turned to see an elderly couple. The tall man in jeans and a white shirt leaned lightly on a cane. The woman similarly dressed stood close beside him with a four-foot section of a broom handle clutched in her right hand. "Yes."

The man studied Cade closely. "Why do you want to see Sabrina?"

"We work together. I'm Dr. Mathis."

"You have any proof?" the woman asked.

Cade pulled out his wallet. They were right to be cautious.

Opening his wallet, he showed them his driver's license and a wallet-size replica of his medical degree.

Both peered at the identification a long time as Cade waited. He had several patients with visual problems who refused to wear their eyeglasses.

Lifting their heads, they smiled. "That's her car, so she's at home. She likes to swim in the evenings. The gate isn't locked, but I keep telling her it should be."

"Ms. Thomas likes to follow her own dictates," Cade said.

"Most women do," the man said, looking affectionately down at his wife with a smile.

"Nothing wrong with that," the woman added. "Please tell Sabrina the Goldens said hello."

"I will," Cade assured them as the couple continued down the sidewalk. Turning, he went back up the walk and around the side of the house. As the woman had said, the gate of the eight-foot wooden fence was unlocked. The neighbors didn't have to worry. Ms. Thomas struck him as a woman who could take care of herself, Cade thought.

Rounding the corner of the house, he stepped onto lush grass in a flower-filled backyard. To his right was an eight-foot stone fireplace with a cushioned group seating in front. He heard a splash, looked deeper into the yard. He saw the water rushing over a rock waterfall into an odd-shaped swimming pool close to the back fence. His eyes narrowed as Sabrina climbed out of the water.

His gaze slowly swept from the soft features of her face over the black two-piece swimsuit, then narrowed on seeing the skin-graft scars that resembled a faded patchwork of skin that ran from her left forearm, beneath her left breast to mid-thigh. He'd done a rotation in the burn unit in medical school.

Gauging from the extensive scars and the smoothness of the skin grafts except beneath her left arm, she'd suffered third-degree burns at a very young age.

Unconsciously his mouth tightened at the thought of the pain she must have endured. Burn therapy had come a long way in the past fifteen to twenty years. But before that time she would have had to suffer the excruciating pain of dressing changes to help heal and debride the wounds without any anesthesia or medication to dull the pain.

She had suffered.

He now knew another reason she fought so hard for her patients. She knew what it was to rely on others for the best medical care, and be at their mercy when it wasn't given.

Sabrina climbed out of the pool, a daily ritual to keep the mobility in her left arm, and reached for the towel she'd tossed on the chaise, and froze. Her head jerked up. Dr. Mathis was the last person she expected to see, even if she had been thinking about him since she left the hospital.

Mrs. Ward had called Sabrina to tell her she'd spoken with him. She'd said he was as abrupt as usual, but he also sounded concerned that she wasn't feeling well. She and her husband had decided, if they had to choose between bedside manners and skill, they'd choose skill. They—

Her thoughts slammed to a halt as she remembered the burn scars. She reached for the towel. Her fingers clutched the soft material, but something inside her refused to hide behind it. So let him be disgusted like Howard in high school when he'd come over unannounced and saw her in a halter top and shorts. That had put an end to their dating.

She hadn't even thought of dating again until she was a freshman in college. Again disaster struck when Kent saw the scars on her arm when her knit sleeve rode up. She hadn't tried dating again.

Her chin jutted the tiniest bit. Let him get a good look. His reaction would put an end to those crazy thoughts she was having about him.

Yet as seconds passed, his expression remained unchanged. He slipped his hands into the pockets of his tailored slacks, his direct gaze on her, and remained silent. She waited for his gaze to flicker over the scars she'd carried since her mother, high on meth, spilled boiling water on her. Nothing. His expression remained impersonal. For some odd reason, that annoyed her.

"What are you doing here?" she snapped.

"I rang the doorbell and no one answered," he said by way of explanation.

"That didn't give you the right to enter private property."

"The Goldens said I should. They said to tell you hello."

She didn't doubt him. She and Kara were the only single women in their neighborhood association. A few of the older couples had made it no secret that they'd like to see them married.

"Aren't you going to ask?" she questioned. Her voice carried a note of irritation. There was no reason to explain further.

His gaze flickered over her, detached and clinical. "Third-degree burns on the left side of your torso and upper thigh. Extensive skin grafts from your right leg." One hand motioned toward her. "It would be my guess that you were swimming to keep the full range of motion in your left arm."

He'd said it so clinically, so remote, but at least there hadn't been revulsion in his face or in his voice. Even a coworker had stared transfixed last week when Sabrina had taken off her jacket. Underneath had been a sleeveless blouse. Sabrina had slipped the jacket back on.

Yet, for some odd reason she was beginning to feel uneasy with him looking at her. She wrapped the large towel beneath her arms, and used a hand towel to partially dry her hair and keep water from dripping in her face. "Why are you here?" she repeated.

"To find out how we can work together without the conflict," he told her.

"I'm not sure that's possible," she said honestly.

"I refuse to believe that." He took a step toward her. "Surely we can find common ground."

She studied the narrowed, determined eyes. He probably wore the same expression when he was in surgery. He didn't have to come. One word from him and she'd probably have to look for another affiliate. "Why don't you just report me? The board thinks you walk on water."

"One, I fight my own battles. Two, although you're misguided, you care about patients. Since we have a common goal, there should be no reason we can't have a respectful working relationship."

"Why bother?"

Annoyance flickered in his beautiful black eyes and across his handsome face, then it was gone. His other hand came out of his pocket. "Conflict is counterproductive. I prefer working in a calm environment."

Sabrina wrapped the small towel around her neck and continued to study him. Her scars didn't bother him. She wondered what did. "Have you had this conversation with anyone else at Texas?"

One eyebrow lifted in annoyance. "It hasn't been necessary."

Sabrina smiled, feeling a small amount of pleasure that she was the only one at Texas that got to the great Cade Mathis. Seems he did notice her—if only that she annoyed him.

"I see nothing laughable about this," he said, clearly ticked.

Sabrina's smile widened. "I've never seen you smile or laugh."

"What? What has that got to do with our discussion?"

Everything, she thought, but this time she kept her thoughts to herself. "You are pragmatic and straightforward. You point out the risks. I look for the endless possibilities, for the positives. Like having you for a surgeon."

"I don't walk on water," he said, as if the very thought irritated him.

No one could say Cade Mathis was egocentric. "No, but you're a hell of a doctor. You fight for your patients, you just don't always fight *with* them."

"I don't have time to pamper them like you do," he said. "Mrs. Ward is a prime example. Letting her postpone the surgery without pointing out the risk would have been negligent of me."

Sabrina thought of pointing out that he hadn't had to scare her, but then perhaps he had. "Dr. Mathis, you have your ways and I have mine. I'll promise to try and see your point, if you'll agree to try to see mine."

"There'll be no more confrontations?" he asked, staring intently at her.

"I'll do my best," she told him.

He didn't like the answer. She could see it in his clenched jaw. She smiled inwardly. Who would have thought it, that she was the one person Cade Mathis couldn't ignore.

"I don't want to have this conversation again," he said.

She tossed the towel on the chaise and folded her arms. "I wouldn't bet on it, but just remember, we're on the same side."

"Good-bye, Ms. Thomas." He turned.

"Sabrina."

He glanced around at her. His expression was stoic.

At that moment, she decided that she'd see him smile. "Since we're going to have a better working relationship we shouldn't be so formal, don't you think?"

"Something tells me it doesn't matter what I think," he said, and kept walking.

Sabrina smiled, then laughed. "You might be right."

"Did she pay you for the painting?"

Kara signed inwardly, and fought to be patient with her mother, but it was becoming more and more difficult. Nothing Kara did pleased her, but at least she hadn't started in on her the moment she got home. "It was a gift, Mama. Sabrina is a friend."

Her mother, sitting at the small table in the kitchen, tsked and punctuated the remark with a thump of her cane on the tile floor. "If she was a true friend, she wouldn't take advantage of you."

Her back to her mother, Kara continued stirring the shrimp in the skillet. Reasoning with her mother had always been challenging. Since the death of her father eighteen months ago, it had become impossible. Hazel Simmons had been pampered and sheltered by her husband of thirty years, her every wish granted. She was angry that he had been taken away from her, angry that she had to do with less since his death. In return she made life miserable for everyone around her.

"She's coming over for dinner in a bit," Kara said, steeling herself for the disapproval.

She didn't have long to wait. "Shrimp is expensive."

"Mama, we aren't so bad off that we can't invite a friend over for a meal." Kara set the sizzling shrimp aside and faced her mother. "I enjoy cooking and having friends over."

"Then invite Burt."

Kara shoved her hand through her hair. Her romance with Burt Collins, an internist at Texas, had lasted only three weeks. "Burt doesn't want to be here any more than I want him here."

Her mother pushed herself up on her cane. "He would be if you weren't so hard on him. You could take him back, and we wouldn't have to watch every dime."

Money. It always boiled down to money. Their father had worked hard, but he hadn't saved very much. The money from his life insurance policy had barely paid for his medical and funeral expenses. Near the end of his lengthy illness, he had worried about his wife more than himself. Kara had assured him she'd take care of her mother. She'd known it wasn't going to be easy when she moved back in, but she hadn't realized how demanding it would be.

"Men are entitled to sow a few wild oats before they get married," her mother said. "Take him back."

Kara cursed the night Burt followed her home after she caught him and one of the nurses at the hospital on the couch in the doctors' lounge. The betrayal had slapped her hard. She'd thought Burt was "the one." He'd proven her wrong. Worse, many of the staff members at the hospital knew it.

"Burt and I are over, Mama," Kara told her, and turned back to the stove to check the boiling pasta. "I could never forgive a betrayal." She didn't add, especially not when she was subjected to the smirk of the nurse she'd caught him with each time they saw each other in the hospital. Thanks to an understanding supervisor, she didn't have to work with any of Burt's patients.

"You're making a mistake, but it won't be your last," her mother said sarcastically.

Kara felt the sucker punch to her soul, as her mother had intended. No matter what, she'd never been able to please her. The more she tried, the more she failed.

The doorbell rang. Her mother's lips pressed together as she stood. "It's time for my stories."

"I'll bring your tray to your room," Kara said, well aware her mother would hear the relief in her voice and annoy her further. Her mother kept walking. Shortly, Kara heard the simultaneous close of the bedroom door and the doorbell.

Shaking her head, she went to the door and opened it. Seeing the beaming expression on Sabrina's face for some odd reason made Kara want to cry.

"What's the matter?" Sabrina asked, stepping inside and closing the door after her.

Kara shook her head and willed the useless tears not to fall. "Nothing. Dinner is ready."

Sabrina glanced down the hallway leading to the bedroom. "Is there anything I can do?"

"You're doing it." In the kitchen, Kara drained the pasta.

The loud pop of a cork sounded in the room. "You look like you could use this." Opening the cabinet, Sabrina picked up two wineglasses, filled one and handed it to Kara, then inhaled over the skillet. "Smells delicious. I told my mother this morning that, if I didn't love you, I might hate you. You do everything so well."

"Except please my mother." The words were out before Kara knew it. With anyone else she might have tried to retract them, but if anyone understood ambivalent feelings about your mother, it was Sabrina.

Kara wasn't surprised to feel Sabrina's arm around her for a quick hug just before she nudged the glass to her lips. "My adoptive parents helped me find my birth mother when I was eleven," Sabrina said. "She was thirty-one, looked sixty, and tried to proposition my dad in front of me. She had no remorse for what she'd done to me. She only wanted money to buy more drugs."

Sabrina took the wooden spoon from Kara's unmoving hand and began to stir the pasta and shrimp. "I cried for days. It was my grandfather, my mother's father, who helped me realize that I was giving more thought to my birth mother than the people who had raised me, the people who had loved me, saved my life after I developed an infection in the hospital. If Mama hadn't been volunteering in the hospital and heard me crying, I might not be here today. Life has balances, if we look for them."

Kara picked up the bowl of fresh-cut vegetables and added them to the shrimp. "My daddy was the best there was. No matter how tired he was or how busy, I always knew I could count on him."

"Balances." Sabrina looked at Kara. "I've had friends before, but none who understood me or didn't freak when they saw the scars from the burns." She grinned. "You were the first until this afternoon."

"Who? What happened?" Kara asked with open curiosity.

"I'll tell you as soon as we fix your mother a plate and make sure she's all right." Sabrina went to the pantry and pulled out a tray. "You won't believe who it is."

. . .

"Dr. Mathis!" Kara screeched, then slapped her hand over her mouth.

Sabrina grinned and took another bite of food, relishing the memory of his reaction to her in a bathing suit as much as the fabulous pasta salad.

"Details, and don't leave out a thing," Kara told her, leaning farther over the kitchen table, her food forgotten.

Sabrina was happy to oblige to tell her everything, and ended by saying, "He can't figure me out."

Kara laughed, then sobered. Worry creased her brows. "Sabrina, you have a dreamy smile on your face. You couldn't possibly be thinking of acting on the attraction you have for him, could you?"

"I might." Sabrina picked up a bread stick. "You know, I've never seen him smile."

"I know you enjoy helping people, but they want help. Dr. Mathis impressed me as a man who doesn't want or need any interference in his life. You might not like how things turn out," Kara warned.

Undisturbed, Sabrina leaned back in her chair. "I wonder what made him so self-contained, so remote. Most straight doctors his age are married. I've never even heard of him dating."

"Since he made a special trip to talk to you because he likes a calm work environment, I'd imagine he wouldn't date anyone at the workplace because the breakup would be gossiped about for weeks." Kara's hand clenched on the stem of her wineglass. "I wish I had had such forethought."

"Burt is a butthead!" Sabrina snapped.

Kara grinned. "I couldn't believe you called him that to his face. He was so shocked, it gave us time to get on the elevator."

"He's lucky that's all I called his cheating behind."

Kara sipped her wine. "I thought I was falling in love with him. It turned out my pride was more hurt than my heart. My second mistake with a man. If not for Mama, I would forget him entirely."

"Most mothers dream of their daughters marrying a doctor so they'll have a secure future," Sabrina said.

It was her mother who wanted the secure future, Kara thought, but she was too ashamed to admit that greed drove her mother. "Your mother and grandmother did just that."

Sabrina smiled. "My brother Stephen is going into premed this fall at UT Houston. He'll carry on the tradition. They'd all be thrilled if I was dating a doctor."

"What? Are you serious?" Kara asked, her concern returning.

"I realize you think I'm crazy, but I've been wondering since he left if I might not just disturb him professionally, but on a deeper, more personal level." Sabrina placed her fork on her plate and leaned forward, her expression determined.

"His bedside manners need a major overhaul, but he genuinely cares about his patients. He's dedicated, hardworking, and goes to the mat for them. He's a good man. I see him and my palms gets sweaty, my heart beats like a jackhammer. I think about what it would feel like for him to smile at me, hold me, kiss me. I've never been this hot and bothered about any other man. I want to see if Cade might feel the same way."

Kara shook her head. "You could get hurt."

Sabrina picked up her fork. "I could also miss out on something wonderful. Like you said, I don't think he'll do the pursuing since we work together so it's left up to me. He didn't freak when he saw me in a swimsuit so we've already passed a major hurdle."

Kara opened her mouth to warn her best friend again, then decided to keep her mouth shut. Just because she was too scared to go after what she wanted in life was no reason to dissuade Sabrina from going after what she wanted. Instead, Kara picked up her fork. "Now that you know you have his attention, what do you plan next?"

Grinning, Sabrina picked up her wineglass. "Keep it on me."

Three

. . . .

Garbed in his green surgical scrub suit and cap, Cade went down the hall toward the OR waiting room. Neurosurgeries could be long and grueling. Things could go bad in a split second. It was his job when that happened to quickly correct whatever the problem was. On occasion that didn't happen. Sometimes the problems were too pervasive and too dramatic no matter how skilled a surgeon, and you lost.

For some odd reason, he thought of Sabrina. He frowned. No matter how he tried to keep thoughts of her away, to keep thinking of her as just the patient advocate, he couldn't. Perhaps it was knowing that she'd suffered, perhaps it was the winsome smile on her face. Either way, since last night thoughts of her kept slipping into his mind. They would stop once he scrubbed, then he'd be focused as always. But, before then he'd talk to Mrs. Ward's family.

He'd made it a practice early in his private career to briefly speak with the family. If things went sour in the OR, he didn't want their first sight of him to be with bad news.

He pushed open the door to the OR waiting room. His gaze swept the room and collided with Sabrina's. He understood the slight acceleration of his pulse and it irritated the hell out of him. His lips tightened.

Eyes wide with worry, Mr. Ward rushed to him, closely followed by several other people. Sabrina stood by the man's side. "Is something the matter? What happened?"

"I just wanted to remind you that the surgery is going to be long. I'll send someone out to give you an update if necessary. After she's settled in the recovery room, I'll come out and speak with you again," Cade said.

Mr. Ward bowed his head briefly, then lifted it. Tears glistened in his eyes. "Please take care of her."

"I will." Cade felt a tug on his pants leg and looked down into the big brown eyes of a little girl. Instantly he knew it was their daughter. "Yes?"

"Mama said you're going to make her feel better so she can play with me and she won't be tired and sick all the time," she said.

Cade couldn't help flicking a glance at Sabrina. Adults he could handle. Children were another matter. He knew too well how a small child could be hurt by careless words, the hurt more painful than the stinging bite of a belt, the angry back of a hand. "I'm going to do my best."

She reached her small hands up to her father. He immediately picked her up. As soon as she was even with Cade, she leaned over toward him. Startled, scared that she'd fall, he caught her around the waist. She kept leaning toward him until her lips brushed his cheek. Only then did she settle against her father, her arm going around his neck.

"Thank you," the child said, a wide grin on her cherubic face.

Cade didn't know what to say, so he did as he always did when faced with emotions he didn't want or understand—he walked away. He didn't stop until he was in front of the sink to scrub up for Mrs. Ward's surgery.

Sabrina went back to her office shortly after Cade left the OR waiting room, but no matter what she did she kept an eye on the clock. Three hours later she was back in the waiting room to see if the family needed anything. As she'd gently suggested, their daughter Clarissa had gone home with a friend. The wait was too difficult on a small child.

Mr. Ward, arms folded, jerked his head up as soon as the door swung open. Sabrina smiled.

Blinking rapidly he jammed both hands into the pockets of his jeans and turned to stare out the window. His mother, then his mother-in-law got up from their seats to give him a hug, speak softly to him before again taking their seats. It was a little past eleven, but Sabrina didn't think any of them had used the vouchers for the cafeteria she'd given them.

Waiting was difficult during any surgical procedure, but when you knew the odds weren't in your favor, it was especially nerve-wracking.

Sabrina checked on the family to see if they needed anything and was met with polite no's and shaking of heads. No one was going anyplace until they knew Ann was safely out of surgery.

Finally, she went to Mr. Ward. He hadn't been able to work regularly as an electrician since his wife's illness. Since both of their families lived out of town, he was left to care for his sick wife and his daughter alone. He hadn't seemed to mind. The love he and his wife shared was obvious. Sabrina had almost given up hope that she'd ever find a man to share her life with.

A memory of Cade, his mouth unsmiling, flashed in her mind before she firmly pushed it away. Thinking of Cade in the long term was asking for trouble. Yet, somehow, she realized she was already on that road.

The door opened and a woman in surgical scrubs came into the room. Mr. Ward whirled around and met the woman before she had taken more than a few steps. "Did Dr. Mathis send you?"

"Yes. Dr. Mathis wanted you to know that he encountered more nerve involvement than anticipated so he's going slower in removing the tumor," she said.

Mr. Ward scrubbed his hand over his face, swallowed hard, nodded. "How much longer?"

"An hour. Perhaps two. It depends on what he finds," she said. "If you'll excuse me, I have to get back."

"Dr. Mathis is the best," Sabrina reminded Mr. Ward as the surgical tech walked away.

"So is Ann." His calloused hands clenched and unclenched. "If I lost her—" His eyes shut tightly.

Sabrina knew he wouldn't eat, so she faced the others in the room. "I'll stay with him so you can eat a bite."

Ann's mother shook her head, as did her husband sitting beside her. "I'd rather wait here."

His mother came to stand beside her son, brushed her hand down his arm. "I haven't been able to come and help because of work. I won't leave him now."

His hand covered hers. "You go on, Mom, and eat. You,

too, Mrs. Sims. I need both of you to be strong. Dr. Mathis said the first twenty-four hours will be tough."

Tears sparkled in Ann's mother's eyes. Her husband's arm curved around her waist. "The other doctors couldn't find anything wrong with her. I thought it was all in her mind." She bit her lip. "You never did. If it hadn't been for you refusing to stop looking for a doctor . . ." Her voice trailed off.

Mr. Ward went to his mother-in-law and hugged her. "Ann is the best thing that happened to me. She loves me and Clarissa. I knew when she couldn't be the kind of wife and mother she wanted to be that the doctors were wrong about it being in her mind."

"You got her the help she needed," Ann's father added. "Her doctor is supposed to be the best."

Mr. Ward glanced at Sabrina. "He's the best, and he's going to make Ann well. Isn't that right, Sabrina?"

Several pairs of eyes filled with hope and fear focused on her. She gave them what she hoped was enough. "Dr. Mathis is the best neurosurgeon in the state, one of the best in the nation. Ann couldn't be in better hands." She said a silent prayer that it would be enough.

"I'm sorry to do this, Kara, but we have two social workers out sick and Meredith is still on maternity leave," Lois Nelson said, handing Kara a manila folder.

Kara automatically lifted her hand to take the folder from her supervisor, then she paused. Her head lifted sharply. Her fingers clenched, her hand wavered. *No,* her mind silently shouted.

"Dale Bowler is an alcoholic with cirrhosis of the liver. His doctor has recommended dialysis three days a week, but Mr.

Bowler let his insurance policy lapse," Lois went on to explain. "I just spoke with his wife, Bess, who's understandably upset and scared, and told her that someone from this department would visit them today."

Kara hadn't missed that her supervisor had yet to mention the name of the patient's doctor. Taking the folder, she opened it and confirmed her suspicions. Burt Collins.

"You know if there had been anyone else available, I wouldn't have assigned the case to you," Lois explained, her face troubled.

"I know." And she did. It had been three months since she learned Burt was a liar and a cheat, more than enough time for her to move on. "Patients come first."

Lois relaxed her considerable bulk in her chair. "I'm glad that I never have to be worried that you might forget that."

"I'll go see him now, and determine what we can work out." Taking the folder, Kara left her supervisor's office and went to the elevator. It was a little after two. There was a chance Burt might be visiting his other patients or in his office. If not, she'd just have to deal with him.

Stepping onto the elevator, Kara punched in her floor. Perhaps avoiding Burt had been the wrong thing to do. She was developing a bad habit of not facing her problems. Never a good thing.

The elevator stopped on the eighth floor. The doors slid open. She stepped off and turned toward the nursing station immediately to her right. The first person she saw was Burt at the nurses' station talking to the charge nurse, the nurse she'd caught him with. Kara kept going, glad she didn't feel anything.

"Kara, wait."

Clutching the notebook and folder to her, she waited for Burt to reach her and as she did, she impassionedly studied him. Tall, athletic, handsome with thick auburn hair. It had been easy to fall for the charm, the lies. She'd been flattered, and used. "Yes, Dr. Collins?"

"We need to talk."

Opening the folder, she took out a pen. "Was there anything else I needed to know about Mr. Bowler before I see him?"

Burt's lips pressed together in a flat line. "You know I meant about us."

She looked up, thankfully calm. "There is no us. You made sure of that." Closing the file, she started down the hall.

He caught her in front of Dale Bowler's room, his hand closing around her upper forearm. "Don't be so stubborn. You're taking this hard-to-get act a little too far."

She looked from the fingers on her arm to him. "You're the actor. I advise you to remove your hand unless you want to face a sexual harassment charge."

"You—"

"Excuse me."

Kara jerked around at the sound of the deep, molasses voice to see a man with the most startling green eyes she'd ever seen in a handsome light brown face. Her cheeks heated in embarrassment. "I'm sorry."

"I'm not," he said, a slow grin spreading across his face making him even more gorgeous. Kara blinked and caught herself before her mouth gaped. The man was absolutely breathtaking.

"Weren't you on your way someplace?" Burt snapped.

The man, at least five inches taller and more muscled, slowly turned to Burt. He stared at him so long, Burt shifted nervously.

Not wanting to be the subject of more gossip, Kara said,

"Dr. Collins, if you'll excuse me." Leaving them both, Kara entered the room. The door had barely swung shut before it opened again. Seeing Burt she was tempted to leave and return later.

He stopped when the stranger tried to follow him. "This is a private room."

"I know." Brushing by Burt, the man entered the room and went to the bedside. "Hi, Dale."

The thin man in the bed opened his eyes. The corners of his mouth in his unshaven, jaundiced face lifted slightly. "Tristan." He looked at the elderly woman beside the bed who was holding a glass of water with a straw. "Told the old lady you'd be here."

Tristan smiled and nodded to Dale's wife by the bed. "Hello, Bess. Still giving you lip I see."

"Always. Hello, Tristan." Bess looked from the thin man in the bed back to Tristan. "Thank you for coming. I don't know what to do."

"I'm here now."

"Are you a relative?" Burt asked abruptly.

"No," Tristan answered, his hand on the man's emaciated shoulder.

"Then I'll have to ask you to leave. Patient confidentiality," Burt said with entirely too much enjoyment.

The man's annoyed gaze swung to Mrs. Bowler. "Is that what you want, Bess?"

"No, and Dale don't either," she said, setting the glass of water on the nightstand. "I want you here. If I got to sign some papers that says so, I will."

"That won't be necessary," Kara said, annoyed that Burt was being so strict. She extended her hand to the woman. "I'm Kara Simmons, a social worker with Texas. I'm here to help Mr. Bowler with his out-patient care."

Bess rounded the bed and took both of Kara's hands in hers. "Lordy, thank you. The doctor was talking about dialysis, but the insurance said the policy lapsed. Our kids ain't able to help."

"All of Zachary's employees in his construction company have insurance," Tristan said, a frown on his face.

The man on the bed looked away. His wife folded her arms around her waist and swallowed before she said, "After Zachary had to let Dale go, he paid the insurance until Dale got another job, and said he didn't need help anymore. But he got fired six months ago. This time the man he worked for left it up to Dale to make the payments." She shook her gray head. "He never made a one."

"Just because I missed a few days they let me go," Dale snapped, his angry gaze on Tristan. "I'm the best tile man in the city. Zachary knows that. I thought Zachary was my friend. Ain't no one better than me." He pointed a dirty, yellowish thumb to his chest. "You know that, Tristan."

"Perhaps once, Mr. Bowler, but your drinking ruined your liver. One kidney has shut down and the other one is failing. Dialysis is the only way to keep you alive," Burt said. "You can't drink anymore."

"A man should be able to take a shot now and then," Dale grumbled.

"You keep on, and you'll be dead in three months."

Dale cursed and tried to lift himself up in bed. "I'll be alive when they put dirt on your face."

"If no dialysis center takes you, you won't live three months," Burt predicted. "You have no one to blame for your condition except yourself."

"Oh, lordy," Bess said, wringing her hands.

Kara curved her arm reassuringly around the woman's

trembling shoulders, and glared at Burt. He was being an ass because he was ticked at her and angry with Dale's visitor. "We'll find a place for your husband. Don't worry."

Burt's handsome face contorted with anger. "I'm discharging you today. There's a list of medications you need to be on. The nurse will bring your discharge orders. Good-bye." The door swung shut behind him.

"It's the eighteenth. We don't get our checks until the first of the month." Bess moaned, placing her hand on her husband's foot beneath the bedcovers.

"Don't worry, Bess. I'll see that Dale gets what he needs," Tristan said, going to Bess.

"Thank—"

"I ain't taking no charity," Dale grumbled, his face belligerent as he cut his wife off. "I called you to help Mama. Those sorry kids of ours ain't worth spit. Been here three days, and we ain't seen a one of them."

Embarrassment touched Bess's thin face. "They're busy, Dale, working and taking care of their families."

"You make excuses for them just like you always do," he said. "You spoiled them so they're no good to themselves or us."

Bess tucked her head and folded her arms around her waist.

Tristan was at the head of the bed in seconds. His voice was hard when he spoke. "Dale, if you weren't already on your back, I'd put you there. Bess put up with your bad temper and hard drinking for forty-odd years. She never gave up on you, just like she hasn't given up on your children. If she were a less loving woman, she would have walked away and left all of you."

There was silence on the bed.

Kara had been caught in family arguments before, caught in her parents'. She could walk away from the latter, but never from her patient no matter how uncomfortable it made her. "Mrs. Bowler, do you have any other resources?"

The older woman shook her head. Kara expected as much. The man might want to help, but dialysis was expensive. "There are programs available to help with the dialysis and the discharge medication. Don't worry." She pulled a card from her pocket. "Here's my card. I'm going to look at the discharge orders and start working on finding a treatment center close to where you live."

Bess clutched the card. "Thank you."

"That's what I'm here for." She pressed her hand to Bess's. "Discharge is often slow. Do you have a way home?"

"I'll take them," Tristan said.

Her gaze flickered to him. "It might be awhile before everything is ready."

"No matter. I'll be here."

"All right. Good-bye," Kara said, and left the room, all the while aware of Tristan's intense green eyes on her every step of the way.

"Excuse me for a moment," Tristan said, and rushed out the door, ignoring Dale's "chasing skirts" comment. "Ms. Simmons." At least he hoped it was Ms. He hadn't seen a ring. Obviously she and the rude jerk of a doctor had a history.

She turned to face him, and what an exquisite face it was. "Yes?" Although her expression was calm, there was something a bit off. If he didn't know better, he'd think she was wary of him.

"I just wanted to thank you again," Tristan said, and extended his hand. "Tristan Landers."

After a moment's hesitation, she lifted hers. "Kara Simmons."

He was surprised to feel the calloused palm, the strength, the slight trembling. "Dale talks big, but he's scared. So is Bess. You helped."

She nodded, sweeping thick, curly black hair over her shoulder. "Any chance he'll stop drinking?"

"No," Tristan answered, giving himself points for not staring at the high, firm breasts revealed when she lifted her arm and her drab gray jacket parted. "He's too stubborn. Even with all that's happened to him, he thinks he's in control of his life."

"Dr. Collins might have been abrupt, but he's a good internist," she said. "At least try to slow him down."

"We will. Do you mind if I have your card?" he said, then added when she hesitated, "In case I think of anything else."

"Of course." She pulled out another card. "Good-bye, Mr. Landers."

Trying boyish charm, he smiled. "Tristan, please."

She didn't smile back. "Mr. Landers," she said, then walked away.

He hadn't thought she would be easy, but he had no doubt about the outcome. He refused to think of the other time he'd been so sure about a woman only to be proven so horribly wrong. Life had bit him on the backside, but he'd finally, thankfully moved on.

Shoving the card into the pocket of his cotton shirt, he went back into Dale's room. "Dale, if you keep going like you have been, none of us are going to be happy with the way things turn out."

"You ask her out yet?" Dale asked, a sly grin on his thin, grizzly face.

"Did you hear me?" Tristan asked.

"We all gotta go sometime, I might as well go out doing what I want," he said, crossing his arms across his frail chest.

Tristan threw a glance at Bess. Her arms remained tightly wrapped around her waist. She lowered her head. "What about your family?"

"Bess knows me better than anyone and loves me in spite of it." He almost smiled. "Now, answer my question. You ask her out yet?"

Aware Dale was going to live his last days the way he wanted, Tristan finally answered his question. "Not yet, but I'm working on a plan."

Dale chuckled. "About time you moved on."

"I couldn't agree more," Tristan said, returning the smile.

Four

. . . .

Less than an hour later Tristan easily located social services on the first floor of the sprawling hospital complex. He saw no reason not to put his plan into motion sooner rather than later. Kara impressed him as a woman who might take a lot of persuasion.

Touching the brim of his Texas Rangers' baseball cap to two passing nurses, he continued down the narrow hallway, looking for Kara's office. The sharp-eyed receptionist said she was in her office. She wasn't impressed with him. He didn't mind, just as long as Kara was.

Locating her door, he knocked.

"Come in."

Even through the door, he liked the sound of her slightly husky voice. He could well imagine it whispering in his ear, just before biting his earlobe. With that titillating thought on his mind, he opened the door.

She was sitting behind her neat wooden desk, a plain manila folder in front of her. The smile on her beautiful face faded.

Slowly, she straightened and leaned back in her chair, her slim fingers clenched around the pen in her hand.

He was right. She was leery of him. Smart woman, but it wouldn't do her any good. This might be your biggest challenge yet, Tristan thought, but he had no thought of not coming out victorious. He closed the door. "Good afternoon, Kara."

Her eyebrow lifted imperiously. She certainly didn't like him calling her by her first name. He planned that and more. "Mr. Landers."

Tristan was undaunted by the frost in her voice. He had a feeling the pleasure of getting to know Kara was going to be well worth the effort. "Tristan, please, since, as I said, we're going to be working together to help Dale."

She closed the folder in front of her and placed her slender hands on top. "I wanted to talk to you about that. Please have a seat."

She'd sidestepped that nicely. He always liked intelligent women, liked them even better when they had a figure that could make a man drool. Kara had both. Tristan took the straight-back padded chair in front of her desk and removed his cap. "He's a good man who made some mistakes."

"How long have you known him?"

"Five or six years," he told her. "He's right about being the best tile man in the business, or at least he once was. He worked for Zachary Holman, owner of Holman Construction Company. He did the tile on the project Zachary did for me."

"Is Mr. Holman the man who continued to pay the insurance premiums after Mr. Bowler was fired?" she asked.

There was no sense evading the truth. "Yes. Zachary tried every way he could think of to keep Dale, including going by his house every morning to pick him up, direct deposit of his check, taking him to AA meetings. Dale balked at everything. In the end, Zachary had to let Dale go."

"No one could get him to understand that he has a problem with alcohol?"

"Dale kept saying he's just living his life the way he wants, so rehab or AA was out," Tristan explained. "He was showing up late and, when he did get there, the work was shoddy. Zachary didn't have a choice. His reputation was on the line."

She braced both arms on the chair. "You and Mr. Holman are friends?"

"Yes. We hit it off when we were working together," he explained, thankful she was relaxing more and more, and that Dale was more than a case number.

"If you don't mind, what type of work are you in?" she asked, then rushed on. "I only ask because you offered to take care of things for Mr. Bowler. They have no financial resources. I assume you meant you'd help them financially."

"You assumed right. I write for a magazine," he told her, then laughed at the surprised expression on her face.

"You're a writer?"

"Yep. Believe it or not." He'd probably never get used to seeing the disbelief on people's faces. His unexpected career had surprised him as well, but it allowed him to do what he wanted when he wanted and enjoy life.

A pensive expression on her beautiful face, she tilted her head to one side to study him. "I wouldn't have pictured you as a writer."

"Believe me, you aren't the first."

"I suppose," she said. "I don't want to invade your privacy, but dialysis is extremely expensive. If I can't get Mr. Bowler into a free program, you could be looking at two thousand a week. I need to know if you can handle that much so I can plan for any eventualities."

"That much, huh," he said, rubbing his cheek. "Well, if that's what it takes, we'll come up with the money somehow."

A frown darted across her dark brow. "We?"

"Zachary and his other friends," Tristan explained, although he had no problem paying Dale's entire medical bill. "Dale had a lot of friends in the construction business who'd want to be there for him. He's helped a lot of people when he was up. Now it's his turn."

She opened the folder. "Thank you for helping me to better understand Mr. Bowler. I spoke with his nurse just before you came. He should be discharged within the hour. Pharmacy is on this floor. I'm hoping to have a company lined up soon to pay for his medication. You can pick up his prescriptions on the way back to his room."

Tristan shook his head and leaned back into his chair. It certainly didn't take long for her to give him the boot. "Since we're finished talking about Dale, I figure we can get on to the second reason I'm here."

"And that would be?"

"I'd like to take you out."

"No, thank you." She came to her feet. "Good-bye, Mr. Landers."

Good manners dictated he stand. He put his cap back on. "You mind telling me why?"

"I'm not interested."

He stared at her, his disbelief plain on his face.

She glanced impatiently at her watch. "I have an appointment arriving shortly."

"Could you answer one last question?" he asked.

"Mr. Landers," she said, annoyance in her voice.

"What is it about me that you don't trust?" he asked.

Her arresting brown eyes widened. Her full mouth, a dark berry color, gaped.

He liked the idea of taking Kara by surprise. It had been a long time since he'd met a woman whose emotions were so open and honest.

"Good-bye, Mr. Landers."

"For now." He turned to leave, trying to come up with his next move and saw the four oil paintings that framed the door. There were vivid slashes of color, power and restraint in the progression of a baby in her mother's arms, to a toddler, next a young man ready to meet the world, and finally to a gray-haired man standing on a moon-draped cliff, the wistfulness in his gaze palpable.

Entranced, Tristan moved to the paintings and looked for the name of the artist. KMS was written in flowing script in the right corner. He whirled to stare at Kara, then looked back at the paintings. It was almost impossible to reconcile the de-mure woman in a white blouse and prim gray suit with the emotions swirling in the pictures. "You painted those?"

After the briefest hesitation, she said, "Yes."

He glanced around the room looking for other paintings, and was disappointed to see none. Finally his gaze settled on her. "You're very talented." She shrugged the tiniest bit. It an-noyed the hell out of him, that she had so little faith in herself or him. "Do you think I'm lying to get you to go out with me?"

"You wouldn't be the first."

"I don't have to lie to get a woman to go out with me," he told her, his annoyance growing. "Was Collins the first?"

"You were on your way out."

He studied her a long time. He should walk, but he knew he wouldn't. He'd already decided Kara was worth the extra effort. "Are they for sale?"

"Three thousand dollars."

She'd tossed out the number carelessly, obviously thinking to get rid of him. He pulled out his billfold and removed a check. She'd learn he didn't bluff. "Who shall I make it out to?"

"No!" she said, catching his arm when he started for her desk.

"Then you didn't paint them?" he asked, disappointed.

"Of course I did, but they aren't for sale. They're of my late father," she explained, glancing at the last painting, her face softening despite the sorrow he glimpsed in her eyes.

"You thought I was trying to con you?" he asked, and when she didn't answer, he continued. "Some men can be trusted."

"The trouble is finding them," she said.

"No, the trouble is misjudging them when you find them." He replaced the check and pulled a card from his billfold. "Call me if you ever want to discuss paintings or honest men." Placing the card on the desk, he left.

He'd give her a week and then he was coming back. Kara was proving more interesting by the minute. He wanted to see, to feel, the passion beneath her cool exterior. One day, he promised himself, he would.

Kara picked up the ecru card with neat black lettering. TRISTAN LANDERS—FREELANCE WRITER. The words were elegant and simple. She looked at the blank backside. No free cards for him.

Kara lifted her gaze to the paintings she had done of her father the year before he died. She had come home from New Jersey for the weekend. That night after her mother had gone to bed, she and her father sat outside on the porch steps talking.

He'd looked so wistful talking about his dreams to own a big rig and travel the country, but he'd never done it. He said he'd never had the courage. Kara had understood he had courage in abundance; he'd sacrificed his dream to ensure that his wife and child were cared for.

After seeing the paintings she'd done to honor him, there had been tears in his eyes. He'd hugged her and then left her to go work his second job as a night watchman at a warehouse. As long as she could remember, her father had worked two or three jobs to give his wife all the things she said she needed to be happy.

Kara was unaware her hand had closed over the card until she felt the edge of the paper dig into her palm. Her fingers uncurled and she stared down at the rumpled card.

Tristan Landers was trouble in designer blue jeans. Sexy, incredibly handsome with mesmerizing green eyes and café au lait complexion, he was tall with a trim, muscular build. He was dangerous to any woman breathing.

She'd known that the second she'd laid eyes on him. He was the kind of man that made a woman forget caution, the kind of man that, when it was over and it would be, made it impossible for a woman to forget.

She dropped the card in the wastebasket. She'd been down that road twice before. Never again.

No matter that she had been ridiculously pleased that he seemed so taken with her paintings. Tristan Landers was off-limits professionally and socially.

. . .

Friday afternoon, Cade worked his shoulders, lifted his hands over his head as he tried to get his stiff muscles to relax. The two-hour surgery he'd planned had turned out to be almost four. The tumor had been evasive and tenacious. He pushed open the door to the OR waiting room.

Mrs. Ward's family rushed toward him. He didn't realize he'd expected to see Sabrina until disappointment hit him when she wasn't there.

"Is Ann all right?" Mr. Ward asked, his family surrounding him as if to give him support. At times like these, Cade occasionally let himself wonder what it would feel like to have a family, for someone to care about him for purely unselfish reasons. Patients and their families needed him, but when that need was past, he ceased to be important to them.

"Dr. Mathis?"

"She's resting comfortably in the recovery room," he told them. "She's still a bit groggy from all the anesthesia, but coherent and all neuro signs are good."

Mr. Ward blew out a relieved, shaky breath. "When can I see her?"

"The nurse will let you know. I'll see her again before I leave." Cade looked at his watch. "I have another surgery. Goodbye." He turned to leave and felt a hand on his arm, and glanced around.

Mr. Ward extended his hand. "Thank you."

"We're not out of the woods yet," Cade said. Above all he was honest with his patients and their families.

The hand remained steady. "You told us about the risks, but you also gave us hope. No other doctor did that."

Cade refused to let the words touch him in any way. The man had wanted to hit him yesterday. If things had gone differently, he might have done just that. People's emotions were flighty and that's why he preferred his own company. People said and did what benefitted them.

Cade finally took the man's hand for one strong shake, then turned and headed back to the surgical suites to do what he did best.

Sabrina was waiting for Cade when he came out of his last surgery. It was almost five. He looked tired. No wonder. He'd been in surgery for over nine hours that day. After Ann's surgery, he had done two spinal procedures.

He stopped when he saw her leaning against the wall, then slowly continued. "There can't be a problem with Mrs. Ward."

She held up a thermos. "Coffee, and not from the cafeteria. Kara is holding a table for us in the cafeteria. And don't worry, it's takeout."

He didn't move. She smiled into his frowning face. "Come on, doc. You're been on your feet all day. What can it hurt to have a meal with your newest associate? Or you can have the leftover dried chicken I saw languishing in the warming tray in the cafeteria."

"Let's go."

They'd barely reached the table in the cafeteria before Kara Simmons spoke briefly and then left. On the table were a woven picnic basket and one place setting with real flatware.

"You aren't eating?" he asked, holding her chair.

"Late lunch. Please sit." She removed the top of the picnic basket and served him veal cutlets and steamed vegetables, then poured him a cup of coffee. "Cream and sugar?"

"Black." Cade took his seat, picked up his fork, and took a bite. "It's good."

Sabrina laughed. "I told you I didn't cook the food." Propping her arms on the table, she leaned over toward him.

He didn't have to look around to be aware that probably every staff member was staring at them. He'd only eaten in the cafeteria a handful of times, and that was when he'd been desperate. The food was probably good when freshly prepared, but he'd always been late.

"You can't cook?" he asked, enjoying in spite of his best efforts the way she seemed to enjoy life and being with him.

"I tried, but there were always more interesting things to do." She grinned. "I was into a lot of extracurricular activities in high school. I went to college at home, but I was just as heavily involved."

He could believe it. She was probably very popular. His cell phone rang. He pulled it from his waist. "Dr. Mathis." He came to his feet. "I'm on my way. Mrs. Ward is asking for me."

Sabrina came to her feet. "Let's go."

Standing, he glanced at the picnic basket, her dinnerware. "What about your things?"

"She's more important. Let's go." She reached for his arm.

Less than three minutes later, Cade entered Mrs. Ward's cubicle with Sabrina on his heels. Sitting by her bedside, her husband held her hand. He rose on seeing them. "Baby, the doctor's here with Sabrina."

Cade went to the other side of the bed. "Mrs. Ward, what is it?"

Her lashes fluttered open. She blinked. "Dr. Mathis."

"Yes, are you feeling all right?"

A slow smile spread across her face. "I woke up."

"That was the plan," he said matter-of-factly.

"Your plan, but His might have been different."

"His?" Cade questioned, looking across the bed at her husband.

"God," he explained.

"You—you gave me a chance to see Clarissa grow up. Thank you. Sabrina was right. Thanks to both of you," she murmured, her eyes closing again.

"She needs to rest," Dr. Mathis told her husband. "You can stay for another five minutes. I want her to be moved to ICU just as a precaution for the night."

Fear flashed in her husband's eyes again. "You said everything was all right."

"It is. She can be monitored more closely there."

"What if she needs you?" he questioned.

"The nurses will call. Five minutes." Taking Sabrina's arm he left the room. "Thanks for the meal. I won't keep you. Goodbye."

He was dismissing her. She'd let him . . . for now. "Good night, Dr. Mathis."

Kara went to bed, but she couldn't sleep. She kept thinking about Tristan, second-guessing herself about throwing away his card.

Three thousand dollars.

Did he really think they were worth that much? What kind of freelance writer was he that he could write out that kind of check as if it were for three dollars? She needed to talk to someone.

At 7:56 A.M., the longest she could stand it, Kara rang Sabrina's doorbell, then rang again, hoping she hadn't gone to the hospital or for a donut run as she occasionally did on weekends.

The door opened. Sabrina, in a lacy pink silk robe and matching short nightgown, yawned. "What's up?"

"I need to talk to you." She held up a bag. "I have food."

Sabrina's eyes widened. She reached for the bag, digging inside as she headed for the kitchen. Then she stopped. "Are you all right?"

"Yes."

Sabrina continued to the modern kitchen in the back of her house. The Viking appliances were seldom used, but as Sabrina often said, it looked pretty. She grabbed the orange juice from the refrigerator while Kara got the plates and napkins. In less than half a minute, they were sitting down to French toast, scrambled eggs, and bacon.

Sabrina blessed the food and took a bite. "Talk."

"I met a man."

Sabrina blinked, grinned. "Hot dog. When?"

"Yesterday," Kara explained and told her about Tristan. "He liked my paintings."

"And you liked him?" Sabrina said, licking the powdered sugar from the French toast off her finger.

"What woman wouldn't?" Kara twisted in her seat. "What I want to know is about my paintings. He was prepared to pay a lot of money for them. I can't get it out of my mind that I might be able to make money from my paintings."

"About time you believed someone."

Kara put her hand on Sabrina's arm. "You're my friend. I haven't let many people know I paint. Even the people in my office. They think they're nice, but nothing special."

"Believe me, they are." Sabrina pulled her leg under her. "I gave one to Mom and Dad for their wedding anniversary. They both love it."

Kara smiled indulgently. "Again, because you gave it to them."

"If I didn't love you, I'd hit you." Sabrina folded her arms. "So, you have to decide if you want to see Tristan because he turns you on or because he might be able to help you market your paintings. I think you should consider both."

Kara shook her head. "Paintings only. With the extra money, Mama could do some things she wants. Maybe take a trip." And stop blaming me for losing Burt.

"What about you?" Sabrina asked, her eyes narrow, her tone a bit sharp. "You mother has a new car, new clothes, regular trips to the beauty salon. You, on the other hand, make do with a ten-year-old car, haven't purchased anything new to wear in months, and do your own nails and hair. Shall I go on?"

"I don't need much, and those things help her feel better," Kara said, trying not to squirm. "I'd be in the beauty shop for hours waiting for this head to dry."

Sabrina grunted.

Kara rushed on. "Then you think I should try to find him?"

"Yes. Sadly the janitors are on it when emptying trash, if nothing else. His card is probably long gone, but there are other ways." Rising from the table, Sabrina went to the computer workstation in the kitchen and turned it on. "We'll Google him."

Kara peeked over her shoulder and chewed her lower lip. "Don't you think that's being a bit invasive?"

"Being invasive is using Google Earth to find a picture of his house."

Sabrina typed in his name. TRISTAN LANDERS WRITER popped up.

"Wow." Sabrina grinned and looked over her shoulder at a hovering Kara. "You can pick them. That is one gorgeous man."

Kara didn't like the strange motion in her stomach on seeing his picture. "I'm only interested in what he can do for me with my paintings."

"He asked you out, didn't he?"

Kara frowned and continued reading his stats. "Yes, but he understands I'm not going out with him."

"From looking at his picture and his accomplishments, he doesn't strike me as a man who gives up easily. He's written for some of the top magazines in the country, including *Luxury*. That took perseverance," Sabrina mused.

"I said no and I meant it."

"Whatever you say. From all of these awards and accolades, he might be connected to a lot of influential people in the arts."

"That's all I care about," Kara said, trying and failing to not let the picture of Tristan with two beautiful women in tiny bikinis bother her.

Sabrina leaned back in her chair and grinned. "If you change your mind later on, I won't blame you."

Straightening, Kara quickly shook her head. "I won't."

Holding up both hands, Sabrina stood. "Just saying. You can jot down his information and call him while I clean up the kitchen."

"Now?" Kara squeaked.

Sabrina picked up the cordless phone with one hand and gently guided Kara to the chair with her other. "The sooner you call, the sooner you two can meet and get your new career rolling."

Kara's stomach knotted. "What if he was just bluffing? What—"

Sabrina dialed the phone number listed on the Web site. "Yes, I'm calling for Kara Simmons, please have Mr. Landers call her at 999-287-5555. He'll know what the call is about. Thank you."

Kara just stared at her best friend as she replaced the phone and went to the kitchen. When she didn't say anything, Kara followed. "Well?" Kara asked.

Picking up their plates, Sabrina went to the sink and emptied the fragments into the sink disposal. "His answering service, and not a girlfriend."

"It wouldn't have mattered," Kara said. At least in that she was being truthful with herself.

"It would if you'd let it. If you'd start living your life and not factor in your mother," Sabrina said gently.

Kara picked up their glasses and flatware. "I promised Daddy I'd take care of her just like he did, and that's exactly what I plan to do."

"What about what *you* want?" Sabrina asked.

"She's my mother," Kara answered, aware from the knowing look on Sabrina's face that she recognized duty not love in her response, and that made Kara ashamed. Maybe she hadn't tried hard enough. Her mother loved other people, why didn't she love her own daughter?

"All right." Sabrina turned on the faucet and rinsed the

dishes. "One thing I'm not letting go is that, if you have an opening for your paintings, you're getting a sinfully sexy gown. People will be talking about the beautiful artist *and* her paintings."

Relieved that Sabrina had intentionally changed the subject so as not to embarrass her further, Kara tried to smile. "And you'll be there to support me, with Dr. Mathis at your side."

Sabrina leaned against the edge of the counter. "He needs me, Kara. He needs to relax and enjoy life. I don't think he does."

"I'd tell you to be careful, but it's obviously too late," Kara said.

Sabrina grinned and opened the dishwasher. "Yep. After yesterday I'm even more determined. He could have blown me off about going to the cafeteria. He didn't. He doesn't do anything he doesn't want to. He feels something. He might not even be aware of it himself, but he's going to. I'm going after him, and he's going to like it."

Kara didn't doubt Sabrina's determination. She just wasn't sure about the results. Sabrina always went after what she wanted. Kara had tried that—twice—and had her pride kicked in. Never again.

Five

. . . .

Saturday morning Tristan climbed out of his mint condition '68 Chevy truck and went to the front door of a one-story home on a quiet residential street in East Dallas, his latest project. Tucking the zipped leather folder beneath his arm, with two fingers he pulled the key from the pocket of his jeans and let himself inside. He didn't stop until he was in the small kitchen. Placing the key on the discolored countertop, he surveyed the room.

Like many of the older homes built fifty years ago it had a single oven, gas stove, refrigerator without an ice maker, a single sink, and no dishwasher. All the appliances were copper colored. All were woefully outdated. Not for long.

Leaving the kitchen Tristan easily found the two small bathrooms. The master bath wasn't much bigger than the hall bath. Serviceable, but with no punch. Nothing about either of them would make a person happy, make them feel pampered and like they could start the day in style.

Again, Tristan would change that.

Pulling the notebook from beneath his arm, he opened it. They'd start tearing out on Monday to remodel the house. He'd gotten the rehab bug after doing research for his first article for an interior design book. The article, "Luxury Living Without a Luxury Price Tag," had been a step-by-step remodeling of his favorite rooms: the bath, kitchen, and bedroom. To him they, not the family room or great room, were the heart and soul of any house.

His thoughts veered to Kara Simmons. If he didn't like a challenge, he might let it go. Her paintings, with their power and passion and hope, wouldn't let him. She had talent. He hated to see people waste what God had given them.

People like Dale Bowler. They'd gotten Dale home a little after six last night. The first thing he did was try to go to the kitchen for a beer. He'd cursed, and Bess has wrung her hands as Tristan poured the four cans out, then searched out the three-bedroom frame home for any liquor that Dale might have stashed.

It hurt to see the house Bess and Dale had been so proud of when Tristan first visited in disrepair. There were cracks in the ceiling, the panel in the den buckling, water damage on the walls. Along with the health insurance policy, Dale had let the house insurance policy lapse and made no repairs.

Tristan had brushed aside Bess's embarrassment. He'd already called Zachary and asked if he could send a crew over the first day Dale was in dialysis to start working to repair the house. He just wished Dale could be repaired as easily. Tristan had no idea why Dale was an alcoholic. He just knew if he didn't stop, he wouldn't be alive when winter came.

Shrugging off the depressing thought, Tristan remeasured the bath and bedroom. Most people called him anal because he checked and rechecked facts, but he'd seen too many costly mistakes in time and money when all it would have taken was a remeasure or a recheck of facts.

Tristan didn't like making mistakes. His metal tape crackled. He'd made a doozy! He shook his head. Before yesterday it had been over three months since he'd thought of his failed marriage. Perhaps he was thinking of it now because his mother had broadly hinted when he was over for dinner Thursday night that she had a nice designer friend she wanted him to meet.

No way, he thought as he grabbed the notebook and headed back to the kitchen. Getting serious was the last thing on his mind. The tape crackled again as he checked the kitchen measurements. He hadn't had a clue that Gizzelle wanted a divorce until she asked him to pack his things. She'd shown more emotion asking him to take out the trash.

She was one of those self-assured overachievers who never doubted she'd make it to the top. She'd explained in the logical, analytical way she was known for in the courtroom that they were heading down different paths, had different career goals. That marriage wasn't working for her.

He didn't learn until weeks later that she had been offered a junior partnership in the law firm where she worked. He'd already asked her to scale back her hours at work. They'd seen less of each other in their nine months of marriage than during the six months they'd dated. Too often he'd come home to an empty house and an empty bed. It hurt his pride that she had chosen her career over him.

The divorce was final a year ago. He'd jumped back into dating as if to prove to anyone who might be interested that he was still capable of getting a woman. Tristan blew out a breath and shook his head at his stupidity. His ex had her life, he had his.

His cell phone rang. He pulled it from the case on his belt buckle. "Tristan."

"It's Zachary. I just left Dale and Bess. He's still upset about his beer. I told him I would have done the same thing."

Tristan leaned against the counter. "It's hard to look at the man he is now and remember the man he was."

"Yeah, but we get to walk away and take a break. Bess can't."

"She'd fight anyone who tried to make her." Tristan almost smiled. "Some women stick."

"I got lucky and blessed," Zachary said. "Madison and the kids are my life."

"Don't I know it. I might have to wait until Manda grows up to find me a good woman," Tristan teased, referring to Zach's five-year-old daughter.

"Don't even jest," Zachary said, a shudder in his voice. "She's growing up much too fast and so is Zachary Jr. It's hard to believe he'll be two in a couple of months."

"He'll be going out on jobs with you before you know it, just like Manda," Tristan said.

Zachary chuckled. "I thought she'd be more interested in TV broadcasting like her mother, but whenever I fix something around the house, she's right there with me. Which reminds me, Bess said Dale's dialysis is scheduled for Monday, Wednesday, and Friday. I'll go over since the crews will be busy at your site and two others."

"Thanks. I'll pay—"

"If you want to stay my friend, you'll forget about money where Dale is concerned," Zachary said. "I just wish I had known his situation before now."

"He didn't want you to know that he was having such a

hard time. That he's messed up," Tristan told him. "Pride got in the way."

"My daddy always said a man who said he hadn't made a mistake was a liar."

"Your daddy is a smart man." Tristan sighed. "I've made my share."

"Same here," Zachary said. "Thankfully we've learned from them."

Tristan caught a hint of something in Zachary's voice. "I think you've moved from generality."

"You were always smart—at least in some things," Zachary said. "Bess likes the social worker, and was a bit concerned that she might be next on your hit list."

Tristan squirmed. "I'm not that bad."

"If Manda was of age to be dating men your age, I wouldn't let you within ten miles of her," Zachary said.

"Bess doesn't have to worry. Kara turned me down flat," Tristan said, his irritation rising all over again. He really wasn't that bad. "She said she wasn't interested."

"It sounds as if it wasn't the answer you expected," Zachary said.

"It wasn't."

"No never stopped you in the past," Zachary said. "I don't think it will this time either."

"You're right, but there's another reason. She's a fantastic artist. Her work deserves to be seen."

"If only that was all you planned to see."

Tristan burst out laughing. "Bye, Zachary. Kiss that beautiful wife and the kids for me."

"I will. The crew should be there at eight to start tearing out. You still plan to be there every day?"

"Yes," Tristan answered, looking around the kitchen. "Unlike the first job, when I let your crew do all the work, I want to show that the homeowner with no experience can do a lot of the remodeling and save money."

Zachary grunted. "There's nothing like experience, but I'll let you find out for yourself."

"With the cameras rolling and a photographer here, the entire world is going to find out. Bye."

"Bye."

Tristan closed the phone, finished measuring, and then walked through the house once again, seeing in his mind's eye the changes that would make the house come alive with warmth and charm.

His phone rang just as he closed and locked the front door. "Tristan."

"This is your answering service, Mr. Landers. You had eight calls."

Opening the door of his truck, Tristan grabbed his day calendar. "Shoot."

"Your mother said for you to call her. Jiles, the editor of *Luxury* magazine, and Sandra Collins, associate editor for *Interior Design,* both called twice. Here are the numbers," she said, then gave him the information. "Patrice Wilson three times. She said you have her cell, home, and work phone number."

Tristan winced. He and Patrice had been out three times, to bed once. A big mistake. She was too clingy and too demanding. He'd told her it was over several times. He didn't look forward to telling her again.

"A person called for Kara Summers—"

"What?"

"A woman called for Kara Summers and asked that you call her back at 999-287-5555. She was the last call."

"Thank you. Good-bye." Frowning, Tristan stared at the hastily written phone number. Why had someone called for Kara? Was it about Dale? Or did she want to talk about honest men or her paintings? There was one way to find out.

He got a dial tone and punched in the number.

Kara freely admitted she was a coward. She'd showed her mother Dillard's sales paper, knowing full well she wouldn't be able to resist going. Kara would pay for it later when the bill came, but she wanted to be able to talk freely if Tristan called.

Too restless to remain inside, she'd taken her easel and canvas, and set up in the backyard a few steps away from the patio covered with pink peace roses. The elm tree cast dappled shadows over her, but not the canvas.

Paintbrush in her hand, she paused. There was a face instead of the strand of forest with wildflowers she'd planned. No matter how she tried to think of him by his last name, she thought of him as Tristan. While she'd told Sabrina to be careful when she'd left a short while ago to go check on Mrs. Ward and see Dr. Mathis, Kara would do better to tell herself to be careful. Now, she was painting him.

If her mother knew—

The ringing of the cordless phone startled her. With trembling fingers she drew it out of the pocket of her apron. Seeing Tristan's name, her hand began to shake even more.

The ringing came again. She swallowed and pressed TALK. "Hello."

"Kara."

She came to her feet, moistening her suddenly dry lips. "Yes, Tr— Mr. Landers. This is she." She wanted to groan. Of course he knew it was her.

"Is this about Dale?"

"No, I wanted to discuss my paintings."

"Do you have others I could see?"

"Yes." She laughed nervously. "A lot. They're in the attic."

"The attic! You're kidding, right?"

Her mother hadn't liked the clutter when she'd moved in to help care for her father when he'd become so ill. "I tend to do larger canvasses."

"I understand. Can I come over and see them?"

"No, I mean—" She moistened her lips.

"If it's not convenient for you now, perhaps you can tell me when," he said. "I start a new project Monday and I'll be tied up every day except Sunday for the next six weeks or so."

Coming to the house made sense. There were too many paintings to take to him. Plus, he could see which ones he liked.

"What exactly do you plan for my paintings?" she asked.

"I have an idea, but I'd want to see the other paintings to see if they have the same appeal."

Kara wrapped her arm around her waist. If they didn't . . . She looked at her watch. Her mother had been gone for an hour. She'd be gone for at least two hours. She might even go to Patrizio's restaurant in the Uptown shopping mall and have lunch or go to Barnes & Noble for books and magazines.

"Kara, you do understand, don't you?"

He was trying to reassure her. "I live in Glen Oaks off thirty-five." She gave him the address.

"I know the area. I can be there in twenty minutes."

"All right. Good-bye." She disconnected the call, scared

and excited. Soon she'd know if her work was salable. She
didn't know why she trusted Tristan's opinion, but she did.

Sabrina stepped off the elevator on the sixth floor of Texas
with a smile on her face. She was dressed in one of her favorite
outfits, a slim-fitting pair of black pants, ruffled yellow-and-
white checkered blouse with bouffant sleeves, a thin red belt,
and red skimmers. She'd checked on Ann twice during the
night and this morning after Kara had gone home. Each time
the report had been good. On one of those calls, the nurse had
reported Dr. Mathis was there as usual.

When Sabrina had asked what she meant, the nurse had
gone on to explain that if Dr. Mathis sent his surgical patient to
ICU, he always visited the patient sometime during the night.
He understood the critical nature of patients and made himself
available. He was one doctor who didn't mind being called.
He'd only had to take one nurse to task for not checking one of
his patients' vital signs on time for nurses to get the message.

Waving to the nurses at the nurses' station, Sabrina pushed
open the door to Mrs. Ward's room. Her husband's head was on
the bed by her elbow, his hand holding hers. Both were asleep.

Smiling, Sabrina let the door close, turned to leave them,
and came face-to-face with Cade. Her heart knocked crazily
in her chest. "Good morning, Dr. Mathis."

His gaze flickered to the badge on the pocket of her frilly
blouse. "Aren't you off on Saturdays?"

Sabrina would have been happier that he knew her schedule
if he wasn't frowning. Otherwise, he looked as yummy as he
always did, even if he was in surgical scrubs and running shoes.

A stethoscope hung around his neck. "Yes. I wanted to check on Mrs. Ward."

He peered down at her with suspicion. They both knew she could have called.

She smiled and forged ahead. "She's resting."

He grunted. "I suppose her husband is still with her."

"I was trying to figure out a way to break the news to you gently."

"I okayed it." He brushed by Sabrina and entered the room.

Surprised, Sabrina followed. Dr. Mathis was known as a stickler for protocol. Doctors made exceptions for the strict ICU visiting hours, but she'd heard him order Mrs. Ward's husband to let his wife rest. She wanted to know what had changed his mind.

Rounding Mrs. Ward's bed, he gently touched her arm. "Time to wake up again."

Mr. Ward jerked awake. "You can't wake her up?"

Cade looked at Mr. Ward as if he'd like to toss him from the room.

"We just came in," Sabrina supplied.

"I'm sorry." He looked from her to Dr. Mathis and rubbed his hand over his face.

Sabrina patted his hand. Dr. Mathis looked as if he might toss her out after Mr. Ward.

"Mrs. Ward."

Her eyelashes fluttered, then opened. "Dr. Mathis?"

"Right." He took her hand in his. "Squeeze. Good. Now, the other hand. Follow the light. How many fingers? Good. I'm going to listen to your heart."

Since she'd turned her head and was looking at her husband, it was Sabrina's guess that she didn't care what he did.

Cade straightened. "I'm going to move you to a regular floor today."

"Then I can see Clarissa," Mrs. Ward said.

"I'm not a proponent of children under twelve visiting patients, especially post surgical. The potential for passing germs and picking them up is too great," he told them.

"I want to see her," Mrs. Ward said, her lower lip trembling.

"I know, honey, but we'll wait if Dr. Mathis thinks it's better for both of you," Mr. Ward said, kissing his wife's hands and looking up at Dr. Mathis. "He's been right so far."

If Cade was surprised by her husband's quick agreement, he didn't show it. Sabrina certainly was. Something had happened between them and she wanted to know what it was.

"Good-bye," Cade said, and strode from the room.

Sabrina followed him out. "I have questions."

"Somehow I'm not surprised, but I have patients to see."

"Then why don't you call me and we can have lunch or dinner as the case might be at my place," she said. The invitation just slipped out, but it made perfect sense. She wanted to be with him, wanted them to get to know each other better. She couldn't cook anything except breakfast food and seldom did that. Maybe she could grill.

"What if I have plans?"

"Do you?" she asked boldly. It was a good thing she fought for what she wanted.

"Good-bye, Ms. Thomas."

She folded her arms and stared up at him. "If I wait for you to call and I don't eat until later tonight, I'll probably be a bit out of sorts Monday, maybe Tuesday as well."

"Ms. Thomas, you're skating on thin ice."

"I don't plan on falling through," she said, and couldn't help the grin that sprang to her face. She found she liked teasing Cade, even liked the way he clipped out her name so formally. "The second you call I'll throw the steaks on the grill so you can eat when you get there, and go home afterward."

He stared down at her. She stared back up at him.

"Late lunch."

"See you then," she said, and walked away, grinning for all she was worth.

Tristan pulled up in front of Kara's house and got out of his truck. Blooming plants were everywhere, huddled beneath the two red oaks in front, bordering the walkway, hugging the house. Red and deep purples were the dominant colors with a smattering of white and yellow peeking through here and there. Kara apparently preferred strong colors. There was passion simmering beneath her calm surface.

It remained to be seen if he would get to sample that passion.

Going up the walk, he rang the doorbell. On the long porch were colorful pots of flowers. He idly wondered if Kara had painted the red clay pots.

The door opened. Kara stood there. She was as strikingly beautiful as he remembered and just as weary. She looked as if she didn't know whether she wanted to close the door or invite him in.

"Hi, Kara. Thanks for letting me come over to see your paintings. I admit I'm anxious to see them," he said, hoping to help her make the decision in his favor.

"Hi. Please come in."

He stepped over the threshold, and frowned. The house was neat and well furnished, but dull with dark woods and dark print fabrics. Kara was wearing dark colors as well. Her curly brownish-black hair was tied back. He got the impression of a self-contained woman, not the passionate woman who had painted the pictures in her office with such power.

"I thought about bringing the paintings down, but decided to wait on you," she said, and bit her lower lip. "It's probably dusty. I haven't been up there in a month."

"I'm used to dirt."

She nodded and didn't move.

He suddenly understood her nerves were related to her paintings as well. He wished he could reassure her, but he couldn't do that until he'd seen her other work. The paintings in her office could have been inspired by the emotional connection and loss of her father. "Which way?"

"Sorry. This way." She led him down a short hallway. The ladder was already down. "It's lit."

Stepping around her, he placed his hand on the ladder. "Are you coming?"

She unwrapped her hands around her waist, then stepped forward. Her hand clamped around the ladder. "If you like the pictures, then what?"

"I have a connection with an interior designer who is always looking for one-of-a-kind pictures to place in upscale homes. The ultra rich don't want to walk into a home and see the same paintings. Even if they have a Picasso or a Monet, it's different of course."

"The price you offered, was that just to get my attention?"

Fair question and he could see in her eyes how much the answer meant even if her hands hadn't been clenched on the ladder.

"No. You might be surprised at the obscene amount of money some people pay for what passes as art. If it doesn't touch me, it doesn't go into my home, and I don't talk about it in my articles."

"For *Luxury* magazine."

His eyebrow lifted. "How did you know I wrote for *Luxury*?"

She blushed, briefly lowered her gaze. "My friend and I Googled you after I, er, lost your card."

He smiled. She'd probably tossed it. "I'm glad you went to the effort. I'm anxious to see your other work."

Nodding, she began climbing up the stairs. "I finished a landscape a little over a month ago. At last count, there were thirty-three paintings."

Tristan tried to focus on the conversation instead of the enticing butt in front of him. "That should give me a good—"

"No! It can't be," she said as her head peered over the edge of the opening, then she was scrambling up the ladder.

His heart slammed in his chest. He almost reached for her leg before he thought, *"Wait for me!"* He quickly joined her. Animals and snakes often got into attics. Standing beside her, he searched for the danger in the clutter and found none.

"They're gone," she whispered, walking past a stack of plastic totes, cardboard boxes, dining-room chairs, floor lamps. "They're all gone."

Immediately he understood. The paintings.

Six

. . . .

Tristan heard the heartbreak, the disbelief in Kara's unsteady voice and bit back a curse. Gently, he touched her arm. She turned to him. Tears glistened in her eyes. His gut clenched at the sight.

"Why would she do that?"

He didn't know who she was talking about, but at the moment it didn't matter. "Could they be someplace else?"

"No. They're gone."

Misery stared back at him. He'd never felt so helpless. "Let's go back down." For a moment she just stood there. "Kara."

Brushing the heels of her hands over her eyes, she went to the ladder and climbed back down. He didn't breathe easy until she was safely standing in the hall. "Why don't we go to the kitchen and get you a glass of water." She didn't resist his urging her down the hall and into the kitchen or setting her in a chair.

After getting her a glass of water, he pressed it to her lips. "Drink." She did, all the while her eyes tightly shut.

"Kara."

Her lashes fluttered, then she opened her eyes. "I'm sorry you made the trip for nothing."

"If you painted one picture, you can paint another one," he told her.

"You don't understand," she murmured.

"Then help me." He placed the glass on the table and took her cold hands in his. "You said you paint large canvases. Is it that you don't paint wet on wet and it takes longer to finish a piece since you work?"

"It doesn't matter anymore."

He didn't know who "she" was, but he didn't like her if she was the cause of Kara's distress. "Are you working on anything now that I could see?"

"It isn't finished."

"It doesn't matter." Standing up, he pulled her to her feet. "Is it here or do you have a studio?"

She rubbed her forehead. "How could she—" She swallowed.

"Where is the picture you were working on, Kara?"

"In the backyard."

"Let's go." Still holding her arm he left the kitchen and went to the connecting den and opened the sliding glass door. His gaze swept the backyard and he saw the easel with a small table with paintbrushes and a couple of tin cans with a chair in front. He started forward, but for the first time she resisted.

"No."

"What?"

"It was just . . . never mind." She held out her unsteady hand. "Thank you for coming."

She was giving up, retreating, and it made him angry. "So you're going to let her defeat you?"

She flinched. "Please leave."

"Not until I see that painting."

Evading the hands reaching for him, he strode to the painting. He stepped around and saw the totally unexpected. His gaze lifted. Kara's hands covered the lower portion of her face.

He stared back at the partially finished painting. Even with only the eyes staring back at him, he recognized them as his own. They were devilish, playful.

"Is that how you see me?"

She brought her arms to her sides. "Could you please leave?"

He went to her. "My mother would probably like to have the picture if you're inclined to finish it."

"Kara! Kara! Whose old truck is in front and what is the attic ladder doing down?"

Her eyes widened with alarm and her head jerked in the direction of the female voice, then back to him.

A slim, middle-aged, attractive woman appeared at the patio door. She leaned on a cane. Her lips were pursed. "Who are you?"

"Nobody, Mama. He was just leaving."

"When he does, get my packages out of the car and put up that ladder so I can get down the hall without breaking my neck. I'm going to get a glass of tea."

Tristan bristled. She hadn't even spoken, just started giving orders.

"I'll show you to the door," Kara said.

In the den he saw the woman slowly making her way to the kitchen. "I came to see Kara's paintings, but they were gone."

"You're wasting your time, so stop wasting hers. I got rid of them."

. . .

Kara heard the strangled, almost animalistic sound, and realized it had come from her. She'd known it, but it was still difficult being slapped in the face with the hatred of her own mother toward her. "What-what did you do with my paintings?"

Her mother continued to the kitchen without answering. Kara followed. "Where are they?"

"Don't you dare raise your voice to me," her mother said. "I birthed you."

And take pleasure in my misery. "The paintings are important to me."

"You waste time painting when you could be doing things around the house I can't do anymore. You promised your daddy before he died you'd help out, not waste your time." She snatched up a glass from the counter. "You're using that little incident against Burt because he agreed that your paintings are worthless."

"I'm willing to pay for them."

Kara had forgotten Tristan was there. She wanted to go through the floor.

"How much?" her mother asked, her eyes narrowed.

"I would have to see them first." Tristan entered the kitchen.

"You know where they are?" Kara said. "Mother, please."

"Your truck outside ain't worth much, so you can't be," her mother said.

"Mother, please," Kara admonished, aware it wouldn't do any good.

"I know people," Tristan said, his expression unchanged. "Where can we find the paintings?"

Her mother held out her glass to Kara. Taking the glass, Kara filled it with ice, then tea from the refrigerator, and gave it back. Her mother drew out the moment.

"She won't sell for less than fifty dollars apiece," her mother said after she'd taken a long drink.

"I need to see them first," Tristan repeated.

Her mother took another sip of tea. "I needed room for my winter clothes and other things since you're in the other bedroom."

Kara was always to blame. "Where are they?"

"I told Fred to take them to the city dump."

"Still no answer," Kara said, clutching the cell phone in her hands. She couldn't stop the trembling of her body. Fred Roberts was a friend of her late father. He'd begun taking care of their yard and doing things around the house for them when her father became too ill to do the work himself. "He could be in his woodshop. He helped me with the frames."

"Then there's a good chance he kept the paintings," Tristan said.

Kara hit REDIAL. She thought Fred valued her work, but it wouldn't be the first time she'd been wrong about a man. "Mother said she had him take the paintings a week ago. He should have called me."

"I imagine he had his reasons."

Kara listened to the phone ring and said nothing. She'd gone past embarrassment. She wanted her paintings back. She'd let him drive because they could load the pictures in his truck and the rest in Fred's truck—if he still had them.

She disconnected the call. "Turn on the next street. Fourth

house on the right," she told him, then scooted forward in her seat. "His truck is in the driveway."

Tristan pulled in beside a gleaming red Ford truck. Kara was out the door before he cut the engine. She hurried on the bricked path to the garage in the back. She heard the buzz of a circular saw from several feet away. Ignoring the sound and the flying wood chips, she stepped into Fred's line of vision.

Her expression said it all. He cut off the power and slowly lifted the protective goggles. "Kara."

"Where are they? Please."

He looked at Tristan. "I—"

She stepped to him. "Please. You didn't do what Mama told you, did you? You didn't—" She couldn't finish.

Anger flashed across his gray whiskered face, in his dark brown eyes. "You think I'd take your heart and soul to the city dump?"

"The only thing keeping me going is the belief that you didn't," she answered, swallowing hard.

"Your mama . . . ," he began, then trailed off.

"Do you still have my paintings?"

"In the house. First bedroom. You go on. I got to get some of this dust off."

Kara didn't need any further urging. She opened the back door and rushed inside. Her heart was thumping so fast she felt light-headed. Her hand closed around the knob, then she opened the door. Paintings were stacked against the walls around the room. Her shoulders sagged in relief. She rushed across the room to touch, to count.

"They're all there," Fred said from behind her.

Kara looked up, tears glistening once again in her eyes. "I'm sorry I doubted you."

"I thought you finally decided to give it up like your mama wanted," he explained. "Your daddy liked your paintings. I hoped she was wrong."

"May I?" Tristan said from just behind Fred. Kara was surprised he'd hung back, then realized he was letting her have her moment. She had been angry with him at first for bringing up the paintings. But if he hadn't, her mother probably would have never revealed where they were.

She stepped away from the paintings, her hope and her fear in her eyes.

Tristan turned first one painting, then another, around to face him, picked it up, studied the subject, and stepped back. He took his time because each picture drew him, but the lure of the next painting pushed him on.

He stopped a third of the way through. There was no need to go on. Kara had talent, but did she have the courage to follow her dream no matter the obstacle or consequences? There was one way to find out.

Propping the picture of a sun-drenched meadow with a stand of oak trees in the distance against the others, he pulled his billfold from his pocket and took out a check. "I'd like to take all of them. Your mother's price is acceptable." He plucked a pen from his shirt pocket.

He watched shock replace hope in Kara's expressive face and eyes. It was all he could do not to go to her. "Shall I make the check out to you or your mother?"

"I . . . I thought . . ."

Tell me to go to hell, he thought, but he said nothing.

Kara shuddered, swallowed. He wondered how many times

life had kicked her in the gut and she'd had to take it. Obviously a lot.

"To me." She went to the nearest picture and picked it up. "I'll help you load."

Feeling like a heel, he watched her leave the room, her steps slow, her head down. She looked alone, and it made his stomach knot to know he was the cause. But she had to learn to go after what she wanted, to stand up for what she wanted.

Picking up another painting, he followed. With each trip, he thought she'd berate him for taking advantage of her. She never did. When he came out with the last paintings, he saw her put the painting she held in the front passenger seat. "Where will you sit?"

"Fred is taking me home," she said, looking over his left shoulder.

The older man glanced from Tristan to Kara, but he didn't comment.

Obviously he cared about Kara. She'd need someone who did. Placing the painting in the back of his truck, he secured the tarp he always carried.

Going to Kara, he handed her the check and a card. "My cell phone and address if you paint any others."

Her hand clutched the check, but she didn't look at it.

"Take care, Kara."

"Good-bye," she said so softly he could barely hear her.

Not by a long shot, Tristan thought. Getting into the truck, he slowly backed out of the driveway. Straightening, he started down the street, his gaze repeatedly going to his rearview mirror, hoping to see Kara signal for him to stop or come back.

She never did.

. . .

Kara watched Tristan take the corner at a snail's pace. At least he was careful with her paintings. She probably should be thankful. She wasn't. Add another man to her growing list of men who had fooled her, used her.

She'd been gullible enough to think he was concerned about her, about her paintings. She was wrong.

"You all right, Kara?"

"I will be." She felt the tentative brush of Fred's calloused hand on her bare arm.

"It's hard parting with something you love and worked so hard to create, but you got paid," he said. "Proves your mother was wrong, doesn't it?"

"Yes." She swallowed the lump in her throat. "If you don't mind, I'd like to go home now."

"Sure. The truck's unlocked. You just climb on in," he told her. "I'll just lock up and get my keys."

Kara climbed inside the truck, her hands clamped in her lap. She'd been so stupid. And wouldn't her mother just love to point it out.

Tristan repeatedly checked his cell phone on the drive to his house. *Call, Kara.* The litany kept repeating itself over and over in his head. Tell him what a SOB he was anything except let herself be walked on and taken advantage of.

His hands clamped on the steering wheel. He'd seen overbearing, thankless parents like hers and thanked God that though his mother might be pushy and nosy, it was because she loved him. Although, admittedly, it drove him crazy at times.

Parking in his driveway, he unloaded the paintings. He made himself not look at them. Kara had so much talent and didn't have a clue. He couldn't wait to see the realization sink in to replace the fear and self-doubt.

Bringing the last picture into the house, he turned it toward him. It was a splash of bright colors that almost looked as if the colors had been carelessly tossed on the canvas, but a closer inspection revealed a yellow vase and multiple stems of flowers reaching almost to the edge of the canvas. Her paintings drew you, just as the woman who painted them did.

However, unless she believed in herself, she'd always be stepped on.

Less than twenty minutes later Kara climbed out of Fred's truck in front of her house, thanked him, and then slowly started up the walk. She'd made it halfway when the door opened. Her mother stood there, waiting. Kara stuck her hands in the pockets of her jeans and glanced down the street. She didn't want to talk to her mother. She was still too angry with her, but Sabrina's car wasn't in the driveway.

"Kara."

There was impatience in her mother's voice. She saw nothing wrong in what she'd done. Kara stepped onto the porch and went inside.

"Well, did he buy them? And don't tell me Fred got rid of them because he was too evasive when I called him that night to ask if he'd done as I asked," her mother said, her hand clamped around her cane.

Hands clenched, Kara faced her mother. "Why? All you

had to do was tell me you needed the space and I would have moved them."

Her mother's lips pursed. "You waste your time painting when things need to be done around the house. You promised to polish the silverware weeks ago."

"You also wanted the hardwood floors polished; the sheers in the bedrooms washed, pressed, and rehung; the windows washed," Kara said, not caring for once that her voice had risen. "I work sometimes ten hours a day, when would I have had the time?"

"Stop that foolish painting and you'd have the time," her mother snapped.

Angrier than she'd ever remembered, Kara pulled the check from her front pocket. "Everyone doesn't think they're worthless." Her mother reached for the check, but Kara shoved it back into her pocket. "The paintings were mine and so is the money."

"If I hadn't given him a price you would have gotten taken," her mother said. "It's only right you share."

"*Right?* You talk to me about right when you sent the paintings you know I loved and worked hours to paint to the dump yard?"

"It was for your own good. You got to stop wasting your time on something that will never matter," her mother said, her voice rising. "I saw the way that man looked at you. You're wasting your time there too. He probably doesn't have a pot to pee in or a window to pour it out. Burt is the man for you."

Her mother would never understand, and there was no sense discussing it. "I'm going to my room."

"You really don't plan to share the money with me?"

"Share?" Kara whirled back to face her mother. "I pay the utility bills, buy the groceries, let you use my charge account.

What do you share except your—" Kara clamped her mouth shut before she said *hate*.

Anger flashed in her mother's eyes. "If your father were alive, you wouldn't talk to me that way. How do you think I feel that I can only get your father's pitiful Social Security check? He promised me he'd always take care of me. So, I go shopping to help me forget my life is practically over. Who wouldn't? You're mean-spirited, and I don't have to listen."

Kara felt the sinking, churning feeling in the pit of her stomach just as she always did when she and her mother had an argument. There was no way to win, and now she didn't even have the paintings to hope.

Cade stared at Sabrina's house but made no move to get out of his car. He wasn't sure why he'd come. He knew she was manipulating him. Mrs. Ward was the only patient they had in common. He should be at his house eating whatever he'd ordered for that day. Try as he might, he couldn't remember what he'd selected. That irritated him as well. Was he in that big of a rut?

Opening the door, he climbed out of the car and closed the door to the Lamborghini, an extravagant status symbol that stayed in the garage more than on the road. The half-a-million-dollar sports car was another sign of his success that the people he wanted to impress would never see. He preferred driving his Jeep, but the foreign car mechanic said the Lamborghini needed to be driven more than once a month.

Once on the porch, Cade rang the doorbell. Waited, rang again. When there was no answer after the fourth ring, he went around the side of the house and opened the side gate to the backyard. He smelled the smoke seconds before he saw the gray-black cloud billowing from a portable grill. A few feet away Sabrina stood by with a bag of charcoal in one hand and a can of lighter fluid in the other.

He thought of the burns she'd suffered and rushed across the yard to her. He didn't realize his heart was beating crazily in his chest until he reached her and started to speak. "Are-are you all right?"

"Yeah." She tossed a glance at him then glared at the grill. "All the stupid thing is doing is smoking. I called Dad, but he forbade me from putting on more lighter fluid."

Cade's heart thumped. He didn't even want to imagine the consequences of such rash actions. His hands actually shook. His hands *never* shook. "Have you ever grilled before?"

"Once or twice," she answered.

Cade saw the grill was new. He didn't know what to say. She'd gone to a lot of trouble to feed him. She wanted information, but he knew instinctually that wasn't the only reason she wanted to be with him. He'd long ago developed an infallible BS meter. He'd had to. Using people was a way of life for some, but not for Sabrina.

"I passed one of those old-fashioned drive-ins where the carhops wear roller skates on the way here. Why don't we go get burgers?"

She wrinkled her nose and took a step closer to the smoking grill. "I promised you a steak."

He already knew she was stubborn. It was interesting to learn she could be stubborn on *his* behalf. "No doubt you'll badger me into having dinner with you again. We can have a steak then."

Her smile was quick. He smiled back before he could stop

himself. She looked fresh and beautiful in a pretty floral sundress, her slim arms bare. "Another woman might take offense at such a gracious invitation, but since we're friends I'll let it go this time."

He resisted the urge to stroke one finger down her cheek. Her skin was probably as smooth and as soft as it looked. He slipped both hands into the pockets of his slacks. "I'll meet you out front."

She caught his arm before he moved away. "You'll do no such thing. I have to change out of this smoky dress. You can wait inside."

In typical Sabrina fashion she didn't wait for him to comply, just went inside assuming he would follow. He did, closing the sliding glass door she'd left open. Like Sabrina, the room was bright and open with generous uses of yellow, the wood on the furniture white.

"Do you want anything to drink?"

"No thanks. Go change."

She didn't move. "The TV remote is in the large white glass bowl on the coffee table." She grinned. "Because I grew up with a father and grandfather who like sports, and later a brother who is just as wild about them, I have all the sports channels."

"I'm not much into sports," he told her.

She frowned, and he gave her the pat explanation. "I was always too busy with other things."

Lifting a brow, she folded her arms over her breasts. "I just bet you were."

Like others, she'd thought he meant women. There had been few dates during high school. Cade's father was a hard man who kept Cade busy with chores on the small farm in East Texas before and after school and on weekends. Cade was never considered a part of the family. What George Mathis called love, others would call free labor.

Cade was up by five every day and was seldom in bed before midnight; he never had a free moment to just relax. In college he was too busy studying to impress the man who, no matter what Cade accomplished, never had a kind word to say.

"You're wasting time," he finally told her.

"Going." Unfolding her arms, she started down the hall.

Too keyed up to sit, he wandered around the beautifully decorated room. There were family photos on the white brick fireplace, on the glass end tables. The family was smiling, happy. It was easy to see that they stood together because they cared, not because they were forced to. Cade didn't have one picture of the people he stayed with the first eighteen years of his life. And he didn't want one.

He heard the water running and glanced down the hallway. He imagined the water running over Sabrina's naked skin before he could stop the image. Cursing his lack of restraint where she was concerned, he grabbed the TV remote. Instead of sports, he let it remain on the news channel, anything to drown out the sound of the water.

She was off-limits to him. He didn't date women he worked with or ones who would object when he moved on—and he always did, always would.

"I hope I wasn't too long."

Cade glanced around and simply stared at Sabrina. She was breathtakingly beautiful in a straight white sundress that stopped just above her incredible knees and a hot pink knit short jacket with rosettes. Desire blindsided him, and he realized what bothered him about Sabrina. He was beginning to think of her as a woman he wanted in his bed.

Frowning, she came to him, placing her small hand on his arm to stare up at him. "What's the matter? Is it one of your patients?"

She always thought of others and he couldn't stop thinking of her. "No." He picked up the remote, causing her hand to slide off his arm. He wanted too badly for her to keep touching him, for him to touch her.

"Let's go," he said, unable to keep the gruffness from his voice, hoping he still had time to stop whatever it was that made his body yearn for hers.

Seven

. . . .

Sitting in the passenger seat of Cade's sports car at the Sonic drive-in, Sabrina silently wondered what had happened between the time she'd left to take a shower and the time she'd returned. Cade had gone from almost teasing to the uptight surgeon. She wanted the other Cade back.

"Is there something wrong with your hamburger?" Cade asked.

Sabrina glanced down at the bacon cheeseburger. She'd taken one bite since he'd handed it to her. That was at least ten minutes ago.

"I can order you something else."

She glanced at him. She could evade the issue or meet it head on. "What changed between the time I went to change and when I returned?"

Broad shoulders beneath the blue-and-white striped shirt stiffened. She could almost see the wheels turning as he tried to think of an answer without outright lying. A man who didn't lie. She'd met pitiful few in her lifetime.

"Never mind. I guess I'm not as hungry as I thought I was." She wrapped the burger back up and put it in the bag between them. You couldn't make someone care. Her birth mother had taught her that hard lesson. "I'm finished, and you must be anxious to get home."

He stared at her a moment, then started the motor and backed out. He slowed down at a waste receptacle and tossed the bag in. He didn't say one word during the drive back to her house.

Parking in the driveway, he opened his door to get out. By the time he stood, Sabrina was passing the front end of the car. The only reason he caught her on the porch was that she had to search for her key. After she opened the door, she turned with a polite smile.

"Thank you again," she said. She'd gambled and lost.

"Does this mean you're going to be out of sorts tomorrow?" he asked.

She'd expected him to make a fast retreat. Amazed, she stared up at him. He looked wary, a bit unsure, two words that she would have never have associated with the great Cade Mathis. He also wasn't the joking type. He was trying. Perhaps he was giving all he could. He'd come a long way since he'd visited her house, trying to get her to back off. He might be able to go further.

"I have cheesecake for dessert. Do you want to take some home with you?"

"No, thanks, but I'd like to check the grill to make sure it's out," he told her.

"I can manage, but thanks." Going inside, she tossed her small purse on the sofa on the way outside. Opening the top, she stared down at the ash white coals. They were finally ready for the meat.

"It would be a shame to waste this great fire. My first, I might add. Neither one of us ate very much. How does steak and salad sound?"

"I'll grill."

She grinned and lowered the top. "Then they might escape being charred. Come on."

Once again he followed her. The kitchen was as neat and as colorful as the den. Here she'd added touches of red to the yellows she seemed to prefer. Opening the refrigerator, she took out a large platter with two steaks covered with plastic wrap and set it on the kitchen island. "Mama gave me her recipe for a marinade."

Cade glanced at the large T-bones before looking at her. "Why did you invite me and go to all the trouble if you've never done this before?"

She removed two glasses from the white cabinet. "Tea or lemonade?"

"Lemonade."

Filling both glasses with ice from the automatic dispenser, she opened the refrigerator for the lemonade, filled their glasses, then handed one to him. "Because I knew you'd be tired and not feel like going out. Most men like grilled steak, and we could talk."

Without drinking, Cade placed his glass on the table. "And you could find out why I changed my mind about Mr. Ward being in the room."

Keeping her eyes on him, she sipped her drink. "The thought had entered my mind, but there was another reason."

"Like what?"

She put her glass down and opened the refrigerator again. "I'll start on the salad."

"Sabrina," he said.

She removed a bag of salad greens, tomatoes, and a cucumber, and then handed him a long-handled meat fork. "It'll wait. The charcoal won't."

Taking the fork, Cade picked up the steaks and went outside.

"You can grill almost as well as my dad, and that's saying a lot," she said, her face soft, a small smile playing on her lips as they sat in the kitchen by the bay window with a view of the pool and blooming rosebushes.

She mentioned her family a lot. "Is your family in Dallas?"

Sighing, she sat back in her seat. "Houston. I miss them like crazy."

"Then why are you here?" he asked, curious in spite of himself. He never asked about anyone's family for fear they'd want to know about his.

She wrinkled her nose. "If you must know, my supervisor and I kept having disagreements on what was best for the patients. She'd worked there for twenty-two years. We'd butted heads almost from the day I arrived. She thought my family got me the job."

"Why would she think that?"

"My grandfather is a former chief-of-staff and retired ENT. My father is an internist and past member of the hospital board," she admitted.

So, he had been right about her having money. "You strike me as the kind of woman who doesn't need nepotism," he said truthfully. "I'm surprised you didn't stay."

"Every day at work was a hassle. I got to the point I hated going in. I didn't want to be miserable every day or for it to affect helping people, so I left." She picked up her glass. "So I know how you feel about a calm work environment."

"I wouldn't have known it."

"I can be a bit pushy at times," she admitted with a laugh. "My mother says that attitude is what kept me alive when I was in the hospital. She was going down the hall and heard me crying. She came into the room and tried to pick me up without hurting me."

Cade didn't want to hear her talk about that part of her life. He was at a loss to explain the sudden tightness in his chest. "How old were you?"

"Eighteen months." She glanced down at her plate. "I didn't know how lucky I was that Mother walked into that room until I was much older. She and my father loved me in spite of my burns."

"Or because of them," Cade said. Sabrina's scars were on the outside, but he knew people who were just as scarred on the inside. "They saw a toddler who needed them."

"That's what they always said. My brother Stephen and I are the lucky ones to grow up in a family of our heart."

Once, foolishly, he'd been envious of people who had grown up with people who loved them. "He's adopted too?"

"Yes."

"Does he live in Dallas?"

She shook her head and gave him one of her quick grins that more and more made him want to grin back at her. "Houston. He's eighteen and going into premed in the fall," she said. "He scored a perfect SAT. He plans to follow granddad into ENT."

"Your father doesn't care?" he asked.

"If he does, he's never shown it. He and Mother want us to be happy." She chuckled. "Dad and I both had to physically restrain Mother from having a 'talk' with my supervisor in Houston."

Cade refused to feel bad because there had been no one to champion him. "You have a nice family."

"How about yours?" she asked.

His expression didn't change. "Dead." He picked up his plate and stood. "Where do I dump this?"

Sabrina came to her feet and took the plate. She'd seen the split second of harshness that crossed Cade's face when she asked about his family. If she didn't miss her guess, his childhood hadn't been a happy one. "I'll take care of this. Thanks for the burger and grilling."

"I don't mind helping clean up," he said.

He'd surprised her again—this time in a nice way. She'd like for him to stay longer, but she didn't want to take a chance that she'd accidentally say or do the wrong thing. "Never let it be said that Dr. Mathis has dishwater hands because of me." She placed the plate on the table and took his arm, felt the muscles beneath. "You're in the free clinic tomorrow, so you'll have a hectic day."

"I could stay," he said at the door.

"Go. You've done enough." She opened the door before she changed her mind. She wanted to soothe away the hurt she'd glimpsed earlier. "Good-bye."

He hesitated. "I let Mr. Ward stay because he was making a nuisance of himself, calling the nurses every fifteen minutes."

Folding her arms, she stared up at him. "Why not let security take care of it?"

"His being there was the only thing that calmed her once she fully woke up," he said. "I didn't want to sedate her."

Sabrina briefly touched his arm. "They love each other very much."

His mouth tightened. "At the moment."

"Some couples make it work for a lifetime," she said. "Like my parents and grandparents."

"I suppose. Good night," he said.

"Good night."

Sabrina watched Cade get into his car and back out of her driveway. He didn't believe in love that lasted a lifetime. If she hadn't been adopted, she might not either. She wondered what made him feel that way. Whatever the reason, she felt sad for him and was even more determined that he know someone cared about him. *Her*.

Turning to go back in the house, she happened to glance down the street. She stepped off the porch to get a better view of Kara's driveway. She'd called earlier to see if Tristan was coming over, but she didn't see a car in the driveway. Sabrina just hoped he'd help Kara believe how talented she was.

Going inside, she began cleaning up the kitchen. She'd learned long ago that if she didn't do it immediately, she wouldn't do it at all. Waking up to dirty dishes wasn't the way she wanted to start the day.

Finished, she propped a hip on the counter stool, picked up the phone, and dialed Kara's number. "So, how did it go?" she asked as soon as Kara answered.

"I-I don't want to talk about it."

Uneasiness wiped the smile from Sabrina's face and had her standing. "Kara, what's the matter?"

"Nothing."

"Bull. I'll meet you in the back in fifteen seconds." Sabrina hung up the phone, grabbed her house keys out of her purse, and headed for the front door. There was something wrong, and she planned to find out what it was.

Kara was waiting for Sabrina in the backyard under a huge elm. She hadn't even attempted to sit on the padded black iron bench. She was too pissed, at herself, her mother, Tristan. They'd walked over her and she'd let them.

Sabrina came through the side gate Kara had left unlocked and hurried across the yard. "What happened?"

Although the garage blocked the view of her mother's bedroom, which was the reason she'd chosen this spot to paint and just get away, Kara stared in that direction.

Sabrina stepped in front of her, blocking her view. "What did your mother do this time?"

Kara flinched on hearing "this time." "Why do I keep letting her treat me this way?"

"Because you respect her as your mother," Sabrina said, rubbing her hand up and down Kara's trembling arm. "You loved your dad and you promised him you'd stay and help your mother no matter what."

Kara swallowed the growing lump in her throat. She hadn't known Sabrina when her father died, but since she'd moved down the street they'd become best friends. Her mother didn't like Sabrina, probably because Sabrina saw through her and didn't cater to her as everyone else in the neighborhood did.

Unfortunately, Sabrina had witnessed on more than one occasion her mother's poor treatment of Kara. In her straightforward way, Sabrina had asked Kara why she let her mother behave toward her that way. Since she wasn't being nosey, and since Kara had seen the wonderful relationship between Sabrina and her own mother, she'd evaded. Sabrina had said nothing, but a couple of days later she'd told her about her birth mother. In her way, she let Kara know she understood.

Kara let out a shuddering breath and told her everything, and ended by saying, "She's angry at me because I didn't want to share the money Tristan gave me."

"She's probably planning a trip to Dillard's as we speak," Sabrina said. "She'll take what she thinks is her share one way or the other."

"True." Kara plopped down on the cushion. "Won't she be surprised if she tries to go over her five hundred dollar limit this time."

Sabrina quickly sat beside her. "You finally did it."

"This afternoon. I can't pay all the bills she runs up. I don't like living from paycheck to paycheck. That's why I was praying Tristan was on the level," Kara admitted.

"I'm not sure he wasn't," Sabrina said thoughtfully. "I kept trying to tell you your work is good. Besides her humanitarian work with children, my mother is on a couple of art councils in Houston. I grew up with art. You have talent."

Kara laced her fingers together. "Before we discovered my paintings were missing, Tristan said he might write about my art, that he had an interior design contact who wanted one-of-a-kind artwork for her clients."

"Sounds reasonable." Sabrina nodded. "The rich want original artwork. Many of them love to tell anyone who'll listen that they have the only one of this or that or it's a limited number, whether it's cars or homes, but especially artwork because art implies class and culture."

Kara jerked around. "Do you mean he might really sell my

paintings for thousands after giving me less than two thousand dollars?"

"Not if you don't let him."

"I've struggled financially since my father's illness when I had to take over his care and bills," Kara mused, coming to her feet. "I did without so he wouldn't have to worry about his medicine or doctor bills. I've taken crap from my mother because she's my mother and I promised Daddy that I'd take care of her. But I won't take crap from Tristan."

Grinning, Sabrina stood. "You want me to go with you and hold your coat?"

"I got this." Kara's hands clenched and unclenched. "My mother had no right to sell my paintings."

"I could follow you, and help you bring them back," Sabrina offered.

"No." Kara's eyes narrowed. "Tristan took them. Tristan can bring them back."

"Go, Kara," Sabrina yelled. "I wish I could be there, but I want a full report tomorrow."

"You got it. Good night, and thanks."

"Good night." Sabrina waved and started toward the back gate. Kara waited until Sabrina closed the gate, then she went inside the house. She didn't stop until she knocked on her mother's door.

She lifted her hand to knock again when there was no response, then let it come to her side. Usually, she knocked again to make sure her mother had heard her, to make sure that she was all right. But not this time. Perhaps, like Tristan, her mother needed to learn that Kara could only be pushed so far.

Grabbing her purse and Tristan's card, she went to the

two-car garage and got into her Maxima. It started immediately. The car was used when she'd purchased it after graduating from college, but it was reliable, unlike many of the people she knew.

Passing Sabrina's house, Kara saw her on the porch with fists clenched and pumping upward. Kara smiled. Whatever else, it was good having a friend you could talk to, a friend who didn't judge, a friend who gave you a swift kick when necessary.

Five minutes later Kara hit I-35. Thirteen minutes later she exited the freeway onto MKL Boulevard. Luckily, she knew the area. Besides the Women's and the African-American Museum on the State Fairgrounds, it was also the home of the Automobile Building. Her father had taken her to the State Fair every year until she was in high school and went with friends.

Turning onto Grand Avenue, Kara checked the address again and slowed. The short street was lined with mansions built in the early 1900s. Many of them had been repaired to their original glory. Because the homes were located in the inner city, she noted that a few were in disrepair and for sale. The ones that had been renovated would probably sell into the millions if located elsewhere. Still, even here they came with hefty price tags.

She slowed on seeing a black truck she recognized as Tristan's. There was also a gleaming red Mercedes two-seat convertible behind the truck. Not giving herself time to become nervous, she parked on the street. The expensive sports car was probably Tristan's other car. Shutting off the motor, she went up the steps.

The house was magnificent, with white rattan furniture tucked on either side of the wide porch. Huge hanging baskets of purple petunias and begonias hung on either side of the white pillars. There was stained glass in the door. But she wasn't there to admire Tristan's house. She rang the doorbell.

The door opened. A stunning woman who appeared to be in her early fifties stood there. She had flawless light-brown skin, a pert nose, and inquisitive brown eyes that studied Kara as intently as she was studying her. Her auburn hair was cut in one of those careless, carefree styles that cost a fortune. Kara could only dream about such styles. Large diamond studs glittered in her ears, an even larger diamond stone surrounded by emeralds shone on her ring finger.

"Yes?"

The voice was cultured and coolly polite. The gaze direct. The black knit trimmed with gold braid unmistakably St. John. The poised woman made Kara a bit nervous. She had been so intent on getting her paintings back, she hadn't thought to change out of the oversized blouse and faded jeans she preferred to wear around the house.

"May I help you?"

Kara straightened her spine. Her paintings were all that mattered. "I'd like to see Tristan, please," she finally managed before the woman could become tired of waiting for her to say something and close the door in Kara's face.

"And you would be?" the woman asked, her gaze going from Kara's dingy old tennis shoes to the hair she hadn't combed since Fred had dropped her off at home hours ago.

Knowing its tendency to curl and escape the ponytail she'd put it in that morning, Kara swiped her hand over one side of her head and then the other, well aware that it wouldn't do any good. Her curly hair had a mind of its own, but it couldn't be helped. "I didn't mean to interrupt, but he has some things that belong to me and I want them back."

"Vera, did you get the door?"

Kara's head jerked in the direction of Tristan's voice. It had sounded as if it had come from upstairs.

"I did and there's a young woman here who says you have something that belongs to her," the woman answered, not taking her gaze from Kara.

"Kara. I'll grab a shirt and be right down."

Kara's gaze snapped back to the older woman. Tristan had a cougar. The thought angered Kara. She didn't want to examine the reason too closely. Once she had her paintings, she'd be on her way and she'd never have to see him again.

"Come in." The woman opened the door and stepped aside.

Kara stepped into the wide foyer and folded her arms. As soon as she gave Tristan a piece of her mind and the check, she was leaving. If he didn't deliver her paintings, she'd hire a lawyer.

She heard the sound of feet hurrying down the stairs. She looked up to see Tristan, barefooted, buttoning his shirt as he came down the curved staircase. "Hi, Kara. Vera, why didn't you offer her a seat?"

"Because I'm not staying long," Kara said, jerking her gaze away from his muscled chest. "I just want what's mine and you can get back to whatever."

The woman lifted a regal, perfectly arched brow. "I don't know whether to strut or take offense."

"Kara Simmons, my mother, Vera Landers-Fiore."

Eight

· · · · · · · · · · · · · ·

Kara's mouth gaped. All she could do was stare at the elegantly beautiful woman. "She can't be. She's too young."

"Definitely strutting time," Vera said, patting her reddish-gold hair.

"Weren't you on your way to the African-American Museum for a meeting with Dr. Robertson?" Tristan asked.

Vera smiled, showing even white teeth and dimples. "This promises to be more interesting than talking about fund-raising projects."

"Vera—"

"What do you have that belongs to her?" Vera asked, her curious gaze going from her son to Kara.

"My paintings," Kara answered, finally finding her voice and her footing.

All playfulness left the other woman. "You're the artist?"

Kara didn't know how to respond. No one had ever called her an artist before.

"Yes," Tristan answered for her.

"Here." Kara pulled the check from the pocket of her jeans. "My mother had no right to set a price for them and you had no right to buy them for fifty dollars each."

"Fifty dollars!" his mother yelled.

"Vera, if you leave now, I'll let you have first look at Kara's paintings—after me, of course," Tristan told her.

"Then she'd better stay because I'm not selling my paintings to you," Kara said, her hands on her hips.

Tristan stepped to her. "I can see how you might doubt my good intentions, but if I had wanted to cheat you I wouldn't have given you my home address and phone number."

Kara wouldn't let herself believe the sincerity in his face or his logic. "You just wanted to use me. You had me fooled once, but no more."

"I never wanted to use you."

She glanced around, away from his compelling face. No man was fooling her again. "Where are they?"

"I'll take you to them, but they aren't leaving this house." Turning smartly, he left the room.

"We'll just see about that." Kara followed him down the wide hallway.

Opening the door, he stepped back. Kara brushed past him to see her paintings propped around the walls of the empty room, face out. She'd never seen so many of them displayed at the same time before. Her chest felt strange.

"You have incredible talent, Kara, but you have to believe in yourself," Tristan said from behind her. "You have to take charge of your life."

She jerked her head around to stare at him. He was referring to her standing up to her mother. Embarrassment and anger warred within her, at him, at herself. Anger won. "You don't know me."

He stepped closer. "I want to, Kara."

She could see it in his eyes, his face, hear it in his voice. She wanted to believe him. It scared her how much. She wouldn't be used again. "So you can steal my work?"

"Now just a min—"

Tristan held up his hand, abruptly cutting off his mother. For a brief moment Kara thought she saw hurt and disappointment in his eyes, then it was gone. He stared at her so long she wanted to tuck her head and say she was sorry. As difficult as it was she made herself not look away. She wasn't going to be taken advantage of again.

Stepping around Kara, he picked up the nearest painting. "What doesn't fit in your car, I'll put in my truck and follow you home."

His mother passed Kara on her way to another painting. "I'll help."

"Touch a painting at your own peril, Vera," Tristan told his mother, then spoke to Kara. "Open your trunk so we can get started."

"I'll get the front door," his mother offered and rushed out of the room.

Kara pulled the keys from her pocket and followed Tristan outside. She didn't know why tears stung her eyes. She was the wronged person here. Or was she? Her self-righteous anger had fizzled and now she wasn't so sure about anything. It took her a couple of tries to fit the key in the trunk's lock. As soon as the lid lifted, Tristan placed the painting inside and immediately went back into the house.

Kara swallowed and pulled an old blanket from a corner to cover the paintings she kept for just such purposes. She stepped aside to see Tristan coming down the steps. He wanted her gone. She swallowed the lump in her throat. "I can get the rest."

"I don't have time to argue. Mother had back surgery a month ago and is on restrictions." He bent to place the painting in the back. "She's just stubborn enough to try and help."

"Why didn't you say something?" Kara rushed back up the steps and into the room to see Tristan's mother reaching for a painting. "Stop!"

The woman straightened and turned. Where there had been mild curiosity in her eyes, there was now reproach. "You insulted my son."

Tristan entered the room and took in the situation at once. "You watch Vera while I load the rest into my truck."

"You don't have any shoes on," Kara said.

He glanced down at his feet. "It won't take me long to put some on and I'll get you loaded and you can be on your way."

Kara closed her eyes. He was giving her what she wanted, so why did she want to cry?

"Change your mind?" his mother asked as Tristan left the room.

"I—" How could she explain what she didn't understand? She wanted to believe Tristan, but she didn't trust her own judgment. Her mother's censure and lack of belief in Kara wasn't helping. She shook her head.

"Tristan, like his late father, will go the distance for you, but question his honor and integrity and he'll walk," his mother told her.

"I didn't mean to. It's just . . ." Kara rubbed her temple.

"Just what? I deserve an answer after your unfounded

accusation," his mother said tersely. "He's honest and dependable. I'm not just saying that because I'm his mother. He goes out of his way to help others."

Kara nodded. Liars and users didn't spend hours in a hospital room or readily give financial assistance without being forced. She hadn't been able to find a provider for Mr. Bowler's medicine by the time he was ready to go home, and Tristan picked it up from the hospital pharmacy at a cost of over three hundred dollars. "He helped his friend, a patient in the hospital. That's how we met."

Tristan came back into the room wearing loafers. Kara imagined they were the easiest to get on. He wanted her out of his house and she couldn't blame him. She'd practically called him a thief when he'd been patient and thoughtful. She had let her fears and insecurities rule her. She was ashamed of the way she had behaved.

She placed her hand on his arm when he stooped to pick up a painting. "I'm sorry. I didn't mean to insult you."

He stared at her a long moment, then straightened. "You don't know me, but I'm hoping to change that. Besides." He smiled at his watchful mother. "Artists are supposed to be temperamental. I grew up with one."

Kara whirled to his mother. "You paint?"

"Pottery, but it was long ago," she said. "Now, I'm an interior designer."

"She took pity on her favorite son and did this place for me," Tristan said, walking over to curve his arm gently around his mother's waist and kiss her on the cheek.

"It's beautiful and restful," Kara said.

"Thank you. It's what I wanted for him." She smiled up at Tristan. "You're also my only son, and you're much better at redoing the room than bringing it all together with furniture and accessories."

"You're blessed to have her, but you seem to know that," Kara said, not bothering to wish that she and her mother were close. It simply wasn't going to happen.

"Vera is my ace in the hole," he said proudly. "I wish you could stay, but I know how strongly you feel about inconsiderate people being disrespectful of other people's time."

His mother frowned up at his teasing face. "It's horrible when your child grows up and uses your words against you."

He grinned. "I love you too."

"Kara, do you have children?"

His mother's words wiped the indulgent smile from his face. "Vera."

"No. I've never been married," Kara answered, feeling a bit restless again.

"Many women these days don't seem to think that's necessary for children," his mother said.

"For me it is," Kara answered. Her father had been her champion. She shuddered to think what her life might have been like if she'd grown up without a father.

"Enough." Tristan urged his mother to the door.

Vera laughed softly. "I'm going. Kara, we'll have to have lunch and I really mean it."

"I'd like that," Kara said, meaning it as well. She and Tristan's mother might have gotten off to a rocky start, but she liked the other woman. It spoke well of her that she and her son had such a close relationship, something Kara had once longed for but had to accept that it would never happen.

"I'm going to walk Mother to the car and make sure she puts the top up on her latest toy," Tristan said.

"If you need to drive her or go with her, I can leave and we can talk later," Kara offered, pulling her keys out of her pocket. She was going to start believing in herself and trust Tristan.

"I'm fine, but thanks for asking," Vera said, picking up her handbag from the table. "I don't mind telling you that I adored your work. I'm hoping we can work together."

"I'd like that," Kara said around a lump in her throat. There would be no reason for his mother to lie to her.

"Vera, you are not getting first refusal so stop trying." Tristan chuckled, urging his mother toward the front door. "Be back in a minute."

Outside, darkness had settled. Tristan closed Vera's car door and waited until the convertible top was secure. "Drive carefully and call when you get to the museum and home."

"Hadn't you better get back to Kara?" Tristan didn't move. "All right, worrywart," Vera finally said. "I think I might like her, although she needs some serious wardrobe adjustments."

Tristan started to say he liked her the way she was, then thought better of it. He didn't want to give his mother any ideas or encouragement regarding Kara. He straightened. "I'm just helping her work get exposure. She has too much talent to let it go to waste."

"I believe your father initially tried to tell his parents the same thing about me."

Tristan didn't know what to say. He'd heard the story a thousand times from his mother. His father had seen her pottery in a small shop in London and sought out the artist. It had been love at first sight for the serious college professor and the outspoken American graduate student. His father's parents had taken considerably longer to warm up to his mother. Tristan didn't remember his father, but Vera made sure he'd never forget him. "I wish I could remember him."

"So do I. He loved fiercely and did everything with passion and drive." She brushed her fingertips across his face. "You're so much like him."

"Call."

"Even if I might interrupt something?"

Tristan flushed, searched for something to say.

His mother laughed. "Good night, honey."

Shaking his head, he watched her back out of the drive. Inside, he went to the empty room, one of many in his house, where he'd put the paintings. He didn't see the need of putting something in a room just to put it there. He hated clutter.

Entering the room, he saw Kara kneeling before a painting of a garden bench in front of a meandering river. "Vera liked that one a lot."

Kara jumped, pushed to her feet, and turned. The weariness was back in her expressive eyes. "Why do you want to help me, especially after the things I said?"

"Why not?" He went to her. "I've said things I later regretted. You have talent. If I can help you get the word out, why shouldn't I?"

"Through your articles?" she asked.

Kara certainly liked things spelled out. He had a feeling it was because she might have trusted the wrong person in the past and paid the price. "One of the ways, but material for a magazine has to be done a minimum of four months before the issue."

"Four months!" Kara was unable to contain her astonishment.

"Don't worry, I have other immediate ideas," Tristan reassured her. Every emotion showed on her beautiful face. "There are newspapers and columnists asking my opinion all the time about what's new or who I think is the next up-and-coming talent. I also Tweet and blog. Both sites get a lot of hits. I'd like to spotlight your work on both. I'm also doing an article for the *Dallas Morning News* in a month. I'd like to mention you there as well."

Her hand pressed against her chest. "You—you'd do that?"

"It would be my privilege and pleasure."

As if having trouble taking it all in, she closed her eyes for a moment then stared straight at him. "I don't want to anger you again, but I want you to know up front that even if you help me I'm not going to go to bed with you."

He reached out and ran a finger down her cheek. She shivered. "No, you'll go to bed with me because you want to."

Surprisingly his self-assurance didn't scare or anger her. "You're wrong, Tristan."

"If nothing else, I got you to call me Tristan. Progress. Now, let's look at the paintings and decide which ones to spotlight first, and which one I'm going to buy to hang in my office."

She'd been about to kneel, but she straightened instead. *Architectural Digest* had nothing on his home. Vera had done a fantastic job. "You—you want to hang one of my paintings in your office?"

He went to an oil painting of a still life. "I told you I don't have anything in my house unless I can enjoy it, and that goes for artwork." He held up the painting in strong blues, yellows, and greens. "This one I think."

It was one of her favorites and already framed. She'd started the painting on the anniversary of her father's death. She'd wanted to honor him, to celebrate his life and what he'd meant to her.

"Two thousand all right?" he asked.

She blinked. Swallowed. Her heart raced. "Dollars?" she squeaked.

"And that's a steal." He looked at the painting again. "You are going to be very famous and I get to say I bought your first painting."

"I—you don't have to pay me that much," she said, trying to get her stomach to stop doing flips. "You're helping me."

He frowned at her. "That doesn't mean I should take advantage of you. Your paintings have value. Don't let anyone tell you differently. Then too, think how impressed people are going to be with me that I discovered you."

"I think your mother is right, you like helping people," she said. "Thank you. I accept your offer."

"Good. What do you say we go see how this looks," Tristan said.

"You make me believe."

His eyes narrowed with regret. She'd said the words with such a mixture of hope and fear that he wanted to touch her, hold her. "Kara."

She shook her head and stepped back. "Which way is your office and do we need a hammer?"

"You can run tonight, but one day . . ." Still holding the painting he left the room.

Kara, girl. Don't be a fool again. Tristan is definitely out of your league.

"Kara, come on."

"Coming," she called, rushing out of the room to follow him. She was a smart woman. She could do this.

"How about here?" he asked, holding the painting on the bare wall across from his desk.

Seeing Tristan, his handsome face animated as he held her work, she wasn't so sure anymore.

"I could see it every time I look up," he went on to say.

He really meant it. Her heart did a lazy roll in her chest. She was definitely in over her head. "It's perfect."

He grinned and lowered the painting. "I'll get the stud finder and hammer. I can't wait."

Kara watched him leave the room, her eyes unerringly going to his butt before she jerked her gaze back to the painting. She was definitely in trouble.

The next day Kara couldn't keep the smile off her face. Not even her mother's closed door when she left to pick up Sabrina for church could curtail her happiness. Tristan and his mother thought she had talent. He'd even purchased a painting. She'd gone to sleep holding the check. She'd told Sabrina what had happened on the way to church.

Sabrina had insisted they celebrate with brunch, her treat. Kara had agreed because she planned to pay. Soon she wouldn't have to watch every penny and Sabrina, as much as Tristan, was the reason. Without her encouragement and faith, Kara would have wallowed in self-pity and doubt. Kara told Sabrina as much while they were eating. Finally, she would be able to please her mother.

Pulling up in her driveway that afternoon after dropping Sabrina off at home, some of Kara's happiness ebbed and guilt nudged her. It was almost three. She couldn't help remembering that her mother hadn't eaten last night and Kara hadn't fixed her breakfast that morning. She'd wanted to get out of the house as quickly as possible to avoid another argument.

Kara had called her mother after church to check on her but there had been no answer. Opening the door, she got out of the car and went inside. She frowned on seeing her mother's door still closed.

She knocked. "Mama? Mama, are you all right?" No answer. She knocked again, ignoring the sting of her knuckles from the wood. "Mama?" She opened the door. Her heart lodged in her throat. Her mother lay on the floor with the bedsheet wrapped around her left leg.

"Mama," Kara screamed, rushing across the room to gently turn her mother's face toward her. Seeing she was awake only eased a portion of her fear. "Does anything hurt?"

"My hip," she moaned. "I waited for you to come. I called over and over."

Guilt stabbed Kara. Her mother had had right hip replacement surgery nine months ago. Kara reached for her mother's phone. "I'm going to call an ambulance."

"No." Her mother grabbed her hand. "No hospitals."

"You shouldn't be moved if-if anything is broken," Kara said, her voice trembling.

"Undo the sheet and let's see." Her mother's eyes closed. "The pain is like after my surgery."

Kara swallowed. If only she had returned or checked on her earlier. Her mother had needed morphine after her surgery. Getting up, Kara supported her mother's legs while pulling the sheet away, watching her mother's face. She grimaced twice before Kara had her free. "I think I should call an ambulance."

"For once don't argue," her mother snapped. "Just help me back into bed."

Kara helped her mother stand, then eased her back into the bed, straightening the covers. "I'll get your pain medicine."

"You know I can't take it on an empty stomach," her mother said to Kara's retreating back.

She whirled. "You haven't eaten?"

"How could I have eaten tangled up the way I was?" she said angrily. "I could have broken more than my hip while you were off having fun."

The hostile comeback had Kara's eyes narrowing. She'd been around enough people in pain to be aware of the catch in their voice, the grimace, even perspiration. Her mother exhibited none of those signs when she'd leaned forward in bed to blast Kara. She was angry at being ignored more than she was hurt. Relief swept through her. Pointing out that she had called wasn't as important as knowing her mother was all right.

"I'll fix you some toast to take your medicine, and then dinner."

Her mother settled back in the bed, closing her eyes. "I want an egg and sausage with the toast. I think I'll try to sleep."

"All right, Mama." Kara left the room and went to the kitchen. So much for her happy day. It seemed pleasing her mother was a long ways off.

Life was good, Sabrina thought. With the convertible top down, the wind blowing in her hair, Sabrina couldn't keep the smile off her face as she cruised down the street. She'd been too revved to stay at home once Kara had dropped her off, and decided to do a little shopping. She would have liked Kara to have come with her, but Sabrina knew her best friend wanted to check on her mother.

Sabrina's smile faded as she pulled into a rare parking spot of the upscale outdoor shopping center. Kara needed to think of herself first more often. She was a fantastic friend and deserved to be happy. Perhaps Tristan was just the ticket. Her smile returning, Sabrina grabbed her handbag from the passenger seat and got out of the car.

She was on the hunt for a dress, perhaps one that would make Cade drop to his knees. Laughing wickedly, she caught the interested gazes of two men walking toward her. They slowed. Her pace increased. There was only one man she was interested in. Cade Mathis. He would be a challenge, but then, her life had been a challenge. He wasn't getting away from her.

Nine

. . . .

The strident buzz of the alarm clock woke Kara up at six Monday morning. She desperately wanted to go back to sleep. After she'd served her mother dinner in bed, she'd needed Kara to fluff her pillows, massage her leg, go to the store for her favorite Blue Bell ice cream, polish the silver, water the houseplants. The list had gone on and on.

A couple of hours after she'd found her mother on the floor, Kara figured out she was being punished, but she'd done her mother's bidding anyway. Her mother's manipulations just showed Kara how much she needed to move. Without the buffer of her father it was impossible for them to peacefully live together. It was even more important that her paintings sell.

Flinging back the covers, Kara showered, dressed, and went to the kitchen to fix her mother a tray. She paused at the entrance on seeing her mother sitting at the table, her right leg propped on a small hassock they kept in the kitchen. She always slept late unless her hip was bothering her.

Despite the doctor's stern orders, her mother hadn't done

the physical therapy as ordered and now she was paying the price. She blamed the doctor for the continued pain and stiffness. Falling had probably aggravated her condition.

"Morning, Mama. Are you feeling better?"

"I've felt better." She rubbed her right thigh. "Staying in bed seemed to make it worse. The therapist said a whirlpool would help. I could sure use it after my fall. I'm sore all over."

"We can't afford to remodel the bathroom." Kara reached for an apron. "What would you like?"

Her mouth tight, she looked up at Kara. "An omelet since I missed breakfast yesterday. I got up so you wouldn't have to fix my tray."

And to take another dig at Kara, and put in another request for a whirlpool. Her mother was back full force. Kara pulled a mixing bowl from beneath the cabinet. *One day,* she thought as she cracked eggs, chopped ham, diced tomatoes, and onions, *I'll be free.*

Kara had barely pulled out of the driveway before the phone rang. "Hello."

"Good morning, Kara."

Tristan. Her hand gripped the phone. For some odd reason his voice made her teary, perhaps because he and his mother reminded her of how lacking her relationship with her own mother was, how gently he'd touched Kara.

"Kara? Are you all right?"

No. "Yes, I'm sorry. Good morning."

There was a slight pause. "You haven't changed your mind about letting me help you promote your paintings, have you?"

"No," she said, then inwardly winced at the desperation in her voice.

"It'll be all right. You have talent, and we're going to show the world."

Swallowing, she pulled through the stop sign. He wanted to reassure her. His voice soothed her, stroked her. She was sure if he had been there he would have given her a hug. Against her better judgment, she wished he was. "Thank you."

"My pleasure," he said, his voice stroking her in an entirely different way.

Kara moistened her dry lips. Tristan was getting to her despite her efforts.

"Vera called back last night with an idea to get your work out there even more," he said. "She wants to use your paintings in a million-dollar spec home she's been asked to decorate."

"What!" Kara screeched, her hand clenching the phone.

"Exciting, isn't it?" he said, laughter in his voice. "When Mother likes something, it's full speed ahead. She's selecting pieces from several interior design studios, but she wants your art."

Kara took the exit ramp to Haskell, her excitement building once the initial fear had disappeared. "Which paintings? They need to be framed." She hadn't had the money or the time or the belief in herself that she could sell her work. "I can go by Fred's house this afternoon to look at the woods I have."

"You framed them too?" he asked, surprise and awe in his voice.

"I wanted to see how different woods, stains, and molding types looked, plus it was cheaper. Fred's grandson is the manager of a lumberyard and he sells me the wood at a discount and then I frame them at a craft store in Uptown Village."

"A true Renaissance woman. You probably already know that Van Gogh, Degas, and Eakins made their own frames. I'll meet you over there to pick up the material and you can frame them at my place. It will keep you from taking the pictures back and forth and risking damage to them. You tell me what you need, including what's at the craft store, and I'll put everything in the room with the paintings," he offered.

"What?"

He repeated his offer. "It makes sense."

The wooden bar lifted in the employee parking lot and she pulled through the gate. "I can't let you do that."

"I'd like to get some photos of your work and start blogging. They'd come off better framed. It would certainly be easier working at my place."

Easier, but definitely more dangerous and Tristan was smart enough to know it. She pulled into a parking space and shut off the engine. "Just business?"

"Whatever you say," he agreed.

Kara frowned. He'd agreed much too quickly. "But you plan to try and change my mind, don't you?"

"Yep," he said, laughter in his voice. "But I'll respect a no."

That was as good as she could hope for. "I can't tonight. It will have to be tomorrow. My mother isn't feeling well."

"Sorry to hear that," he said. "Is there anything I can do?"

"No, thank you. I'll call Fred and let you know what time to meet me there." Getting out of the car, she started for the crosswalk.

"Tomorrow night might be better for me too. I just arrived at my current project and the first days are always long."

"You doing another article?" She stopped on the sidewalk.

"Another house," he said. "I rehab homes. I caught the bug when I did an article on how to make a home look lux for a fraction of the cost. I like doing different things. I bore easily. At least with some things," he quickly added.

Kara could just imagine one of those things was women. "I see."

"If we finish transporting everything early enough tomorrow night, I thought we might go to dinner and afterward a gallery opening. Some important people will be there."

"I don't have a thing to wear," she blurted. Her eyes widened at the admission. She barely kept from slapping her hand over her mouth.

"Whatever you wear, you'll look fantastic."

She smiled at the compliment, but she had to be sensible. Tristan wanted more than to help her with her paintings. "Can I think about it and let you know later?"

"Sure." He sounded disappointed. "One of the workers just walked in. Talk to you later. Bye."

Kara disconnected the call and went inside the hospital. She should have insisted she frame the pictures at Fred's house, but Tristan was right about the possibility of damaging them while taking them back and forth, and it would be easier and faster if everything was all in one place. She just had to remember Tristan was off-limits.

Thus far, she wasn't doing a very good job. Her crack about clothes proved as much. Unlike her mother, she didn't obsess about clothes. There were more important things to think about, like the house payment, food, utility bills. With Burt, she certainly hadn't worried about what she'd wear.

Waving to a coworker, Kara went inside her office. Tristan

was too smart not to have realized what her comment meant. Thinking about Tristan as more than a business associate was a mistake, but she seemed to be heading in that direction.

She turned to look at the last painting of her father. "Daddy, I think I'm in trouble."

Several hours later, Kara was more than ready to call an end to a horrible day. Nothing had gone smoothly since she'd walked into the hospital. One family had even called her supervisor to complain that she hadn't worked hard enough to find them a nursing home. It had all boiled down to them wanting Kara to find a more luxurious accommodation that someone else paid for. Most days she enjoyed her job.

Not today.

A knock sounded on her door. She was tempted not to answer it. "Come in."

Sabrina breezed in with the happy smile she'd been wearing more and more since she'd decided to go after Dr. Mathis. She took one look at Kara and quickly rounded her desk. "Tristan, your mother, the job, life?"

"How about all four?" Kara answered.

Sabrina sat on the corner of her desk. "I have ten minutes."

"Mama and the job aren't going to change. Life is life."

"So that leaves the yummy Tristan. Talk."

Kara leaned back in her chair and told Sabrina what had happened after Kara had come home from church. "Mama doesn't trust him. Tristan admits he wants a sexual relationship. The bad thing is that no matter how hard I try, if I'm honest, I'm attracted to him. I just don't want to make a fool of myself, especially with Mama ready to tell me I told you so." Kara's hand closed around the bottle of water on her desk. "Going over there every night to frame my paintings isn't wise."

Sabrina put her hand on her best friend's tense shoulder. "I wish I could give you the answer. I tend to jump first and look later."

"You aren't afraid to go after what you want." Kara leaned forward and propped her arms on her desk. "Tristan asked me to dinner and a gallery opening tomorrow night. I want to go, but—"

"But nothing." Sabrina cut her off. "You're going."

"I don't have anything to wear," Kara confessed. "Mama has maxed out the charge accounts already, but even if she hadn't I wouldn't waste any of the money he paid me or use my emergency credit card on a new outfit."

"Buying an outfit that makes you feel and look good is not wasteful." Sabrina stood. "I'd buy the dress for you myself if I didn't already know how stubborn you can be."

Kara adamantly shook her head. "No, I'm not borrowing money from you."

"Who said anything about borrowing? It's my gift for all the times you've fed me." Sabrina folded her arms. "I wouldn't have the great house I live in if not for you. You helped me hang curtains when I was lost. I have a beautiful yard because you introduced me to Fred. I could go on, but my break is almost over."

"You're a friend."

"Exactly. Friends are there for each other. There's a boutique near here that has some beautiful things and they're having a sale." Sabrina wrinkled her nose. "I went by there yesterday. They had this sexy white halter sundress I almost bought, but it wouldn't look right with a short jacket or sweater."

It wasn't often Kara thought of the scars on Sabrina's upper body. Like everything else, Sabrina saw the burns as an inconvenience, not as an excuse to be bitter. "I wish I had your outlook on life."

Sabrina shook her head. "And I wish I had your patience. Now, back to the dress to make Tristan drop to his knees and beg for mercy."

A picture of Tristan on his knees flashed through her mind, but she was the one begging for mercy. She flushed, tucked her head.

Sabrina lifted a brow. "Did I miss something?"

"Just thinking," Kara said. "I'll wear what I have."

"Kara, why don't we just go look?"

"No. Thank you," Kara said firmly, afraid she'd weaken. Sabrina was very persuasive. "Tristan is business and I want to keep it that way. It doesn't matter what I wear, it's the paintings that matter."

Sabrina made a face. "You're going to kick yourself ten seconds after the store closes tomorrow at six."

"Probably, but Tristan will have to take me as I am," she said.

"From what you've said, he's ready to take you any way he can," Sabrina said teasingly, and laughed out loud at Kara's blush. "All right, but if you change your mind, call me."

"Thanks, but I won't."

"Bye."

"Bye." As soon as the door closed, Kara picked up the phone and called Tristan.

"Tristan."

Kara rubbed her jittery stomach. She wasn't sure if it was the sound of his strong voice or what was at stake that had her nervous. "If the offer for dinner and the gallery opening is still open, I accept. Fred says he'll be at home after four so we can pick up the wood."

"Give me his number and I'll send someone to pick the material up so you can go home after work tomorrow to check on your mother," he said.

He was a quick thinker, and thoughtful. She gave him the number.

"I'll pick you up at seven tomorrow night. Good-bye."

"Good-bye." Kara hung up the phone and bit her lower lip. Had he sounded impatient? She recalled his earlier words that he became bored easily. Had he already become tired of her? She chastised herself. She wasn't going to do this to herself. He was probably busy.

Kara opened the back door of her mother's house a little after five Monday afternoon. She'd debated all the way home whether to tell her mother about working with Tristan. She finally came to the conclusion that it was cowardly not to. Besides, how was she going to explain being away from home every afternoon for a couple of hours? However, she was not mentioning the check.

Turning on the oven, she went to check on her mother and change before cooking dinner. Her bedroom door was ajar. Kara heard her mother laughing.

Kara pushed the door open farther. Her mother was reclining on the lift chair eating ice cream off her best china. "Hello, Mama. Glad you're feeling better."

She jumped, almost dropping the bowl. She looked at Kara with annoyance. "You scared me. You're home early."

"I wanted to check on you," Kara said. "It's good seeing you're all right. After tonight, I'll be working on framing my paintings in the evenings."

Her mother's eyes narrowed. "You still have too many things around the house to start painting again."

"I won't have to," Kara said, taking a certain amount of pleasure in the announcement. "Tristan returned the paintings to me. He's going to help me sell them."

Her mother straightened. "How much?"

The greed in her mother's eyes didn't surprise her. "I'm not sure. We're going to a gallery opening tomorrow night."

"Don't look at that pretty face of his and get taken," her mother warned. "For once, be smart like me and not gullible like your father. Gallery means money."

To her mother, it always came down to money. "I'll go fix dinner."

Sabrina had anxiously waited almost forty-eight hours for this moment. She'd missed Cade when he made rounds Monday evening, but today, Tuesday, would be different. She adjusted the collar of her crisp new coral blouse, adjusted the twisted coral necklace, checked her makeup, smiled, then left the bathroom across the hall from her office. It was after six and Cade was in the hospital making evening rounds. She'd asked the charge nurse to notify her when he arrived because she needed to discuss one of their patients.

She stepped on the elevator, smiling and greeting people. She was aware she probably had a sparkle in her eyes that wouldn't be there if she wasn't anticipating seeing Cade. Getting off the elevator, she turned and saw his broad back immediately. Her heart rate increased, her breath fluttered over her lips.

If she got all hot and bothered just looking at his back, what would happen when she faced him? There was only one way to find out. She headed straight for him.

"Hi, Sabrina," several of the nurses called to her.

"Hi," she greeted. If she hadn't been watching Cade, she wouldn't have seen his shoulders tense. Two steps forward, two back. It was a good thing she didn't give up on what she wanted easily.

She walked to him and turned, leaning back against the counter of the computer station the doctors worked on to look down at him. "Hello, Dr. Mathis."

His hands flexed the tiniest bit, then he looked up. "Ms. Thomas."

She was hoping he'd call her by her first name at work as he did a few of the staff members. Patience, she reminded herself. "I wanted to speak with you about a couple of your patients."

"Mrs. Ward is doing well. I plan to discharge her Friday," he said.

"She told me when I spoke with her this morning," Sabrina said. "Her family plans a double celebration Saturday for her homecoming and Clarissa's birthday party." She leaned over, just to tempt herself, and just maybe him. His eyes widened, but he didn't move back. "We're invited to both parties."

"I don't have time." He turned back to the computer screen.

Sabrina's temper spiked at his easy dismissal, but she kept the smile on her face. Although she didn't like it, she realized certain things couldn't be rushed. It had taken countless skin grafts and surgeries and two years to try and repair the damage to her body, and even longer to heal the emotional scars of abuse and neglect. She might not remember the pain or the surgeries, but every day growing up she saw the scars and was reminded what her stoned mother had carelessly done to her.

Her early teen years had been particularly devastating. Teenage girls could be unthinkably cruel. She'd hated showering after gym and the whispers that always followed. She could do backflips and yells better than any of the girls in her class, but the coach of the varsity cheerleaders told her she couldn't try out. Sabrina couldn't wear the short skirt and a longer one would look "off." The varsity swim coach hadn't wanted her either. She hadn't told her parents, just cried and wondered why life had been so cruel and unfair to make her ugly and different.

It had taken her parents' and maternal grandparents' unfaltering love and support to help her finally realize and accept that she was more than the scars on her body. If others judged her because of what they saw instead of her character, it was their problem and loss, not hers.

"I wasn't finished, Dr. Mathis," she said with a calmness that she was proud of. Out of the corner of her eyes she saw a couple of doctors stop what they were doing and look over toward them. Sabrina was sure the staff was doing the same thing.

"Yes?" He faced her.

"If you don't mind, I'd like to discuss the case in a more private setting." She glanced at the outside counter where two family members waited to speak to a doctor. One asked for a blanket.

"The cafeteria, I suppose."

"My office actually."

He stared at her. She stared back. "I probably won't finish for another hour."

"I'm extremely grateful for your time, Dr. Mathis. I'll work around your schedule," she said, trying to sound as contrite as possible for interfering with his schedule.

She shouldn't have bothered. His eyebrow went up again. He clearly knew she was laying it on a bit thick.

"A calm work environment is essential." She repeated his words.

"That remains to be seen. I'll see you in one hour."

"Thank you, Dr. Mathis." Smiling, she stopped briefly to speak to the nurses and doctors before going to the elevator.

Cade paused before opening the door to Sabrina's office. The corners of his mouth lifted in a semblance of a smile. She'd thrown a lot of BS at him. She knew it and so did he, but the results were the same. He was here just as she wanted.

Wanted. What exactly did she want from him?

Increasingly, he knew what he wanted from her—her warm, willing, and wild in his bed. His hand clenched on the knob. He'd thought about it with increasing and annoying regularity. He'd caught the look in her eyes a couple of times and knew she might not be thinking of intimacy, but she was definitely interested.

He'd think she was after him if he hadn't approached her first. He usually ignored people who irritated him. Perhaps even then he had wanted her. But it wasn't going to happen. As he'd told her. He didn't date staff members.

"Dr. Mathis, can I help you?"

Lost in thought, he glanced up to see Gwen Owens, a social worker at the hospital. In her late thirties, reasonably attractive with a good figure, she'd made several overtures to him when he'd first arrived. He hadn't been interested then or now. "No, thank you, Ms. Owens. I was just about to go into Ms. Thomas's office."

Gwen shook her head of reddish-gold hair. "I heard about the disgraceful way she acted toward you. You would be within your rights to speak to her supervisor. She had no right to question you."

The door suddenly opened and Sabrina stood there, a hard frown on her pretty face. It was directed at Gwen. "Hello, Gwen. Don't let us keep you," Sabrina said. "I know how busy you are."

The woman's red lips tightened, then she smiled at him. "Dr. Mathis, if there is ever anything I can do for you, please don't hesitate. My door is always open."

"So I've heard," Sabrina muttered.

The other woman glared at Sabrina. The rumors about Gwen's "openness" to doctors was well known.

Sabrina's startled eyes widened with embarrassment. Cade realized that once again, she'd spoken without thinking it through first. He thought to soothe the incensed older woman. He'd heard she could also be vindictive. "I appreciate the offer, Ms. Owens. It's good to know you're there to help if patients need you."

"Thank you," Gwen said, somewhat mollified.

"Good-bye." Urging Sabrina back into her office, Cade closed the door.

"I didn't mean to say that," Sabrina said, staring at the floor. "The way she lives her life is none of my business."

"Then why say anything at all?"

Her gaze flickered to him and away. "Bad manners."

He frowned down at her. "Why don't I believe you?"

Shrugging, she waved him toward a seat in front of her

neat desk. "Please have a seat. I don't want to take too much of your time."

"Still laying it on a bit thick," he said, but he started for the chair. A flash of color caught his attention. Instead of sitting, he stared at the painting behind her desk.

Sabrina saw the direction of his gaze, and came to stand beside him. "It's good, isn't it?"

"Very."

"Kara painted it for me. The next time you see her, you can tell her."

"So she doesn't spend a lot of her time holding a table in the cafeteria for you," he said drolly.

"Hardly," Sabrina said. "We have much more important things to do. Like discuss her amazing work, and how she's going to be rich and famous one day."

Cade stared down at the top of Sabrina's sleek head of hair. She barely came to the middle of his chest. He outweighed and outranked her, but she wasn't afraid to stand toe to toe with him. His attention switched to a safe topic. "The painting is peaceful, but at the same time it grabs your attention."

"A contradiction, just like a certain doctor I know," she said, going behind her desk.

His gaze snapped to her. She had a sassy mouth. He could too well imagine it on his, her mouth roaming over his body.

Her brown eyes narrowed. Her nostrils delicately flared. Her body responded to him with just a look. What would happen if he actually touched her?

He wasn't about to find out. "You mentioned you needed to see me."

She swallowed, swallowed again. "Yes." Bending, she lifted an oversized hot pink gift bag with THANK YOU in large letters on it, and gave the bag to him. "This is for you, from Clarissa and her classmates and friends."

He stared at the bag.

"It won't bite," Sabrina said with a smile. "Her father brought her by this morning. She gave me a hug and a card too."

Cade took the bag. He didn't know what to say.

Sabrina leaned against her desk and folded her arms. "I'd say you made an impression on her." She motioned toward the bag. "She enlisted her friends at her school, the art teacher, and her Sunday school class to write you notes thanking you for helping her mother feel better so she'd come home and they could do things together."

For the first time in months, he thought of his own birth mother. He'd wished for her to come get him, take him away from his hellish life, but she never did.

"The children touch you the most—with their innocence and trust and love," Sabrina said. "Every child deserves to grow up with loving parents."

"That's impossible for some people, and we both know it," he snapped.

"The authorities never found my father. The man my mother was living with refused to take me, saying he wasn't my father. DNA tests proved he wasn't." She folded her arms. "My mother was never off drugs long enough to give a thought or try to get me back from the foster home, which probably saved my life."

"I'm sorry," he said. He knew what it was to be unwanted, unloved, to be reminded every second that you were nothing.

She shrugged carelessly. "It happened. We've both seen cases where the child didn't survive. I was blessed to find parents who love me."

Despite his best effort, his features hardened.

Her arms slowly unfolded. She stared at him a long time. "You didn't, did you?"

A burning rage that he'd thought he'd buried erupted. He never wanted anyone to know his shame.

Sabrina shrank back from him, then took a tentative step toward him. "Cade." She reached for his arm. He stepped back. He didn't want her to touch him. Once he would have given part of his soul for a simple touch.

"Please forgive me. I speak—"

He whirled and headed for the door. She caught his arm, felt the muscles bunch. "Please. Yell at me if you want. Please. I can't stand the thought of me hurting you."

He tugged his arm free, then he was gone, the door snapping shut behind him.

Sabrina stared at the closed door. Tears rolled down her cheeks. She'd hurt him. This time she wasn't sure he'd ever forgive her, and she couldn't blame him.

Ten

. . . .

Tuesday evening Kara stared at her reflection in the mirror over the dresser in her bedroom and wanted to cry. She looked "ordinary" in the dark navy suit and simple white shell. Nothing stood out or invited a man to take a second look. She didn't even have any pretty jewelry to wear.

On her bed were several suits and dresses that she'd tried on. None of them made her look any better. She'd never been this anxious about what she wore on a date. She shut her eyes. This was not a date. Her eyes opened.

Lying to yourself is a bad sign, Kara. She should have listened to Sabrina. Sabrina might not date, but she knew women's psyches where men were concerned. She also wasn't afraid to go after what she wanted. Kara had been tempted to call her. But Kara had made the decision and now she had to live with it.

The doorbell sounded. Kara blew out a breath and picked her purse off the chair in her bedroom.

In the den, she was surprised to see her mother watching

television. After her father died, her mother wouldn't sleep in their bedroom. She'd moved to the guest bedroom down the hall, then complained about being cramped.

Tired of hearing her complain, Kara hired Fred to tear out the wall of the connecting bedroom and remodel the rooms into one for her mother. One of the additions her mother insisted on was a 44-inch TV. The den had the same 19-inch RCA her parents had when Kara was a child.

The doorbell sounded again. Her mother casually picked up her glass of Pepsi and sipped. Kara knew her mother was purposefully waiting for Tristan to arrive. How she'd act was anybody's guess.

Kara went to the door and opened it. Her heart did a quick, unsettling jerk. Dressed in a lightweight wheat-colored sports jacket, white shirt, and chocolate-colored slacks, he looked mouthwatering. "Hello, Tristan."

"Hi, Kara. You ready?"

"Yes." So what if she had vainly hoped to see a hint of appreciation in his green eyes despite her putting him off-limits.

"A man with manners would come in and speak," her mother said from behind her.

Kara wanted to hang her head. Instead she opened the glass door and stepped aside for Tristan to come into the house.

"Good evening, Mrs. Simmons," Tristan greeted.

"Kara might trust you, but I don't."

"Mother," Kara said, embarrassed.

"I hope to change your mind, Mrs. Simmons. Your daughter has talent and I want to help her find an audience for her paintings," Tristan said.

"No doubt . . . for a price." Her mother practically sneered.

"Good night, Mother." Kara left the house. Tristan followed.

On the porch, she paused. In the driveway was an expensive-looking black sports car.

"I didn't know what you'd wear and I didn't want you struggling to climb up into the truck," he explained, leading her to the car and opening the door.

"I might have known you'd have another car." Seated, she buckled the ~~the~~ seat belt he handed her.

"Actually, I prefer the truck," Tristan told her before he got inside and started the motor. "It belonged to my dad. He died when I was three, but Mother kept it for me."

Her mother had sold her father's car a week after they buried him. She said there was no sense paying insurance on a car to sit in the garage; besides, she needed the money to pay bills. She'd used the money to go to an exclusive spa. "I like your mother."

"She likes you too." Tristan took the ramp to the freeway. "She's excited about placing the paintings in the model home."

"I'm grateful she wants to help, especially after my bad behavior," she said, remembering her mother's rudeness tonight. "My mother . . . I'm sorry. She—"

His hand briefly rested on hers. Startled, she glanced up at him. "She's just worried about you."

She wasn't, and they both knew it. "Where are we going for dinner?"

"Someplace quiet where we can relax and talk." He exited the freeway and headed toward downtown. "I thought tomorrow night we'd go over the selection again."

"Fred loves working with wood and helping me frame them," she said, relaxing a bit as he turned into the West End, a popular tourist attraction that had a lot of casual restaurants.

"I still can't believe you frame them yourself," he said as he slowed down to pull behind another car.

"The pricing of odd-size or large canvases is outrageous," she said. "Besides, I like finishing the wood, selecting the matting."

"People are going to be lining up to buy your work once they know it's all handcrafted." He grinned at her. "You're going to be a sensation."

Kara grinned back. "I'm going to hold you to that."

"We're here," he said.

Kara looked around, saw the palm tree neon sign for the Palm, an upscale restaurant, and shrank back against the seat. "We're eating here?"

"Yeah. They have great food and we're early enough to miss the evening crowd."

A smiling young man in white slacks and shirt opened her door. "Welcome to the Palm."

Tristan stared at her when she made no move to get out of the car. "What's the matter?"

How could she tell him she wasn't dressed right? The Palm was a five-star restaurant. She'd passed it several times but, because it was so expensive, had never eaten there.

"Would you rather go someplace else?" Tristan said.

Kara saw two couples, the women in pretty summer dresses, go up the steps leading inside. Once again she wished she had listened to Sabrina. Kara wanted to feel confident, beautiful, and she felt neither.

Tristan pulled out his billfold and extracted two bills. "Sorry, fellows."

"No. This is fine." Reminding herself that this was a business meeting, she got out of the car. Tristan rounded the car and curved his arm around her waist. She didn't think of protesting. She needed the boost his nearness gave her.

"They have great seafood and steaks," he said as they entered.

"Welcome to the Palm," a woman greeted at the podium. "Two for dinner?"

"Yes, thank you," Tristan said. "A quiet table."

"Certainly, sir." The woman led them to a high-backed booth, then moved aside.

Kara sat down in the leather booth, careful not to pull the white tablecloth from the table as she slid in. She expected Tristan to sit on the other side. He sat beside her. She had no choice but to slide over. The hostess handed them menus.

"What would you like to drink, or would you prefer to wait for the wine steward?"

"White wine," Kara said.

"Hennessy."

"They'll be right out. Enjoy your dinner."

Tristan opened his menu. "Anything look good to you?"

You, popped into Kara's head before she could control the thought. She hid behind the menu, but she couldn't ignore him; the heat from his body burned though her clothes.

"I'm having salmon. How about you?"

She lowered the menu and found his face inches from hers. She didn't want to be attracted to Tristan. Somehow she knew he could hurt her worse than any man before him.

His fingertips brushed across her chin. "Believe in yourself. Believe in me."

"Hello, Tristan."

Tristan tensed beside her. Kara looked up to see a beautiful woman in a gorgeous red silk suit. Short stylish black hair framed her face. An onyx enhancer surrounded by diamonds hung from her neck. Matching earrings graced her ears. She exuded confidence and wealth.

"Hello, Gizzelle."

"Aren't you going to introduce us?" she asked, her voice smooth and cultured.

"Kara Simmons. Gizzelle Adams," Tristan said tightly, obviously not wanting to make the introduction.

Kara nodded. Gizzelle did the same, but didn't move. Kara sensed the woman and Tristan had once been more than friends. Had she been one of the things he became bored with?

"How is your mother?" Gizzelle asked.

"Fine," Tristan clipped out.

"Please give her my love," Gizzelle said, staring at Tristan with greedy eyes.

"Sure."

Gizzelle's gaze finally moved to Kara and stayed. Kara felt as if she were being evaluated and found lacking. She sat up straighter.

"The hostess is waiting on you," Tristan said.

Gizzelle didn't even look in the direction of the woman standing a few feet away. "If you ever need a hair stylist or a personal shopper, Tristan has my number."

Tristan shot to his feet. His face was hard. "No I don't, and Kara doesn't need your help."

Gizzelle stared at Kara, smiled coldly, and said, "Spoken like a man who is only thinking about one thing."

"You're pushing it, and you really don't want to do that," Tristan said tightly.

"Just trying to help. People in our influential circle can be so cruel to outsiders," she said, and looked at Tristan. "Perhaps we'll see each other again."

"I can't think of a single reason why either of us would want to."

Her head snapped back, and the self-assurance faded from

her face. She shot a killer glance at Kara then finally moved away.

Trying to control his anger, Tristan sat back down. Gizzelle still got to him, but not in the way she wanted.

"Your drinks. Are you ready to order?"

Tristan gave the waiter their food order and menus. As soon as the waiter left, Tristan turned to Kara. "I'm sorry for that."

He'd overlooked her mother's bad manners so she should reciprocate. Besides, the woman had reminded Kara that Tristan wasn't for her. His association with Gizzelle was none of Kara's business, but she heard herself ask, "Is she one of the things you became bored with?"

"She became bored with me." He picked up his cognac. "We were married less than a year and we've been divorced a year."

Kara placed her hand on his arm. "People do things they regret later on. Like my bad behavior."

He wasn't surprised by her concern or by the way his body reacted to her touch. She got to him in the best way. "You were pissed off and scared. My ex was uncaring and gleeful. She wanted a partnership more than she wanted me."

"I think she's discovered that some accomplishments aren't worth what you give up to get them," she said.

His hand covered hers. "You care about people. Bess said you called today to check on them. You didn't have to do that."

Her hand trembled beneath his, but she didn't pull away. "My obligation doesn't end when a patient leaves the hospital. I wanted them to know I'm still there for them."

"I've met a lot of people who care about the money and not the job. They make everyone around them pay for their unhappiness," he said. "Bess said you helped them get other services. You went beyond what you had to. Just before you called yesterday, Zachary had called to say Dale had another buddy bring him more beer. I could have kicked his butt for wasting his life."

So, that was the reason he had sounded impatient. "It's hard when you care for a person and they don't seem to care about themselves. Alcoholism is a complex disease."

"You're right, but I could still kick his butt."

Kara almost smiled. Tristan didn't appear to be a man who tolerated weakness in himself or others. Her smile faded. He would have put her mother in check long ago.

"I'm glad Bess has you to help her."

"I like helping people. As for those you mentioned earlier who just want a job, I bet you don't have them working for you for long," she said, sure of her answer.

"You would be right."

"Your meal." Two servers placed their entrees along with the family-style servings of vegetables on the table, almost taking up the entire space.

Kara laughed. "I think you ordered too much."

"If it got you to laugh, it was worth it."

She smiled at him. "I'm glad I came."

He picked up his glass. "A toast." She followed suit. "To a new beginning."

"A new beginning." She sipped her wine. Over the rim of the glass she stared into Tristan's green eyes, felt the heated rush, the pull, and realized he wasn't just talking about their business arrangement. She wasn't either. Despite his ex's taunts, Tristan, Kara was finding, was a man worth taking a chance on.

The Myers Art Gallery off Elm Street in downtown Dallas was a modern two-story structure. Mellowed by two glasses of good wine, Kara wasn't as intimidated as she'd thought she'd be when meeting the people inside. Tristan, remaining by her side and introducing her as his newest protégée, helped. From the gallery owner to the other guests, people wanted to know more about her. Laughing, Tristan told them they'd have to wait. They were there to enjoy the opening and the artist.

"I think you're a hit," Tristan said as they moved away to view an abstract by Paul Jakes, the featured artist.

"They're going to expect a lot," she said, gripping the handful of cards that had been thrust at her.

He turned to her, his eyes direct. "And you'll give it to them in spades."

Her body clenched. Her nipples tightened. Sexual attraction blindsided her. His eyes narrowed. His casual arm around her waist tightened.

"Do you like *Emotions*?" the artist asked proudly.

Embarrassed, Kara tucked her head. She definitely liked Tristan and the way he made her feel.

"Standing here, I certainly feel emotional," Tristan answered, his voice a bit husky.

Kara lifted her head to see the tall, slim man in his midthirties with a goatee smiling at Tristan.

"It's a steal at thirty-five hundred," the artist went on to say.

Kara jerked her head back around to the painting, and the discreet price tag tucked in the corner. She studied the painting and though she found nothing to draw her, it had more to do with her personal taste and nothing against the man's talent.

"I want to look around before I make a decision," Tristan said smoothly. "Thanks for coming over. I'll be sure and blog about the event before I go to bed tonight."

"That would be great." The artist stuck his hand out. "If I don't see you anymore tonight, thanks for coming."

"My pleasure," Tristan said. "The world needs art and you bring your own special touch to every painting."

The man's grin widened. Tristan had complimented him loudly enough for those standing nearby to hear. The artist extended his hand to Kara. "I hope you'll invite me to your opening. I'd love to see your work."

The warmth of his smile appeared genuine. They saw things differently when they painted, they touched people differently, but differences made the world more exciting and interesting. "I'd love to."

"Excellent." He enfolded her hand in his. "Good night, and thanks for coming."

"Good night and good luck," Kara said.

"Thanks, and the same to you." He pulled a card from the pocket of his sports coat. "Call me if you ever want to discuss art or other things."

Kara blinked. There had been no mistaking the inflection of his voice. He'd gone from friendly to interested.

Tristan took the card. "She'll be busy."

Kara jerked her head around to stare at Tristan. The smile was gone.

"I might have known," the artist said, then laughed and slapped Tristan on the back. "Don't forget the blog."

"I won't."

The man glanced at Kara one last time, then moved away. She realized as he did that he might be interested in her, but he was more interested in Tristan giving him a plug on his site.

"You ready to go?" Tristan asked.

Kara stared up at Tristan. He had acted territorial, and completely out of line. She didn't need him running interference for her, but it was nice knowing he didn't mind letting the artist or anyone else know she was off-limits. Still.

"Tristan—"

"I know," he interrupted. "I was out of line and you can take care of yourself."

He looked so disgruntled and annoyed, her lips twitched. What woman, deep down, wouldn't be pleased having a gorgeous, successful man warning off other men? Caveman for sure, but she needed the ego boost. "I've picked a couple of duds in my life."

His hand around her waist tightened. "Some men are fools."

"So are some women," she said, aware she was moving into dangerous territory, but unable to stop herself.

He grinned at her, making her heart thud, her blood hum through her veins. "Let's get out of here."

He was going to kiss her.

Kara anticipated the kiss, the warmth of his mouth, the texture of his lips, the taste of him. Kara thought about it all the way back to her house. The evening might have started out as strictly business but, wise or not, they had moved beyond that. While she wasn't sure how far she wanted things to go, she did want to know the feel of his arms holding her, the feel of his muscular body pressed against her.

Her knees actually shook as they walked to the front door. He probably felt it since he held her arm.

"It's all right."

She stopped in the middle of the sidewalk. "What?"

He stepped in front of her and curved his other arm around her waist, then leaned over and brushed his lips gently across hers. Her hands automatically closed around his arms. "See, there's nothing to fear. I'm not going to jump you."

"You don't mince words," she managed, wanting to trace her tongue across her lips to taste him again.

"I find it easier." Leaning over, he nibbled her ear. "You tempt me as I've never been tempted before."

She wanted to purr it felt so good. The man had magic lips. "I—"

The porch light snapped on. "Kara, come inside."

The sensual haze instantly cleared. Kara stiffened. She tried to push out of Tristan's arms and found it impossible. "Please."

"Only for you," he said, finally releasing her.

Kara went up the sidewalk, past her mother standing in the door and into the house, heard the door close behind her. "Why would you embarrass me that way?" Kara asked, trembling with anger.

"I'm trying to keep you from making another mistake," her mother said, unrepentant. "He's just trying to get you to lower your price for the paintings."

The paintings. Her mother had never cared about the paintings before. The only reason she did now was money.

"You don't have good judgment with men," her mother went on to point out. "I just don't want to see you taken advantage of. Perhaps you should let someone else take a look at them."

Money again. "I'm working with Tristan."

"And you'll get taken just like before," her mother said. "I don't know why you believe all the crap men tell you."

Kara didn't have a comeback. She'd believed her college sweetheart Ryan and loaned him money to get his car out of the shop only to find out a few days later that he'd used the money to gamble. Short of embarrassing herself further by trying to take him to small claims court, there was nothing she could do about the two thousand dollars she could ill afford to lose. He might have lied about the reason, but the money was still a loan. Then there was Burt. Another mistake.

Both men had called to try to convince her they were sorry. All the calls had done was convince her mother even more how gullible Kara was. "I'm going to bed. Good night."

"One day you'll thank me."

Kara kept walking. In her bedroom, she closed the door just as her cell phone rang. Picking it up, she activated the call. "Hello."

"Are you all right?" Tristan asked.

She wrapped one arm around her waist. There was genuine concern. She refused to believe it was motivated by greed. "I'm sorry."

"Don't be. You still coming over tomorrow night?" he asked.

"I'll be there, but . . ." She swallowed, pressed her arm around her churning stomach.

"I don't think I want to hear the rest."

"Perhaps it's best if we go back to business only." She didn't want to go through the daily fights with her mother, and that was exactly what it would entail. She wasn't adept at hiding her emotions.

"Best for whom?"

She tucked her head. "Please."

"Sometimes you have to fight for what you want even when the odds aren't in your favor. See you tomorrow. Night."

Kara stared at the phone. He wasn't going to back off. Neither was her mother. And Kara was going to be caught in the middle.

Past midnight, racked with remorse, her eyes red and puffy from crying, Sabrina sat on the side of her bed. She'd hurt Cade. She couldn't get the picture of his face out of her mind. There'd been anger, but there'd also been embarrassment, shame. Her eyes shut tightly. In trying to get him to open up, she'd made him relive memories of his past he obviously wanted to forget.

She wiped at the tears slowly gliding down her cheeks. Her loving parents and grandparents had helped her work through her pain and anger of what her mother had done to her. Who had been there for Cade? Her thoughtlessness had made him feel exposed, even vulnerable when all she'd wanted to do was let him know she cared.

She'd failed miserably and Cade paid the price. Curling up on the bed she let the tears flow.

Eleven

. . . .

I t was past two in the morning and Cade couldn't sleep. In silk pajama bottoms, he stood on the balcony of his condo and stared out at the warm summer night. Eighteen stories up gave him a breathtaking view of the Dallas skyline. Across the way was the W Hotel, and around the corner was the American Airlines Center, where the top musicians in the world played, as well as Dallas's basketball and hockey teams. He was living the life he'd always dreamed of and promised himself he'd have.

Yet, it wasn't enough.

His hands tightened around the top steel railing that ran the length of the balcony. No matter how he tried to run from it, the fact remained, his mother hadn't wanted him. If he believed the heartless bastard who raised him, his birth mother had chosen her reputation and social standing over her son.

He was a bastard no one wanted.

No matter how successful he was, how many accolades and awards he garnered, how his bank account and stock portfolio grew, that gut-wrenching fact remained. From the second he drew his first breath, he was considered a nothing.

And Sabrina knew his deepest secret.

He felt exposed. He wasn't afraid she'd tell anyone. That wasn't her style. Besides, the tears that glistened in her eyes were real, which angered him more. He didn't want her pity. He wasn't one of her patients to try and fix.

Perhaps that was what she wanted from him, to fix him. Fix the damaged, unwanted man that his colleagues revered.

Cade rubbed a hand across his face. He couldn't let this get to him. He had to push it away as he'd always done and get on with his life. To do otherwise would be to let the man who called himself his father, and the woman who gave birth to him, win.

He'd eat glass first.

Straightening, he started back inside. The house phone rang just as he passed. He stared at it on the small glass table. The only time it had rang in the past was to ask if he was ready for his meal. The waiter had delivered his dinner hours ago. It remained on the dining table. Untouched.

He picked up the white receiver. "Yes."

"Dr. Mathis, this is Simpson with security. There's a Sabrina Thomas here. She refuses to leave and insists on seeing you."

"I don't want to see her."

"I understand, sir. I was just checking. The security and privacy of our guests is paramount."

"Send her away."

"Yes, sir. Just as soon as we think she can drive safely."

"What's the matter with her?" Cade tensed in spite of himself.

"She's crying. Bailey took her into the lobby to let her calm down. Don't worry. She won't get past us. Good night, Dr. Mathis. Sorry to disturb you."

Cade hung up the phone, but couldn't quite release it. *She's crying.* His gut knotted. No one had ever cried for him. The wife of the man who pretended to the town he cared had tried to help him, but never when it went against her husband's wishes. She thought of herself first. She'd certainly never shed a tear for him.

He snatched up the phone and punched in the code for security. The call was answered on the first ring.

"Yes, Dr. Mathis. Is everything all right?"

"Security just called about a woman downstairs wanting to see me. Please keep her there until I arrive, but I don't want her to know I'm coming. Understand?"

"Understood."

Cade replaced the receiver and went to get dressed.

"Thank you." Sabrina sniffed, clutching the wad of tissue in her hand. "I can drive all right now."

"We have to be sure," the man in an expensive black suit and silk tie said. No tacky uniforms for the security team of Navarone Place. He smiled easily. "We wouldn't want you to be hurt on the way home."

"I promise I won't sue," she said, coming to her feet and taking a tentative step toward the front door. Her eyes felt like they had sand in them. No wonder, she'd cried off and on all evening and into the morning. Finally, thinking of Cade alone and with no one, she hadn't been able to stay away.

The security guard easily matched her step for step. He'd

probably heard that before. But she just wanted to go home. Cade hated her. Tears formed in her eyes, rolled down her cheeks. The soggy tissue in her hands was no help.

"Sabrina."

Her head came up. Cade, his face unemotional, his body stiff, stood several feet away. She didn't care. "Cade." She ran toward him.

The nice man who had been trying to calm her was suddenly in front of her, his face no longer smiling, his eyes unblinking.

"It's all right," Cade said.

The man stepped aside.

Sabrina took a tentative step toward Cade. He looked untouchable. Cold. She knew he wasn't. He'd been hurt, still hurt. She'd grown up with love. She was positive he hadn't. Love and trust were learned responses. If she had to be the first to reach out, so be it.

"Cade." This time she didn't stop until she had her arms around his waist, her cheek pressed to his chest. His heart thudded in her ear. "I'm sorry. I'm so sorry." She sniffed, but the tears just came faster. "I couldn't sleep. Please don't be angry with me."

"Dr. Mathis?"

"It's all right," he said, one arm lifting to curve around her waist.

She swallowed. Through watery eyes, she stared up at him, blinking to try to see his face clearer. It didn't help. She was caught between needing to release him to wipe her eyes and just holding on. One word from him and the watchful guards would take her away. "Can I please talk to you alone?"

Silence.

"Please."

"Two minutes." Pushing her arms away, he stepped back and started for the elevator. Sabrina followed, going over in her mind what she'd say. Neither spoke on the elevator or as they walked down the wide, beautifully decorated hall.

Stopping in front of the second door near the end of the hallway, he stepped aside for her to enter.

Sabrina quickly entered. She didn't waste time. "I'm sorry. I know I hurt—"

"It doesn't matter."

"It does matter, Cade. Don't be mad at me."

"Do you know what time it is?" he asked.

She didn't understand the question, but at least he was talking to her. "I guess around two," she said. "You probably have to get up early to see patients, but I just needed to tell you I'm sorry. I don't want you upset with me."

"Because we're friends."

She sniffed. Nodded. "And because you matter to me." She might not get another chance. "And not because you're a brilliant doctor and we work together."

"I've never met anyone like you," he said.

Sabrina finally felt secure enough to use the soggy tissue to wipe her eyes so she could see him clearly. His face was no longer harsh and forbidding. "Because I'm pushy?"

His thumb brushed away a lingering tear. "That would be one reason."

The phone rang. He quickly crossed the room and picked it up. "Dr. Mathis."

Sabrina moved closer.

"Get a CAT scan of her arm, stat. I'm on my way." He hung up. "I have to get to the hospital. My patient might have a blood clot. Call a cab and wait here until it arrives."

"I can dr—"

"I don't have time to argue." He grabbed a ring of keys from a bowl by the door, his wallet, his cell phone. Opening the door, he was gone.

Sabrina sat down on the elegant French sofa to dig her phone out of her purse. Occasionally she needed to call a cab for patients. Finding the phone, she scrolled through the numbers, but suddenly decided she might lose her chance to talk to Cade if she left.

She glanced around the penthouse. It was stylishly decorated and sterile. Everything was neatly arranged. She didn't see one picture. Her heart went out to him again. He was alone, but not anymore. He had her. She just had to be patient and wait for him to realize it.

She kicked off her shoes and prepared to wait.

Two hours later Cade opened the door to his condo and saw Sabrina asleep on the sofa. Her hands were pillowed beneath her cheek, her shapely legs drawn up.

He accepted the tug in his heart, the wish that she would always be there for him. She looked right there somehow. He admitted the idea of coming home to a loving, warm, and waiting woman was something he'd never let himself imagine.

Closing the door, he went to the sofa. For a long moment he simply watched her sleep. She was beautiful, her lashes black and silky, her perfectly shaped lips slightly parted.

And she could never be his. Even if they got past their working together, she wasn't the brief affair type. She felt too deeply. As much as he wanted her, he wanted her to stay happy more. The unfairness of life caused him to clench his fist instead of brushing the hair from her cheek, kissing her awake.

"Sabrina." He gently shook her shoulder, a safe place to touch her.

Her eyes opened. She smiled. A warm sensual expression on her incredible face, she reached up to touch his face. He caught her hand. "Sabrina."

She blinked. He released her hand. He should move away. He didn't. "Is the patient all right?" she asked as she sat up.

"Yes. You were supposed to call a cab." *Instead you're here, tempting me with what I can't have.*

She ran a distracted hand through her hair, causing her breasts to rise, tempting him even more. "I started to, but I was afraid if I left you might change your mind about talking to me."

"It's almost five. You should be home."

"Not until you forgive me."

He pushed to his feet. "Let's forget about it."

She stood, coming to the middle of his chest. He could lift her with one arm, and yet she got to him as no one ever had. "Neither one of us can do that."

He hadn't expected it to be easy. The crazy thing was she was being stubborn for him. "My first patient appointment is at nine. I need to check on a couple of patients in the hospital before then," he told her. "I need some sleep."

"You can't just ignore it," she persisted.

He brushed both hands over his head. "Why can't you just let it go?"

"Because ignoring something doesn't make it go away." She placed her unsteady hand on his chest. He felt the softness, the warmth, and fought to keep from crushing her to him. "If we don't get past this, it will always be between us."

She had finally given voice to the growing awareness between them. Only there could never be an "us," but from the look in her eyes when he'd woken her that was what she wanted. Lord help him, he wanted it too. "I'm going to bed."

She folded her arms. "Now who's being stubborn?"

"Since you're staying, you want to tuck me in?" he asked, unsure if he was joking or half hoping she'd take him up on the offer.

Her breath caught. Air fluttered over her incredible lips when she released the breath. "Where's the bedroom?"

Once again, she'd caught him off guard. He frowned down at her. "You know it wouldn't stop there. You aren't the one-night-stand type."

"No, I'm not," she said quietly. Emotions shimmered in her velvety brown eyes. She'd do whatever it took for him to realize she cared.

Fists clenched, he began to speak. "My mother gave me away at birth. The couple who raised me used me as free labor, but never as their son. The man took every opportunity to tell me how worthless I was, how my wealthy mother didn't want me. How I'd never amount to anything."

Tears crested in her eyes again, but she blinked them away. She took his face in her hands. "You proved him wrong. You matter. People are alive today because of you. You matter, Cade."

Her softly spoken words, the touch of her hand broke through the barrier he'd erected. He'd waited and wanted too long. His body burned. With desperation and desire he pulled her to him, his mouth fusing with hers. Pleasure swamped him. The taste, the feel, the warmth of her.

She came to him eagerly, fit perfectly in his arms. Her soft body molded against his. His tongue mated with hers, greedy to take and give. His hand cupped her hips, bringing her against the hardness of his lower body. She whimpered. His hand closed over her breast, felt the nipple push against his palm asking for his mouth. He picked her up.

"Cade," she whispered, her voice unsteady with passion.

He stumbled to a halt, then tightly shut his eyes. She'd made him forget.

"Cade, what is it?"

He glanced down at her face, flushed with desire, her eyes so full of warmth that he wanted to curse whatever fate had shown him what it was to be truly wanted, then snatched it away. Forever wasn't for him. He knew that was what Sabrina wanted, deserved. He wouldn't crush her dreams as his had been crushed.

He set her on her feet, then quickly stepped away. "That shouldn't have happened. I'm sorry."

"Cade—"

"You should go."

For a long time she simply stared at him, then she went to the sofa, picked up her handbag, continued to the door, and opened it. "I'm not sorry. See you at work." The door closed behind her.

"Not if I can help it," Cade murmured.

Sabrina was too jazzed to be sleepy at work. Later that morning sitting behind her desk, she wore a goofy smile on her face and didn't care. Cade wanted her. She'd hoped and plotted, and it had happened. And it wasn't just sex between them. If he hadn't cared, he wouldn't have stopped. She certainly wouldn't have stopped him. She was falling in love with him. He needed her.

She jumped up from her desk at the knock on her door and

rushed to open it. She hoped it was Kara so she could tell her what had happened, and get an update on her and Tristan.

Seeing Kara's unsmiling face, worry replaced Sabrina's happiness. Closing the door, Sabrina asked, "What can I do to help?"

Kara swallowed and told her about what her mother had done. "Mama is going to keep at me and make my life miserable."

"You could tell her you're an adult and to back off," Sabrina suggested.

"She'd have a fit, tell me how ungrateful I am, how disrespectful, and make my life even more difficult." Kara stuffed her hands into the pockets of her slacks. "Besides, Tristan won't be around forever."

Sabrina's eyes narrowed. "You like him, don't you?"

Kara opened her mouth, closed it, then threaded her fingers though her hair. "He's made it no secret that he wants me, but he's just as forceful when it comes to making me believe in my art." She laughed. "My art. It's because of him that I'm beginning to believe."

"About time. So what happened on the pretend dinner date?" Sabrina asked.

"I met his ex-wife who apparently wants him back, went to a gallery opening, and almost melted when he kissed me," she confessed.

Sabrina grinned. "I did melt when Cade kissed me. I forgot my own name."

Kara's eyes widened. "Dr. Mathis?"

"Has some incredible moves." Sabrina loved and trusted Kara, but she wasn't going to discuss Cade's background. "He says it shouldn't have happened, and he'll probably try to avoid me. I'll let him until Friday. He's taking me to Clarissa's birthday party Saturday afternoon."

"I wish I could go after what I wanted without worrying about the consequences like you can," Kara mused.

Sabrina placed a hand on Kara's arm. "I'm not being pulled in three directions. You have your painting, Tristan, your mother. You can possibly have two happily in your life, but I'm not sure about all three."

"I know." Kara wrapped her arms around her waist. "I'm going over to Tristan's place tonight to start framing the pictures."

"Lip-locking time," Sabrina said.

"It will be strictly business," Kara said.

"Only until you see him and then you'll start thinking about the kiss, how it made you feel. You'll want that again, and what your mother says or thinks won't matter," Sabrina predicted.

Unfolding her arms, Kara frowned at her best friend. "Since when did you become an authority?"

"Since I saw Cade an hour ago from a distance. Just thinking about the kiss made my knees weak." Sabrina's eyes narrowed. "If he thinks he's getting away from me, he better think again."

"I'd wish you luck, but I'm not sure Dr. Mathis is the man for you," Kara warned.

"I am. I just have to convince Cade."

Kara stood on Tristan's porch Wednesday evening and chewed on her bottom lip. Sabrina was wrong. Kara didn't even have to see Tristan to think about the kiss, to want to feel his mouth on hers again. She rubbed her sweaty palm against her jean leg and rang the doorbell.

The door opened. Tristan stood there, looking gorgeous in a white T-shirt, sinful jeans that molded to his muscular thighs, and a smile that made her heart sigh. "Hi, come on in. Everything is ready."

On trembling legs, she entered the house. "Hi," she said, hoping he didn't hear the breathlessness in her voice.

"Did you get a chance to eat?" Tristan closed the door.

"Yes, thank you." She would have never heard the end of it if she'd left without preparing dinner for her mother. Kara had been too nervous to eat.

"Great. You're probably anxious to see the setup," he told her. "I put everything in the same room. Come on."

A bit off-balance, Kara followed him down the hall. She didn't know what she'd expected, but it wasn't the friendly businessman. She stepped ahead of him as he indicated the room with the paintings. Everything she needed to start framing was there. With the money he'd given her for the painting, she'd be able to repay him.

She turned to thank him and found herself in his arms, his hot mouth on hers. Thoughts of protesting vanished. She just enjoyed the slow glide of his tongue against hers, the lazy sweep of his hand down her back. He ravished her mouth. She returned the pleasure.

"I'm not going away. I'm not using you."

She discovered she needed the kiss, the warmth of his body against hers. "I know that. It's—"

He placed one long, elegant finger against her lips. "No. Just concentrate on what you want. What you feel is right."

"That's not always easy." She bit her lip. "I've made mistakes."

"If you're talking relationships, I think we can agree that mine trumps yours."

"We can also agree if I go along with you, we'd end up sleeping together."

"Yep. There is that, but I also get you to believe, really believe, in yourself."

Something bristled inside of her. "You think I'm a coward."

"I think you care deeply and try to avoid confrontations," he answered.

"A coward." She pushed against him to free herself, and then went to the lengths of unfinished woods on a long table in the middle of the room. "I plan to start staining the woods this week and begin framing Monday."

"I'll let you get to it. I'm anxious to put up photos of the paintings on my blog," he told her.

She glanced up. She thought nothing bothered him, but recalled hurting him in this very room. Yet, he'd accepted her apology and continued to help her. He was successful, sexy, and charming. He didn't have to go to such lengths to get a woman into his bed. "Thank you. Again. I'll frame the ones you liked first. Do you remember the ones Vera favored?"

He smiled and leaned against the doorjamb. "I do, but she'll be here any minute so she can point them out."

"Your mother is coming?"

"She insisted when I told her you were coming by." He straightened. "I'll be in my office if you need me."

"All right."

Tristan stared at Kara as she ran her hand lovingly over the length of wood for framing, and his body hardened. He wanted to feel her hands on him, his on her. He'd take his time stripping away the unflattering clothes until there was only bare tempting skin. But not now, not until she gained confidence in herself and trusted him completely.

Leaving, he started for his office, then changed direction at the sound of the doorbell. Opening the door, he smiled on seeing his mother. "You're early."

"You knew I would be," Vera said, coming inside. "I saw Kara's car so everything is going as planned."

"Getting there," he told her.

"Good," Vera said, then, "Gizzelle called today and invited me out to dinner." Vera wrinkled her nose. "As if I would. She upped the ante by asking me to redecorate her place." Vera's eyes flared. "It took everything not to hang up on her."

"It's over," Tristan told her.

"She hurt you," Vera said sharply, clearly not ready to forgive or forget.

He hugged his mother. She loved fiercely. No matter what, he could count on her. "She means nothing to me." The only emotion she'd been able to elicit at the restaurant was anger when she had tried to talk down to Kara. "I've moved on."

Vera glanced in the direction of the back room. "I believe you have."

"Whoa." He held up both hands. "We're just getting to know each other while I help her with her paintings. She's a special young woman."

His mother lifted a perfectly shaped brow. "Hmm."

"Vera, don't get any ideas." He didn't like the way the conversation was going.

"Wouldn't dream of it." She tapped his chest with her clutch. "I'll think I'll go say hello."

He caught her arm. "No matchmaking."

With her free hand, she patted his face as if he were two instead of thirty-two. "You know I'll always do what I feel is best for you."

"That's what I'm afraid of."

Laughing, she walked away.

Shaking his head, Tristan went to his office. He cared about Kara, wanted the best for her, but it wasn't forever. He'd been down that slippery slope and wasn't going again.

His ex had taught him that love wasn't always forever, and when the woman you loved walked away with a smile on her face, it made you feel like you'd been run over by a semi. You felt like a fool for being so clueless, questioned yourself over and over why you hadn't been good enough in bed and out. Never again! This time he was being smart.

Twelve

· · · · · · · · · · · · · · ·

H i, Kara."

Startled, Kara whirled around and saw Tristan's mother and felt heat flush her face.

Frowning, Vera came farther into the room. "I'm sorry, I didn't mean to startle you."

"You didn't," Kara managed. It had been her own naughty thoughts about her son that was the problem. She moistened her dry lips. "Tristan said you were dropping by."

"Oh," Vera said.

For some reason her direct gaze made Kara nervous. "Y-yes. I'm staining the wood for the frames this week. I wanted to know which pictures you were interested in so I could frame them once I finished with the ones for Tristan."

"All of them," Vera said, then laughed at what Kara knew was her stunned expression. "I agree with my son, you're very talented and a special young woman."

Kara was stunned again, this time by what Vera had said.

Tristan thought she was special. She tucked the words in her heart.

Stepping past Kara, Vera went to the paintings propped against the wall facing her. "There are several that would look fabulous in the spec house I'm decorating. You said Tristan has already picked out the ones he wants."

"Yes," Kara said. "He's already hung one. The others are in his office."

Vera nodded. "I don't blame him. If I had room, I'd select a couple for my home. I still might." She reached for a picture.

"No!" Kara snapped off her gloves and rushed over. "You point and I'll do the rest."

Vera wrinkled her nose. "Tristan is just being his overprotective self. I can lift the painting as well as you."

"No disrespect, but I've seen too many patients back in the hospital or having prolonged therapy for not following orders," Kara told her. "I don't imagine you liked the restrictions your doctor imposed on you. You certainly don't want the time extended or worse, to not get the optimum results from your surgery."

"Pain doesn't wake me up in the mornings anymore," Vera said. She sighed and pointed. "That one, please."

Kara picked up the paintings as Vera directed. By the time they finished, Vera had selected seventeen paintings.

"Can you have those ready in a couple of weeks?" Vera asked.

"I don't . . ." Kara began, then said, "They'll be ready." This was her chance. Whatever it took, she'd have them matted and framed.

"Good. I have another appointment, so I'll run and let you get back to work."

Kara followed Tristan's mother to the door. "Thank you for believing in me."

"Thank Tristan," Vera said.

"I have," Kara told her. "He's changed my life."

Vera smiled. "You might have changed his as well. Good-bye, Kara."

"Good-bye." Puzzled by Vera's last comment, Kara watched Vera walk down the hall to Tristan's office, then dismissed it. She had work to do. Tristan and his mother were giving her a chance, but she had to do her part.

She picked up a cloth and a dark mahogany stain and began applying it to the wood. No more sinful thoughts about a man who was just passing through her life no matter how sexy he was, no matter how much she wondered what it would be like to kiss him again.

Two hours later, her back and neck in knots, Kara placed the stained molding on the table and pulled off her gloves. She'd made good progress. If she continued, she could possibly start framing next week since she didn't need molding for all thirty-two pictures.

She started from the room, but took one last look back and then bumped into a solid wall of temptation. Air fluttered over her lips. "Tristan. I'm sorry."

"I'm not." His head descended.

She didn't even make the effort to evade the kiss, not that he gave her a chance. His hungry mouth captured hers, taking her on an easy ride of pleasure. He made her body hum, want. She'd gotten her wish, and it was better than the first time.

"You taste better each time I kiss you."

Her stomach did a slow roll. So did his. What she wouldn't give for another forbidden taste. "I-I was just leaving."

"You never even took a break."

"I'm used to working nonstop. My mother . . . I should go," she said, trying to step away and finding it impossible.

"I'll grab my keys."

"For what?" she asked as he released her and moved toward his office. He couldn't be thinking of following her home.

"I need to make a run," he called as he went into his office, and almost immediately reappeared. "Let's go."

Outside, he walked her to her car, which was parked behind his truck. "See you tomorrow. Drive safely." He kissed her on the cheek, then went to his truck.

Kara stared at him, then got into her car when his engine started. She wondered where he could be going, then shook her head and backed out of the driveway. He was young, handsome, rich. It was barely nine. She straightened and glanced into her rearview mirror, saw his headlights.

Dammit, she wasn't jealous, but he'd kissed her as if she meant everything to him.

Kara took the ramp to the freeway and Tristan was still behind her. Her gaze flickered to the rearview mirror when she passed the exit for downtown where there were lots of places a man on the prowl might find what he was looking for. He stayed behind her when she took her exit.

He was following her home. He didn't have to, but she knew somehow it was his way.

Fifteen minutes later she pulled into her driveway and activated the garage door. Lowering her window, she waved good night to Tristan and pulled inside, letting the garage door back down. A little smile on her lips, she went inside. Her mother met her.

"At last you're learning some sense and came home at a decent time and alone." With that her mother turned and went to her room.

Kara stared after her. "I certainly am, Mama. I certainly am."

Thursday evening, her hands gripping the steering wheel, Kara pulled into Tristan's driveway. It was 7:23 P.M. She slammed out of the car and hurried to the front door. It seemed as if everything had conspired against her efforts to stay on track and finish staining the molding. She hadn't been able to leave work until 6:15. She'd run into a traffic jam, and then arrived home to her mother waiting like a baby bird to be fed. She'd fixed her a roast beef sandwich from leftovers, ignored her disapproving face, and left.

Tristan opened the door. "Sorry." She brushed by him, already going over in her mind what she had to do. She entered the room and came to a complete stop, then closed her eyes.

"I had the time."

Opening her eyes again she saw almost all of the moldings that she'd planned to stain tonight were already stained and varnished. She turned and he was there. She leaned into him, closing her arms around him.

"Bad day?" he asked, stroking her from her head to her hips.

"Horrible," she said, fitting herself more comfortably against him.

"Maybe this will make it better." Lifting her chin, he kissed her. Her lips and body softened, yielded to the mastery of his mouth, the comfort of his touch.

Lifting his head, his mouth hovered over hers. "Better?"

"Better." Reluctantly, she pushed out of his arms. "Thanks for following me home and for this." She picked up a pair of gloves. "I won't be able to come over this weekend."

"Why?"

"This is my weekend to clean the house." She began to rub varnish into the wheat-stalked molding.

"I don't suppose you'd consider hiring someone." He picked up a length of molding.

"Not in the budget," she said frankly, then continued. "I'm saving the money you paid me." One way or another, she was getting a place of her own.

"What if I gave you an advance on the other paintings I know will sell?" he asked.

"Thank you, but I'd have to find someone, check them out." And hear her mother gripe about the waste on something Kara could do, and then bring up her hot tub again. Kara placed the three-inch molding aside and picked up another piece. "I'll stay a little longer tomorrow night to get more done. You've been a big help."

"I wish I could do more."

She glanced up and saw the sincerity in his face. "You've given me more than I ever dreamed."

"Kara—"

She averted her head. She was feeling too vulnerable, too needy. If he kissed her, they'd probably end up hot and sweaty in his bed. And lose more time. "I need to finish."

"The day is getting closer when I won't let you run."

"I know." Her hands tightened. "I have to make this work."

He picked up his cloth and began rubbing the wood. "So, what happened at work today?"

She breathed easier. He was giving her the time she needed,

but one day he wouldn't. She shivered. One day she wouldn't want him to.

Sabrina decided after a restless Wednesday night that if she got hot and bothered seeing Cade, he might feel the same about her. With that thought in mind, she asked the charge nurse on the surgery floor to call her when he came up to make rounds. Sabrina had gone up Thursday afternoon to find Cade dictating on the computer.

Out of the corner of her eye she saw him stiffen when she spoke to everyone. She'd made it a point to speak and place a friendly hand on his shoulder. He'd jerked around. The heat and desire in his eyes scorched her, taking her breath away. Then it was gone. He whirled back to continue dictating.

The second time was by accident in the X-ray department later that afternoon. By Friday she decided it was time to put them both out of their misery. Seeing him sitting in the cafeteria, a place she'd seldom seen him, she decided he might have the same idea.

"Hi, mind if I join you?' she asked, a soft drink in one hand.

"You know this can't work," he said.

Smiling, she took a seat. "A drink and conversation?"

"Is that all you want?" he asked.

Heat zipped though her body. "I might ask you the same thing."

Desire burned hotly in his eyes. "Don't push this," he warned.

Sabrina took a sip of her Pepsi to ease her dry throat. There was nothing to be done about her accelerated heart rate. "Have you picked up a birthday gift for Clarissa?" Sabrina asked. Surely that was a safe topic.

Cade hadn't. In fact, he had hoped he could escape going to the child's birthday party. He should have known better. "I thought I could give you some money to pick up a gift."

Sabrina folded her arms. "No can do."

"Why not?"

Her arms came to her sides, a grin on her pretty face. "Clarissa and her parents want you."

He knew, and that made him a bit restless. In the past, he had kept his relationship with patients strictly professional. He wasn't sure how it had changed. Then he stared across the table at Sabrina looking up at him with her saucy smile that he was becoming all too used to, and knew the exact reason.

"Stop frowning unless you want to make an appointment with Dr. Snyder," Sabrina teased, referring to the plastic surgeon.

She continued to amaze him. No one teased him or seemed to care about him if it wasn't professionally related. No one but her. No matter what, nothing seemed to faze her. "I suppose you can't wait."

"That's right. I might even take my turn at the bouncey house Mrs. Ward said they're having. I had one at my birthday when I was a kid."

A shadow flittered across his face. There had been no celebrations of his birthdays. He still didn't celebrate the day. It had been a bad day for all concerned.

"After we leave the party, we can drop by Patrizio's, an Italian restaurant in Uptown Village, grab a bite, and go to a movie."

"I'll drive."

"All right. You can pick me up at four." Sabrina picked up her soft drink and walked away.

He'd meant he'd take his own car. He needed to stop her

to explain, but as the seconds ticked by he sat there and did nothing.

Saturday afternoon Cade sat in Sabrina's driveway, unsure of how he'd gotten to this point. Yes, he was. He enjoyed being with Sabrina. She intrigued him. She was smart, beautiful, had horrible scars that hadn't made her bitter. If nothing else, he admired her for that reason alone.

He just had to make sure he didn't cross over the line again. He could do this. Life had stuck it to him in the past; he wasn't going to let it take the pleasure of Sabrina's friendship away.

Getting out, he went up the steps. The door opened. Sabrina came out in a green leopard-print cardigan, a matching shell, and black pants. As always, she looked pretty and happy. No one could guess the pain she'd gone though as a child.

"Hi, Cade. You decide on a gift yet?" she asked, stopping beside him on the porch.

"An American Express gift card."

She stuck her tongue in her cheek. Obviously she was amused.

"It's practical," he defended.

She looped her arm through his. "Cade, my birthday is in November and if you decide to get me a gift, I just want you to know that I'm not a practical kind of girl."

"I'd already figured that out."

"Good. Let's go have fun."

Sabrina thought Cade might loosen up once he was around the other people, but he never did. He kept himself apart. It was almost as if he expected them to reject him. She thought more and more of his childhood. He wasn't on an ego trip, he cared about his patients, but who cared about him? She was determined that she'd show him that she cared.

When Mr. Ward herded everyone back into the house for ice cream and cake and opening the presents, she held Cade back.

"Have you ever been in a bouncey house?" Sabrina nodded toward the inflatable contraption in the shape of a clown.

"No." He glanced at his watch. "I think we can leave now."

"I'd say you were long overdue. Let's go give it a try."

Cade pulled back. "You can't be serious?"

She smiled into his horrified face. "I most definitely am. It will be fun."

"Not if you break something," he said.

"Then it's a good thing I have a doctor with me." Tugging his hand, she moved closer. When they were within five feet, she released him, placed her handbag on a table, pulled off her shoes, and crawled though the opening flap of the clown's mouth. Inside, she beckoned him to follow. "Come on, Cade. It's more fun if someone is with you."

He folded his arms. "No."

She lowered her head briefly then lifted it. "Please. I really want to do this, and it's more fun with someone like I said."

Unfolding his arms, he toed off his loafers, and he slowly and carefully crawled inside as if he were going to his doom.

"Now stand up and jump." Sabrina demonstrated as she hopped around. "You're gonna land on your butt if you don't."

Cade went down and stared up at her, his eyes promising retribution.

Sabrina smiled. "Told you. Let's see who can jump the farthest."

"You really want that broken arm, don't you?"

"Come on, Cade, help me out with a little competition. The loser buys dinner. I won't tell anyone, including Kara, that you lost."

Slowly he pushed to his feet. "We'll see who loses."

She might have known he was competitive. "I'll let you warm up a bit."

He was awkward at fist, as if testing his balance, then he became more self-assured.

"Here goes," Sabrina said, then bounced a good six feet. "Beat that if you can."

Wordlessly, Cade sprang up and came down inches ahead of her. She fell against him, taking both of them down with her on top. Laughing, Sabrina stared down at him, then she sobered. She felt the hard impression of his body, but most of all the heat of his searing gaze. Desire swirled through her. His mouth was so close, so tempting. She leaned toward him.

Taking her arms, he quickly came to his feet. "I believe you owe me dinner."

She swallowed her disappointment and tried to control her longing. "I'll even spring for the movie tickets," she said, glad her voice sounded almost normal as she moved to the exit to put on her shoes and grab her handbag. "We'll go watch Clarissa open her gifts and say good-bye."

Cade slipped on his shoes. "I bet you also like birthday cake and tearing into presents."

"You know it." She slipped her arm through his and headed back into the house. She felt his reluctance and continued. Opening the back door she was greeted by the high-pitched sounds of children's laughter.

In the center of the den, Clarissa was surrounded by mounds of presents, torn wrapping paper, children, and adults. Several adults were taking pictures. Her beaming mother sat in a chair beside her. Her happy father, who had been on the floor handing Clarissa gifts, saw Cade and came to him.

"Dr. Mathis, thanks doesn't say enough. You gave me my family back." Mr. Ward swallowed, scrubbed his hand over his face, and stuck out his hand. "Thank you."

Cade was stunned by the effusive thanks and even more by the applause in the room, the tears in Mrs. Ward's eyes. He'd received accolades before from many prestigious organizations, but none affected him as much. Sabrina smiled proudly up at him. With her beside him he didn't feel like an outsider or alone. "You're welcome," Cade said and shook the other man's hand.

"Don't forget you're invited to Clarissa's wedding," Mr. Ward said to Sabrina. "You too, Dr. Mathis."

"We'll be there," Sabrina said as Clarissa's father went back to helping his daughter open gifts. His mother served them cake while they watched Clarissa work through her presents.

A short while later her father handed his daughter an envelope. "This is from Dr. Mathis."

"Thank you, Dr. Mathis." Clarissa tore open the envelope and frowned at the gift card. "How do I play with this?"

"I'll happily show you," her mother said, and laughed as the adults joined in. Cade was surprised to feel a smile on his own face.

The birthday party hadn't been bad, Cade thought as he and Sabrina left thirty minutes later, perhaps because the Wards seemed so happy. In a small way he had helped that happen. It felt good. "You're paying for dinner."

"Don't worry, I know it's not a pretend date like Kara's," Sabrina said from beside him on the sidewalk.

"What's a pretend date?" Cade asked.

Sabrina tucked her head. "Inside joke between friends."

Cade wasn't used to a shy Sabrina, then guessed she must have inadvertently mentioned something she was supposed to keep secret. He didn't want to put her on the spot.

"Ms. Simmons is a good social worker. I enjoy working with her," Cade said, opening the door of his car.

"Unlike working with me?" He was glad to see the smile back on her face. "One day I hope you can say the same thing about me."

"I already can," he said without thinking. "You care. You're a little exuberant, but that can be a good thing."

Pleasure spread across her beautiful face. "Thank you, Cade. That means a lot coming from you."

He didn't like the way she was looking at him, or the way his body hardened with need. They were just friends, nothing more, although he had almost forgotten when she was on top of him in the bouncey house. He'd never known wanting could be so fierce.

Thankfully, she got inside the car. "Cade, why don't you come over to the neighborhood block party next Saturday?"

"They still have block parties?" he asked, getting in the car and pulling out.

"In my neighborhood they do." Sabrina twisted in her seat toward him. "We're going to have food galore. This is my first, but I hear from Kara that it's fantastic. The city even blocks off the street. I'm cooking."

He lifted a dark brow. "I'm not sure that's wise."

She playfully swatted him on the arm and chuckled. "You

might have a point," she went on to say. "I seldom cook. I should buy stock in the restaurants near the house, I eat at them so much. Kara takes pity on me more often than not. How about you?"

"Me?"

His face had closed off. Sabrina forged ahead. "Do you cook?"

"No. Navarone Place has a chef. I simply order what I want," he told her as he parked the car near the restaurant.

"That must be nice. You don't even have to stop or get in line."

"I suppose," he said, but he didn't sound convinced as he got out of the car.

"What movie do you want to see?" she asked, holding her breath, afraid he'd refuse.

"So long as it's not silly, I don't care."

Sabrina wanted to do a happy dance. She hoped her facial expression didn't give her away. He still wanted to be with her. "I think that can be arranged."

Thirteen

. . . .

Late Saturday night Sabrina opened the front door of her house and went inside, silently inviting Cade to follow. After the briefest hesitation he did. "Thank you for a wonderful evening."

"There is something that needs to be repeated and made clear."

"Yes?"

"I don't date people I work with."

"So you said, but we've already figured that out."

"We?" he asked sharply.

She wanted to kick herself.

"Sabrina, I'd like an answer."

"You're not going to like it."

"I already figured as much, but I still want an answer."

She sighed loudly. "Actually it was my best friend."

"Do I know this best friend?"

She could see him retreating and wanted to cry. "Kara Simmons."

His eyes chilled. He actually took a step away from her. "You discussed me with someone who works at the hospital?"

She reached for him. "It wasn't like you think."

"If you'd let go of my arm, I'd like to leave."

"Don't you dare take that tone with me, Cade Mathis. We're friends."

"My arm," he repeated.

Her hand flexed, but she didn't dare release him. She didn't think she'd get by security at his place this time either. "All right, but you just remember you forced the issue. You don't remember our first meeting, do you? Of course not. You were getting off the elevator, Kara and I were getting on. I thought you were hot and I told her."

He looked stunned.

She released his arm. She wanted to tuck her head, but didn't. "After you came here, I mentioned it to Kara. She thought that since you wanted a calm environment you didn't date staff members. Which I understand, because neither do I," she said, thinking that added a nice and true touch.

Puzzlement pushed away the anger in his face. "You don't?"

"Nope."

"But you've only been here six months," he said, as if that explained everything.

She folded her arms and lifted a brow. "I was asked out three times the first week. Five times the next week. Shall I go on or don't you believe a man could want me?"

"I believe you," he said, his gaze drifting to her mouth.

Heat pooled in the pit of her stomach. She wanted his mouth on hers again and she was going to get it. "Good. Block party starts at noon. Bring an appetite. Use the code 'neighbor' to get your car past the barricades in case you have to leave."

His hands slipped into his pockets. "I'll be busy all this week. I'm speaking at a symposium Tuesday evening. I'm giving a talk at the medical school on Wednesday. There's a charity function Friday night."

"Then by Saturday you'll need to kick back and relax," she told him. "The party will go on until nightfall from what I understand. Come when you can or just to pick up a plate."

"I don't know."

He was retreating again. Time to pull back and let him mull things over. Unlike her, Cade thought things through. He also wasn't the type of man to be pushed or rushed. She stepped around him and opened the door. "I understand. Good night and thanks again."

Looking a bit unsure, he said, "Good night."

Sabrina closed the door and smiled. If he didn't feel something for her, he wouldn't have felt the need to mention he didn't date coworkers. She just had to build on it. She had all weekend to plan.

Kara arrived at Tristan's house Monday night, ready to start framing and, despite her best efforts, longing for the sight of him. She'd missed him. Being cooped up in the house with her mother all weekend hadn't helped. Her one outlet was finishing the painting of him. It was the least she could do for his mother.

Kara might have ambivalent feelings about Tristan, but Sabrina knew exactly what she wanted. Dr. Mathis. That day at lunch Sabrina had confided that Dr. Mathis was being stubborn, but it wouldn't do him any good. He was going to be hers.

Getting out of her car with the small canvas, Kara wished she could be as confident about her future. When Sabrina asked Kara about her and Tristan, Kara hadn't been sure how to answer except to say that he gave her hope.

The door opened. Tristan pulled her into his arms and kissed her. When she came up for air, she held up the canvas. "For your mother."

He took the picture and stared at it so long she became nervous.

"Vera will love it."

"But you don't," she said, unable to hide the hurt in her voice.

"It's impossible not to like it. You kept the teasing look in the eyes, but the stubborn chin is there as well." He looked at her. "Once again, you've amazed me. Thank you. I'll go put this up for Vera."

She stared after him, then continued to the room to work. She never knew what to expect from Tristan. Yes, she did, she decided as she pulled on her gloves—his easygoing manner, his faith in her, and kisses that left her wanting more. Not a bad combination. Not bad at all.

Hours later when she was ready to go home, he'd followed her as usual. The next night and the next were a repeat of the night before. With one major difference, the kisses were getting hotter, longer, more intense.

She was getting used to his touch and wanting more. Each night took Kara closer to finishing framing the pictures, and realizing her dream. Promising her mother a shopping trip to Dillard's at Uptown Village kept her reasonably mollified with quick meals and the house not being as spotless as Kara usually kept it.

Thursday night, she'd arrived to find the glass and matting

for the pictures. She'd simply asked for the receipt. She was paying Tristan back every penny.

"Only if you kiss me," he said, a teasing grin lifting the corners of his too tempting lips as he held the receipt over his head.

She wasn't so slow that she didn't recognize he was asking for more than a kiss, he was asking for her trust. He'd asked so little of her, and when he had, it had been for her benefit. She curved her arms around his neck and kissed him on the forehead.

"Pitiful."

The next one was on his cheek.

"Better."

She smiled up at him. With Tristan, she could relax, be herself. He pushed her, but he was always there for her, something few people had been in her life. For him she could let herself go and let her body press against him, the way she'd wanted for so long.

His heart leaped, her pulse thudded. She watched his beautiful eyes narrow, felt him go hard. Still he waited. He was also patient with her.

Her lips brushed once, twice against his, enjoying being held by him, enjoying the softness of his mouth, the muscled hardness and warmth of his body. She wanted more. Her tongue slipped into his mouth, seeking, finding the hot, intoxicating taste of him.

His arms closed tightly around her waist, dragging her closer. Between one breath and the next, he took charge, deepening the kiss, taking her higher. Pleasure rippled though her as his mouth plundered hers, leaving her weak and pliant and needy. Very needed.

As if reading her thoughts, his large hand cupped her hips, bringing her closer to his erection. Her leg lifted to wrap around his hips.

He groaned her name. She moaned his. They broke apart at the same time.

Their breathing labored, she tucked her head between his neck and shoulder, and tried to clear her mind of the sensual haze, fight the need rippling though her to rip off his shirt and feast on his body.

"You make me forget," he breathed, nibbling on her earlobe.

She tilted her head to give him better access and let her leg slide down. "Same here."

"If this wasn't important to you . . ."

He didn't have to continue. He'd stopped for the same reason she had—if they didn't, they'd end up in bed and it would be a long time before he let her out. If only . . .

She drew in one studying breath after the other until her blood no longer rushed hotly through her veins, until her legs supported her. She stepped back.

He handed her the receipt. She was surprised, and a bit pleased that his hand was as unsteady as hers when she took it and shoved the slip of paper into her pocket.

"Thank you."

A slow, sexy grin spread across his handsome face. "My pleasure."

She grinned back. "I better get to work." With one last lingering look, she went down the hall, away from temptation.

By Friday night, Cade was restless and on edge. The reason had nothing to do with his being in a long line of cars slowly making

their way to the waiting valets. He didn't like social events, but
that wasn't why he was out of sorts. As difficult as it was for him
to admit, let alone accept, he missed Sabrina. He had caught a
glimpse of her Tuesday afternoon in the ER, but nothing since.

Apparently, she had finally realized there could never be
anything between them. So why couldn't he stop thinking about
her winsome smile, the way she melted in his arms, how she
blew his mind with a kiss?

Annoyed with himself, Cade stopped in front of the many
valets in red vests. A waiting hand opened his door. Climbing
out of his car, he thanked the valet, accepted his parking ticket,
and joined the other guests climbing the white steps to the
hundred-year-old front doors of Hempstead Mansion, a twenty-
five-thousand-foot monstrosity of a home.

Bill Hempstead was a billionaire and he shared the wealth
he'd made in the dot.com business. He had a heart of gold and a
wife who had the misguided thought that every surface needed
to have an object on it. The house was an expensive, cluttered
mess.

Cade thought of how inviting and restful Sabrina's house
was in comparison and snarled. The matronly woman beside
him quickly moved through the open door the butler held. Just
inside the door were four perky young women, checking names
off the guest list.

Bill might have a heart of gold, but he detested moochers
and gate crashers. No one got past the front door who wasn't
on the guest list, proof that they'd paid the two-thousand-dollar
ticket price. At least the food was always good and substantial,
the booze the best money could buy.

Once cleared, Cade walked farther into the cathedral-like
entryway. Perhaps the diversion would keep the mild headache

away that had been plaguing him most of the day. He never got headaches. He resisted the urge to rub his temple and stepped into the great room.

The huge room, done in red and gold, was packed and loud. No one seemed to be paying attention to the woman singing an old Anne Murray song. A horde of waiters in white dinner jackets served food and drinks. Although he hadn't eaten since breakfast, Cade wasn't hungry. If the chief-of-staff, Tony Davenport, hadn't asked him to come, Cade would have sent a check and his regrets. Since Tony left Cade alone, Cade felt it would be in his best interest to attend.

"Dr. Mathis. Dr. Mathis." Lena Hempstead waved. Wineglass in hand, she hurried toward him, at least as much as the low-cut, skintight red dress would allow.

"Hello, Mrs. Hempstead," he said.

She placed her hand on his arm and smiled up at him. "I'm glad you could join us again this year. Tony said you'd be here," she said. "I know you're busy."

"Texas appreciates what you and Bill have done," Cade said, and meant it. He might not want to be there, but he could appreciate the Hempsteads' commitment to helping others. Lena might dress a bit provocatively, but she was genuine and she loved her husband. She was good people in Cade's book.

She glanced around with a pleased smile. "I think we're going to reach our goal to build a serenity garden at the entrance of the Lois Hempstead Cancer Center by summer's end. Bill's mother was a strong believer in prayer and meditation."

Bill's mother had succumbed to cancer several months before. "I never met Mrs. Hempstead, but I heard a great deal about her."

Lena leaned over. "She didn't like me at first for Bill, said I was all wrong for him. I understood after I had children of my own. You want the best for them. Before we lost her, she loved me like a daughter. There's nothing like a mother's love."

"Yes," Cade said. Instead of thinking about himself, he thought of Sabrina and what she had endured at the hands of her birth mother. Rage surged though him.

"You all right?" Lena asked, her eyes going wide.

"Yes," he said, working to bring his anger under control. "I was just thinking."

"Well, it's time to relax. There's plenty of food and drinks." Lena patted him on the arm. "I see someone I need to speak with. Please excuse me."

As she moved away, Cade glanced at his watch. He'd circulate, give it another fifteen minutes, thirty tops, and then he was going home.

Accepting a glass of wine from a passing waitress he had no intention of drinking, he moved around the edge of the crowd, seeing several doctors and staff members as he did. He spoke, but he kept moving. It didn't bother him that they didn't invite him to join them; he'd always been on the outside looking in. Besides, he wasn't much on small talk.

Halfway around the room, he heard a woman's familiar laughter. The sound went though him like leashed lightning. He jerked around to see Sabrina talking with two men. She wore a fitted black dress with red-and-black ruffles at the hem, her slim back partially bare. She faced away from him, but he knew the happy sound of her laughter, the elegant shape of her body. He was moving before he realized it.

"Good evening."

Sabrina turned to him, her eyes twinkling. His narrowed. There wasn't a shred of surprise in her beautiful face. Then he recalled he'd mentioned the charity event to her. "Dr. Mathis, I'd like you to meet Jeff Kennedy and Bobby Rush."

The men barely nodded. He'd be an idiot not to realize they saw him as a threat. Smart.

"Well, gentlemen, it was nice meeting you. I should go. I have a busy day tomorrow," she said, placing her full glass of wine on the tray of a passing waiter.

"Please stay," Jeff urged. "I could get you another glass of wine."

"Would you like a plate?" Bobby asked. "Uncle Bill and Aunt Lena always have great food."

"Thank you both, but I really must go. Night." Smiling, she walked off. Cade and the two men were left staring after her.

Sabrina handed her parking ticket to the valet and refused to look back to see if Cade had followed her. She'd almost given up hope that he'd attend the charity function, and then he'd walked in. Her heart had done a crazy jitterbug, the way it always did when first she saw him. Mercy, he was one gorgeous man. In his black tux, he was devastating, his unsmiling face giving him an aloofness that had woman after woman watching him. He didn't seem to notice.

She'd debated on the best way to get his attention, then Mrs. Hempstead had rushed over to greet him. Sabrina hadn't been worried about anything romantic between them. For the Hempsteads, like her parents, obviously had a love that grew stronger with each passing year.

Once the hostess left, Cade began to circulate. Sabrina saw her chance to "accidentally" meet him and made her way across the room to place herself in his path. A few minutes before Cade showed up the two men had approached her and introduced themselves.

"They're complaining that they didn't get your phone number," Cade said from behind her. He didn't sound pleased with her. *Good.*

Was that jealously in his voice? "There's only one man I want to have my phone number," she said without looking at him.

"Car number two-eighty-eight."

"That's me. If you'd like to continue this conversation, you know where to find me." Despite her shaking legs, she got inside her car and drove away.

After debating about going home and finally taking something for his headache and the wisdom of going to Sabrina's house, he'd ended up in Sabrina's driveway. She was the one and only temptation he couldn't resist. Despite everything, she loved life.

He *lived* life, but he wasn't sure he had ever enjoyed it. He'd never had the chance. He couldn't remember having one carefree day. The man his birth mother and her family sent him to live with spouted Bible verses and made Cade's life hell. In college, he had been too busy studying and working. He'd been determined to succeed, to show the old man that he wasn't stupid as he'd told him every day the sun rose, show him that he could make something of himself.

Cade had done that and more.

He and Sabrina had little in common. He hated the woman who gave him away. Sabrina had forgiven her birth mother for scalding her. Her scars were on the outside. His were on the inside. He should just go home. And then what? Opening the car door, he got out and went up the steps to ring the doorbell.

Before the sound ended, Sabrina, still dressed in the pro-
vocative black-and-red dress, opened the door. "Hi, Cade. Please
come in."

He stepped over the threshold and stuffed his hands in the
pockets of his slacks. "I'm not sure this is wise."

"That's debatable." She closed the door. "Why don't we go
out on the patio?" Not waiting for him to answer, she walked
away.

Cade got another arousing view of the slim curve of her bare
back, the enticing sway of her hips. He hardened with need.
Definitely, not a wise idea. The slight headache that had plagued
him off and on all day, brutally reared its ugly head again.

She stopped at the sliding glass door. "Coming?"

He was trying his best not to.

"Cade?"

Removing his hands from his pockets, he followed her outside, and realized immediately that he was in trouble. Several
flickering candles in brass lanterns of varying heights sat around
the grouped seating arrangement in front of the bricked fireplace, casting the patio in undulating shadows. The pool light
and water rushing over the waterfall added to the air of seduc-
tion.

Sabrina took a seat on the cushioned sofa. "I have Hennessy and tea. Coffee in the kitchen. What would you like?"

"To be able to stop thinking about making love to you," he
answered, not sure if he wanted to frighten her or entice her.

She paused as she reached for a glass. Slowly, her head lifted.
"Why?"

"Why?" he repeated. "I think that's obvious."

She picked up the glass, sipped, then leaned back. "No, it's not. At least not to me. I think the reason is more than just us working together."

"I don't do relationships," he told her bluntly.

"Why?"

He shoved his hand over his head, paced. The pounding in his head worsened. "People lie and try to paint sex as anything but a basic human need. My way is more honest."

"And meaningless." She placed her glass on the table and stood. "I'll show you out."

His eyes widened in surprise. "What?"

She stopped mere inches from him. "I might care about you, but I'm not going to be intimate with you or any other man just because you have an urge. The man I give myself to for the first time is going to want me for all the right reasons."

"The first—" He stared at her. "You can't be— You're beautiful."

"And scarred."

He jerked her to him. His black eyes blazed with anger. "Don't say that! There's nothing wrong with you."

"Neither my one boyfriend in high school or the one in college would agree with you," she told him. Her voice and body trembled for a second, then firmed. "You're the first man who didn't look at my scars with revulsion. I'll keep searching until I find a man who wants more than sex."

His hands flexed on her slim arms. Jealousy swept through him. He stared down at her. Her eyes were sad and determined. They made him ache to be what she wanted. She moved him as no other person had ever done. "Sabrina, I don't know how to have a relationship, but neither do I want to walk away from you."

A small smile curved the corners of her mouth, taking the sadness away. Staring up at him, she slid her arms around his waist. "Then this will be a first for both of us. We can learn together."

"I don't want to hurt you," he said, his gut knotting at the thought. "But I don't want to let you go."

"Then don't. But if you mess up, I'll let you know."

Cade blinked, then laughed, hugged her slim body to him. "The staff at Texas and most doctors quake in their shoes around me. Not you."

"That's because I see the man behind the accolades and awards." Her hands cupped his cheek. "Just like you see me."

"Sabrina." He kissed her. He couldn't wait any longer. The taste of her was even more intoxicating than the first time. She felt right in his arms, as if she were made just for him.

His hand stroked the smooth, bare curve of her back, felt her shiver, press closer. His mouth slid along the curve of her jaw. His other hand cupped her breast, felt the nipple harden and push against his palm. He wanted the material gone, wanted his mouth on her bare skin. If he got this hot with a kiss, what would happen when she was naked under him, his body pumping into hers?

His cell phone rang. He cursed.

"Now I know how Mother feels." Sighing, she stepped back. "Answer it."

The ring came again. "I wish—" He snatched it from his belt and answered. "Dr. Mathis," he snapped. Sabrina flinched. He briefly closed his eyes, and reached for control. "Sorry, what is it?"

He listened, nodded. "I'm on my way." He ended the call. "I'm needed in the ER for a consult."

"Then go." Taking his hand, she started back inside.

"I don't know how long I'll be gone."

Sabrina opened the front door. "I'll be here. Tomorrow is the block party. I'm grilling."

"Don't you dare light that grill," he ordered.

She kissed him on the cheek. "Good luck and drive carefully."

He hesitated, then pulled her into his arms for a quick kiss, then ran to his car. The motor rumbled to life. Returning Sabrina's wave, he pulled out of the driveway, feeling much better than when he'd pulled in, his headache gone.

Fourteen

· · · · · · · · · · · · · · · ·

A little after ten Friday night, Kara slowly secured the wire of the last painting Vera had ordered. She should be elated. She wasn't.

With the last painting for the spec house done, there would be no reason to keep returning to Tristan's house. Sadness swamped her. She enjoyed being with him, enjoyed the peace and happiness of being around a person who valued and respected her. That pleasure increased several times when that person was a man she cared about.

Out of the corner of her eye, she saw Tristan studying one of her paintings. He never seemed to tire of looking at them or of encouraging her. Despite her initial reservations and plan to keep their relationship strictly business, she'd failed miserably. She really cared about him. Those unexpected feelings still scared her a bit. Tristan might care about her as well, but he wasn't looking at anything long term. His helping her wasn't tied to their being intimate. As he'd said, he'd accept a no. She just wasn't sure she wanted to keep saying no.

Was the hurt and misery she'd feel when he walked out of her life worth the pleasure of following her heart? Placing the painting with the others, she stepped back. "It's finished. We did it."

"You did it." Tristan walked over and pulled her into his arms. "I thought of champagne, but I decided this might be better." He mouth closed over hers in a lazy kiss that slowly heated, just the way her body did.

His head lifted and he stared down into her face. "You better grab your things while I have the willpower to let you go."

She stared up at him and said what was in her heart. "What if I want to stay?" She kissed him, a highly erotic mating of tongues, her breasts pressed against his chest, her thighs against his legs.

Tristan had planned to keep it light, but lost it. Kara made him horny as hell and protective. He wanted to shake the world and make things right for her. She made him feel emotions he'd never felt for another woman. She got him hot with just a look, and pissed him off that she had so little faith in herself. Yet, like her wonderful paintings, he never grew tired of looking at her, being with her. He wasn't sure he ever would.

He broke the kiss and finally came up for air. His breathing ragged, he stared down into her desire-filled eyes. Her decision hasn't been an easy one and he wasn't going to take her incredible offering lightly.

"Are you sure?" he heard himself ask. He needed her so badly he wanted to whimper, but he wanted it to be right for her with no regrets. He couldn't stand the thought of her having regrets afterward.

Smiling, she brushed her lips across his, suckled his lower lip, then bit his earlobe. "If you're up to it."

The challenging words were barely out of her mouth before

he captured hers again. This time the intense heat and desire leaped like a current between them. He'd never gotten this hard this fast. He'd never wanted this badly. From the way she clung to him, making the little whimpers that were driving him crazy, she felt the same urgent need.

Scooping her up in his arms, he hit the stairs, hoping he'd make it. His legs were actually shaking.

"I'm too heavy," Kara protested.

Tristan would have snorted if he had the extra air in his lungs. Shouldering his bedroom door open, he stumbled toward the bed. Standing her to her feet, he jerked the covers back then tumbled them down into the sheets. He had a split second to thank the housekeeper for changing them, then he caught the intoxicating scent of Kara, felt her lush breasts brush against him, heard her sweet laughter. His body clenched.

"In a bit of a hurry are you?"

He smiled, enjoying her laughter. "A bit, but other things take time." He straddled her, his hands going to the buttons of her blouse and slipping each free. Slowly he parted the material to reveal incredible smooth satin skin, a plain white bra. Kara's arms suddenly covered her breasts. His eyes lanced up to her.

"Not very sexy, is it?"

Gently, his eyes on hers, he removed her arms. "I've never seen anything more beautiful. Let me show you." His finger followed the curve of the top of the bra, then his tongue followed. He heard a little whimper, then quickly sat her up to unfasten the bra and toss it aside.

He was the one to whimper then. Her breasts were full and tempting, rising and falling with her accelerated breathing. He leaned forward and took the turgid point into his mouth, suckling. Strawberries and cream. He laved one nipple, then the other.

Her hand cupped his head, holding him to her. The nipple hardened along with another part of his body. If he didn't get them undressed . . . Reluctantly releasing her nipple, he jerked off his shirt and kicked off his jeans.

Kara's eyes widened. He thought it was because of his blatant arousal, then she licked her lips. He shut his eyes to blot out the image of her doing that to him.

"What?"

His eyes snapped open. He saw the uncertainty replace desire and wanted to rile against the person who had taught her not to trust herself or anyone else.

Tenderly, his hand cupped her cheek. "I want you so badly. Seeing you do that almost drove me over the edge."

"Do what?"

He licked his lips. Her eyes widened with knowledge. "Yes," she breathed.

She wanted this night with him. For once, she just wanted to forget everything else, except what she wanted. She placed her hand on his chest. It was time she gave as well. Here. Now. "You make me want things I never thought about before."

She was intrigued and there was no doubt about it. Pleased, he hugged her, then leaned her away from him. He'd never met a woman so sensually unaware of her sexuality or so desirable. "I want to kiss and lick every inch of your delectable body. I want to be buried so deep in your satin heat that we're one. And when I finish, I want to start all over again."

"Yes," she breathed, leaning toward him. She ached with wanting him, and the wanting grew stronger with each ragged breath she drew.

He caught her to him, his mouth locking on hers. Heat and need pulsed through her. Her body was on fire.

Breathing hard, he broke the kiss. Somehow he managed to get her walking shorts off, giving brief and profound thanks they weren't jeans. He'd planned a more leisurely undressing. He hadn't been joking about kissing and licking, but that would have to wait for next time.

Then they were both naked, his hands free to roam freely over her incredible body, his mouth to taste silken skin, to incite and plunder. Her mouth and hands were just as busy, arousing and stroking and pushing him to the point of no return.

Untangling himself from her arms and legs, he jerked open the nightstand for the condoms he'd put there the day after he met her. Even then he'd somehow known they'd end up here, the first and only woman he'd ever made love to in this house.

Sheathing himself, he rose over her and stared deep into her passion-glazed eyes. What he saw there made his chest tight, made him harder. He saw desire, but he also saw trust. His lips brushed over hers as his hand skimmed down her body to find her damp and hot.

"Please." She moved restlessly beneath him.

With one sure thrust of his hips, he joined them. She clenched around him, the fit tight and exquisite. He began to move, bringing them together again and again. Pleasure built. Her long legs wrapped around him, holding him to her, urging him on. The pace quickened. They came together.

Their breathing erratic, he rolled to one side, refusing to release her. He'd never felt anything so right. Kissing her, he tucked her body closer to his, heard her contented sigh. She went full-out every day. She had to be tired. He kissed her forehead.

"Tristan," she murmured sleepily.

"I'm here." He kissed her again, managing to pull the covers up over her bare shoulders. His lower body reacted predictably to her naked length pressed against his, but he had no intention of acting on it. She needed to rest. He felt oddly pleased that while she did, he would watch over her.

Kara woke with a smile on her face, snuggled closer to the warmth. Her eyes snapped open to see Tristan beside her. Panic hit. Flinging back the covers, she jumped naked from the bed.

"Honey, what is it?" Tristan clamped his hand around her wrist.

"She'll know." It was too late to be modest. She pulled on his arms, scanning the room for her underwear. She saw her bra several feet from the bed. How could she have been so careless to fall asleep? "I have to go."

"No, you don't. You can stay with me."

"For now. But what about when you get tired of me? Then what?"

His silence sliced through her, but it was no more than she'd expected. It wasn't his fault she didn't believe in forever.

"So, that's all our being together meant to you?" Frost coated each word.

"No, but I still have to go. Please understand." Kara shook her head, trying to bring some order to her hair. "She'll keep at me until I feel worthless and ashamed."

"All the more reason to stay."

She tried to pull her arm away. His hold was unyielding. "I can't. I have to go home. I promised my father I'd take care of her."

"Take care of, not let her abuse you," Tristan said, his voice tight.

"I have to go." She snatched her arm free, stepped into her walking shorts, snapped on her bra, and shoved her arms though the sleeves of her shirt. She didn't have time to search for her underwear.

In jeans and an unbuttoned shirt, he stepped in front of her. "I'm taking your car keys if you don't promise to drive the speed limit. I mean it. "

"Let go." She brushed by him. He caught her arm again.

His eyes blazed. "It's not over between us."

"I need to get home."

Muttering, he released her and grabbed his keys. Kara was already on the stairs.

Inside her car, she kept glancing at the clock on the dashboard. 12:03 A.M. Each time she sped up, a horn sounded. Tristan. *Her mother would know.* She certainly had when she came home late with Ryan. After he proved he was just using her, her mother hadn't let Kara forget it. Although she hadn't been intimate with Burt, she realized her mother wouldn't have said anything. Burt was wealthy. She'd bite her tongue off before she told her mother that Tristan was probably just as well-off.

Pulling into the driveway, she slammed out of the car and went inside the house. She didn't have time to put the car in the garage. She breathed a sigh of relief when she didn't see her mother in the den, and tried to creep silently down the hall to her room.

"Kara."

She swallowed, tensed. "Yes, Mama."

"Get in here."

Wiping her sweaty hand over her pants, she opened the

door to see her mother in bed with a bag of Oreo cookies and a pint of Blue Bell. She glanced at the clock. "It's late."

"I know." Kara muffled a fake yawn, stretched her arms over her head. "I didn't want to stop until I finished. Tristan's mother is decorating a speculation house and she's using seventeen of my paintings. There's a good chance when people see the house they'll want to buy a painting."

Her mother's eyes widened. She sprang upright in bed. "Seventeen paintings, and you never said one word!"

Greed won over motherly concern every time with her mother. "Because nothing is certain."

Her mother looked thoughtful. "Maybe I can get the whirlpool tub for my bathroom, and go to that spa I read about near Austin."

Lake Austin Spa cost upward of fifteen hundred dollars a day. "The paintings won't bring in that kind of money," Kara said.

Her mother didn't look convinced.

"Good night." Kara left with her mother still staring at her. Neither trusted the other.

A little after eleven Saturday morning, Kara finished frosting the second German chocolate cake and placed it in the cake carrier. Five houses on the block had been chosen to host events for the neighborhood block party. Before her father died, they'd been one of the stops with card games and dominoes in the backyard. Her mother had declined this year because she said it was too painful. Kara's hand clenched as she picked up the cake carrier. She knew the real reason—her mother didn't want to be bothered and thought the beer and other refreshments her father always provided were a waste of money.

"Did you leave me some cake?" her mother asked as she entered the kitchen.

"Yours is on the table," Kara said.

"It's about time you remembered I'm your mother." She walked over to the three-layer cake. "Those people just want to use you."

"Daddy always had me make two cakes along with lemon pies," Kara said, wanting to end the conversation so she could leave.

"And you see where he left me financially." Her mother's lips pursed. "I shouldn't have to depend on anyone."

Kara heard the anger, but also something that sounded suspiciously close to fear. "Daddy did the best he could. You know that. I realize it's hard for you, depending on me, but you have to know that I'm here for you."

"No, you're not. You've always been your daddy's child more than mine," her mother said.

Kara started to ask whose fault that was, but instead said, "I gave up my position at the hospital in New Jersey to move back here when Daddy was sick. I stayed for you once we lost him."

"We both know it's because he asked you to stay and help out." Her eyes narrowed. "He promised me so much, and I got nothing."

"He loved you."

"If he had loved me, he wouldn't have left me with nothing," she snapped. "I can't buy one thing on my own."

Material things were all that mattered to her mother. She'd grown up with poor parents and fourteen other siblings. For as long as Kara could remember, she'd never seemed satisfied or happy. In spite of that, her father had loved her. For that very reason, Kara would continue to try and close the gap between them.

"I tried putting money in your account, but you were always overdrawn," Kara reminded her.

"A measly two hundred dollars a month. Your daddy's Society Security check is less than that. How can I live off that?" She scoffed, taking a seat. "If you had married Burt, I wouldn't have to do without. I'd have the things your daddy promised."

Kara gave up. Nothing she could ever say would change her mother's mind and she was becomingly increasingly tired of trying. "I'm going to take this cake to Sabrina's."

"There you go. Rushing to take care of other people," her mother said. "You've been late getting home all this week. I'm tired of eating leftovers."

"That was just for two days," Kara said. "I was here yesterday and cooked. Besides, there's food to cook."

"I get tired standing on my feet. You know that." Her hand flexed on her cane. "But you're so busy with your life, you don't think about how difficult mine is."

"That's not true, Mama. Anything you want, within reason, I try to get for you," Kara told her.

"As long as it's what you want," her mother said. "You're listening to Sabrina and that man. Nothing good can come of it. He's conning you about your paintings. You'll see. But I still want that shopping trip and the spa you promised."

Kara opened her mouth to say she hadn't promised the spa, but she let it go. She had to get out of there. She reached for the door handle. "I'll bring you a plate."

"Don't listen to me. You never did anyway and see what happened? Mark my word, they're using you. He's using those paintings to get what he wants. His mother will probably only give you a pittance of what she gets for them," her mother warned.

Keep walking, Kara told herself. Her mother just wanted to hurt her, make her doubt herself. Opening the front door, she went down the steps and continued onto the sidewalk. Three boys skateboarding and yelling momentarily snagged her attention. She didn't believe she'd ever been that carefree and happy.

A warm, calloused hand closed around her upper forearm. Startled, she swung around and saw Tristan. The teasing smile on his face faded. She'd wondered how she'd feel when she saw him again. Now she knew. She wanted to crawl up in his lap and cry.

"What's the matter?"

Too many things to count.

"Kara, are you all right?"

How can I be when my mother hates me?

He gently loosened her grip on the carrier handle. "I'll take this. Where were you headed?"

She swallowed, swallowed again. She would not cry. She would not. "Sabrina's house. Two doors down on the right."

He took her elbow and continued in the direction she had been going. "Glad I'm here in time to get a slice of cake. I bet you're a fabulous cook. Across the street, they're setting up a net. Can I hope it's for volleyball?"

He wasn't prying. He was trying to help, although since he'd met her mother he probably had a good idea what the problem was. "Badminton."

"Do you play?" he asked, going up the steps of Sabrina's house.

With each step, the knot in her chest and her throat lessened. "Yes."

"I bet I can take you."

She stopped, stared at him, and then looked away.

"What is it?" he asked, his hand rubbing up and down her bare arm, sending heat rippling in its wake.

Finally, she faced him. "My mother thinks that's what you plan to do. Take me."

His green-eyed gaze remained direct. "What do you think?"

"Hello, Kara. Young man," an elderly man greeted as he went up the walk of the house next door. "Save me and Sheila a piece of that cake."

"Yes, sir." Kara waved to Mr. Golden who had a bag of ice in each hand. He and his wife had been the first to welcome her parents to the neighborhood, the first ones to offer help when her father became bedridden. Whatever they needed, the Goldens were there for them. "I will," she said, and then faced Tristan. "It might have taken me awhile, but I trust you. You want me in your bed, but you won't use my art to get me there."

The tightness eased only marginally around his mouth. She frowned. "I said I trust you."

The fingers of his free hand trailed down the curve of her cheek. "You shouldn't have to defend me or your art."

She shivered and briefly tucked her head. That was the same thing Sabrina said, but they didn't have to live with her mother. Kara wished she didn't either. She should feel ashamed of such thoughts, but she couldn't. "We better get this inside."

Unmoved, he stared at her a long moment. "You and me. Badminton before the day is over."

He wasn't going to let her hide from him or shut him out. She was slowly learning that he was someone you could trust to always be there for you, no matter what. "You're on," she said, trying to smile and failing miserably.

Behind her, she heard the rumble of a powerful engine and turned. "He came."

Tristan stared at the expensive black foreign car as the driver whipped into the driveway. The skateboarders stared in awe. "Before I go macho, please tell me you aren't interested in him."

Before she could answer, the door behind them opened and a young woman rushed onto the porch. Speaking to Tristan and Kara as she passed, she continued to the man climbing out of the low-slung car. "Cade, you're here! Thank goodness."

"What is it?" Cade asked, straightening and slamming the car door.

The woman caught his hand and started back up the walk. "The fire, what else? Don't fuss. I thought I could do it. I'm supposed to grill the franks and burgers for the block party."

"Don't worry," he said, nodding to Tristan and Kara as he passed.

"Does that answer your question?" Kara asked, a tiny smile on her face.

His arm curved around her shoulders, glad to see the semblance of a smile. It was a start. "Then he can live."

Seeing the teasing glint in his eyes pulled a real smile from her. She could either enjoy herself or be miserable—just as her mother wanted. "I'm glad you came."

"Me too."

Fifteen

. . . .

Sabrina didn't stop until she stood in front of the grill. "I started the fire an hour ago. I thought I just needed to let the coals cook longer or something like you did. But . . ." She lifted the top.

The coals, peeking though a mound of scorched wood chips, looked as if they'd just been poured from the bag. "I looked out about fifteen minutes ago and I thought, because it wasn't smoking, it was doing okay."

"When did you put the wood chips on top?" Cade asked, using the end of a twig he'd picked up to push the chips aside.

"After it flamed up a bit," she said, then hurriedly added when he stared at her, "They were in a pan and I kind of tossed them on and closed the lid. I messed up."

He placed his hand on her shoulder. "Building a good fire takes practice. It didn't help that the vents are closed. The fire simply smothered out."

She looked up at him with wide, beseeching eyes. "Cade, I promised. What will I do? I don't want to let everyone down.

This is my first get-together. All of my neighbors have been so good to me. They had a party to welcome me to the neighborhood. When we had the last power failure, three men came over to check on me."

She'd turned to him for help. It meant more to him than he wanted to admit. His patients and their families wanted his help, but it would benefit them. Sabrina wanted it to repay her neighbors for welcoming her.

He didn't know one resident in Navarone Place. There was a monthly tenant meeting, but he'd never bothered to attend. He spoke to people on the elevator—if they spoke to him first. He didn't engage in conversation with them and, if they tried, he always gave short, one-syllable answers.

He caressed her shoulder. "Don't worry. I sort of took precautions in case something happened. Come on." Without thought, he took her hand and headed toward the sliding back door.

Outside, the three skateboarders had been joined by several other men. Cade nodded. Sabrina waved and spoke.

Opening the trunk of his car, Cade took out two twenty-pound bags of charcoal and then handed a large can of lighter fluid to Sabrina. "We'll have the fire going in no time."

"Thank you." She pressed the container to her chest as if it were flowers.

"Mister, how fast will it go?" one of the teenagers asked.

"Two-twenty," Cade answered.

Appreciative comments floated around those staring at the car as Cade and Sabrina went back inside. In the backyard, Tristan and Kara waited.

"You must be Tristan," Sabrina greeted as she passed them. "As soon as we get this fire started, we'll introduce everyone."

"Do you need any help?" Tristan asked.

"Thanks. Cade, do we need anything?" Sabrina asked, looking up at Cade.

Cade sat the charcoal on the ground. "Something to scoop the charcoal out and something that won't burn to put it in."

"I've got a spade. There's a ceramic planter by the fireplace that I bought and never put anything in," Sabrina said.

"I'll get them," Kara said.

"I'll help." Tristan followed.

"With everyone helping and you telling us what to do, I'll be cooking in no time," Sabrina said happily.

Kara handed the spade to Cade. Sabrina wrinkled her nose. "I wanted to do this myself."

"Here you go." Tristan placed the light blue planter beside the grill.

"Thanks." In a matter of minutes Cade had replaced and lit the charcoal. "In ten minutes it should be ready to cook the meat. Start with the burgers because they'll take longer."

Sabrina hugged him. "Thank you. Now, I won't have to hide my face when I see my neighbors."

"They would have understood," Kara said. "They still talk about Mrs. Golden substituting salt for sugar when she made the lemonade and tea last year."

"Still." Sabrina straightened away from Cade. He felt bereft. "I'll get the tablecloths."

"I'll help," Kara offered.

"I'd say you saved the day," Tristan said when the women walked away.

"Sabrina isn't much on grilling or cooking, but she likes people and hates to disappoint them."

"Kara is the same way."

"I know. Kara and Sabrina work together at the hospital."

"Do you work there as well?" Tristan asked.

"Yes." Cade stuck out his hand. "Cade Mathis."

"Tristan Landers."

The back door opened and out came Kara with an armload of tablecloths and napkins. Tristan moved to help.

"Dr. Mathis, Sabrina is finishing the patties. She could probably use some help."

"Doctor? You didn't mention you were a doctor," Tristan said.

Cade shrugged carelessly. "Doesn't matter. I'm not sure how much I can help, but I'll go see. Excuse me."

"You can't be any worse than Sabrina," Kara said to his retreating back and spread the tablecloth. Laughing, Tristan reached for the other end.

Inside the kitchen, Cade discovered Sabrina slicing onions and blinking back tears. She really needed help. "I'm told holding a piece of bread in your mouth helps," he advised.

"Then please stuff a slice in my mouth." She closed her eyes. "I'll certainly appreciate onions served at a restaurant much more."

Removing a slice of bread from the bag on the counter, Cade tore it in half and held it out to Sabrina. She opened her mouth, biting down. Her lips brushed against his finger. They both jumped. Their eyes met, clung. "Later," he promised.

The phone rang on the counter. "Please get that."

Cade picked up the phone. "Sabrina Thomas's residence."

"Who's speaking please?"

"A friend. Cade Mathis. Who's this?"

"Her mother. Christine Thomas."

"Hello, Mrs. Thomas. Just a moment please." He held out the phone to Sabrina, but she had already snatched a paper towel to clean her hands. "Hi, Mother. Kind of busy here preparing the food for the block party I told you about."

"Is he anyone special?" her mother asked.

"Mother, I have thirty or more hungry people descending on me in less than thirty minutes," Sabrina said, tossing a quick glance at Cade who was rolling up his sleeves. "And I'm still cutting vegetables." She slapped her hand over the receiver. "What are you doing?"

"Helping you cut up the vegetables. Where can I wash up?"

"You're a guest. Doing the fire was enough."

"Sabrina, what is going on?" her mother asked.

"Love you, Mother. I'll call later." Sabrina hung up. "Really, Cade. This I can do."

"Your guests will be here soon. You can't grill and prepare things in here as well."

She blew out a breath. "I wanted to do this myself."

He went to her. "Why is it so important?"

"To prove I'm not completely hopeless in the kitchen," she told him.

"Hopeless is not a word anyone who knows you would ever associate with you. If I or Kara needed help, would you think less of us if we asked for it?"

"Of course not," she answered.

"Then where do I wash up? And do I grill or slice?" he asked. "I'm good at both."

"You can use the sink over there. The burgers are in the refrigerator." She picked up the onion. "Thank you."

"You can thank me later," he said, his voice stroking her,

heating her body, leaving no doubt as to how he wanted her thanks.

She grinned. "Count on it."

Tristan had gotten his badminton game, and planned to take Kara home with him before the day was over. He hated seeing the defeat in her beautiful eyes where there had been so much passion and happiness last night. He knew the reason for her unhappiness, her mother.

Kara took her responsibilities seriously. No matter how much the situation saddened her, she was sticking. All he could do was to be there for her. There was no way he was letting her mother keep them apart. It wasn't just the sex, although it had been incredible, Kara drew him. She was an amazing woman. He'd keep telling her until she believed him.

From the sideline, women, especially Sabrina, cheered Kara, while the men cheered Tristan on. The score between him and Kara was tied. He grinned and sent the shuttlecock back over the net, enjoying her laughter as much as the agile quickness of her long legs, legs he kept remembering wrapped around him last night as he pumped deep into her.

Suddenly, the laughter left her face. She straightened, the racket clutched in her hand. The shuttlecock fell unnoticed to the lawn. Groans came from the women. Kara didn't seem to notice as she stared across the street. Tristan cursed, knowing before he turned he'd see her mother.

Mrs. Simmons, her face unsmiling, stood on the porch, both hands propped on the cane she leaned on. Tristan wondered briefly how Kara had managed to grow up so caring when her mother treated her like a hired servant.

"I'm sorry. I need to check on her," Kara said.

"I'll go," Sabrina said, already walking away. "You stay and finish the game."

Kara shook her head. "No."

"You both stay," Mrs. Golden told them. "Your mama probably wants to watch the game."

With a resigned expression, Kara handed the racket to Sabrina. "Finish the game for me," she said, then briefly touched Mrs. Golden's shoulder. "Thank you."

"You coming back?" Tristan asked.

Kara swallowed, her smile tremulous. "Probably not. Good-bye." Her hands clenched, she crossed the street.

"Beer and cards at our house," Mr. Golden said to the milling crowd. "Sheila and I are defending our reign as bid wiz champions. Who wants to fall first?"

The neighbors moved away, laughing, making bets, but not until Kara and her mother had gone inside. It seemed that Tristan wasn't the only one who noticed her mother's less than caring attitude.

"Why does she do that?" Sabrina asked, anger in her voice. Out of the corner of his eye, Tristan saw Cade curve his arm around her shoulders. Tristan wasn't sure if she meant Kara or her mother; either way it came down to the same thing.

He wasn't seeing Kara again tonight. Unless. He pulled out his cell phone. Kara's mother wasn't the only one who could pull out the big guns.

Less than thirty minutes later, Vera's red Mercedes roadster convertible stopped in front of Sabrina's house. Tristan, Cade, and Sabrina met her on the sidewalk.

"Hi, Vera," Tristan said, and introduced everyone. "Security let Cade drive his car because he's a doctor. How did you get past?"

Vera, beautiful in an Oscar de la Renta print, lifted a regal brow. "I simply showed him my heels."

Sabrina grinned. "Once he put his tongue back in his mouth he waved you on."

Vera smiled. "What's the use of looking good if no one notices?"

"There is that," Sabrina said. "Tristan, I don't think Kara's mother has a chance."

"We're going to find out." He nodded down the street. "Two houses down. I'd take you, but she doesn't like me."

Anger flared in Vera's brown eyes. "Oh?"

Tristan felt better with each passing second. His mother was fiercely protective of him.

"Let me handle this." Getting back in the car, she drove away and parked in Kara's driveway. Picking up the Nancy Gonzalez clutch from the passenger seat, she went up the walk.

Tristan folded his arms and glanced at his watch. "Ten minutes top. Kara's mother won't know what hit her."

Kara heard the doorbell and tensed. *Please don't let it be Tristan,* she thought. Her mother had finally stopped talking about the spectacle Kara had made of herself playing badminton. The doorbell rang again.

Her mother came out of her room. She didn't say a word. Her face said it all.

Rubbing her hand on her pants, Kara went to the door and opened it. Her mouth gaped.

"Hello, Kara. Can I come in?"

"Who is it?" her mother called.

Kara snapped her mouth shut. She didn't know how to answer. Nor could she close the door in Vera's face. Indecision and dread kept her immobile.

"Who are you?" Hazel asked, from behind Kara.

"Vera Fiore, an interior designer, working with your talented daughter." Vera glanced over Kara's shoulder. "You must be her mother, Mrs. Simmons. Is it all right if I park in your driveway?"

Hazel stepped around Kara, saw the expensive sports car, then snapped her gaze back to Vera. Her mother's entire demeanor changed. "Of course. Kara, get out of the way and let her in out of the heat."

Kara opened the door, caught between embarrassment that her mother's greed was so obvious and hope that Vera's showing up meant Kara might see Tristan tonight.

"Would you like a glass of iced tea?" Kara asked, waving Vera to a chair.

"No, thank you, Kara." Vera sank gracefully in the dark, floral-print side chair. In her colorful print dress, the dark furniture looked even worse. "I realize how busy weekends are, but I wanted to drop by and take Kara to see some of the designer pieces I plan to pair her art with. The million-dollar spec home I'm in charge of decorating is fabulous and the perfect place to showcase Kara's work."

"Million dollars." Hazel's annoyed eyes snapped to Kara. "You didn't tell me how much the house cost."

"I'm not sure she knew," Vera put in smoothly. "Kara's focus has been on finishing framing the paintings. And rightly so. Some very important people will see her art. Tristan will make sure of that."

"I don't trust him," Hazel said. "He wants more than the paintings and is using his looks to get them."

Kara tensed. Vera didn't take kindly to anyone maligning Tristan.

"I can understand your caution. Mothers love their children." She leaned forward. "Just as I love Tristan, my son."

Hazel straightened. "Your last name isn't the same as his," she stammered.

"My professional name. My late husband was an Italian count." Vera's mouth softened. "He was always supportive of anything I did."

"A count," Hazel whispered, awed.

Vera waved her hand negligently. "I didn't come here to talk about me. Kara, I'd love to show you what I envision for your paintings. Please say you'll come with me."

"Yes," Kara said, coming to her feet. Vera had given her a chance and she was taking it. "I'll go change."

"You look fine." Vera rose.

"Maybe I should go," Hazel suggested and stood.

No. Kara swallowed.

"If only you could." Vera took Kara's arm and steered her to the door. "I'm in the two-seater. If I had thought, I would have driven my other car."

"What's your other car?" Hazel asked, avarice in her voice. Kara winced, but kept walking.

"A Phantom Rolls."

Hazel actually licked her lips and followed them onto the porch. "You plan to put all seventeen pictures of Kara's up?"

"Yes." Vera went down the steps.

"How much does she stand to make?" Hazel asked, one hand on the cane, the other pressed against the brick post.

"That depends on a lot of things. There are costs involved. Commission, overhead, supplies that have to be taken into account and subtracted." Vera slid into the driver's seat as Kara got in on the other side. "I'll try to have her home before midnight. Good-bye, and thank you."

Hazel watched them leave, her face unsmiling.

Kara buckled her seat belt and waited until Vera had pulled into the street and her mother had gone back inside. "I'm sorry about my mother."

"You have nothing to be sorry for," Vera said, and activated the Bluetooth. "We'll meet you at my shop," she said, then disconnected the call. "There's only one thing you can do for me."

"Yes?"

"Live your life the way you want to live it," she said, stopping at the barricade.

Kara clenched her hands in her lap. Easier said than done. The two off-duty policemen acting as security for the neighborhood party grinned and waved them through.

"We're meeting Tristan at my office," Vera explained as she headed for the freeway. "I detest liars—unless necessary," she said, then laughed.

With the wind blowing in her hair and the anticipation of seeing Tristan, Kara should have been feeling carefree as well, but all she could think of was her mother's greed.

Tristan was waiting for his mother and Kara when they pulled up in front of Vera's store, Fiore Design Studio, located in the design district off Oak Lawn. He pushed away from his truck and walked over. Kara got out of the car, but stared at her tennis shoes. "Thanks, Vera," he said, then took Kara's hand. "You all right?"

"Kara has to come inside the shop before you two disappear," Vera said, continuing inside.

"Kara?" She finally lifted her head. She looked unbearably sad. He swept his hand over her wind-tossed hair. "Talk to me."

"My mother loves money more than she loves me," she whispered.

He bit back a curse. His heart turned over. He drew her into his arms, felt her tremble. He searched his mind for something to say to ease the pain he'd heard. The words *I don't* flashed through his mind. He had to clamp his teeth together to keep from saying them. He shifted uneasily.

Kara pushed out of his arms and started inside the shop. He caught her arm. She glanced back at him, misery in her eyes.

"Her loss," he said, his hand sliding into her hair, angling her head up. "You count in all the ways that matter. You're beautiful, talented, and courageous."

Her laugh was ragged. "Hardly."

"I see what you don't. What you see as weakness, I see as strength," he said, meaning every word. "It takes more courage and more love to stay than to walk away, which would be the easy thing to do. You chose love over easy."

She let her head fall against his chest. "Your mother is the only person I've ever seen that outmaneuvered mine."

"That's my mother. Why do you think I called her?"

Her head lifted. "I thought so."

"I was worried about you," he confessed, his mouth hovering inches from hers.

"I wish life was simple."

"Let's make a pact that when we're together, it will be." His mouth moved closer.

"I might forget." Their warm breaths mingled.

"Then I'll just have to remind you." He kissed her, a gentle press of his lips, then lifted his head. "Let's go see what Vera wants, and then we're going to the movies, sit in the back row, and make out."

She stared up at him. "How about we switch locations to your house? I don't have to be home until midnight."

His smile was sad. "I don't want your mother on your case."

"And you wouldn't want to use Vera that way."

"Yeah," he confessed. It was more important that she be happy than they go to bed.

Kara finally smiled and curved her arms around his neck. "You're an honorable man, Tristan. Thank you."

He hugged her to him, resigned to be horny, but Kara's trust and smile were well worth it.

Sixteen

. . . .

Sabrina sat on the cushioned sofa on the patio with Cade, her head on his shoulder, his arm around her. The full moon cast a golden glow over them. She'd never felt more at peace.

"Today was fantastic," she said, snuggling closer.

"You have good friends, good neighbors," Cade said, kissing the top of her head. "If one of us had to be adopted by people who loved them, I'm glad it was you."

She turned to him, her heart aching for him. "Cade." The tips of her fingertips trembled as they brushed across his lips. "I wish I could do something to make up for what you went though."

He stared down at her. "You already have."

Both moved at the same time, their lips meeting, softening against the other. Sabrina turned in his arms, wanting to give, to erase the unhappiness he'd experienced as a child, and was unable to forget as an adult.

"I want to make love to you," he said, his mouth hovering inches from hers.

Standing, she took his hand. She didn't stop until they were in her bedroom. The lamps on the twin bedside chests were dim, the covers drawn back on the queen-sized bed, the air fragrant from the group of candles on the dresser.

"I was sort of hoping you did."

"Sabrina," he breathed, taking her into his arms again, his mouth finding the sweetness of hers. She was open and honest. He hadn't known what it was to be really happy until she came into his life. As always, she came, giving herself totally to him. His tongue mated with hers. His breathing hitched along with hers. He'd never known a kiss could be so wildly erotic.

His hand swept up under the white tunic top and moved upward. The instant his hand touched the skin graft, she jerked, trembled.

He didn't hesitate. He went to the lamps and turned both up, then came back to her. "I can't imagine how difficult this must be for you, but I'm hoping you know that it's difficult for me as well."

She frowned. "For you? Why?"

He smiled, brushing her hair back from her irresistible face. Sabrina always wanted answers. "Since this is your first time, you probably have very high expectations, maybe a fantasy or two."

She looked up at him. "Maybe. I'm reasonably sure you'll see me and not change, but . . ."

"You could feel the same way about me. Let's see." He tossed off his polo shirt, toed off his loafers. His slacks followed.

Her eyes widened. "You're beautiful."

"So are you." He pulled the ties free at the wrists of her tunic, reached for the hem. "May I?"

She nodded. "It's only fair. Right?"

The barrier he'd erected around his heart melted. She wouldn't let fear rule her. She humbled him. He had to be just as brave.

He pulled the blouse over her head in one smooth motion. Her gaze locked on his face. He let his eyes slowly move downward over her left shoulder to the barely there lace bra. The scars, from midway on her left breast to the waistband of her pants, were flat and resembled a patchwork of skin. As he'd noted before, skin had been grafted from her stomach. He saw it with his eyes, but also with his heart.

His hungry gaze came back to hers. "I'll say it again. You're beautiful. You humble me with your courage, your capacity to forgive and love life." His hands settled on her small waist. "You also drive me crazy with wanting you."

She blinked, swallowed, and slowly smiled. Her arms curved around his neck. "We can't have that." She kissed him, sliding her tongue into his mouth to taste and tease as she pressed against him.

Pleasure and passion swept through him. He wanted this to be as perfect for her as she was making it for him. His mouth moved with maddening slowness over the curve of her jaw, the slope of her shoulder, hovered as he unhooked her bra. Her breasts were high, firm, and exquisite.

"I'm a lucky man," he said, his warm breath teasing her nipple, just before he pulled it into his mouth. She jerked, then arched, holding his head to her. He moved to the right, licking and teasing and blowing.

"Cade." She moaned out his name.

Sweeping her into his arms, he placed her on the bed, enjoying the sight of her flushed face and full breasts, before pulling the wide-leg pants from her legs. His heart almost stopped on seeing the lacy scrap of material masquerading as panties. He swallowed.

Leaning over, he kissed her there then stripped her panties away. He tossed his briefs after her panties and pulled her back into his arms, kissing her, allowing his hands to freely roam her incredible body. She was an unexpected gift that he treasured.

Soon, kissing and touching ceased to be enough. He groaned when he realized his condom was in his wallet.

"What?"

"Protection's in my pants and I don't want to move that far away from you."

"You don't have to." Reaching under the pillow she held up a package, then tore off the wrapper and straddled him. "Let me."

The indulgent smile on Cade's face faded as Sabrina, with an intensity that strained his willpower, slowly rolled the condom onto his straining flesh. She seemed to take great pride in getting it on just right, running her hand over it repeatedly.

He tried to remain still, but with her breasts moving enticingly in his line of vision, he lost the battle. Rising up, he was once again on top, his mouth kissing her as his fingers tested her readiness and found her hot and wet. He thrust into her, felt her clench around him. He moved slowly, allowing her to adjust to him. He didn't have to wait long.

Her hips lifted, her legs wrapped around him, urging him deeper. She met him thrust for thrust, bringing them closer until they exploded together. His breathing harsh, he gazed down into Sabrina's flushed face.

His heart stumbled. She stared up at him, a serene smile on her face. "If I had a fantasy it would be you. This," she breathed.

"Sabrina." He rolled, bringing her with him, unwilling to release her. She got to him. It no longer bothered him. She was the one joy he'd looked for in life and never found. Kissing her on the forehead, he closed his eyes and followed her into sleep.

Tristan pulled up in front of Kara's house at half-past ten Saturday night, turned off the engine, and reached for her hand. It trembled. "I'm calling in ten minutes."

She laid her head on his shoulder. "If only—"

Twisting his head, he kissed her on top of her head. "If only what?"

She straightened and looked at him. "Too many things to count." She briefly pressed her lips to his then jumped out of the car. Pulling her house key out of her pocket, she let herself inside and cocked her head to listen.

Her mother usually watched TV on Saturday night. Since she claimed sitting in the pews at church aggravated her hip, she watched church services on television as well. Two cautious steps later, Kara paused, closed her eyes.

What are you doing, Kara? Now she's got you sneaking to your room. Her "if only" had been if only she had a mother like Vera, but the flip side would mean she would be as bold as Tristan. He loved his mother, but there was no way he'd let her run his life.

Kara continued down the hall, humming the theme song from a movie she'd only seen snatches of. When she wasn't kissing Tristan, she just enjoyed being close to him, enjoyed being held by him, knowing he wanted her, but he put her first.

"Kara?"

Still thinking of Tristan, Kara opened her mother's bedroom door. Several issues of *Southern Interior* magazine were scattered around the chaise longue she was reclining on. The picture on her television screen had paused. *Not good.* "Hi, Mama. You need anything?"

"I asked Sheila about that decorator," she said, plainly still miffed about being left behind.

Kara waited. Sheila and Calvin Golden had the only two-story house on the block. Their warm, inviting home was beautifully and expensively decorated.

"Sheila had heard of her. She's decorated some of the best homes in the city." Hazel glanced down at a magazine. "She's not cheap, which means your paintings won't be either."

Money, first and always.

"You watch her and that son of hers." Hazel snorted. "Commission my foot, but with that many paintings we should make out pretty good."

We. "I might not sell anything."

"They wouldn't be trying to butter you up if they thought that, and that's why we're going to the open house, to keep tabs on them," her mother said smugly. "There's nothing to keep us away."

No. Please no. "There's no need. It will probably be boring and long. You can't sit that long," Kara said, walking farther into the room. "The home is two stories. You'll never be able to get upstairs."

"Then you'll go where I can't. At least you can do that—if you stop thinking about that son of hers," Hazel snapped. "They won't get one over on us. You keep working with them, but be smart about it. This is our chance. I won't let you mess this up for me."

Me. It would be a waste of time to point out to her mother that she had maligned Kara's paintings, had tried to destroy them. Now that there was a chance to make money, she was on board all the way. *Too late*. "I'll do whatever it takes."

"Good." Her mother picked up the remote control and started the TV program again.

Dismissed, Kara went to her room. Her cell phone rang. Picking it up, she plopped on her bed. "My mother believes you and Vera are out to take *us*. She wants to come to the open house to watch you. I'm to keep working with you to make sure *we* get our money."

"What time should I pick you up tomorrow so we can watch each other?"

Tristan took it better than she'd expected. "Why aren't you as angry as I am? Vera would be."

"Let's say I have ulterior motives, all of them having to do with—" He whispered something naughty and intriguing to her.

"Noon." She and Sabrina went to church together and lunch afterward, but Sabrina probably had plans of her own from the way she and Dr. Mathis kept looking at each other. She'd understand.

"See you then. Dress casually. I can't wait to hold you again. Night."

Her heart sighed. "Me either. Night." Kara disconnected the call. Tristan might not be forever, but it was wonderful having him in her life now.

Cade woke up early Sunday morning with Sabrina wrapped around him. He didn't think, he just went with his emotions, brushing his lips across her forehead. She snuggled closer, whispered his name softly.

Even asleep, she responded to him. She was the one bright constant thing in his life. For the first time in his memory, he was content.

He glanced down, wanting to see her reaction when she came fully awake. Her eyes opened; happiness shone in them. "Good morning," she said, climbing completely on top of him.

His body stirred. "It certainly is."

She chuckled, brushed her lips across his. "I thought I'd dreamt you."

His hand swept over her naked butt, pressing his arousal against her woman's softness. "Does that seem real enough?"

Sabrina moaned softly, rubbing against him. "Very." She nipped his lower lip.

He twisted and then she was on the bottom. His gaze swept over her naked torso with greedy appreciation. "I see you and I want you."

Her eyes softened with an emotion he couldn't identify. "Good, because I feel the same way about you."

"Good." Putting on a condom, he brought them together.

She clamped around him, her arms tightening as he pumped into her. She reached completion seconds before he did. His breathing harsh, he rolled, taking her with him. Her warm, uneven breath fanned his chest.

"I'm so glad you made the exception to your dating rule," she murmured, kissing his chest.

He glanced down at her. "Because you make me look forward to every day. Before you, it never really mattered that much."

Tears sparkled in her eyes.

"No." He kissed each eye. "I never thought about harming myself. It's just that growing up, the next day always meant verbal abuse or a belt if he felt like it. It got to the point I dreaded the next day, dreaded tomorrows. I grew up with the attitude that if tomorrow never came, it didn't matter."

"I intend to make sure you keep on looking forward to each morning." She kissed him and rolled out of bed. "You stay here. I'm going to take a quick shower and make you breakfast in bed."

Cade caught her several steps away, picking her up. He enjoyed holding her, hearing her happy laughter, the softness of her slim body against his. "How about we shower together and I fix *you* breakfast?"

She gave him a quick kiss as he set her on her feet in front of the glass enclosure. "Breakfast I can cook."

Opening the shower door, Cade stepped inside, bringing her with him. He turned on the water, adjusting the temperature. "Never doubted it. I'd rather be with you."

"Cade." His name trembled across her lips.

"And I get to do this." He pulled her into his arms, his mouth finding hers.

Kara was ready when Tristan pulled up in front of her house at noon. After he came in to speak briefly with her mother, they were on their way. Kara glanced down the street toward Sabrina's house. Dr. Mathis's car wasn't there. He hadn't made it back, but Sabrina had said he would. She and Kara had talked that morning before and after church.

Sabrina was happy and on top of the world. Yet, while Sabrina freely admitted she was in love, Kara wasn't ready. She felt deeply for Tristan, trusted him with her paintings, but not her heart.

"You all right?" he asked, pulling out of the driveway.

She glanced around at him, felt the tug in her heart and almost panicked.

"Kara?" He pulled over to the curb a couple of houses from hers and took her into his arms. "What is it, honey? Did your mother say something else to upset you?"

No, I did this all by myself.

His hand stroked her arm. His lips brushed the top of her head. "I'm here."

But for how long, she thought, then chastised herself. Tristan had been totally honest with her, had pushed her to succeed when she'd doubted. If any man deserved her love, it would be him. If he didn't return it . . . well, she'd cross that bridge when she came to it.

She lifted her head to see the unmistakable concern in his eyes. "Whatever happens, I'm glad we met."

He frowned. "That sounds like a brush off."

She laughed because he looked so angry at the thought. Then she plastered her lips and as much of her body against his as possible in the cab of the truck. "Did that feel as if I'm going anyplace?"

He dragged her to him for another long kiss, then sat her in her seat and started the engine. "I'd planned brunch and the art museum, but they'll have to wait."

Kara smiled and snuggled closer as he pulled off. She ran her hand over his thigh. "I'm going to make a feast of you," she told him.

Tristan groaned. "I couldn't sleep last night for wanting you. So behave."

Seeing the proof of his words, Kara inched away from him. "For now, but just you wait, Tristan. Just you wait."

In the kitchen Sunday afternoon, Sabrina eyed the caller ID just before she picked up the ringing phone. "Hello, Mother."

"Hello, baby. You sound happy."

"I am." Sabrina hit the speaker, replaced the receiver, and continued cleaning up the kitchen. She hadn't gotten around to it because she'd wanted to spend every moment with Cade before he left to go home to change and then make rounds at the hospital. Shortly afterward, Kara had picked her up for church. She'd only recently arrived back home.

"Any particular reason?" her mother asked.

Sabrina felt too good about Cade to be embarrassed. She smiled, shook her head, and picked up their plates. "Mother, I thought you were more subtle than that."

"I'm fifty-seven so I have certain privileges," she said. "Is there a reason for the cheerfulness I've heard in your voice lately?"

Sabrina leaned against the counter and crossed one ankle over the other. After last night it was time. "I met a man."

"Who is he? What does he do? When did you meet?"

"Mother." Sabrina chuckled. "You've never been this inquisitive about my dates before."

"Because you never dated much when you were home," her mother said. "There are some wonderful men out there, and then there are the others."

From the time she started having an interest in boys, her mother had warned her about the ones who only wanted a good time. Since Sabrina's father was devoted to her mother, Sabrina assumed it was just a mother's fear.

"Sabrina," her mother urged, worry creeping into her voice.

"His name is Cade Mathis. He's one of the top neurosurgeons in the country." She paused, trying to think of her mother's other questions. "He has privileges at Texas. You spoke to him on the phone yesterday."

"I knew it!" her mother said, excitement chasing away the worry. "How long have you been dating?"

Sabrina shifted from one foot to the other. "Not too long."

"Is it serious?" her mother asked again.

For me it is, Sabrina thought. She was 90 percent sure that it was for Cade as well, but she understood that with his traumatic childhood it would take longer for him to admit his feelings. "We're just dating, Mother."

"I know you're grown, but you're still my baby," her mother said. "I worry."

"Don't," Sabrina said, going to the table and picking up the coffee cups. "He's a great guy. He saved me when the grill wouldn't work and I had to do the meat."

"Where is he from?"

Sabrina realized she couldn't answer. "I don't know."

"You don't know? What about his family? Are they in Dallas?"

She was on slippery ground. Family was a touchy subject for Cade. "His parents are dead."

"What about the rest of his family?" her mother asked, concern in her voice.

Sabrina didn't know the answer to that question either. "Mother, we're just dating. He doesn't know that much about me either."

"You just be careful. I'll ask your father if he's heard of him," she said.

Sabrina picked up a serving dish from the table. It wouldn't do any good to ask her not to. Her mother was in full protective mode. "Don't worry, Mother. Cade is a great guy."

"I hope so."

"Gotta go. I need to finish the breakfast dishes," she said, then could have bitten her tongue.

"You've started eating breakfast?"

"Occasionally," Sabrina said, feeling her face heat up. "Give Daddy a hug for me and tell that little brother of mine to call once in a while."

"Stephen is shadowing Dr. Crenshaw in ENT, and loving every moment," her mother said proudly. "He can't wait to start premed in the fall."

"He's going to make a great doctor," Sabrina said. "He's wanted to practice medicine as long as I can remember."

"We'll have another doctor in the family," her mother said, then added, "Is there a possibility that there might be another one?"

Sabrina would like nothing better. "We're just dating, Mother. And I really have to go."

A long sigh drifted though the receiver. "All right. Love you and take care."

"Love you too, and I will." Sabrina hung up the phone. She reached for the flatware and heard a car door slam. She ran to the front door and opened it. Cade was there, taking her in his arms, kissing her, closing the door behind him.

"Is everything all right?" she asked.

He swept her up in his arms and started for the bedroom. "It is now."

Sabrina couldn't agree more. She didn't give another thought to the dishes or her mother's concerns then or later.

Seventeen

· · · · · · · · · · · · · ·

Hand and hand, Tristan and Kara ran up the stairs. They burst into his bedroom, reaching for each other's clothes and trying to kiss at the same time. They laughed when they bumped noses. Her knit top flew in one direction, his shirt in another. Her bra followed. She unsnapped his jeans. He shucked them off, while she did the same to her slacks.

"Let me," he said, his eyes hot when she reached for her panties. He pulled them slowly from her body, his mouth following.

"My turn." She reached for his black briefs and pulled them down. He sprang free, proud and ready. Kara licked her lips.

"No." Tristan stepped back, reached into the nightstand for a condom, and took her into his arms. "I missed you last night."

"Show me," Kara said, running her hand over his broad chest.

"My pleasure." Curving his hands under her hips, he surged into her waiting heat. Sensations swept through him. There had never been a woman his body and mind were so attuned to.

He moved in and out of her satin heat, the fit exquisite as he filled her. She locked her arms and legs around him and met him thrust for thrust. Soon she stiffened, her arms clamping around him. With a hoarse shout he followed, holding her as aftershocks swept through her. Not wanting to release her, he rolled until she was on top.

"Tell me about Tristan Lowell Landers," Kara asked when her breathing returned to normal.

Tristan brushed Kara's thick black hair from her beautiful face, wanting to catch every nuance of the happiness he saw there, enjoying her trim body against his. She was an exceptional woman, in bed and out.

"Tristan," she urged, her finger curving down his face playfully.

"Hmm." Happiness looked good on her. Her playfulness was as unexpected as it was pleasurable. He simply enjoyed her. He wasn't a slam-bam type of man, but he wasn't known to linger after sex. With Kara, he was content to just watch her.

"You aren't asleep because your eyes are open."

When women began asking questions about his background, they usually wanted a deeper relationship, which meant it was time for him to make a quick exit. He didn't feel the slightest urge to move and he attributed it to the fact that Kara might be with him now, but she was still cautious.

"I'm waiting, Tristan. You already know about me."

Not enough, he thought, but her past wasn't a happy one. "You already know my father was a count. He was also a scholar. He and my mother met while he was teaching and she was studying in London and they fell in love. His family didn't like him marrying an African-American woman because she wasn't wealthy or famous or titled more than because of her race. In Vera's interminable style, she won them over. You never saw such crying as when I was thirteen and we left to come back to America to live."

"Why do you call her Vera?"

He smiled. "My father lived with his parents when he married my mother, and continued afterward. I grew up calling her Vera because that's what I heard. I understand they tried to get me to say Mother, but I resisted."

She grinned down at him. "Stubborn even then."

"I guess," he replied.

"I know, but no one is going to run over you," she said, her smile gone.

She was thinking of her mother, Tristan thought. He wanted to see her smile again. "I posted pictures of your paintings last night on my blog and the response has been incredible."

"Really?" Her eyes widened with happiness.

"Really." His hand swept her hair back from her face. "I'll let you see for yourself. Afterward we can run over to the house I'm remodeling. I'd like to see what you think, then we can grab a bite to eat and go by Dale and Bess's house."

She blinked, swallowed. "I'd like that."

"Good." Coming upright, he picked her up and headed for the shower. He'd only gone a few steps before the unexpected thought of wanting to keep her with him, to not let her go back to the woman who seemed to take pleasure in hurting her, hit him. His hold tightened.

She snuggled closer, then sighed. "Mama was grumbling all morning. I'm not sure if I can go out anymore this week."

He kissed her forehead. "Then we'll make today count, and snatch moments when we can."

She lifted her head to look at him. "Thank you for understanding."

"I'm not letting you go," he said with a fierceness that was foreign to him. In the shower enclosure, he let her slide down his body and stared into her face, trying to imagine where those impossible thoughts came from, why they wouldn't leave.

"What's the matter?" Kara asked.

"Nothing." He turned his back on her and adjusted the shower pressure. He was just being protective of her because her life was so difficult, that's all. It didn't mean anything. Sure of his feelings, he faced her with a lazy smile and slow hands.

Monday morning Cade woke up missing Sabrina. He realized that last night, for the first time in his adult life, he'd gone to sleep anxious for morning to come. Sabrina was the reason.

He quickly dressed and went to his office. Iris, always the first one there, greeted him with a smile and a list of his patients for the day.

He smiled back. "Thank you. How was the weekend?"

She blinked. "F-fine."

"Good." He continued to his office. His question had taken her by surprise. He wasn't that bad, was he? Admitting he was, he opened his door. Perched on one corner of his neat desk was a beautiful bouquet of cut flowers with red and yellow balloons. Crossing the room, he plucked the card.

Missing you. Have a great day.
Sabrina

Rounding his desk, Cade picked up the phone and punched in Texas's main number. "This is Dr. Mathis, please connect me with Sabrina Thomas."

"Yes, Dr. Mathis."

"Good morning, Sabrina Thomas. How can I help you?"

"You already have," Cade said, watching the balloons dance in the cool breeze from the vent. "I've never received balloons before."

"You haven't seen anything yet."

He chuckled and reached for his cell phone. "I'm looking forward to it. In the meantime, could you give me your phone numbers and I'll give you mine." They exchanged information. "I'll be at the hospital later. Maybe we'll have time for some bad hospital coffee."

"I'd like that. Kara and I plan to grab a bite around noon, which means we'll get to the cafeteria around one if we're lucky."

"I'll look for you then. Bye."

"Bye."

Cade hung up the phone, leaned back in his chair, and enjoyed looking at his flowers.

In the coming days, Cade received a cookie bouquet and Texas Motor Speedway NASCAR tickets. Thursday morning he received an invitation to a Wine Walk in Uptown Village for that night. He wasn't surprised that Sabrina made the event fun, even taking their picture.

Each night she left a note in his pocket, always saying the same words, *"Missing you. S."* He was touched that she was making sure he looked forward to each morning. She did that just by being herself. He told her as much as they sat in a quiet booth at Bailey's in Uptown Village Friday night having dinner.

She blinked rapidly. Sniffed.

"If you cry, you won't be able to read this." He handed her a business envelope.

She brushed her fingers across each eye and opened the envelope, gasped, then threw her arms around his neck. "You never take a weekend off."

"Then it's about time," he told her, enjoying her excitement. "A chartered jet will take us to San Francisco, a chef from the Ritz-Carlton will prepare the food for the plane trip, and a limo will pick us up at the airport and take us to the Ritz there. The weekend will be ours. You just pick the weekend you want to go and I'll clear my schedule."

"Is two weeks enough time?"

"I wish we were already there," he told her.

"Me too, but Mother is coming tomorrow."

He tensed. "You didn't mention her visit before."

Sabrina twisted in her seat. "She called a little bit before you picked me up. She wants to meet you. She's a great mother. You'll see. She's not pushy or anything."

Cade saw all too well that her mother wanted to protect her. In one way he was pleased, in another he was shaking in his wingtips. "Is she flying or driving up?"

"Flying in on American. I'm picking her up at the airport," Sabrina said, looking uncertain.

He took her hand. "How about *we* pick her up?"

She leaned into him. "I'd like that very much."

Saturday morning at Love Field Airport, Cade was no less nervous than when Sabrina had first told him that her mother was coming. Sabrina loved her mother. If the woman didn't like him, he'd have a problem.

"There she is. Mother!" Sabrina yelled, waving happily.

A tall, attractive, well-dressed woman in a white suit waved back. As soon as she passed the checkpoint, she and Sabrina were embracing. "Oh, baby, it's good to see you."

Sabrina laughed. "You just saw me three weeks ago."

"It seems longer," her mother said, then she looked at Cade.

"Mother, this is Dr. Cade Mathis," Sabrina said, her eyes shining up at him proudly.

Cade extended his hand. "Good morning, Mrs. Thomas. Sabrina has been excited since she knew you were coming."

Sabrina's mother curved her hand around her daughter's shoulders. "Hello, Dr. Mathis. Sabrina is very precious to us."

Sabrina rolled her eyes. "Mother."

"I can see why," Cade said. "She's a unique woman."

Sabrina reached for his hand. Cade caught it and squeezed. He wasn't the demonstrative type—or at least he wasn't until Sabrina. Her mother caught the motion. Was there censure in her gaze?

"Do you have any bags?" Cade asked.

"No. This will be in and out," Mrs. Thomas said.

"My car is waiting. Would you like to have lunch or go to

Sabrina's house?" Cade asked as they started up the concourse with Sabrina between them. "I have reservations, but I can always change them or cancel."

Sabrina stepped on the escalator first and smiled back up at her mother. "It's at your favorite restaurant."

Mrs. Thomas glanced at him before stepping on. "Why don't we go to the restaurant and get to know each other?"

Translation, grill him about his family. Sabrina might accept his life, but he didn't think the woman in the designer clothes would. "All right."

Sabrina excused herself and her mother before they were seated at the table and took her to the ladies' room. They stopped just beyond the door. "I don't want you grilling Cade about his family."

"I wouldn't grill the man, but there are questions any concerned parent would want to know about the man in her daughter's life," her mother told her.

"No, Mother, and I mean it. He's told me about his childhood," Sabrina said.

"What did he say?" her mother asked, moving closer.

"He told me in confidence and that's the way it will remain," Sabrina said. "I ask you to respect his privacy and trust my judgment."

"What could be so bad that he can't disc—" Her mother stopped abruptly.

"Exactly. Stephen and I were both abused. He refuses to talk about his past even now. I'm not saying that's Cade's issue, I'm just reminding you that it isn't as important how you got to where you are as it is where you are now. For some, the past needs to be left in the past."

"You know being cryptic makes me nervous," her mother told her.

"I'm sorry, but Cade means a great deal to me," Sabrina said. She wasn't going to be like Kara, miserable and torn because her mother distrusted the man she wanted to be with. She and Tristan hadn't been out all week. Every night her mother had a physical complaint or something for Kara to do. Sabrina refused to let her mother keep her from the man she loved. "He knows how much I love you, and I can tell he's worried that you'll try to break us up. It's not happening."

"Sab—"

"I love you, but it's not happening," Sabrina repeated sternly.

Her mother stared at her a long time. "He better not hurt you."

Sabrina hugged her mother. "He won't. Now let's go put him out of his misery."

Cade rose as they neared the table. He held the chair out for her mother. Sabrina winked at him. He breathed a sigh of relief. For the moment at least, he was safe.

Christine Thomas couldn't put her finger on exactly what it was about Cade Mathis that made her feel uneasy, but it was there nonetheless. Perhaps it was Sabrina not wanting to discuss his background. He was handsome, attentive to Sabrina, courteous to her. Her husband had balked at having him checked out except for a few discreet questions. He didn't want Sabrina to think they didn't trust her judgment.

But Christine knew how a smooth-talking man could sweep a woman off her feet. Her hand clenched on the steering wheel. She hadn't thought of her own bad decision and the consequences in a long time. She'd go months without thinking about it, and then something would trigger the memory of that night. Her father had patiently helped her through that dark period in her life, made her see that her life wasn't over. Like her husband, her father was the rock of the family.

Her father. She activated the Bluetooth.

"Hello, Christine," he said when he answered on the second ring. As a doctor, he'd always been a light sleeper.

"Daddy, everything is all right, but I need to talk to you," she quickly said. It was past eleven. Late phone calls never boded well for a man in his profession.

"I'll be downstairs waiting."

"Thank you, Daddy. I'm ten minutes away. Bye." He'd always been there for her. Why hadn't she remembered that sooner?

Christine took the next exit, still thinking about the past. For months she'd been so ashamed and unable to look at her father or mother. They'd been patient, supportive, and loving when she thought she didn't deserve to be loved. Eventually she'd put the past behind her and started to live.

She turned into an upscale neighborhood of stately homes. She'd grown up riding her bicycle down these streets, playing tennis on the private courts a couple of blocks over. She'd been sheltered, but had learned the harsh truth at nineteen that men lied as easily as they smiled.

Flicking on her signal, she turned into the driveway of a two-story white brick mansion with dark green shutters. Getting out, she went up the steps and rang the doorbell. The door swung open.

"You're sure you're all right?" her father questioned as she stepped into the wide foyer.

"Reasonably," she said. "Marshall isn't due back until tomorrow and I needed to talk to someone tonight."

He took her arm. "Your mother is asleep. Come into my study."

Christine smiled in spite of the tension she felt. Her father's study was the place for family discussion. Other people might converge in the family room or media room, but for them it was her father's large study with its book-lined walls, large windows, and comfortable chairs.

He sat on the leather sofa she'd grown up sprawled on, reading while he worked. "Now, tell me."

In his direct gaze, she saw patience and love. "I love you, Daddy."

His hands closed around hers. "I love you too. You're the best part of your mother and me."

She wanted to glance away, but didn't. "You haven't always been proud of me."

"That's not true."

She shook her head. "We both know there was a time I let you and Mama down, let myself down."

"Now, you hold on a minute," he said, his voice tight. "You were fooled by scum masquerading as a man."

Her eyes briefly shut. "I thought he loved me," she whispered. "How could I have been so foolish, so gullible?"

"Because you're honest and thought he was too. I wanted to take my forty-five and go find him."

She gasped, her hands closing on his. "Daddy, no."

"I realized that if I did, I wouldn't be here for you and your mother. That bastard had taken enough from us," he said tightly.

"Do-do you ever think about that night?" It was a question she'd been afraid to ask all these years.

"All the time," he admitted. "It was hard on all of us."

"He was your first grandchild." Tears sparkled in her eyes. "Not being able to have other children is my punishment for giving him away."

"You stop that nonsense," her father told her. "Lots of women have only one child. You did what you thought was right."

"But you didn't agree with me, did you?"

He looked tired, but resigned. "You were so adamant on what you wanted to do. You wouldn't even look at your mother or me. If we had kept the baby we wouldn't have been able to keep you, and that would have killed us."

"Daddy, I'm sorry I made you choose."

He patted her hands. "I thought for a while you might change your mind."

"It wouldn't have done any good. I had signed the adoption papers."

"But they weren't filed until later."

She frowned. "What do you mean?"

A muscle ticked in his jaw. "You thought we were ashamed of you. Disappointed that you had gotten pregnant by that scum. I had hoped you'd realize that we loved you more because of what you were going through and that you'd change your mind about giving the baby up."

"I didn't know he was married. He was so cruel when I told him about the baby." She lowered her head. "How could I have been so stupid?"

"You loved the wrong man."

Her head lifted. "That's why I came. I'm worried about Sabrina and the man she's dating. But, first, what do you mean about the adoption?"

"He wasn't adopted until later," he said. "I had the baby placed with a church-going couple who were upstanding members of the community my lawyer found. If you changed your mind about the adoption in a month or so, I wanted you to be able to get the baby."

Wide-eyed with disbelief, Christine came unsteadily to her feet. "What?"

Her father stood as well. "I'd hoped time would help you to realize you had nothing to be ashamed of, to stop blaming yourself. You never did. Whenever I tried to bring that night up, you'd withdraw into yourself. Then when you couldn't have children you blamed yourself even more. It tore me up to see you so miserable, but by then it was too late to get him back."

"Then-then you know the family who adopted him? You can find him?" she said, feeling almost light-headed.

"I've always kept my distance. The first time I had my lawyer check on him was when he graduated from high school. I was afraid if I actually saw him, I wouldn't be able to stop myself from trying to meet him," he confessed.

"Oh, Daddy. I cheated you and Mother out of so much. I'm so sorry."

"You were barely nineteen. You were hurting. You made what you thought was the best decision for both of you."

"I didn't want him called names or gossiped about. But he's all right? Where is he?" she asked, excitement growing with each passing second.

"In Dallas."

"Dallas?" Christine repeated, the strange feeling of fore-boding returning.

Her father almost smiled. "You'd be proud of the man he's become. In a strange twist of fate, he's a doctor, and a darn good one."

A chill raced down her spine. "Do-do you know his name?"

"Dr. Cade Mathis."

Eighteen

. . . .

'm not sure your mother likes me," Cade said later that night with Sabrina sprawled on top of him.

Sabrina kissed his chin. "She doesn't want me hurt."

"I don't either."

The phone on the nightstand rang. Sabrina eyed the phone. Cade glanced over as well, then looked at her. It was almost midnight. "She called you from the Houston airport to let you know she'd landed safely."

The phone rang again. He lifted her off him. "I'll give you a moment."

She caught his arm when he stood. "No matter what, I'm not going anyplace."

"Answer the phone," he said, and continued out of the room, picking up his pants as he went.

"Hello," Sabrina said, picking up the phone just before it would have gone into voice mail. She only had to think about the misery she saw daily in Kara's face to remain strong.

"Oh, Sabrina. You can't see Cade anymore."

Her mother sounded almost hysterical. Sabrina did not want to have this conversation. Sighing, she sat on the side of the bed, drawing the sheet up over her naked breasts. "Mother, we've been over this."

"Things have changed."

"Nothing has changed. Mother, I love you, but you can't dictate whom I date," Sabrina said, trying to keep her voice low so Cade wouldn't hear her.

"Sabrina, please. I'll explain everything in the morning. Your father and I are flying back to Dallas in the morning."

"Mother, ple—"

"Just do as I say," she said. "He isn't there with you, is he?"

"No, he isn't here with me," she said, which technically was the truth. He was in the other room.

"Thank goodness." Her mother sounded relieved.

"Mother, Cade is a wonderful man. He—"

"Sabrina, you don't understand. We'll be there in the morning."

"All right. Good night," Sabrina said.

"Good night."

Hanging up the phone, Sabrina went to the closet for a robe. She found Cade on the love seat on the patio in front of the fireplace with his bare feet propped up on the ottoman.

She sat beside him and leaned her head on his shoulder. "When I couldn't find you, I thought you might have gone."

"I probably should have."

"I'm sorry, Cade. I don't know why she's so upset," she said, misery creeping into her voice.

His hand cupped the back of her head, angling her head upward. "I'm the first man you've been serious about. I have a reputation for being a coldhearted bastard."

She straddled him, her knees denting the padded cushion, her arms around his neck. "That's not the man who makes my heart beat faster with just a look, the man who makes every day brighter, the man who touches me with such tenderness."

His hands clenched around her waist. In the lamplight she saw the glitter in his eyes. "None of that matters to your mother."

"It does to me." She took his face in her hands. "As she pointed out, I'm a grown woman. I'm where I want to be, and nothing she says will change my mind."

"Your mother—"

"I love her, but she doesn't run my life." She leaned closer. "Perhaps you need a demonstration that I'm not going anyplace." She pressed her lips to his, her woman's softness rubbing against his turgid manhood.

Air hissed between his teeth. Gathering her to him, he stood. Her arms clamped around his neck. "No. I won't let you go," she said.

His forehead rested against hers. "It would take a stronger man than me to do that."

"Then where were you going?" she asked when he kept walking.

"Bed. Protection," Cade groaned just before he tumbled them back into bed.

Sabrina was up and dressed the next morning when she heard the doorbell. Cade had left thirty minutes earlier. She had wanted him there, but he wanted to give her time alone with her parents. Since her father was coming and he was less protective of her than her mother, Sabrina thought together they would be able to ease her mother's worries. She had a feeling that her father and Cade would get along.

Sabrina opened the door and was surprised to see her maternal grandparents as well. Even more surprising were the red, swollen eyes of her mother.

Fear swept through Sabrina. "Is Stephen all right?"

"Stephen's fine," her grandfather answered. He looked tired and worried. Beside him, her grandmother kept blinking her eyes as if she was fighting tears.

"Oh, my baby," her mother wailed and pulled her into her arms for a fierce hug. "I'm sorry. So sorry."

Sabrina hugged her back, felt her tremble. Over her mother's shoulder she sought her father's gaze. He was always steady. Today he looked as if he hadn't slept in days.

Sabrina pushed away from her mother. "Would somebody please tell me what is going on?"

"Sabrina, baby—" her grandfather began, but her mother cut him off.

"No. I'll do it." Her mother brushed tears from her cheek with the heel of her hand.

"What is it?" Sabrina asked, her fear growing stronger.

"Your mother will explain." Her father curved his arms around their shoulders and seated them on the sofa in the den. "I love you both." He kissed them and stepped back.

Her mother took Sabrina's hands. "This is difficult."

"It's my fault," her grandfather said. "I should have told you sooner."

Her mother looked up at her grandfather. "No, Daddy. It's my fault for not taking responsibility for what I'd done."

"Mother, please." Sabrina scooted closer, putting her arm

around her mother's trembling shoulders. "Whatever it is, we're family and family always sticks together."

Her mother tightly shut her eyes. "Oh, lord. What have I done?"

Sabrina's father sat on the other side of her mother. "Do you want me to tell her?"

"No." Her mother opened her eyes. "I have to do this." She took a deep breath. "This is about Cade—"

"Mother," Sabrina said, pulling her hands free and standing. "You had me scared to death that you were critically ill or something. Cade is the man I've dreamed abo—"

"He'll hurt you." Her mother stood as well.

"No, he won't." Sabrina took a step backward. "Nothing you can say will change my mind. Bringing Father and Granddad and Grandma won't help. I love him."

Her mother palmed her face. Her husband drew her into his arms.

"I'm sorry if you disapprove, but I'm hoping you'll come around."

Her mother lowered her hands. "That will never happen. He won't let it now."

"That's not fair. Cade is—"

"The son I gave up for adoption."

Stunned, Sabrina stared at her mother. Her mother had never been pregnant. They'd adopted because she couldn't conceive. Sabrina almost laughed, sure it was some kind of crazy joke until she noticed the shattered expression on her parents' and grandparents' faces.

"No," Sabrina managed. "That can't be. Why would you give your child away?"

"Because his father was married and didn't want either of us," she said, misery in every word.

Sabrina felt sick. She and Cade weren't related by blood but . . .

"Your mother didn't know at the time he was married," her father told her. "She thought the adoption was best."

"Best," Sabrina said. "He was abused and degraded every day he lived with the people who raised him. How could you have put your child through that?"

"Oh, no," her grandfather said, looking shattered. "I didn't know. My lawyer never mentioned the child wasn't being cared for and loved. I would have intervened. Your mother didn't know his name until last night."

"His name is Cade," Sabrina said, angry that fate had played such a cruel joke on them. "You know what he said to me? He said that if one of us had to be adopted, he was glad it was me."

Her mother wiped away fresh tears. "I'm sorry for the way things turned out for him. I–I did what I thought was for the best. I didn't want him taunted and teased as a bastard."

"Instead he was taunted and teased by the man you left him with. For so long, he dreaded tomorrow because of it," Sabrina said, her body shaking. "Cade hated him and his birth mother and her family. And when you tell him he'll hate me."

Cade slammed out of his car and rushed up the steps to Sabrina's house. He patted the note he'd found on his car seat when he'd gotten inside this morning. *I miss you. Hurry back.*

Grinning, he rang the bell. Every day since he'd confessed he didn't look forward to tomorrows, she'd made sure that changed. She cared. He saw it in her eyes, the soft touches, the way she smiled at him.

He'd waited almost thirty-eight years to wholly love anyone. The idea didn't scare him. He was tired of being alone. Sabrina made life better, brighter. He was about to ring the bell again when it opened. Sabrina stood there, her eyes red and puffy.

He reached for her, but she shook her head, and evaded his touch. "Honey, what's the matter?"

"Hello."

Cade jerked his head around to see Sabrina's mother and three other people. His gut clenched. His gaze swung back to Sabrina. "Did they get to you?"

Shaking her head, she circled her arms. "Cade, I'm so sorry."

He opened his mouth, not quite sure what he'd say, then snapped it shut. He wouldn't beg no matter how much he wanted to plead with her not to leave him as everyone else had. "Good-bye."

"Please wait."

Frowning, he stared at Sabrina's mother, her hand clenched with the man's standing next to her. "Why?"

"There-there's something you need to know," she said.

He could just imagine. He folded his arms across his chest, well aware his pose was defiant. "And what would that be?"

She swallowed, swallowed again. "I'm your birth mother."

His arms dropped to his sides. He stared at her, hearing a rushing in his ears. He released the breath he'd held. Rage and resentment he'd fought to bury long ago surfaced.

"Why didn't you just abort me?"

Her gasp cut through the room. He didn't care. "You cared about your social position more than a baby who couldn't defend himself."

"I didn't know you weren't cared for," she cried.

"And that excused you?" Cade snapped. "I made a successful life in spite of you and the cruel man who reminded me
every day how worthless I was."

"Don't blame her." A white-haired man stepped forward.
"I'm her father. It was my decision to leave you with the Mathis
family."

"So your daughter didn't have to worry about the bastard?"

"I'm sorry," the woman cried. "I thought I was doing what
was best for you."

Cade's laugh was ragged. "Lie to yourself if you want. You
tossed me away because I was an inconvenient embarrassment.
Well, I don't need you, and I could care less about your apology."

He whirled to go and went still. Sabrina stood by the door
with tears streaming down her face. His stomach knotted. His
birth mother had deprived him of a normal childhood, and
now she made it impossible to have the woman he loved.

"Please," the man beside Sabrina's mother said. "She's punished herself enough."

Cade whirled toward him, his fists clenched. "Did she go
to bed hungry almost every night? Was she worked from sunup
to sundown? Did she have to wear castoff clothes? Was she—"
He stopped, his breathing uneven. "No, she was loved and
pampered. She still is. I never was."

Cade worked to get his temper under control. "What about
my birth father? Were you at least honest enough to tell him
you were pregnant with me?"

"She told him," the older man said. "He didn't want you."

"Just like you didn't." Cade looked at them with scorn.
"And now I don't want you. I hope you rot in hell."

. . .

Cade wanted to put his fist through something, test the car's speedometer. He did neither. He'd learned early to control his anger or suffer the consequences. But this was more difficult than anything he'd ever had to do.

His hands flexed on the steering wheel. He'd tried to forget the woman who gave birth to him. He'd thought he'd succeeded. He'd been wrong. Looking at her brought back all the hurt and fears he'd had as a kid, that it was his fault that he was unlovable. He didn't know anyone at school who didn't live with a relative. He was different—unloved and unwanted.

Pulling into the garage of his condo, he quickly parked and rode the elevator to his floor. Punching in the code, he went inside, slamming the door, at last able to vent some of his building rage.

His birth mother's attack of conscience had done two things: irrevocably taken Sabrina away from him and confirmed that the man who'd raised him was right when he said Cade was an embarrassment to a rich socialite.

His birth mother gave him away and adopted two other children. To her he was just something to be tossed away and forgotten. She would have never given him a thought if he hadn't been dating Sabrina.

Restless, he went to his bedroom to change into his gym clothes. He'd never been to the fitness center in the building before, but he needed to work off his anger.

Unbuttoning his shirt, he tossed it on the bed. One sleeve landed on the nightstand next to the picture Sabrina had given him of them at the wine tasting. He remembered clearly her smile, her wanting to place the picture where he'd see it every day when he woke up.

He had liked having the picture, liked knowing that some-one cared and made him happy. She'd taken the picture of them with her phone camera. They were standing in front of the dancing water fountain in Uptown Village, both were grinning because she'd whispered something naughty to him.

He jerked up the picture, started to fling it across the room, but remembered her tears. This was hurting her. But for them there could never be anything else.

The doorbell rang. He opened the drawer on the night table, put the picture inside, and went to answer the door. He expected the waiter with the brunch he'd ordered. He'd planned to bring Sabrina back and spend a lazy day in bed and out. He never tired of her or being with her. And she was lost to him forever.

He jerked open the door. Sabrina stood there with tears glistening in her eyes. She brushed past him. He swung the door shut and turned to faced her. Pride dictated she never know how much losing her hurt.

"It might be rude to barge in but I was afraid you'd close the door in my face."

Oddly, that hadn't occurred to him. "What do you want?"

"For things to be the way the were, but that wouldn't be fair to any of us," she said.

He knew by "us" she'd included her mother. He'd never think of her as his mother.

Her hand shoved impatiently through her hair. "Perhaps we shouldn't have ambushed you, but none of us wanted to tell you over the phone."

"How long have you known?" he asked, his voice gravelly.

"Since this morning." She swallowed. "They arrived shortly

after nine. Although we aren't related, I felt . . . funny learning you were my mother's son."

He flinched. "I'm not her son."

She reached toward him, then let her hand fall to her side. "Placing you for adoption wasn't taken lightly."

"I don't want to hear about her and her lies."

This time she did touch him, placing her hand on his bare chest. His heart raced. "I care about you. Nothing can change that. I hope you feel the same way."

"I hate the woman you call your mother."

Sabrina shook her head. "She's your mother too, and she's hurting now."

"You think I care what she feels?" He whirled away, spun. His chest heaved. "Whatever she's going though, it can't be a fraction of the pain and hurt I went through because she didn't want to be embarrassed."

"It wasn't like that," Sabrina said. "She thought it was best for the child—for you. She's a wonderful, loving woman."

"Just not to me." His face hardened. "She could have cared less what happened to me. She went on with her life without a thought of me. She adopted two other children." He wouldn't be jealous of Sabrina or her brother. He'd succeeded in spite of all of them.

"She adopted us because she and Father wanted children," Sabrina explained. "She learned after they were married for three years that she couldn't have children."

"At least there's some justice in the world," he spat.

"Cade, we can work through this. Please. I know it's hard and you're angry. I can't blame you, but please don't turn your back on what we have."

He slowly shook his head. "Every time I see you, I think of

her and what she did to me. The rage and hate I thought I'd buried boils to the surface. I can't think of anything else."

"Cade." Sabrina's voice trembled. She stepped closer. "Give it time. You can't let this break us up."

"There is no 'us' and there never will be."

"Please, Cade. I love you."

He stared, transfixed by the words no other person had ever spoken to him. He cared for her as well, but it was too late the instant he'd learned her adoptive mother was his birth mother. "Please leave."

"Cade, did you hear me?"

He went to the door. "Good-bye, Sabrina."

"I'm not giving up on you, on us."

She wouldn't. She was too stubborn. "I don't want to work with you on any new patients. You can talk to your supervisor or I can."

Hurt and surprise flashed in her face. "If you think you can run from me, you're mistaken, Cade. You'll remember my lips, my arms around you, the warmth of my body next to you, the—"

He jerked the door open. "Leave or I'll call security."

"You can't stop caring any more than I can. When you realize it and accept that it breaks my heart knowing what you went through, what seeing my mother does to you, I'll be waiting." She walked through the door, her fingertips briefly touching his arm and then she was gone.

Cade closed the door, lonelier than he ever thought possible. And this time there wasn't even the hope that one day he wouldn't be because his hope, his life was Sabrina, and she could never be his.

Nineteen

· · · · · · · · · · · · · · · ·

Monday morning, Cade didn't need the alarm clock to wake up. He hadn't slept all night. He couldn't get Sabrina's tear-stained face out of his mind or the face of his birth mother. Muttering a curse, he picked up the controls and turned the television on, hoping noise would keep his thoughts off the two women.

It didn't, and neither did the car radio. He was in a pissy mood when he entered his office. Iris looked at his face and silently handed him his schedule.

"Is there a delivery in my office?"

"Yes."

"Get rid of it. Now."

Iris took off. He stared at the list of patients.

"It's gone."

He glanced up. "Don't accept anything else," he said. He'd forget Sabrina. It might take a lifetime, but he'd do it.

. . .

Sabrina dragged herself out of bed and went to work despite the concerned protest of her mother. She hadn't liked Sabrina going to see Cade last night; she liked it even less that Sabrina was subjecting herself to more pain by not giving up on getting back together with Cade. She hurt for Sabrina and blamed herself. She didn't believe Cade would ever forgive her, and thus Sabrina. If Sabrina didn't believe otherwise she wouldn't be able to go on.

With her sun shades on to conceal her red eyes and puffy lids, Sabrina went to the neuro floor. The nurse-in-charge said Cade was there and in a mood.

Sabrina's heart ached for him. He was hurting. She had no idea what she'd say to him. Then the elevator door opened and he was there. His face was hard, his eyes blazing with anger. She thought he would take another elevator, but he stepped on. So did three visitors. They all got off at the ground floor. She quietly followed Cade outside.

He turned at his car. "Do us both a favor. Don't speak or come near me again." Getting into his car, he drove away, taking her heart with him.

Cade glanced in the rearview mirror, saw Sabrina standing there, her head bowed, and knew she was crying. He gripped the steering wheel to keep from slamming on the brakes and going back to her. Then what? He saw her and remembered the woman who had tossed him away and loved her. He wasn't so low to be jealous that his birth mother loved her and not him, but neither could he push it from his mind.

He sped through the security gate as soon as it lifted. At a red light, he called Sabrina's house. Her mother wouldn't have left so soon.

"Hello."

"Your maiden name? Who's my father and where can I find him?" he asked, recognizing his birth's mother's voice.

"You have to—"

"His name, dammit. You owe me that!"

"James. Christine James. A.J. Reed. He owns a car dealership in Sugarland."

Cade disconnected the call, then called his office. "Iris, clear my schedule for tomorrow." He hung up. Maybe there was a chance he could find one person who wanted him. He thought of Sabrina, pushed it away, and sped through the green light.

Tuesday, a little after noon, Cade sat in a rental car and stared at the Mercedes and Cadillac dealership that spanned half the city block. And his father owned it. He didn't doubt she'd told the truth. She was too upset not to. Cade's mouth tightened. She should have been that conscientious thirty-eight years ago when she'd given him away to a man who made his life hell and took enjoyment in it while doing so.

Cade got out of the 550 Mercedes sedan he'd specifically requested. He wanted to get the man's attention. He would have driven his car, but he knew his mind wouldn't have been on the four-hour drive, plus he was too anxious to take the time. There was still a chance his birth mother and her father had lied. They might not have wanted him, but his father could have.

He hadn't been able to find anything personal on the Internet about A.J. Reed. There'd only been information on his dealership. There hadn't even been a picture of him.

His palms sweaty, his heart rate irregular, Cade opened the spotless glass door. No salesman in the modern and elegant showroom rushed to greet him although he saw three milling around. Obviously, in the strained economy they were doing well or they had learned that some people preferred to look. All the men wore ties and white dress shirts. One finally moved away from the other two and, smiling, came to Cade, extending his hand.

"Good afternoon, sir. I'm Charlie Waters."

"Dr. Mathis," Cade said. He wanted to impress so why play around?

A predatory gleam entered the man's eyes. "Welcome, Dr. Mathis. How can I help you today?"

"I'm looking for a CL series. I heard you had a good selection," Cade said. He'd looked online and planned this moment. The car started at $94,000.

"What do you drive now?"

"A Lamborghini."

The man practically drooled. "I was in Houston for a medical conference and decided I'd like to drive back to Dallas," Cade said. "I'm prepared to write a check for the full amount, of course."

"You've come to the right place." Waters waved his hand toward a shiny gray car on the dais. "We can start with this beauty." He went on to extol the virtues of the car that included a heated steering wheel and pedestrian detection.

"Sounds good, but if the owner is available, I'd like to speak with him. It's been my experience that the owner can give me a good feel if I'd like to do business with the company."

There was the briefest hesitation. Cade couldn't tell if the man was afraid of losing the sale or of the owner. "Of course, I'll match any commission for you if the owner completes the sale."

"That's not necessary, but that's awfully nice of you. I'll get A.J."

A.J. Reed. His biological father. Cade tensed, but nothing showed on his face. Seconds ticked by, then he saw the salesman returning. With him was a tall, well-dressed man in a tailored suit and polished ostrich cowboy boots, a wide grin on his brown-skinned face.

Cade took an immediate dislike to the man. He wasn't sure if it was because he had abandoned him or because the fake grin on his face had a high BS reading. A.J. stuck his wide, manicured hand out two feet away, his grin widening. "Good afternoon, Dr. Mathis. Welcome to my dealership."

"Good afternoon," Cade said, hoping, waiting for some sign of recognition, but there was nothing. He didn't look like either parent, although Cade's eyes were black like his birth mother's father.

"Thank you. Charlie was telling me about the car on the dais. Is it possible for us to take a test drive?" Cade inquired.

"Get the keys," A.J. ordered.

Cade looked at his wrist long enough for A.J. to follow the direction of his gaze and see the thin platinum watch. "I hadn't realized the time. I don't want to keep you from lunch. I can come back."

"No. No. Have you eaten?" A.J. asked.

Cade shook his head. "I just drove in from a medical conference in Houston."

"Then, I insist you let me buy you lunch." As Cade had

expected, A.J. wasn't about to let a man willing to pay cash for a car walk out of his showroom with just his word that he'd return.

"All right. I'll drive, if you'll point me in the right direction."

"Sure. I know just the place."

The place was Party Palace, a gentleman's club. The parking lot was packed. At the door, A.J. flashed another grin, and gave a twenty to the man at the door.

"Welcome back, Mr. Reed," greeted the smiling hostess.

A.J. winked at Cade as if they shared an inside joke. Cade followed as the woman in a black miniskirt and plunging V-neck top showed them to a table near the center of the stage. "Mr. Reed, do you want your usual?"

He grinned, another inside joke. "A drink for now. We'll talk later."

The woman kept the smile on her face, but Cade could tell it was forced.

"And you?"

"Hennessy please, and a lunch menu."

"We serve from the buffet, but I'll be happy to bring your food," she said, and named the entries.

"Just a spinach salad with vinaigrette," Cade said.

She smiled and turned to A.J. "What about you?"

He wasn't smiling. "You know what I like."

"Yes, sir."

"And stop calling me sir."

"I didn't mean anything." She placed her hand on his shoulder. "Whatever you say."

The smile returned. He was appeased. It seemed the hostess

had a bigger BS meter than A.J. did. She probably loathed him and he'd never know it.

"I'll send the drinks over right away and personally go into the kitchen and prepare your food," she told them, and left.

A.J. leaned back in his chair. Obviously he thought he was the big man and wanted to be treated accordingly. He didn't like that the hostess had paid more attention to Cade, which meant he was insecure and petty.

"You come here often?" Cade asked.

A.J. grinned and looked around. "A man's gotta have a little diversity."

"Here you are." A woman in a revealing red bustier and short shorts set the drinks on the table, serving A.J. first. "Scotch for Mr. Reed. Hennessy for his guest."

Another twenty hit the table. She swiped it up and ignored the hand on her butt. If ever a man disgusted him more on such short notice, Cade couldn't remember. He sipped his drink and watched A.J., who watched the dancer on stage.

Cade motioned toward the ring on his hand. "Aren't you concerned?"

A.J.'s eyes hardened. "No. My life is my own. You single?"

Cade thought about Sabrina, the life they might have had together and then pushed her away. "Yes."

"Smart man." A.J. leaned closer. "But you'd be surprised at the women who fall for the old trick about not being happy, especially when they see I'm loaded. Get more tail than I can handle."

Cade clenched the glass to keep from shoving his fist into A.J.'s crude mouth. "What about the consequences?"

"Here you go, Mr. Reed," the hostess said, serving A.J., and then Cade. She wasn't making that mistake again.

"He's a doctor from Dallas. He drove from Houston to buy one of my cars," A.J. announced proudly, then he picked up his knife and fork to cut into his steak.

"You made the right decision. Mr. Reed is known for miles around because of his dealership. If you need anything else, just let me know." She moved away.

"What kind of consequences?" A.J. asked around a mouthful of bloodred beef.

Cade's hand tightened around his glass. "Children."

A.J.'s dark brown eyes hardened. "You mean bastards," he snapped. "I only had one child I claim. A son." His voice quivered, strengthened.

Cade's heart raced. He had a brother. He wasn't alone. "Where is he?"

A.J. visibly swallowed. "Gone. The governor and mayor came to his funeral. He was an important man. The world loved him."

Grief hit Cade. He leaned forward in his chair. "When? How?"

A.J.'s face contorted with fury. "Almost five years ago. Damned drunk driver. If he'd just done what I taught him about women he'd be alive today." Bitterness coated each word. He snatched up his drink and downed half the contents.

"I'm sorry," Cade murmured, wondering if A.J.'s son had been as careless with women as his father.

"Maybe you heard of him? Wes Reed." A.J. said the name proudly. "He was a nationally known news correspondent and lived in Dallas."

Cade had. If he had come to Dallas sooner he might have met him. "Wasn't he married to a Dallas talk show hostess?"

"Madison Reed," A.J. snarled. "I hope she rots in hell. If she'd been the kind of woman Wes needed he wouldn't—" He emptied his glass. The waitress quickly refilled it and moved away.

Wheels were turning in Cade's head. Madison Reed still lived in Dallas. Hadn't he seen her on TV in one of his patients' rooms talking about her family a couple of months ago? "I seem to remember seeing Madison on TV with a little girl around five. Is she your grandchild?"

A.J. looked as if he wanted to lunge across the table and choke the life out of Cade. "It ain't fair that Wes died and that whelp lived. She should have died with her no-good mother. That bitch Madison let that bastard step into Wes's shoes just like he always wanted. But I'll never claim—" A.J. snapped his mouth shut and straightened.

Cade's agile brain, which had helped him finish in the top 3 percent of his class, quickly processed A.J.'s rage-filled words. "So the little girl is Wes's and Madison's husband is Wes's half-brother," he guessed.

A.J. quickly glanced around as if to make sure no one had heard Cade. He reached for his drink only to push it away. "I never said that. We're here to talk about cars."

Cade wondered about the reason behind the flash of fear in the other man's eyes, and casually picked up his drink. "I always heard grandparents doted on their grandchildren."

"I didn't say anything about a grandchild." A.J. cleaned his hands with a paper napkin. "We need to get back."

Cade wanted to keep him talking, but he could see A.J. retreating. He was mean, hateful, and angry. If A.J. had loved anyone, it was the son he'd lost. But . . . "What if you had another son?"

A.J. jerked his head up and stared hard across the table at Cade. "I just told you I only had one son. The rest are bastards."

It was now or never, Cade thought. "Christine James is my birth mother and she says you're my father."

A.J.'s eyes narrowed, his expression hardened. He started to rise then sat back down. "She meant nothing to me. Anything she birthed means even less." He picked up the glass he'd pushed away and drained the contents. "Wes was my *only* son. I'd trade every bastard who ever claimed my seed and the women who birthed them for Wes to be alive."

There it was. He wasn't wanted.

"And you can get it out of your head if you think to get my money. You aren't the first one to come crying to me. Just like the rest, you mean nothing to me," A.J. flung.

"You mean even less to me." Cade pulled out his billfold, making sure A.J. saw the black Centurion American Express credit card, the platinum and diamond stud cuff links as he tossed a hundred-dollar bill on the table. He came to his feet. "I could buy and sell you if I wanted. I've succeeded. People respect me. They loathe you and you deserve every second of their scorn. One day you'll need someone, and no one will be there."

Cade walked away. He didn't look back. He had the answer he wanted. No one wanted him, not then and not now.

Cade hit the freeway with a burst of speed, leaving Sugarland behind him. He'd be in Houston soon. He was driving straight to the airport. His hand gripped the steering wheel. He'd hoped his father— He gritted his teeth. He wasn't going there.

At least he'd learned he had a half-niece, and a half-brother. Perhaps he could connect with them and finally be a part of a family. Or would they turn their backs on him as well? He had an abysmal track record for people who wanted him to be a part of their lives.

Sabrina's smiling face flashed in his mind before he could stop it. He ruthlessly tried to push the image away. He succeeded only for it to be replaced with one of tears sparking in her eyes. He muttered a curse.

His ringing cell phone blessedly chased the image from his mind. He eagerly snatched it from the inside of his coat. "Hello."

"Cade, oh, God, Cade."

His grip on the phone tightened. She sounded frightened. The overwhelming need that she be safe overruled everything else. "Sabrina, what is it? Are you all right?"

"No. Yes."

Cade slowed on the busy freeway, and pulled over to the outside lane to take the next exit. "Sabrina, are you hurt?" He tried to stay calm, but his hands were trembling. She wasn't a hysterical or indecisive woman. "Sabrina?"

"It's Stephen. He's been hurt."

The younger brother she loved. Taking the exit, he pulled into a service station and parked. He didn't have to ask if it was bad, he heard the fear in her voice. "Has the doctor had a chance to evaluate him?"

"He-he says the head injury is too extensive for anything to be done, but he's wrong. You have to come and see Stephen. You can save him. Please."

"Sabrina, I'm sorry." Families often found it difficult to accept the truth. He'd give anything for her to have been spared this. Rubbing the back of his neck, he paced beside the rental. "Who saw him?"

"Dr. Fielder. Dad says he's supposed to be the best, but he's not. You are."

Cade knew Fielder, had done a consultation with him several weeks ago, but he lived in Houston. "Fielder has a good reputation."

"But he's not you. I want you."

He wanted too, wanted to be there for her, wanted her. He'd learned long ago you didn't always get what you want. "I'm out of the city."

"Where are you?"

He paused. "Outside of Houston."

"You saw him, then?"

Her mother must have told her. His hand flexed on his thigh. "Yes."

"I'm sorry it didn't work out for you. His loss."

My loss. The way it had always been. "I'm driving to the airport to catch a plane back to Dallas."

"Thank God. Stephen is in Texas Hospital in Houston. I came back with my parents. Please come."

His fist clenched, he shook his head. "I can't."

"Cade, please. He won't make it if you don't. The doctor hasn't given him much time. Mother is hysterical. Father isn't much better. Neither are my grandparents."

No matter how selfish, one thought ran through his mind. "Stephen has people who love him, cried for him. I never have."

"Yes, you have. Me," she told him.

How he wished that was possible. "I can't help you."

"Cade, don't blame Stephen for what happened to you."

"I don't blame him. I envy what he had. I have to go."

"Cade, please. The man I fell in love with, the man who fights for his patients, the man who overcame incredible odds to rise to the top of his profession, wouldn't turn his back on a young man who desperately needs him."

"He has a doctor," Cade reminded her.

"He's not you," she said. "Stephen needs the best to make it. He needs you. We both do."

Cade silently shook his head again. She was asking too much.

"I love you, Cade. You have to come for your sake as much as Stephen's. You care. Helping people is not just a job to you, it's who you are. He's on the eighth floor in ICU. You can't turn your back on him."

"Why not? Everyone turned their back on me," he said, and disconnected the call. He didn't want to see Stephen's mother crying for her son when she'd never shed one tear for him. He couldn't.

Starting the motor, he got back on the freeway and headed for the airport.

Twenty

· · · · · · · · · · · · · · ·

I s he coming?" her grandfather asked, his face strained.

Sabrina briefly shut her eyes. "I don't know."

He nodded and turned to look at his daughter, who was softly crying in her husband's arms. "I've only felt this helpless one other time in my life."

Sabrina leaned her head against his shoulder, her arm going around his waist as his went around hers. "The night Cade was born."

She felt his sigh rather than heard it. "She changed from an outgoing young woman to a depressed, fragile thing who wouldn't even look at me or her mother. Giving him up wasn't easy."

"Thirty-eight years ago it wasn't as accepted for an unwed mother or the child," Sabrina said. "I know you and Mother meant well, but his childhood was horrible. The emotional scars run deep."

Her grandfather faced her, then he lowered his head for a moment. "I didn't know. I swear I didn't. He was my first grandchild. I would have moved heaven and earth to have kept him, but your mother was too fragile. The family he went to was supposed to be decent, hardworking Christians. I thought he was all right."

He visibly swallowed. "I stayed out of his life until he graduated from high school. I asked the lawyer who located the couple and handled the paperwork to check and see which college he planned to attend. I wanted to ensure he had the opportunity and learned he wasn't going because they couldn't afford it. Through the lawyer I arranged for a 'benefactor' to pay for his full tuition."

"You," she guessed.

He almost smiled. "He graduated summa cum laude and continued to be the best."

"Medical school is expensive," Sabrina said.

"He was my first grandchild," her grandfather said as if that explained everything. "I wanted him to have every chance in life."

Sabrina kissed him on the cheek. "Thank you. Cade thinks no one has ever cared for him, cried for him. I'm glad I'm not the first."

"And I'm glad he has you."

"I just hope he does," she said, turning as the door to the ICU opened and Stephen's doctor came out. She and the family members and friends waiting converged on the thin, weary-looking man.

"Is there any change?" Stephen's father asked.

"Not for the better I'm afraid," Dr. Fielding said. "The swelling has increased. His neuro signs are decreased."

"No. No," her mother sobbed.

"I'm sorry. As you know, closed head injuries are tricky.

The baseball was hit with an aluminum bat, which propels the ball faster, which in turns makes the injury worse."

"Can't you go in and relieve the pressure?" her grandfather asked.

"Ordinarily we could, but another problem has presented itself. The CT scan revealed a tumor exactly in the area we need to go in."

"A tumor?" Sabrina said.

"Yes. He was probably having vision and depth perception problems, which explains why he missed the line drive and the ball hit him in the head," Dr. Fielding went on to say.

"He thought his vision problems were because he was studying so much," his mother said softly. "He didn't want to be bothered with contacts or eyeglasses. I should have insisted he be checked."

"It's not your fault, Mother." Sabrina gently touched her mother's arm. "Is surgery our only hope?"

"Yes," Dr. Fielding answered.

"We'll sign the consent," her mother said.

For the first time Dr. Fielding looked uncomfortable. "Marshall," he began, calling Sabrina's father by his first name. "Can I talk with just the immediate family?"

Sabrina clutched the hands of her grandparents, as everyone except her parents and grandparents left them with the doctor. She knew before he spoke that none of them were going to like what the doctor had to say.

"All right. Say it," her father said tersely.

Sabrina understood and hoped that Dr. Fielding did as well. Her father was angry at the situation and his helplessness to help his son, not at the doctor.

"There's nothing more that can be done," Dr. Fielding told them.

"You're the best. You have to operate," her father said.

"I'm sorry. I won't go in," Dr. Fielding repeated. "I don't know of any doctor who would."

"I do." Sabrina pulled her cell phone from the pocket of her slacks.

"Put the phone away, Sabrina," her grandfather said.

"No, Cade has to come," Sabrina said, fighting tears.

"He already has."

Sabrina jerked around to see Cade walking toward them. He wore the forbidden expression that intimidated people. Sabrina intimately knew and loved the man behind the façade. With a shout of joy, she rushed to him, her arms going around his waist, just holding on.

"I knew you'd come. I knew it."

She felt the hardness of his body, the warmth, then his arms curving loosely around her. For now it was enough. She made herself straighten and look up at him.

"Thank you."

"I'm not promising anything," Cade said.

"You're here." Taking his hand, she started back to Dr. Fielding. Her parents and grandparents stepped away. Sabrina hurt for all of them, but Stephen came first. "Dr. Fielding, I think you know Dr. Mathis."

"Dr. Mathis," Dr. Fielding greeted, extending his hand.

"Dr. Fielding," Cade said. The handshake was brief.

"Dr. Mathis has agreed to consult on Stephen's case," Sabrina said.

Dr. Fielding's stance changed. He turned to her parents who were standing a few feet away. "Marshall, is this what you want?"

"I want Stephen to have the best, and you two are the best," her father placated. "Would you want any less for your child?"

Dr. Fielding seemed to lose some of his hostility. "Dr. Mathis, if you'll follow me, I'll show you the reports and you can examine him."

Cade glanced down at Sabrina, then followed Dr. Fielding through the double doors of the ICU.

"Will he help Stephen?" her mother asked, her voice unsteady.

"Cade fights for his patients." Sabrina hugged her mother, aware she had evaded giving her a direct answer. From the expression on her grandfather's face he hadn't been fooled. The first hurdle was Cade's assessment of Stephen's condition. He very well might agree with Dr. Fielding, but if he didn't, would he try to save Stephen's life?

Cade had wrestled with his decision to come all the way to the hospital. His birth mother and her parents had turned their backs on him and now they expected him to save their son, their grandson. His love for Sabrina had been stronger than his hatred of them. He'd finally stopped fighting that truth at least.

"As you can see, the tumor is sitting in a delicate place," Dr. Fielding said. "Even if you were to try and remove it, the chances of him dying on the table are high. If he did make it off, he might never come out of the coma or he might have permanent brain damage."

Cade studied the X-rays on the screen. Fielding was right.

"The risk is high, but if you don't go in, he won't make it through the night."

"I know." Fielding blew out a breath. "Marshall lives two blocks over. Stephen went to prep school with my oldest. They're on the same baseball team."

Cade recalled seeing several young men in baseball uniforms in the waiting room. Stephen had everything Cade had wanted and had been destined never to have.

That's a lie. You have me. Sabrina's words came clearly to him. "I'd like to see him."

Dr. Fielding studied Cade for a few moments. "I realize you have a reputation for pulling off the impossible, but Stephen is beyond help."

Cade simply stared at Fielding. Nothing pissed him off more than someone telling him what he couldn't do. He'd learned early in his medical practice that people with limits wanted to limit you. He'd promised himself the day he set foot at the University of Texas at Austin that he'd never let anyone define him again the way the man who raised him had tried to do.

"I'll take you to him," Fielding finally said.

In Stephen's room, Fielding silently gave Cade his stethoscope and penlight. Cade looked down at the pale figure on the bed, his respirations uneven, his blood pressure low. He might have had everything, but illness was the great equalizer. It didn't care about your social status, race, nationality, gender.

Putting on the stethoscope, Cade thoroughly checked Stephen. The neuro signs were as depressed as he'd thought, but he paid particular attention to the heart and lungs. Finished, he handed the equipment back. "Thank you."

"Well?"

"You're right about his chances," Cade said.

Dr. Fielding stuck the stethoscope in the pocket of his lab coat, along with the penlight. "I imagine they're waiting on us."

"I imagine." Cade left the room with Fielding close beside. When Cade pushed open the door to the ICU, he saw more young people had joined those who were waiting. Sabrina, holding her grandfather's hand, rose from her seat and started for him. Her grandmother, sitting with her daughter and son-in-law, did the same.

He saw the hope in Sabrina's face, the faith in him that he could make her world right again.

"Dr. Mathis agrees with me that nothing can be done," Dr. Fielding said.

Her father swayed unsteadily on his feet, then held his softly crying wife in his arms.

Sabrina's gaze never left his. She stepped closer. "I want to hear you say it, Cade. Is that what you think?"

"I already said—"

"Dr. Fielding," her grandfather interrupted. "My granddaughter asked Dr. Mathis a question. I'd like to hear his answer as well."

Sabrina stepped forward to grip Cade's arm. "If you tell me there's nothing that can be done . . ." She briefly closed her eyes. "I . . . I'll believe it."

Her faith and trust in him shouldn't make his chest tight, his arms ache to hold her, to keep her with him always.

"Surgery is his only chance and even then he might not make it off the table. If he does, he might be paralyzed or remain in a coma," Cade said.

"I won't operate," Dr. Fielding reminded them.

"Can you do it, son?" her grandfather asked.

Cade jerked his head around, ready to shred the old man to pieces. Now he was a "son" when they needed him.

"No one can do the surgery," Dr. Fielding said. "Marshall, I know you're grieving, but don't put your family or Stephen through this."

Sabrina whirled angrily on the doctor, then seemed to gather herself before turning back to Cade. "Stephen is a fighter. He'd want to take the chance if there was one. Cade, do you think there's a chance if you went in?"

His sister was also a fighter. "Fielding is right—to a degree—but a chance is sometimes all any of us ever get. Your parents have to make that decision."

"Does that mean you'd do the surgery?" Sabrina asked.

His hesitation was brief. "Yes."

Tears flowed from her eyes. She hugged him.

"Sabrina—" he began, but she cut him off.

"You're giving Stephen a fighting chance." She stared up at him with love and gratitude. "I know it wasn't an easy decision. I understand the odds. Thank you."

How could he not love her? She didn't expect the impossible from him. She knew his faults and fears, and it didn't matter. He allowed his hand to sweep up and down her slim back. "His parents have to agree."

"We do, and we're grateful." Her father spoke to Dr. Fielding. "Bring us the consent forms."

His body rigid, Dr. Fielding walked away. Cade turned to follow.

"Dr.-Dr. Mathis," Sabrina's mother said softly. "Thank you. Please save Stephen."

Cade ignored her and the pleading expression in her face, her eyes. She had never been there for him or cared about him. If it wouldn't upset Sabrina, he'd tell her he wasn't doing it for her.

Cade felt a hand on his arm and saw Sabrina's grandfather smiling up at him. "I had no way of knowing sending you to college and med school would affect us one day. You worked hard for your success."

Cade stared at the older man and tried to take it all in. He'd paid for his education?

The smile on the man's face faded. "There haven't been many days that I haven't thought of you. I'm proud of the man you've grown up to be. Forgive me for not protecting you better."

Cade wanted to believe his grandfather really cared, but he couldn't. He squelched the softness unfurling inside him. He just needed him. He had to remember that.

"The consent forms," a nurse said, handing the forms to Mr. Thomas.

Cade noted Dr. Fielding standing a short distance away. He was pissed, but he was also a good neurosurgeon. "Dr. Fielding, I'll need another pair of eyes and hands. I can't think of another surgeon I'd rather have with me."

Fielding stared at him. He was aware that Cade was feeding him a line, but the other people didn't know that. "Of course. I'll show you where to scrub in."

Cade knew he'd accept. He was scrubbing in as an assistant, taking none of the risk if things went bad and part of the honor if they didn't. Giving Sabrina a brief hug, he followed Dr. Fielding.

. . .

Sabrina stared after Cade until he disappeared through the double doors, then turned to her immediate family. "Mother, Father, Granddad, Grandmother, I need to talk to you, please. It's about me and Cade."

They followed her a short distance away. "I love Cade. It won't change, it will only grow stronger."

"Sabrina, baby," her father said. "Are you sure? He seems like a hard man."

"Because for most of his life that was all he knew," she said.

"My fault," her mother said, choking back tears. "I let both of my sons down."

Her father held her closer. "Christine, don't blame yourself for any of this."

She shook her head and straightened away from him. "Who else? I told myself it was best for him, but I was also ashamed of being an unwed mother."

"You did what you thought best," Sabrina's father said, taking her mother's shoulders in his hands and staring down at her. "I told you that when you thought to leave me because we couldn't have children, and I'll keep on telling you. You gave him up out of love."

"He hates me," she cried, tears streaming down her cheeks. "And I can't blame him."

"Then we'll all have to work hard to help him come to know us, and hopefully forgive us," her grandfather said. "We have a chance that I thought we'd never would."

"Carlton is right," her grandmother said. "Cade is our first grandchild. We'll give him time, but we won't give up. Never again."

Her mother squeezed Sabrina's hands. "If I couldn't care for him, I'm thankful that now he has you."

"Yes, he does. He's hard at times, but he fights even harder for his patients. He'll fight the devil himself for Stephen," Sabrina said. She just prayed it was enough.

Sabrina had never been good at waiting. She paced the surgery waiting room, declined coffee and the offer of food from well-meaning relatives and friends. There were so many people waiting that many of Stephen's classmates and friends were in the hallway. She kept throwing glances at the big clock on the wall.

It had been two hours since Cade had left with Dr. Fielding. He'd sent a technician out an hour ago to give them an update. There should—

"Code blue in OR. Code blue in OR."

"God, no!" Sabrina cried, turning to her mother who was already on her feet. People piled into the room from the hallway.

"It doesn't have to be Stephen," her grandmother said, but her voice quivered.

"Of course not," her grandfather said.

"I'll just go check," her father said, gently trying to disengage himself from his wife.

"No, you don't have to go," her mother cried. "Like Mother said, it-it doesn't have to be Stephen."

Sabrina had never seen her easygoing father look so torn and afraid. Sabrina made her legs move toward her mother. "Why don't we sit down?" They were surrounded by friends and family, but none of that mattered.

Sabrina held the hands of her mother and grandmother, but she couldn't help thinking of Cade, who grew up with no one. Thinking of him helped keep her mind off the operating room. She refused to think it was Stephen in trouble, and began praying.

Cade was the best. She swallowed the growing lump in her throat. Sometimes even the best lost.

"Please, let me through. I need to speak with Mr. Thomas's parents," requested a female voice.

People parted, but Sabrina and her family were already rushing to the same technician who had come before. She didn't waste time.

"Dr. Mathis got his heart beating again," she said.

Her mother's nails dug into Sabrina's hand. Sabrina fought tears and said a quick prayer of thanks.

"Dr. Mathis told me to tell his sister that she was right about Stephen being a fighter," the technician said, smiling briefly at Sabrina. Then she was gone.

"So, it seems, is my first grandson. Thank God for him," her grandfather said.

Sabrina wasn't sure what people standing nearby thought of her grandfather's comment, and she didn't care. *Keep fighting, Stephen. Please keep fighting.*

Cade stared down at Stephen's still body in the recovery room. Cade had done all he could. Stephen still wasn't out of the woods. If he hadn't fought so hard to live, they would have lost him on the table. That, and Cade was sure, a higher power had a hand in this. Cade knew his limitations and Stephen's operation had stretched them to the limits.

"You're as good as they say or the luckiest man alive," Dr. Fielding said from the other side of the narrow bed.

Cade glanced up. "Luck had nothing to do with it."

"I imagine his parents want to see him. I'll go get them."

"Wait," Cade said, staring at the monitors. Sometimes you got a warning the patient was going bad; other times it happened in a blink of the eye. "His vitals are shaky. I don't like it."

"After what he's been though, it's not unusual," Dr. Fielding said, but he moved to the other side of the bed.

Cade's gaze flickered to Stephen even as his breathing altered the tiniest bit, then stopped completely. The eerie wail of the alarm sounded. Cade cursed beneath his breath and started chest percussions as Fielding grabbed the ambo bag.

Sabrina held it together by sheer force of will. It had been twenty-two long minutes since Stephen's last cardiac arrest. No one had come this time. She tried not to let her mind think of what that meant. Stephen was a fighter. Cade was the best. Her brother would come through this. She refused to think any differently.

"Please, God. Please. Don't take him," her mother prayed softly.

Sabrina noticed how quiet it was and glanced around. Others were praying as well. She swallowed the lump in her throat, then reached past her father to close her hand over her mother's. She wanted to say it would be all right, but the words wouldn't come.

Her mother, sitting between her own mother and Sabrina's father, lifted her gaze to Sabrina. Tears silently ran down her cheeks. "I can't lose again."

Choking back sobs, Sabrina knelt in front of her mother and hugged her around the waist, much as she had done as a child. "They're both fighters," she said, praying it was enough.

"Don't give up on them," her grandfather said, hunkering down to reach past Sabrina to her father. He grasped his hand and his wife's. "Don't lose faith."

Her mother blinked away tears. "Daddy, I'm scared."

"I know, baby," he said, fighting his own tears. "We all are, but we're going to get through this as a family."

Her mother nodded. Her breath shuddered out over her lips. Her hands clenched Sabrina's. "I'm sorry. For everything."

Sabrina said the only thing she could. "I love you. I'm glad you're my mother."

"Me too," her mother said, the corners of her lips curving upward slightly.

"Mr. and Mrs. Thomas."

She glanced up to see the technician who had given them news before. Her lower lip quivering, she blinked back tears. Sabrina turned into her grandfather's arms and sobbed.

Twenty-one

· · · · · · · · · · · · · · ·

Hours later Sabrina readjusted her weight in the uncomfortable straight chair. Through the blinds she could see a pale hint of daylight. The night had been long and harrowing. She watched as Cade stretched his long arms over his head. He had to be tired yet he was still here.

He turned his warm gaze first to her, then to Stephen resting quietly. She shivered despite the two blankets Cade insisted she have. All too vividly she recalled the anguish before the technician said that Stephen was all right. She hurriedly explained that she was crying because Cade had refused to give up.

"He's holding his own." Cade straightened from examining Stephen. "Go home and get some rest."

Standing, she went to Cade and curved her arm around his waist and leaned into him. "Not until he wakes up."

"At least go find someplace to stretch out," he said.

"I'm fine," she said, then forged ahead. "Can Mother come back in?"

There was the briefest pause. "Briefly—if she's calm."

Her mother hadn't wanted to leave Stephen's bedside when they'd been allowed to see him after his second cardiac arrest. She'd been almost hysterical.

"I'll go get her." Rising on tiptoe, she kissed Cade on the cheek.

Cade watched Sabrina leave, then turned his attention to Stephen. He was a good-looking kid and, from what Sabrina had said, he'd had a rough beginning. But he'd been adopted by people who cared. He'd had the life Cade should have had.

He heard sniffles behind him, but didn't look. Slowly, Christine Thomas approached Stephen on the other side of the bed, her body trembling, her eyes red and puffy. Regardless of how right or wrong it was, no matter how many times, he couldn't let it go that she cried for a man she adopted, but never for him, her own son.

Gently, she brushed her shaky hand over Stephen's forehead. "I love you, Stephen. We all do."

"Send in his father," Cade said, unable to keep the anger from his voice.

Her gaze jerked up to his. He expected to see annoyance at the very least. There was such a mixture of emotions, he couldn't decipher them all.

"Thank you." With one last look at her son, she was gone.

Almost immediately, her husband entered. Cade didn't expect the strong hand on his arm, the extended hand. He didn't know how to react to either. Stephen's father didn't wait, just reached for Cade's hand and firmly shook it once. Releasing Cade's hand, he went to the other side of the bed and leaned over.

"It's going to be all right, Stephen. Your family and friends are here and praying for you. You've got the best doctor in the country." Upright, he looked at Cade, then left.

Cade turned to see Sabrina. Her gaze lingered on her brother and then she was wrapped around him. Tears dampened his scrub shirt. "Shh. He's a fighter."

Sabrina lifted her head, brushed away the last tears with a tissue. "I know. Just like you, but I wasn't crying for him." She went to the bed and placed her hand on her brother's forehead. "There's a wonderful man I want you to meet when you wake up." She gently kissed him. "When you do, we'll be here. Granddad and Grandmother send their love."

"That might not be for a while. Go home and rest," Cade told her.

She shook her head. "Watch over him for us, Cade."

She knew him well. "Please call my service and have them contact Iris. Let her know I won't be in today."

"All right." On tiptoe, she kissed him on the cheek. "I love you."

Cade watched her leave. Sabrina was a fantastic, intelligent, and loving woman. He couldn't deny he was glad she'd come into his life, no matter the circumstances.

Cade turned to stare down at Stephen and in doing so finally understood why he fought so hard to help people, stayed close by after they had major surgery. He wanted them to have a chance for the life he'd never had, to be happy and loved.

Maybe, just maybe he had a chance after all.

Texas Hospital in Dallas was buzzing with the news that Dr. Mathis had operated on Sabrina Thomas's brother after he'd been injured by a line-drive baseball. The operation wasn't speculated on as much as the reason Dr. Mathis was in Houston. The staff had noted they were getting chummy, but on Monday Dr. Mathis had been a bear to work with and Sabrina'd had red, swollen eyes.

Kara was barely in the hospital lobby before she heard the "juicy" gossip. Frightened and worried, she quickly went into her office and called Sabrina's cell phone number. The call went to voice mail. She picked up her desk phone and called Texas Hospital in Houston. In less than a minute, the phone in the ICU waiting room rang.

"Hello."

"Sabrina Thomas, please. Kara Simmons."

"Just a moment."

"Morning, Kara. I guess you heard about Stephen through the grapevine. Sorry. I haven't called," Sabrina said, sounding tired.

"Stop talking nonsense." Kara wrapped her arm around her waist. "What can I do to help?"

"Just keep praying," Sabrina said. "He came through the night all right. Cade is with him now. He made the difference. If . . ."

"He was there, and that's what matters," Kara said, hearing the strained emotions seeping through Sabrina's unsteady voice. "I can be on a plane and there by noon."

"No. I appreciate the offer, but there isn't anything you could do."

"I could be with you." Kara sat behind her desk. "You've been there for me too many times to count."

"And you for me," Sabrina returned. "Besides, you'll be able to tell me all the gossip when I get back."

Aware that Sabrina needed to get her mind off Stephen if only briefly, Kara said, "I was barely through the hospital door before I heard people talking. The big question is if Cade was already there with you or if he flew down to do the surgery. I gather his office manager isn't talking."

"I wish others would take a clue from her," Sabrina said, a hint of annoyance creeping into her voice.

There wasn't enough privacy in the waiting room for Sabrina to tell her whether either speculation was right. The important thing was, he was there. "Is everything all right between you two?"

There was a slight pause. "I'm not sure. It's complicated."

Kara leaned forward and propped her arm on her desk. "I know complicated. Mother can't stand Tristan. We had lunch here yesterday since Mama is still complaining that she doesn't feel well and I don't want to leave her. I can tell he questions my sanity for staying with her."

"And you love them both."

"Tristan kind of snuck up on me," she admitted. "I actually teared up last night when he dropped by unexpectedly just to check on me. I wanted to go with him so badly."

"Why didn't you?"

"I'm not up for hearing any more of Mama's criticism," she admitted. "Besides, I have enough on my mind with the open house this weekend. His mother is showcasing my paintings."

"You're going to be a sensation. People will love the paintings as much as the house."

Thankfully, Kara didn't become nervous as she usually did. Tristan was making a believer of her with regard to more than just her paintings. "I've made two sales already. The builder's wife came by, and she wants the paintings in the dining room.

She and her husband live a couple of houses down from Tristan. They're coming over to his place tonight to look at more."

"I knew it! You're going to be a sensation. I want a full report."

"You'll have it. By the way, is your phone off on purpose or do you need to charge it?"

"On purpose," Sabrina admitted. "I knew you'd track me down. I took the week off, but I left a message for my supervisor yesterday about Stephen. Most of my friends and relatives are here. I figured you'd send an e-mail to the neighbors."

"Good thinking. I'll let you go. Call me if there's anything I can do."

"I will."

"Bye. Love you."

"Bye. Love you too, and thanks for the call."

Kara hung up, then punched in Tristan's number.

"Hi, honey."

Just hearing that made the tears she'd held at bay threaten to fall. "I—" She swallowed.

"Are you hurt? Is your mother at you again?" he asked, his voice rising.

She wasn't surprised by his question. "It's Sabrina. Her brother was injured yesterday. Cade is there. He-he did the surgery. She didn't say, but it must be bad since he's still there. He always monitors his patients if they're critical."

"Do you want to fly down? I can go with you."

It didn't surprise her that he'd asked. "No. I asked, and she said not to come. I-I don't know."

"She's your friend and you feel helpless since you're not there for her."

"Yes." Was there ever anyone who understood her better?

"You have an incredible capacity for love."

And the reason people ran over her. Instead of making her feel better, she felt worse.

"I have a lot of contacts in Houston. Why don't I come over? I can make some phone calls and at least we can make sure they have some decent coffee and food. Call Sabrina back and ask her to find a place to set things up and ask how many people."

That would be costly. She didn't hesitate. "Can you take any of the paintings to pay for everything? I put the money you paid me in a CD."

"Don't worry. It's a gift from both of us. I'll be there in fifteen."

"We could handle everything over the phone."

"But I couldn't hold you, kiss you, reassure you. Bye, honey."

Kara replaced the receiver, a small smile on her face. It was wonderful having a man you could count on, a man you didn't have to be afraid was using you. She just couldn't let herself believe it would be forever. She'd just enjoy the time they had—at least try to with her mother's outspoken disapproval.

Lifting the phone, she called Sabrina back, pushing her own problems away.

Sabrina had forgotten what money, power, and respect could accomplish. When she told her grandfather what Kara and Tristan planned and that they needed a place to set up, he'd made a phone call. In less than five minutes a representative from the hospital was there to show them a room on the same floor. They even brought in a recliner so her mother could stretch out if she wanted.

Food for at least thirty people along with two servers arrived thirty minutes later. Kara hadn't listened to her when she said six people. She probably remembered that her parents had lots of friends and associates.

It didn't take her long to appreciate the refreshments when, besides the people coming to visit them, the chief of staff, the head of neurosurgery, and a couple of board members stopped by. They knew her father and grandfather, but Cade was the big draw.

She didn't have to be a mind reader to know they wanted him to relocate there. They hadn't been so insensitive as to say anything, but between their effusive praise and their repeating "we need a skilled neurosurgeon like you" it wasn't hard to get the picture.

Cade had quickly drank his coffee and gone back to Stephen's room. The men were left looking uncertain, and Dr. Fielding miffed.

She'd waited until the room was empty to go get Cade so he could eat and relax in peace. Her mother had called her over and asked her to make sure Cade ate something. "I will," she said, happy that her mother had noticed and cared.

It took a bit of doing, but he came back to the makeshift lounge. She prepared him a plate and placed it on the table. "Please sit down and eat."

"Quite a spread." Cade took his seat at the conference table. He'd changed into another scrub suit.

"Thanks to Kara and Tristan." She made a face and stepped behind him to massage his shoulders. "I told her six people. This is for thirty people easily. I told the two servers we didn't need them. This is costly enough. Kara can't afford this."

"She's probably not worried about cost. She wants to help a

friend." He leaned back and stared up at her. "You're a good friend."

She couldn't resist brushing her lips across his. "Some people make it easy to love," she said, her mouth inches from his.

"Sabrina, I told you—"

"And I told you I'm not giving up on us, so tell the bigwigs here that they can't steal you from Texas Hospital in Dallas." She laughed. "You can bet the people in Dallas won't be happy when they hear about this."

"I've already had two 'important' calls. One from the hospital administrator and the other from the chief of staff in Dallas. They wanted to know if there is anything else I need to keep me happy."

"Smart thinking on their part. Stop picking at your food," she said. "You think I can go peek in on Stephen when you're finished?"

"I thought he would be fully awake by now." Twin furrows raced across his brow.

Her hands trembled. "Stephen was always a sleepyhead. He made me late to school more times than I can count."

Cade squeezed her hand. "I bet you were a bossy big sister."

"I prefer decisive."

"Figures." He finished his quiche and juice, then stood and reached for her hand, squeezed it again. "Let's go."

Cade didn't pay any attention to the people waiting, or at least he tried to tell himself that. But it seemed, each time he entered the room, there were more people there. They might have been visitors for the other patients, and perhaps a few were, but the majority of them were for Stephen. Cade was glad for the young man. He needed their prayers.

Inside the cubicle, he released Sabrina's hand and went to

the bedside. Removing a penlight from his pocket, he lifted Stephen's eyelid. The pupil constricted. He breathed a sigh of relief. Progress. The vitals were stable and good. It was up to a higher power now.

He looked up to see Sabrina watching him closely. She trusted him to make this right for her. He did what he never had in the past, said a prayer and offered hope when he wasn't sure. "What are you going to tell him when he wakes up?"

Her smile trembled. Going to Cade, she slid her arms around his waist and just held on. "That I love him. That I found a man to love and he can play the overprotective brother. That he can't—" Her voice broke.

Cade's arms closed around her protectively. "Don't give up hope. You're the strong one."

She sniffed and lifted her eyes to his. "Because you're here. If you weren't, I don't know how I would have gotten through this."

"Bree."

Cade and Sabrina jerked toward the bed. Stephen's eyelids fluttered. Opened. "Bree."

Laughing through her tears, Sabrina caught her brother's hand and tried to stay out of Cade's way as he checked her brother's neuro signs. "I'm here, Stephen. I'm here and so is Mother, Daddy, and our grandparents."

"How do you feel?" Cade asked.

"Head hurts."

"I'll bet." Cade took Stephen's hand. "Squeeze. Good. What's the last thing you remember?"

Frown lines pleated his brows. "Playing ball."

"You were hit by a line drive, but you're going to be all right," Sabrina said. "Can I go get Mother, please?"

"Mother's here?" Stephen asked.

"Where else would she be?" Sabrina asked. Then, realizing what she'd said, looked up at Cade. His face was closed. "Cade—"

"Go get his mother."

"We're going to talk," she said, then rushed out of the room to tell her parents.

Where else would she be? Sabrina's statement rang in Cade's ears as he slipped from Stephen's room and left the ICU. There was no place for him there. He'd served his purpose, just as he had when the man who raised him used him for free labor, just as the patients did when he helped them. No one wanted him for just himself.

Lifting his hand to push open the waiting-room door leading into the hallway, he wondered if anyone ever would. The people who loved Stephen certainly hadn't.

"Cade Mathis, you come back here."

Cade spun on hearing Sabrina's voice. He was as surprised to see her as to hear the sternness in her voice.

Sabrina caught his hand. "I love you. I'll keep telling you until you believe in us. I'm not letting you go. We had a shock, but we can get though this."

Cade wanted to love her, but seeing all the people who should have been his family, he felt like an outsider. "There is no place in this family for me. I gave them Stephen back. Good-bye."

He turned away from the tears in her eyes. *Just keep walking,* he told himself as he headed for the doctors' lounge to change clothes. *Don't hope. You always end up with the shaft.*

In his street clothes, he rode the elevator down to the first floor. The sun was bright, the air muggy. He'd never felt worse or more alone. He was afraid this time the ache wouldn't go away.

He stepped off the sidewalk and started across the drive to his rental. He needed to call his office and have Iris get him the first available flight back to Dallas, but putting one foot in front of the other took all the strength he had. He fished the car keys from his pocket.

"Cade Mathis!"

Hearing Sabrina's voice, he hung his head, silently admitting to himself why he was walking so slow. He wanted to see her again. Yet, he wasn't sure how he could handle seeing her, wanting her, and knowing their impossible situation.

Or was it? His steps slowed.

The man who had raised him had been a cruel, lying bastard who wanted to hurt Cade with every self-righteous breath he drew. He took pleasure in Cade's pain. The best way to do that was by telling him his socialite mother hadn't wanted him.

"Cade."

Sabrina cared about people. She fought for what she believed in. She wouldn't love a selfish woman who only thought about herself and her social standing.

Finally, he turned and frowned. Sabrina wasn't alone. Besides her parents and her grandparents, it looked as if most, if not all, the people in the waiting room were following them. "Why aren't you all upstairs with Stephen?"

Swallowing, Sabrina's mother briefly touched his shoulder. Her teary gaze held him. Her lips trembled. "Because I wanted to introduce my son."

He felt a tightness in his chest. He swallowed, swallowed

again to ease the constriction in his throat. *Son.* He'd waited all of his life to hear his mother say that one word. Sabrina stepped beside him, slipped her hand into his and squeezed.

Mrs. Thomas's smile tremulous, she faced the people behind her. "Thank you for coming with me. I want to introduce someone I'm very proud of, my son, Dr. Cade Mathis, a gifted neurosurgeon. Because of him, Stephen is alive."

People stared from Cade to his mother, their mouths gaping. Questions swirled around them. A young man in the back cracked, "I defy anyone to do our unusual family tree." People laughed.

Sabrina briefly leaned her head against Cade's shoulder. "He might be fighting it, but he's also the man I'm going to marry. You'll all receive wedding invitations."

There were more shocked whispers from the older adults, and the younger ones applauded. Smiling, her mother's parents ushered everyone back into the hospital.

Cade was too emotional to speak. His mother and her parents had looked at him with pride and love. His mother's husband had slapped him proudly on the back.

"You're not alone anymore." Sabrina hugged him. "You just have to believe it, and we'll go from there."

He wanted that more than anything.

"Mother and Granddad made a horrible mistake, but they did it out of love," she whispered. "Sometimes love isn't easy, but it's worth the risk."

Staring down at her, he realized again how much courage Sabrina possessed. She wasn't afraid to lay her feelings out there for him and all the world to see. He pulled her to him. He had to be just as brave. The past needed to stay in the past. "You make me weak, but you also make me believe."

She hugged him harder. "I love you, Cade. Nothing will ever change that."

He smiled. "I finally believe you." Lifting his head, he told her about meeting his father and finished by saying, "Grandfather"—he paused as if savoring the word—"was right. My father hadn't wanted me."

On tiptoe, she kissed him on the lips. "We do."

"I might have a half-brother and a niece," he said, excitement in his voice. "When things settle in my head a little bit, I plan to do some checking."

"I'll help. We'll find them."

He placed his forehead against hers. "You're always there for me."

"Where else would I be?" she said softly.

He recalled her saying the words in relation to her mother and Stephen. Loving someone meant being there for them. "When you come back, we need to talk."

Uneasiness entered her eyes. "Am I going to like this talk?"

Laughing, he kissed her long and hard. He never wanted her to regret loving him. "I certainly hope so. I'll call you tonight."

Her smile returned. "I'll be waiting."

Cade got in the car and pulled away smiling.

Twenty-two

· · · · · · · · · · · · · · · ·

Kara should be feeling great. Sabrina had called to tell her that Stephen was awake and steadily improving. And Kara was days away from the open house. She should be hopping with excitement. She wasn't.

She was driving to Tristan's house later. The sundress she had on was five years old, the small yellow-and-purple flowers faded. She wished she had a pretty summer dress to wear to meet the wife of the builder whose luxury home her paintings were displayed in.

Kara was sure the wife would look great, and so would Tristan's mother, if she happened to drop by. Kara always felt like an old shoe next to her. She'd caught his mother a couple of times looking at her with a frown. She could almost hear her thinking Kara needed a major wardrobe makeover.

Unwillingly Kara recalled Tristan's ex-wife's condescending comments about her clothes. Yet, not once had Vera ever made Kara feel uncomfortable in any way. She was always warm and solicitous, but she still probably wondered what her gorgeous, well-dressed son was doing with Kara.

Kara wondered herself. She heard the kitchen timer go off and headed in that direction. All she needed was to burn her mother's food. Opening the oven, she took out the smothered steak and sat it on the stove, then mashed the potatoes with real butter and cream. Her mother demanded both.

"Dinner ready yet?"

Kara kept whipping the potatoes. "Almost."

She heard then saw her mother lift the top of the casserole top with a pot holder. "I thought you meant a real steak when you said we were having steak."

Kara clenched the handle of the whisk. "T-bones and rib eye are seven ninety-nine a pound."

"You can't afford eight dollars to feed your mother?"

Kara carefully scraped the potatoes into the Lenox dish her mother preferred her food served in. It wouldn't have occurred to her mother that Kara might want a steak as well.

"I asked you a question."

"We have to save every place we can."

"You act like we're paupers. What about those paintings? You promised your daddy to take care of me. We still haven't gone to Dillard's for my shopping trip. I can't do anything fun," her mother complained.

Kara whirled. "Did it ever occur to you that neither can I? You spend four times as much as I do. I pay the house note, the utility bills. You ran up my Dillard's card so much that I can't even use it. What more do you want from me?"

Her mother's lips tightened. "I took care of you and never said a word while you went to college and moved to New Jersey.

The least any self-respecting daughter could do is help out a bit and not complain."

"Father and I paid for my tuition. I worked all through high school and college. I paid for my move. You never worked."

Her mother's chin lifted belligerently. "That doesn't mean I wasn't there helping him manage things. Without me, he would have had nothing. I pushed him every step of the way."

Too hard, Kara wanted to say, but she turned to pour the green beans into a companion serving dish. "Dinner is ready." Stepping around her mother, she placed the dishes on the table. She'd already set the place setting for one. Wordlessly, her mother took her seat and briefly bowed her head.

"I'm going out," Kara said. "I'm not sure when I'll be back."

Her mother turned and pinned her with a look. "I know I told you to watch them, but if you get into trouble you're no daughter of mine. That man is no good, I can tell. He just wants to use you."

The only person using me is you. "I have to go," Kara said. Arguing with her mother never solved anything. It just left her feeling miserable and trapped.

"You just be sure you don't let him cheat you out of the money for the paintings."

Halfway out of the kitchen, Kara stopped. "I trust Tristan. He believes in my paintings."

Her mother sucked her teeth and went back to her food. Kara noted she had a big slice of smothered steak on her plate. "We both know the reason for that."

"Good night, Mother." Trembling with anger, Kara couldn't get to her car fast enough. She had never wanted to be away from her mother as much as she did now.

She was still shaking when she pulled up in front of Tristan's house twenty minutes later. She closed her eyes and leaned back against the seat. She didn't know how much more of this she could take.

The door suddenly opened. Startled, she turned to see Tristan, his brow furrowed. She didn't give herself time to think, she just reached for him. His arms closed securely around her.

"I got you, baby. I got you."

She tried to stem the flow of tears and lost. Tristan placed her on her feet, grabbed her purse, car keys, and then swept her into his arms again. He didn't stop until they were inside and he was sitting on the sofa with her in his arms.

His lips brushed against hers. "I'm here. I'm here."

She felt his warmth, his solidness, enjoyed the comfort he generously offered. He didn't question her, badger her, belittle her. "Why can't she ever be satisfied or happy for me?"

He tensed. His arms gathered her closer. "Baby, I'm sorry."

She looked up at him through tearstained eyes. "Nothing I do pleases her. She always wants more."

He lifted her chin. "You might not like to hear this, but I'm going to tell you anyway."

She pushed upright. "I probably won't."

He caught her face in his hands. "She does it because you let her. When was the last time you said no, gave her back some of her own?"

"She's my mother and I promised Daddy that I'd take care of her," she reminded him.

"Which she uses to her advantage. Stand up to her," he told her, his face hard.

He thought she was weak and a coward. She stood. He was right. "When do you think your friend and his wife will be here?"

Tristan stared at her a long time. "If you don't fight for yourself, you only have yourself to blame."

She picked up her car keys. "I made us some sandwiches. They're in the trunk."

He pushed easily to his feet and took the keys from her. "I might have known. You know where the wine and wine-glasses are and the rest of the things. I'll get the sandwiches while you set up the kitchen." He took a couple of steps away, then turned back and kissed her on the cheek. "You know you can tell me to go to hell and I'll still help you, don't you?"

"I do and I would if you weren't right." She glanced away. "I'm all she has."

"You're all she has, and that hasn't stopped her from telling you what she thinks."

"She's my mother."

"And that's why I bite my tongue when I'm with her. You're a strong, caring woman. One day I hope she'll see that."

Kara shook her head as he walked away. He was wrong. She was weak, not courageous as he'd once said. Worse, her mother would only become more critical and demanding as the years passed.

Once outside, Tristan cursed all the way to Kara's car and all the way back with the tray. She did so much for others, and her mother treated her like crap. She seemed to enjoy belittling Kara. Tristan stopped on the porch and took one, then another, calming breath.

Tonight was important for Kara. It was another person vali-dating her work. In the coming weeks and months she was going to be extremely popular, and he was going to make sure, at least in her paintings, that no one took advantage of her.

Going inside, he went to the kitchen. She had everything set up. He liked seeing her there, could easily imagine her there cooking one of her incredible dishes.

She glanced up, sadness in her eyes. Putting the tray down, he pulled her into his arms and kissed her long and hard. "Think about that or how you're going to be very famous. Nothing else."

Her eyes softened. "Can I think about what a great kisser you are?"

Chuckling, he let her take the easy way out. She wouldn't let herself believe. "You inspire me."

The doorbell rang. She tensed and her eyes widened.

Taking her hand in his, he felt the tiniest tremble. "It's Mother or Zachary and Madison."

"Zachary Holman? Your friend, and the one who helped Dale is the builder of the spec house?"

"One and the same. He's a great guy and so is his wife." Still holding her hand, he went to the front door. He was keeping her close to him. He wasn't going to give her time to get scared or worse, think about her uncaring mother.

Opening the door, he grinned. On the porch was an attractive couple in their thirties. Madison was stylishly dressed in a multicolored sundress. Zachary wore a chambray shirt and jeans.

"Hi, Zachary and Madison, come on in." He grinned and looked behind them. "Where's Zach Jr. and Manda?"

Madison laughed softly. "Mother's night out. Zachary's parents came up for their doctor's appointments, and decided to spend the night. The kids are loving it."

Zachary grinned and kissed his wife on top of her head. "Yeah, I get my wife to myself for a change."

Tristan closed the door. "Zachary and Madison Holman, meet Kara Simmons, the next sensation of the art scene."

Still smiling, he expected Kara to roll her eyes at his introduction. However, she just stared open-mouthed at Madison. "Kara?"

Kara snapped her mouth shut and stared at the nationally known talk show hostess, Madison Reed. "You're famous!"

Madison smiled easily. "On television maybe, but now I'm wife to a man I'm crazy about, and mother to an inquisitive five-year-old and a rambunctious twenty-two-month-old."

"In other words," Tristan said mildly, "she puts her panty hose on the same way you do."

Everyone laughed, including Kara. "I'm sorry. Pleased to meet you. I just admire your work. I only record a couple of shows, and yours is one of them."

"Thank you. I admire your work as well," Madison said. "I can't wait to see more. We have lots of walls to cover and I want quality work, work I can hand down to my grand-children."

Zachary frowned. "I'm not sure I want to think of Manda dating."

Madison patted his arm affectionately and winked at Sabrina. "Then we won't."

"There's food in the kitchen," Kara offered.

"And wine," Tristan added, placing his arms around her. He was pleased that she didn't jump or pull away.

"You didn't have to go to the trouble, but since I was late getting home and haven't eaten, I'm glad you did," Zach said. "Only I'd like a beer."

"Got you covered. Come on into the kitchen." Tristan motioned in that direction.

"I want to see the paintings first," Madison said with a mischievous grin. "I know I should wait and give others a chance to look, but friendship has its privileges."

"You really liked them?" Kara asked.

"Loved would be a better word," Madison said, linking her arm carelessly through Kara's. "The two I already have will go perfectly in the dining room, but then I decided I'd like a couple for the master bedroom. One over the bed and possibly one over the antique accent piece Zachary's mother gave us."

"I'll show you where they are." Grinning broadly, Kara led her from the room.

"I suppose you want to follow them instead of getting my beer," Zachary asked.

"You know I do, just like you want to be with Madison," Tristan said.

"Yeah, but I love Madison," Zachary mused. "I've never seen you this concerned and careful of a woman, not even your ex."

Tristan jerked his head around and held up both hands. "Whoa. We're just seeing each other."

Zachary arched a heavy brow. "Tell that to someone who hasn't been around you and other women."

Tristan was shaking his head before Zachary finished. "She's had a rough time. Any decent person would care."

Zachary grunted. "I fought falling in love with Madison too, but it was the smartest thing I ever did."

"You're wrong," Tristan protested.

"Zachary, come on," Madison called from the other room. "I found a painting I think would be perfect for the guest bedroom."

"I don't think so," Zachary said to Tristan, then louder, "Coming, honey." Zachary left Tristan standing there with a shell-shocked look on his face.

Kara still couldn't believe it. Madison and her husband purchased two more paintings. Neither blinked nor protested when Tristan quoted two thousand dollars each—which included the friends and family discount—if she didn't mind.

Kara wildly shook her head and felt light-headed as she watched Zachary pull a check from his shirt pocket and make it out to her. Her hand shook when she took it. She stared at the amount. She'd pressed it to her chest with trembling hands, then looked at it again. "Thank you."

"Thank you," Madison said.

"I'm ready for that food," Zachary said.

"I'll fix your plate." Kara hurried to the kitchen, still finding it difficult to believe she'd sold four paintings. Placing the check on the counter, she began preparing their plates while Tristan poured the wine. He winked at her. She grinned.

It was real!

Tristan lifted his glass. "To Kara and a long, successful career as a professional artist."

"To Kara," Zachary and Madison echoed.

Kara's grin widened. She touched her glass to theirs, sipped her wine. She turned to Tristan. "Thank you. If not for you—"

"It would have happened," he interrupted. "You're too talented for it not to have happened." He slung his arm over her shoulders. "But I'm glad I was there to see it happen."

"Me too," she said, tempted to kiss him.

"You know I'm going to want to hang them tonight, but we'll have to wait until tomorrow for Manda to help," Madison said.

"Your little girl?" Kara asked.

"Yep," Zachary said proudly, finishing off his beer. "She has her own tiny tool set. One day Holman Construction will belong to her and her brother." He glanced at his watch and came to his feet, holding Madison's chair as she did the same. "We better get going. We try to read the kids a story and tuck them into bed whenever possible."

Kara couldn't remember one time her mother had tucked her into bed or read her a story, just her father. "You're both lucky people."

Zachary and Madison smiled at each other. "We think so," he said. "One day I hope you're as lucky."

Kara didn't dare look at Tristan for fear he'd see the love and longing in her eyes. "I hope so too."

"I'll help you load the pictures in your truck." Together, he and Zachary wrapped the paintings in a heavy mover's blanket and put them into Zachary's truck.

"Once all the pictures are hung, I'd like to invite you and Tristan over to see them," Madison offered from the passenger seat a short time later.

"I'd like that." Kara stepped away from the truck as it came to life. "Good night."

"We'll see you this weekend at the open house," Madison said. "Good night."

"Good night." Tristan waved. His arm around her, he led her back inside. "Happiness looks good on you."

"It feels good too." Her arms slid around his waist. "Thank you."

He frowned down at her. "Are you standing here because you're grateful?"

"Does it make a difference?"

"With you, it does."

Her smile was slow and seductive. "I'm here because I want to be. You make me feel things that scare me, excite me."

He pulled her closer. "I feel the same way about you."

"Good." She reached for the hem of his knit shirt. "Now, let's go celebrate in style."

Cade was busy until late Thursday night. He seriously considered chartering a plane back to Houston for the night but he'd had an emergency surgery. He missed Sabrina. In the doctors' lounge, he plopped down in a chair and called her.

"Hi. I was waiting for your call," Sabrina answered.

He came upright. "Is everything all right?"

"Yes, Stephen is getting stronger by the hour," Sabrina said. "He wants to meet you when he's not so out of it. Father and Grandfather told him the four of you would catch a Rangers game before the summer is over."

"I've never been to one of their baseball games," Cade said, relaxing back in the chair and admitting to himself he'd like that. "When do you plan to come back?"

"If Stephen keeps improving I'm thinking of Saturday."

Cade blew out a breath. "I hope I can last that long."

"I'll make it up to both of us."

He grinned. "I'll pick you up. Give your family my phone numbers. We'll have dinner at my place." Afterward, he was taking her to bed, and he didn't plan to let her out for a long, long time.

"Thank you. We'd all feel better if we stayed in touch."

He'd put it off long enough. "How-how is she? There must be questions about me."

"There are, but Mother just tells them she chooses not to discuss it. You're her son and that's all that matters."

He'd had time to think and knew there would be a lot of gossip associated with her announcement. She hadn't had to tell anyone about him. Stephen was out of danger. Perhaps there was hope for them.

"Have you done anything about locating the people who might be your half-brother and niece?" she asked.

"No." He started to say he'd been busy, but if anyone would understand it would be Sabrina. "I didn't want to be disappointed again, but it should be easy to find Madison Reed since she's so well known, and through her her husband and their daughter. Getting the opportunity to speak to them privately is another matter."

"I'll start on the research while I'm here. When I get back, we'll find a way to meet her and the rest of your family," Sabrina told him.

His family. He'd never allowed himself to hope. Sabrina had changed his life in so many ways.

"You have me now," she said.

"That's finally sinking in."

"Good."

He smiled. "Good night, Sabrina. We'll talk tomorrow."

"Good night, my love."

Kara refused to go to the open house in an old dress. She'd thought about it all day at work and warred with herself about the expense, then decided a little after three that afternoon, that for once, she wasn't going to think about the cost. She deserved a new dress.

Opening her office door, she took a seat behind her desk and picked up the phone. Sabrina would know the perfect place.

Tristan didn't seem to mind what she wore. Kara smothered a giggle as she dialed. Perhaps because she didn't keep it on for long once they were alone.

"Hello."

"Hello," Kara said. "I'm glad you have your phone on. You sound like your old self."

"Cade is responsible for both," Sabrina said happily. "Stephen is going to make it, and I think Cade finally realized he can't live without me."

Kara's laugh joined Sabrina's. "He never had a chance."

"How about you and Tristan?"

Kara sobered. "He cares, but I'm not sure if it's the forever kind."

"But for you, it is." It was a statement not a question.

Kara gazed at the pictures of her father. "Yes."

"Love has a way of doing that. I thought it was lust," Sabrina whispered the last word. "But it was so very much more."

"I'm happy for both of you," Kara said.

"Tomorrow is the beginning of your big weekend. You're exited?"

"And terrified," Kara confessed. "I'm thinking a dress would help a great deal."

"Now, you're talking. Patrice is a fantastic boutique off Lemon and also the name of the owner. Ask for her, and tell her I sent you. She's fabulous. You won't go wrong."

"I knew you'd help me. It might be a little vain, but I'd like to at least try and hold my own with Tristan's mother and Madison Reed. Both look terrific."

"What did you say about Madison Reed?"

"She's married to Zachary Holman, the builder of the spec house Vera is decorating with my paintings. I told you she bought two paintings. Well, last night she and her husband came over to Tristan's house and they bought two more. I wanted to pinch myself. She looked even more fabulous in person than she does on television," Kara explained.

"Oh, my goodness."

Kara caught the change in Sabrina's voice. "What is it?"

"I hope to explain soon, but know everything is all right and I have to call Cade."

"You're sure everything is all right?"

"Positive. I want to hear about the two fabulous dresses you're going to buy."

"Two?"

"You can't wear the same dress for Saturday and Sunday," Sabrina said.

"You're right. Go call Cade. I think I'll leave early for once and go shopping. Good-bye."

"Good-bye." Sabrina disconnected the call, started to call Cade, then changed her mind. This news needed to be delivered in person. Slipping the cell phone into the pocket of her slacks, she went to tell her family she was flying back to Dallas. Cade needed her.

Twenty-three

. . . .

Kara's plan to leave early hit a snag with the unexpected discharge of a patient living alone who needed help finding a home health agency for daily dressing changes that accepted his insurance. By the time she'd matched the patient and the agency, it was after five. She grabbed her purse and hit the door. Luckily, Patrice was on the corner of the busy shopping complex and the parking spot gods were with her as a car pulled out a few doors down.

Sabrina was right again, Kara thought as she hurried past the beautiful clothes displayed in the window that ranged from casual to elegant all with style and glamour. She opened the door of the spacious shop and headed for the counter, noting several other shoppers in the store and three deep at the two cash registers.

Kara glanced at her watch: 5:27. The shop closed at six. She went to the closest cashier. "Please excuse me," Kara said to the woman waiting in front of the line, then to the cashier, "This is sort of an emergency. My name is Kara Simmons. Sabrina

Thomas said I should ask for Patrice and to tell her that she sent me."

The cashier smiled at Kara, then spoke to the woman waiting. "Is it all right if I take a moment to call?"

The well-dressed woman with several items of clothes looked from Kara's wind-blown hair, past the seven-year-old navy blue suit to her sensible pumps. "Definitely an emergency. Make the call."

"Thank you," Kara said, trying not to notice that the other women in line were looking at her as well.

"You wanted to see me?"

Kara turned at the slightly husky voice and blinked. The woman was at least five-nine, stunning, with a figure to match. She wore a sleeveless coral and black sheath that stopped mid-thigh, and silver bangles jingled on both of her toned arms. She looked elegant and earthy.

"Ms. Simmons," she prompted.

"Sorry," Kara said, extending her hand. "I didn't expect you—I mean . . ."

"That's all right. I caught you off guard. I'm Patrice Solomon, how can I help you?" The handshake was brief.

Kara quickly explained the situation. "I don't want to look like this."

"That won't be a problem," Patrice said drolly. "Come with me."

Kara followed. True to her word, in less than fifteen minutes, Patrice had found four dresses that Kara fell in love with and accessories to match. Although she said she wouldn't, she took a peek at the price tags and almost swooned.

"I like the peach and the white. Both can take you from a pool party to a night on the town with just a simple change of jewelry and shoes," Patrice said. "It's almost closing. I'll leave you to decide."

Kara nodded. She was aware that Patrice had seen the sticker shock on her face and was giving her time alone. She wanted to be sensible, then thought why? For once, just go for it. She picked up the two dresses, the accessories, and hurried to the cashier. Patrice said there was a shoe shop a couple of doors down that closed at eight.

"I see Patrice worked her usual magic," the middle-aged cashier Kara had spoken to earlier said, smiling. "Will that be cash, check, or charge?"

"Charge." Kara opened her wallet, drew out the credit card she saved for emergencies, and handed it to the smiling woman. It would be the only charge on the card when the bill came in and she could pay off the balance with Zachary's check in her wallet.

The cashier's smile faltered as she swiped the card for a second time. "Do you have another card? This one has been declined."

"Declined! There must be a mistake. The card has a zero balance. Please run it again." Kara remembered paying off the balance when the water heater burst in the end of December.

"I'm sorry." She handed the card to Kara. "Do you have another card?"

"There must be a mistake," Kara said, taking the card and pulling out her cell. "Please hold these things while I call."

"Of course," the cashier said, moving the merchandise aside and motioning for the next woman in line.

Kara went to a quiet corner and called customer service for the credit card. In less than a minute, she was talking to a representative. She shook her head. "There must be a mistake. I can't be over my credit limit or behind on a payment. You must have my account mixed up." She repeated her credit card number and was given the same information. Perhaps someone had stolen her card, she was told.

"I have the card in my hand," Kara replied. "Where and when were the charges made?" she demanded, ready to dispute each one. But as the man on the other end went through the charges and dates, Kara's anger shifted in a different direction.

"Do you recognize any of those retailers or the merchandise?" the man asked, then repeated the question when Kara didn't answer.

"How could she?" Kara whispered.

"What did you say?" the man asked.

"Good-bye." Kara had never felt so angry or such embarrassment when she turned to see Patrice a short distance away. Stiffening her shoulders, Kara went to her. "I'm sorry to have wasted your time."

"Helping a customer is never a waste of time," Patrice said graciously and handed Kara her card. "We open at ten on Saturdays, but I'm usually here by nine."

With over a five-thousand-dollar bill hanging over her head, there was no way she could even think about buying the clothes. She slipped the card into her pocket. "I'm sorry. Please put everything back. Good-bye." Kara walked from the shop, her anger growing with each step. Her mother had finally crossed the line.

Sabrina grabbed a taxi and went straight to Cade's office. She'd spoken briefly to his office manager and knew he was scheduled to be there until six to see the patients he'd had to reschedule. During the taxi ride, Sabrina Googled Zachary Holman and located his construction company. By the time she arrived at Cade's office, she had an appointment with Zachary at the open house site at seven that night.

After reading several articles about him and the scandal of Madison's announcement that they were going to get married and raise her husband's child by another woman, Sabrina thought Cade might be right about Zachary possibly being his half-brother. She'd thought of requesting the appointment as newly-weds or newly engaged, but she didn't want Cade to think she was being pushy. In the end she'd given a false name.

Paying the driver, Sabrina went to Cade's office and straight to the reception window. "It's extremely important that I see Cade when he's free. Please tell him that Sabrina Thomas is here."

The older woman's eyes narrowed. "You sent all those things."

"Yes."

"I don't guess you'd be here if your brother wasn't doing well." She came to her feet. "I'll show you to his office and tell him you're here." She met Sabrina at the door leading to the exam rooms. "Iris Johnson. Glad to finally meet you. You did what I was beginning to think impossible."

"I love him," Sabrina said simply.

"It shows. On both of you." Iris opened another door. "Make yourself comfortable."

"Thank you." Sabrina stepped inside the office, where she was struck by all the degrees, certificates, accolades, the shelves that held books and journals, but none of the family mementos and items her father and grandfather liked. That would change.

The door opened behind her. She whirled to see Cade. "I found Zachary Holman."

Kara screeched to a halt in her drive and slammed out of the car. She went straight to her mother's closed door. She opened it without knocking.

Her mother rose up from the chaise longue. "What's wrong with you?"

Kara went to the walk-in closet and pushed open the sliding doors. "Where are they?"

"Where's what?" her mother called. "Get out of my closet."

Kara ignored her mother and went to the back of the closet. Her teeth clenched on seeing the dust covers for four designer handbags. There were six hanging bags with clothes.

"You get out of there," her mother called from directly behind her.

Kara whirled, stepped around her mother, and went to where she kept her jewelry. The diamond earrings were in a velvet case by themselves. Kara picked them up and faced her mother. "Why? Just tell me why?"

"I need things and you're too stingy and mean to give them to me," she said, reaching for the earrings.

Kara kept them out of reach. "So badly that you stole my credit card?"

"Don't you dare talk to me like that," she said. "I saw that check in your wallet." Kara's eyes widened. "You weren't planning to tell me, were you? If you were paid that much for four paintings, you stand to make a small fortune when you sell the rest, so stop complaining."

"Why did you have me?" Kara asked. "Why? Answer me!"

Her mother flinched, then her eyes narrowed. "Because your daddy kept on me about having a baby," she shouted. "I grew up with nothing. There was never enough to go around with fourteen children, not food, not clothes, not love. I swore when I got grown and married I'd have it all." Her eyes fired. "Your daddy promised he'd give me anything I wanted. He promised."

"And worked two jobs, sometimes three, that sent him to an early grave, to give it to you," Kara said, her voice and body trembling. "Did you ever love either of us?"

"I wanted someone just for me," she said.

"That's what you had, but you were too greedy and too selfish to recognize it." Kara tossed the earrings on the bed. "I'm leaving."

"Where're you going?"

"Anywhere, as long as it's away from you." In her room, she grabbed an overnight bag and stuffed things inside.

"If you think he wants you for anything more than what you're giving him, you're wrong," her mother said nastily. "He doesn't want you."

Kara jerked up her bag. "Neither do you."

"You come back here! You promised your daddy!" her mother screamed, trailing after her. "Who's gonna take care of me?"

Kara whirled at the door. "That's no longer my problem. Good-bye." Kara went through the door, hearing her mother screaming her name. She got in her car, backed up, and drove away with absolutely no idea where she was going.

. . .

Cade pulled up behind the big black truck at a quarter to seven. He'd never been this anxious, not even the first time he'd assisted in the operating room.

"It's going to be all right," Sabrina said from beside him.

He caught the hand that reached out to him. She was his one constant. "As long as I have you, it will be. Come on." Releasing her hand, he got out. By the time he rounded the car, a tall, brown-skinned man with broad shoulders was coming down the walkway. Cade paused, then felt Sabrina join him and curve her arm around his waist.

"You must be Mr. and Mrs. Thompson." The man extended his hand, tipped his baseball cap to Sabrina. "I'm Zachary Holman of Holman Construction."

Cade had been studying the man for any resemblance so intently it took him a moment to remember he and Sabrina were the Thompsons looking for their second home. The handshake was firm, the eye contact direct. "Thank you for seeing us on such short notice," Cade said.

"No problem." Zachary glanced back at the two-story mansion with a balcony on the second floor. "It gave me a chance to look everything over again before the open house. Come on, I'll show you and your wife around."

"Thank you," Sabrina said.

"If you like to cook, Mrs. Thompson, the kitchen has all Viking appliances with a Sub-Zero refrigerator, warming oven, and wine refrigerator. After seeing the hardwoods on the floor and the cabinets, my wife has been hinting at remodeling our kitchen." He opened one of the iron doors and stepped back for them to enter first.

Although Cade wasn't interested in a house, he was impressed by the extensive use of molding, the wide Italian marble entryway, the double staircase, the infinity pool beyond the wall of glass in the living room. Sabrina paused to look at the paintings in the entryway.

"They're good, aren't they? The artist, Kara Simmons, will be here tomorrow. You'll see her work throughout the house. She's a talented young woman," Zachary said.

"You don't mind spotlighting someone else's work at your open house?" Sabrina asked, almost positive of the answer.

"Of course not," he said easily. "Her work shows the house better. Besides, I was always taught that if you could help someone, do it."

"Did your father teach you that?" Cade asked.

"And my mother," Zachary said.

Cade couldn't wait any longer. "What about your biological father?"

Zachary frowned. "What?"

"A.J. Reed," Cade answered.

Anger swept across Zachary's face in a heartbeat. His weight shifted. "Get out of my house. Now!"

Cade realized he had to talk fast. "I was given up for adoption when I was less than a day old. I grew up not knowing about my biological parents until recently. I learned a few days ago that A.J. Reed, no matter how despicable, is my father. I went to meet him and he talked about Wes, the only son he'll ever recognize, but he also talked of you finally stepping into Wes's shoes. He was livid and stopped short of saying he wasn't going to 'claim' you.

"I guessed you were his son, and the daughter you and your wife are raising was Wes's. A.J. became nervous and denied the little girl was his granddaughter. Since I later found out it's public knowledge that Manda was Wes's, I reasoned he must be afraid of you. There has to be a compelling reason for a braggart like A.J. to fear you." Cade swallowed. "Are you my half-brother? Do I have a niece?"

Zachary stared at Cade a long time.

"Please," Sabrina said. "All he wants is to know if you're related. You can ask Tristan about him. Kara is my best friend."

"Let me see your driver's license," Zachary said.

Cade pulled out his wallet and flipped it open. "We didn't give you our real names because Sabrina just found out today from Kara that you were married to Madison and how to locate you. I wanted to meet you privately. What other information do you need?"

"I was looking for your birth date," Zachary said.

Cade lifted his head. "What?"

"A.J. is scum."

"No argument there." Cade's mouth flattened. "He talked of his conquests. He uses women and thinks it makes him a bigger man."

"What do you think?"

"Besides hoping his balls fall off, that my mother was better off that he walked away. His poor wife must be miserable."

"Vanessa is cut from the same mean cloth as A.J. They hate each other and make each other miserable," Zachary said.

"Then you do know them," Cade said.

"Unfortunately."

"Are you my half-brother? Is A.J. your father?"

"Ben Holman is my father."

"I see." Cade tucked his head.

"You still have me," Sabrina said softly.

His head lifted. "Sorry to bother you, Mr. Holman."

Zachary walked them to the door. "No more questions?"

Cade shook his head. "I guess not."

"Mind if I ask one?" Zachary asked.

With his arm around Sabrina, Cade stopped. "I guess you're entitled."

"Why did you believe me and not A.J.?" Zachary asked.

"Because you don't have a BS meter that's off the chart. A.J. hates you, Madison, and his son's daughter. I just met you, but you impressed me as a man I would have enjoyed getting to know," Cade answered. "Any other questions?"

"Just one."

"Yes?"

"What kind of little brother do you think you'll make?"

Stunned, Cade stood there. Zachary slapped Cade on the shoulder and stuck out his hand. "Nice to meet you, Cade."

"I don't understand," Sabrina said.

"Ben Holman married my mother when I was eight years old." Zachary's face hardened. "I don't think of A.J. as my father."

"I understand," Cade said, and he did. It was difficult to believe you came from a man so totally without morals or values. "I know it's asking a lot, but do you think I could meet Manda in the near future?"

"No time like the present. My parents came up for the open house so you can meet them as well, and don't worry, Mama is the best." Zachary set the alarm and closed the door. "Let's go meet the rest of your family."

Kara got as far as the registration desk of the hotel, then returned to her car. She knew where she wanted to be and it wasn't crying alone in a hotel room. Getting back in her car, she drove to Tristan's house and parked behind his truck. Getting out, she left the overnight bag and rang the doorbell.

The door swung open. "Where've you been? I've call— What did she do—" He broke off, caught Kara's arm, and didn't let go until they were in the kitchen. Muttering, he poured her a glass of wine and brought it back. "Drink."

She did because he wasn't taking no for an answer.

He surged to his feet, slammed the glass down on the table, paced, then came back to hunker before her. "You are not going back there tonight or ever. Mother was going to tell you tomorrow, but I think you need to hear it now. Zachary gave her permission to take clients by the spec house. You sold seven more paintings. You have more than enough money to find another place."

He didn't want her. Tears rolled down her cheeks.

"Don't you do that." He picked her up and sat back down with her in his lap. "Stop it. If she wasn't your mother—" He bit off and rocked her, stroked her hair. "You're staying here tonight. Tomorrow is going to be the beginning of a fabulous career as an artist and a new life."

Kara choked back a sob. "I don't have a dress. Mama maxed out my credit card." She showed him Patrice's business card and told him what had happened at the dress shop and at home. "I've never been so embarrassed. I can't go tomorrow, not wearing this, but it's all I have."

Tristan cursed silently. "It will be all right. I promise. No one is going to hurt you again. No one."

He knew she heard him, but she didn't answer. Rising, he took her upstairs to his bed, removed her jacket, skirt, and heels and tucked her under the covers. "I'll get your bag and be right back." He kissed her on the cheek.

Partially closing the door, he went downstairs to get her keys out of her handbag. He reached inside as her phone rang. He picked it up and saw her mother's name. His anger hit the boiling point. Knowing he shouldn't didn't keep him from activating the call. "You won't hurt her again."

"I want to speak to Kara," the woman screeched. "You're just using her."

Tristan's temper went up a notch. "Unlike you, I care about her and want what's best for her. I don't degrade and belittle her every chance I get."

"No, you sweet talk her and use her for a convenient bed partner. Using her stupid dreams against her."

"She isn't stupid, and neither are her dreams."

"What do you call thinking you're going to marry her. Ha! You'll use her and move on. I warned her, but she wouldn't listen. She was a fool to fall in love with a pretty face. You'll get tired of her, but I want what's mine when she sells those pictures. You hear me?"

Tristan disconnected the call, then shut it off. He turned and went back upstairs. Curled in a fetal position, Kara had gone to sleep.

She loved him. He waited for the fear, the urge to flee, but all he wanted to do was get closer, fight to make her happy. Zachary and his mother had tried to tell him that for him, Kara was different, but he hadn't wanted to listen. She'd quietly captured his heart. She gave so much and received so little in return. That was going to change.

He picked up the card that had fallen from her hand off the floor and left the room. He hit speed dial on the kitchen phone.

"Hello."

"Hello, Vera." He quickly explained. "I don't think I can stand to see her crying or feeling less. Can you help me?"

"What kind of woman would do that to her own child?" Vera questioned, anger in her voice.

"And despite it all Kara still loves her. How can anyone toss away that kind of love?"

"Her mother is selfish and greedy, but there are others who are so busy running that they don't see what's right in front of them."

Tristan shifted. He was sure the conversation had become personal. "Can you help me find the shop's owner?"

"Be stubborn," Vera said. "I've heard of her shop. Let me make some phone calls. If all else fails, we'll be there in the morning when the shop opens."

"You'll be late," he reminded her.

"So, we're late. This is more important."

"I love you, Mother."

"I love you too. Bye."

Tristan hung up the phone. If it were possible, Vera would come through for him. Grabbing the keys, he went to get Kara's bag from her car.

Twenty-four

. . . .

want you to meet Sabrina Thomas, and Dr. Cade Mathis, my younger brother."

With those words, Zachary introduced Cade to his family. Since there had been no hesitation, no strange looks, Cade was sure Zachary had called ahead. Still, it was surreal sitting there talking to them over a delicious strawberry pound cake and coffee.

Manda was a charmer. Cade had become Uncle Cade to her almost immediately. She'd tried to use his presence as an excuse not to go to bed. She'd explained she and her brother, Zach Jr., deserved to stay up. The little boy had a winning smile and quick laughter. The family was obviously happy, as was Zachary's mother. Cade didn't try to figure out why she'd kept Zachary while Cade's mother had chosen to give him up. It no longer mattered. Life had taken, but it had given him so much more. It had made him the man he was today.

Cade whispered in Manda's ear and put something in her hand. She giggled, then walked directly to Sabrina.

"Uncle Cade said this belongs to you." She opened her hand. In the center of her palm was a glistening princess-cut eight-karat diamond solitaire.

Sabrina gasped and her eyes teared.

Cade plucked the ring from his niece's hand, got down on one knee. Neither seemed to notice the phone camera Zachary aimed at them. Taking her trembling hand, he slipped the ring on her finger. "You are everything I ever wanted before I knew what it was. I wasn't really living until you pushed your way into my life and made me like it. I love you with all of my heart. Once I had no one. Because of you I'll never be alone again. Will you to marry me?"

"Yes! Yes!" She launched herself at him, propelling him backward, kissing him. Thinking it a game, Manda and her brother joined them on the floor, giggling.

Cade came up with one arm around Sabrina, the other around Manda. Zach Jr. was in his lap. "Tomorrow after the open house we have reservations to fly to Houston. I'll ask your father's permission to marry you, and we can check on Stephen."

"I wanna go," Manda said.

"Me too," Zach Jr. joined in.

Everyone laughed. Zachary plucked up one child, then the other, sending them into peals of laughter. "Not this time."

"But soon," Cade promised, holding Sabrina tighter as he handed her his phone to call and speak with her parents.

Neither he nor Zachary had discussed how or if they'd let friends and coworkers know they were related, or the possibility of their mothers meeting. For Cade, he was content to let Zachary make the decision. Cade had what he'd always wanted and dared not let himself believe, family.

But he couldn't help but think about the "others" A.J. had

mentioned. What kind of life had they had? Were they looking for a family just as Cade had been? Were they as lucky as Zachary had been? Cade didn't want to upset Zachary's mother or his—he didn't choke as he thought of her—but Cade knew that before long, he'd seek out the answers to his questions and hoped Zachary would help.

Tristan hadn't thought it possible, but Vera hadn't been able to come up with a private phone number for Patrice. He would have laughed at Vera's annoyance if the situation hadn't been so important. He stared at Kara still asleep, then her phone.

Sabrina might know Patrice's number. He'd already crossed the line once by answering Kara's phone. He'd invade her privacy if he scrolled though her phone numbers. It couldn't be helped. He turned back to her phone to call Sabrina, looking down at Kara.

She loved him. She'd forgive him. He looked at her again as the phone powered up. He'd shout like a kid with a new toy, strut like a rooster if she were happy. If tearstains weren't on her cheeks.

He stepped out of the room, prepared to do whatever necessary. He found recent calls, Sabrina's number, and hit CALL BACK.

"Kara, I've been trying to call you. You'll never guess or maybe you will."

"Sabrina, this is Tristan. Kara is all right, but I need your help. Do you know how to reach Patrice?" he asked.

"Why do you have Kara's cell?"

He wasn't sure how much to tell her. "She's upstairs. She

wasn't able to get her clothes at Patrice's shop. I'd like to get them for her."

"I'll take care of it. Was her mother the reason?"

"I'd rather not say," he said.

Sabrina muttered something unladylike. "Listen, Tristan, my grandmother has a saying, make your move or move along. You get my meaning?"

"Perfectly."

"Good-bye."

For a man who thought he was pretty smart, he certainly hadn't acted like it. He stepped back into the bedroom. He might be slow, but he was a fast learner. Now that he'd stopped denying his feelings for Kara, he was going to do everything in his power to keep her love and make her happy.

Kara woke up slowly. She felt the warmth pressed against her back, her legs, and she knew Tristan was in bed with her. "How long have I been asleep?"

He snuggled closer and kissed her ear. "A bit. You hungry?"

"No."

"You should eat something. I can order takeout."

She angled her head to look at him. "You hungry?"

He shrugged.

Patting his leg, she sat up. "What do you want?"

"Whatever I can get."

Kara glanced at him and stood. He was looking at her so intently that she wondered if she might have said she loved him in her sleep. "You all right?"

"Getting there."

"Tristan—" The doorbell interrupted her.

He rolled from the bed and took her hand. "That's for you."

Frowning, she allowed him to pull her downstairs to the front door. Shock widened her eyes when she saw Sabrina and Cade. Then they were hugging, and Kara wasn't sure when the tears started. She accepted the handkerchief Tristan handed her. "I'm sorry."

"You have nothing to be sorry for," Sabrina said. "Do you want to talk about it?"

"No." Kara emphatically shook her head. "Since you're here it means Stephen is still improving."

"Yes," Sabrina told her. "We're flying back to Houston tomorrow after the open house."

Kara teared up again.

"No, you don't," Tristan said in a panic. "Please, honey, stop crying."

"You don't understand," she said.

"You might be wrong about that." Sabrina handed her a garment and a shopping bag. "Patrice said these belonged to you."

Kara gasped, reached for the dresses, then jerked her hands back. "How—" She shook her head. "I can't afford them."

Tristan took the dresses and held them out to Kara. "Yes, you can. There'll be lots of media there tomorrow. You'll look great in anything, but you wanted these."

"Thank you," Kara said, taking the dresses and the shopping bag, but she still didn't sound happy. She placed everything on a nearby chair.

At a total loss, Tristan stared at Sabrina for a clue and she stared back. Cade picked up her left hand.

"You're engaged," Tristan burst out, and earned a look of annoyance from both.

Kara grabbed Sabrina's hand and hugged her, then Cade. "I'm so happy for both of you." She picked up Sabrina's hand again, stared at the ring, then looked at Cade. "She never wavered. She always knew you were the one. You two have something very precious. I can't even begin to imagine how happy you both must be."

For some reason, Kara's statement annoyed Tristan. "You aren't happy with me?"

Kara turned, her smile tremulous. "Of course, but it's not the same."

"What's that supposed to mean?"

Kara threw an embarrassed glance at Cade and Sabrina. "We'll talk about it later."

"No. I want to know why I don't make you happy," he said, then only had to look at her tear-ravaged face for his answer. He muttered a curse, shoved both hands over his head. He recalled Kara saying that Sabrina never wavered and always knew. He'd made no secret that he'd wanted to get her into bed. He'd offered her nothing but good times between the sheets and she had given him so much more.

"This isn't your fault," Kara said.

"It still tears me up inside to see you with tears on your face. I should be able to make things better for you, and I can't."

"Yes, you can," Kara said, taking his shoulders. "You gave me hope. No one, not even my father, was able to do that."

"But it's not enough to replace the tears on your face," he said, his voice ragged.

"Tristan, it's not your fault."

"Whose then? A man who loves a woman as much as I love you should be able to keep her happy!"

Kara went still. Her mouth opened but nothing came out. She trembled all over. "You love me?"

Gently he took her into his arms. "I'm not sure when it happened, but you mean everything to me." His hand brushed the hair from her face. "As much as I hate to admit it, I probably would have kept on denying the truth if your mother hadn't said you love me."

"What!" Kara pushed out of his arms. "So you feel sorry for me?"

"That's so stupid I won't even answer."

"Are you calling me stupid?"

"I'm calling you my heart, the air I breathe, the reason I wake up with a smile in the morning, the woman I want to grow old with. The woman I'd fight the world for." He took her face in his. "Will you marry me?"

Tears crested in her eyes. Panic filled Tristan. "Please don't say no. I don't know what I'll do if you're not in my life."

"I feel the same way about you. I didn't know what living and being loved truly felt like until you came into my life." Her lips curved upward. "Yes, I'll marry you."

"Kara," he whispered, kissing her with a tenderness that caused tears to well up in her eyes again.

"Congratulations," Cade said, extending his hand to Tristan. "You're going to have a lot to celebrate tomorrow."

Kara smiled. "With the dresses, I won't embarrass you or your mother."

He glared at her. "That could never happen. We're both proud of you. She'll be showing you off tomorrow as much as I will. What you wear doesn't matter."

"Spoken like a man," Sabrina said. "Patrice picked your

shoes and accessories out in less than five minutes. She's awesome."

"Not as awesome as you are," Cade and Tristan said, staring at the women they loved. Sabrina and Kara melted in their fiancées' arms.

"We're lucky men, Cade," Tristan said.

"I know," Cade replied with a grin. "I'm sure they won't let us forget it."

Sabrina laughed. "You're so right."

"I still can't believe it," Kara said, leaning against Tristan.

"I'll remind you of this on our silver wedding anniversary." Tristan pulled her closer.

"Give me a hug so we can leave you two alone to talk," Sabrina said. "We'll have a long talk when I get back. Tomorrow you'll be too busy. Maybe we'll lock ourselves in my office Monday once news gets out we're both engaged and about your success."

"The hospital grapevine will be jumping," Kara agreed, grinning back. "I don't know how you did it, but thanks for the dresses. I'll pay—"

Sabrina held up her hand to silence Kara and Tristan. "No to both of you. I helped my best friend and got to see her become engaged to a wonderful man on the same night I became engaged. That's a priceless memory." Sabrina blinked back tears. "We're outta here. See you tomorrow."

To cries of good night, Cade and Sabrina drove away. His arm around her waist, Tristan and Kara went back inside. "Let's call Vera and tell her the good news, then we'll go celebrate."

"In bed," Kara said, leaning into him.

"Why break a great tradition?" he said, his mouth finding hers.

"You sure you want to do this?" Tristan asked as he stopped in Kara's driveway a little after nine the next morning.

Kara grabbed his hand. "She's my mother. She might not feel the connection, but I do. No matter what, I can't turn my back on her."

"I'm going with you."

She squeezed his hand. "She can't hurt me anymore. I have you and a future."

"You amaze me." Tristan kissed her hand.

"It's because of your faith and love that I can do this." She looked at the house she had grown up in, recalled the good memories, the bad. "Last night I was a miserable wreck."

"I didn't realize until later that Cade held up Sabrina's hand to demonstrate the power of love," Tristan said thoughtfully. "I get that now."

"We both do." Kara opened the car door and got out. At the hood of the car, Tristan reached for her hand again. They went up the steps. On the porch, she rang the doorbell and waited.

The door opened. Her mother's angry gaze went from Kara to Tristan beside her. "He get tired of you already?"

Kara felt Tristan tense beside her. "I tried to love you, tried to do what Daddy asked, but I can't. I can't live with hate."

"You promi—"

"It's over, Mother. I'll set up a household account that should take care of the bills and give you a reasonable amount to spend," Kara said calmly. "If you go over that amount, you'll have to live with the consequences."

"Now that you're going to be rich, you want to forget about me," her mother screeched. "That dress is new. So are the shoes and the jewelry. You ungrateful sl—"

Tristan said one precise word. "Don't."

Fear widening her eyes, her mother grabbed the lapels of her silk robe and staggered back.

"Tristan and I are engaged," Kara said, and watched the disbelief, the unexpected anger in her mother's face. She wanted Kara to be as unhappy as she was. Kara felt sorry for her. "Goodbye, Mother. I'll send someone for my things." Turning, Kara went back down the steps and got into the car.

"You all right?" he asked, backing up and pulling off. "Kara?"

Her smile was shaky, but it was there. "With your love, I'll get there. My life is ahead of me, not behind me. I'll forever regret that we can't be close, but I thank God with every breath that I have you."

"Always."

She caught his hand. "Always."

Half past ten Saturday morning Cade held Sabrina in his arms and thanked God for her. Sleeping on top of him, she stirred. He kissed the top of her head, murmured for her to go back to sleep. She had to be worn out. They'd made love most of the night. The thought brought a smile to his lips, and a hardening to his lower body.

He chuckled softly. Seems he couldn't get enough of the woman who had captured his heart, and made life fun.

"What's so funny?" Sabrina murmured, lifting her head from his chest to smile at him.

"A certain part of my anatomy can't get enough of you," he

told her, sweeping the hair back from her face. It was easy to talk with her.

She grinned, wiggled. "You notice I'm not complaining."

"No." She was always there for him. "I didn't know what living and loving really meant until you came into my life."

Her smile trembled. She placed her hand over his. "Loving you is what I was destined to do."

"I'm a blessed man," he said, meaning it with all of his heart. "I've found what I wanted all of my life. I can't help but wonder . . ."

"About the others?" she asked.

He nodded. She understood him so well. "I was going through the motions of living. Zachary was lucky, but what if the others were like me? I want to know the answers, but I realize it just doesn't involve me."

She tenderly palmed his face. "Together we'll figure this out."

"Together." He had so much and it had all begun with the woman in his arms. "I love you. You fill my days with love and my tomorrows with happiness."

She blinked back tears. "The best is yet to come."

"And I'm looking forward to every incredible second." He kissed her, loved her, eagerly looked forward to every precious moment ahead of them.

Epilogue

Carlton James was a happy man. He'd waited over thirty-eight years for this moment. His family was finally intact. With his wife by his side, his grin widened as he looked around the hospital room.

Stephen, looking almost like his old self, sat up in bed holding a Texas Rangers baseball cap that Cade had given him. At the moment Cade stood at the foot of the bed holding Sabrina's hand as she held her mother's. His son-in-law was beside his wife. The initial awkwardness when Cade and Sabrina first arrived had slowly disappeared. It was clear that love—Cade's for Sabrina, and hers for her family—would help them get past the mistakes and pain.

"Cade, I hope you know what you're getting into," Stephen said with a teasing grin. "She's bossy, opinionated, and can't cook."

"He knows and loves me anyway." Sabrina gazed adoringly up at Cade. "And I love him."

"I think you forgot stubborn," Cade said easily. "I certainly have my job cut out for me and I'm looking forward to every incredible moment."

"Just as I am," Sabrina said.

"I'm happy for both of you," her father said. "We appreciate you bringing her home, and asking for her hand."

"I love Sabrina. She loves her family, and I hope . . ." Cade paused. His gaze moved from Sabrina's father to her, then to her mother. "Her family will possibly become my family."

Sabrina's mother brushed tears from her eyes and faced Cade. "You *are* a part of this family. My bad judgment doesn't negate that." She lifted her hand toward his shoulder, paused, then lightly grasped his arm. "I always hoped and prayed that Sabrina would find a man who would love and honor her, a man she could trust and be proud of. You're that man. I'll never have to worry about her because I know she has you." She swallowed. "And although you have her, I–I hope you don't mind me still worrying a little bit about you."

Cade stared at his mother, watched tears slide down her cheeks, felt the warmth and strength and love of Sabrina by his side. His mother had given him away, he had suffered because of it, but in adopting Sabrina, she had done what he couldn't, protected and loved her and kept her safe until his heart found her. Priceless. His hand lightly covered his mother's. "I don't mind at all."

Sabrina hugged Cade and her mother. Sabrina's father joined in. Stephen gave a thumbs-up.

Carlton pulled his wife closer, wiped away her tears, and then his own. His family still might hit a bump or two, but they were going to be all right. *His family.*

Finally, his firstborn grandson had come home.